Praise for *Half-Blood*

A USA Book News BEST BOOKS 2011" Finalist

"Amazing doesn't even do this book justice."
— The Magic Attic

"This book is made of awesome."
— Muggle-Born

"Jennifer Armentrout has delivered an action packed book full of twists, romance, and paranormal powers and a great unique Greek Mythology."
— Mundie Moms

"I was completely blown away and left utterly speechless."
— Amy G., The YA Sisterhood

"*Half-Blood* is an action-packed thrill ride that pulled no punches. Full of fantastic mythology, great storytelling, forbidden love, and danger at every corner, *Half-Blood* has something for everyone. "
— Reading Angel

"*Half-Blood* is pure awesomeness. I loved this book from beginning to end."
— Bookittyblog

"Armentrout's writing and characters kept me entertained and thrilled about the world that she has created… This book is sexy, kick-ass, and entertaining."
— Fantastic Book Review

"Alex may just be one of the most kick-butt heroines of YA fiction here lately."
— Letters Inside Out

"*Half-Blood* is a book that will sink its teeth into you and won't let go."
— fiktshun

"When I finished *Half-Blood*, all I wanted was more."
— Collections

"Intense, dramatic, and downright un-put-down-able."
— 365 Days of Reading

"It pulled me in and didn't let me go until the final page. Actually, it never really let me go because I am completely aching for the next in the series."
— Two Readers Review

"One of those books that you open to read and then set it down four hours later, head spinning like you've spent an afternoon on the tilt-a-whirl with the biggest grin on your face."
— The Irish Banana Review

"*Half-Blood* is so complete in its great pacing, developed characters and balance between mythology, romance, and action."

— Read Me, Bookmark Me, Love Me

"Can I just say wow, wow, and wow? Yeah, I loved this book that much."

— Book Passion for Life

"*Half-Blood* takes the WOW factor to a whole new level."

— Mindy, Books Complete Me

"*Half-Blood* completely blew me away! I could not put it down and stayed up till 4 am just to finish it. It's one of those rare books I've added to my "must read again" list!"

— Confessions of a Bookaholic

"This book was awesome!"

— Crystal's Reviews

"Jennifer has this amazing way of sucking me into the story and making it so I never want to leave. I absolutely could not get enough of this amazing book."

— My Bookish Fairy Tale

"Very captivating, it's a great debut novel."

— The Fable Faerie

"*Half-Blood* is fast-paced and full of action. It's definitely a great read that brings in elements of mythology, but stays fresh."

— Letters Inside Out

"This book has everything: the scary monsters, the dangerous quests, the annoying family members, the steamy scenes... I just couldn't get enough."

— iLive, iLaugh, iLove Books

"A wonderful new YA series that no one should miss reading."

— Books to Brighten Your Mood

"Oh. My. Goodness... I really wanted to just enjoy this one and let it soak in slowly. Please read this!"

— I'm a Book Shark

"*Half-Blood* is an exciting first book in a series that promises to get even better (if that is possible!)"

— Books to Brighten your Mood

"If you want to lose yourself for a couple of days, just plain out fall-off-the-face-of-the-planet-and-not-remember-what-else-is-going-on-in-thc-world, lose yourself... THIS BOOK WILL DO THAT! I was completely blown away."

— YA Bound

"This is a book you will finish, and weeks later still be mind blown about, just trying to think of the words to use for how much you loved it."

— Ya-Aholic

"Oh, how I loved this book!"

— Book Loving Mommy

"An awesome debut that shouldn't be missed."

— Birth of a New Witch

"If I could describe this book in one word it would be: AMAZING!!"

— Catching Books

"I can not express how much I enjoyed this book."

— Moonlight Book Reviews

"It will entrap you from page one and seduce you all the way through."

— Shortie Says

"*Half-Blood* is a book you cannot put down! A one sit read!"

— Ivy Reads

"Oh my gods, I can't even tell you how much I love this book! ...Completely entertaining and utterly compelling, *Half-Blood* has definitely earned its place high up on my favourites list! Even if you're not a fan of Greek Mythology, I recommend this book wholeheartedly. It's the kind of book you want to go back and read again immediately."

— Mimi Valentine

"This is definitely my favourite mythology-based book to date... I definitely give this 5/5 and I cannot wait for the next installment, *Pure*."

— The Cait Files

"I was blown away."

— Going from Nobody to Somebody

"Armentrout officially has me hooked on this series, and I may go crazy waiting for the next installment."

— IB Book Blogging

"Jennifer L Armentrout has written a page turner worthy of a one sitting read. Clear your day. It's literally impossible to put *Half-Blood* down until totally devoured....and then you are licking your lips for more."

— Novels on the Run

"Ms. Armentrout has created a world filled with magic and danger... I really, really enjoyed it and was bummed when I arrived at the end."

— Nightly Reading

"5 Stars—A must read."

— Stuck in Books

"I'm addicted, and I want more."

— Dreams in Tandem

"This is a 2011 must read!... Jennifer has written an absolute Masterpiece!"

— Blkosiner's Book Blog

"*Half-Blood* was everything that I love in a book. There was romance, action and drama! I would not change one single thing about it! This book quite literally took my breath away!"

— Two Readers Reviews

"I've found my new favourite series."

— Safari Poet

"*Half-Blood* is one of my favorite books this year. I'd advise everyone to pick it up." — The Reading Housewives

"*Half-Blood* was a fantastic read that refused to let me put it down until it was over. It was well paced, had interesting characters, and quite the romance."

— Poetry to Prose

"This is one book to remember, THE one you definitely wanna read and reread... This book is perfect! A total MUST READ!!"

— Darkest Sins

"By book's end I had tears in my eyes and couldn't wait to get my hands on Covenant book two, PURE."

— All Things Urban Fantasy

"I was drawn to *Half-Blood* like a daimon to aether... I would recommend *Half-Blood* to anyone who is looking for a story with a strong female protagonist, an intricate world with descendents of gods, daimons, hierarchy and oppression, a little romance and some kick-butt action."

— Quill Café

"From all the daimon killings to all the heart-pounding OMGs, this is one debut that will rock you off your toes!"

— Books Over Boys

"Paced with precision, the story unfolds gradually to the perfect end, filled with unanswered questions and a desperate longing."

— Writing Jewels

"Nothing short of an absolutely amazing read."

— Omnom Books

Spencer Hill Press

Contact: Spencer Hill Press, PO Box 247, Contoocook, NH 03229, USA

Please visit our website at www.spencerhillpress.com

First Edition: April 2012.
Second Printing: September 2012.

Armentrout, Jennifer L. 1980
Pure : a novel / by Jennifer L. Armentrout – 1st ed.
p. cm.

Summary:
Seventeen-year-old Alexandria has to fight daimons to survive – and fight her growing attraction to the man she can never have. If she loses either fight, she could lose everything.

Cover design by K. Kaynak with artwork by Misha.

ISBN 978-0-9831572-2-9 (paperback)
ISBN 978-0-9831572-3-6 (e-book)

Printed in the United States of America

Pure

The Second Covenant Novel by

Jennifer L. Armentrout

Spencer Hill Press

The *Covenant* Series

Daimon (A short prequel to *Half-Blood,* available as a free download at www.SpencerHillPress.com)
Half-Blood
Pure
Deity (November 2012)
Apollyon (Spring 2013)

Also by Jennifer L. Armentrout

From Spencer Hill Press:
Cursed (September 2012)

From Entangled Publishing:
Obsidian (Book 1 in the Lux Series)
Onyx (Book 2 in the Lux Series) (May 2012)
Opal (Book 3 in the Lux Series) (November 2012)

Writing as JL Rogers:
Unchained (Fall 2012)

Coming from Disney-Hyperion:
Don't Look Back

To my family and Loki

(yeah, I'm dedicating *Pure* to a dog)

Pronunciation Guide for *Pure*

Daimon:	DEE-mun
Aether:	EE-ther
Hematoi:	HEM-a-toy
Apollyon:	a-POL-ee-on
Agapi:	ah-GAH-pee
Akasha:	ah-KAH-sha

CHAPTER 1

I STARED AT THE CEILING OF THE GYMNASIUM, LITTLE black splotches dancing in front of me. Man, my butt hurt. No surprise, as I'd landed on it about fifty times already. The only thing not burning with pain was my face; it was on fire for an entirely different reason.

My Gutter Fighting class wasn't going well.

This style of hand-to-hand combat wasn't exactly second nature. My muscles screamed as I pulled myself off the mats and faced our Instructor.

Running a hand through his thinning hair, Instructor Romvi looked disgusted with the entire class. "If he'd been a daimon, you'd be dead now. Do you understand? Dead, not alive, Miss Andros."

Like there was some other definition of "dead" I wasn't familiar with. I gritted my teeth and managed a nod.

Romvi shot me another scathing glare. "It's difficult to believe you have any amount of aether in you, Miss Andros. The essence of the gods is wasted on you. The way you fight, you might as well be mortal."

Hadn't I killed *three* aether-craving daimons? Wasn't that worth something?

"Square off. Keep your eyes trained on muscle movement. You know the drill," he instructed.

I turned back to Jackson Manos, resident Covenant heartthrob and my current opponent. With his swarthy looks and those dark, sexy eyes, he could be quite the distraction.

Jackson winked at me.

I narrowed my eyes at him. We weren't allowed to talk during sparring. Instructor Romvi felt it took away from the authenticity of fighting. Really, even in all of Jackson's glory, he wasn't the reason I kept missing his heel strikes and spin kicks.

The source of my absolute failure leaned against the training room wall. Dark waves tumbled over his forehead, falling into gunmetal gray eyes. Some would say Aiden St. Delphi needed a haircut, but I loved the wilder look he'd been favoring recently.

An instant later, our gazes locked. Aiden returned to the stance I was all too familiar with—well-defined arms crossed over his chest, legs widespread. Watching, always watching. Now he communicated a look that said I should be paying attention to Jackson and not him.

Tight coils sprung within me—another thing I'd grown accustomed to. It happened whenever I laid eyes on him. It wasn't so much the near perfect curve of his cheekbones or the way his smile hinted at a set of dimples. Or that impossibly ripped body of his—

I snapped out my reverie with a moment to spare. I blocked Jackson's knee with a brutal swipe of my arm, and then I went for a throat strike. Jackson countered it easily. We circled one another, delivering blows and dodging them. He stepped back, dropping his arms to his sides. I saw my opening and went for it. Spinning around, I aimed my knee for his midsection. Jackson darted to the side, but not quickly enough. I caught him hard in the stomach.

Surprisingly, Instructor Romvi clapped. "Good—"

"Oh, crap," Caleb Nicolo, my best friend and partner in mayhem, moaned from the group of students standing against the wall.

The thing about defensive kicks—once we made contact with our opponents we either needed to go for the kill shot or back up. I'd done neither. Jackson doubled over my knee and went down, taking me along for the ride. We hit the mat, and somehow—and I seriously doubted by accident—Jackson ended sprawled atop me. His weight knocked my head back and the air out of my lungs.

Instructor Romvi yelled, slipping into a different language—maybe Romanian or something. Anyway, whatever he said sounded suspiciously like cursing.

Jackson lifted his head, his shoulder-length hair shielding his grin from the class. "Always on your back, huh?"

"Yeah, that's more like your girlfriend. Get off." I pushed at his shoulders. Chuckling, Jackson rolled and stood. Ever since the whole "my mom murdered his girlfriend's parents" incident, Jackson and I hadn't gotten along. Actually, courtesy of my dead daimon mother, I wasn't getting along with most of the other students, either. Go figure.

Flushing with embarrassment, I scrambled to my feet and stole a quick glance at Aiden. His expression may have appeared blank, but I knew he'd already compiled a mental list of all the things I'd done wrong and filed it away. But he wasn't my immediate concern.

Instructor Romvi stalked across the mats, stopping in front of Jackson and me. "That was absolutely unacceptable! You move away or dispose of the opponent."

To drive his point home, he threw his arm out, hitting me square across the chest. I stumbled back an inch and clenched my jaw shut. Every cell in my body demanded that I do the same in return.

"You do not wait! And you." Romvi whirled on Jackson. "Do you plan to lie on daimons for fun? Let me know how that works out for you."

Jackson flushed, but didn't respond. We didn't talk back in Romvi's class.

"Off the mats now—not you, Miss Andros!"

I stopped, eyeing Caleb and Olivia hopelessly. They stared back, their expressions mirroring mine. Resigned to what I knew was going to happen next, because it'd happened every class with Romvi, I turned to the Instructor and waited for the epic smackdown.

"Many of you aren't ready for graduation." Romvi prowled the edge of the mat. "Many of you will die the first week on the job, but you, Miss Andros? You're an embarrassment to the Covenant."

Romvi was an embarrassment to the male race, but he didn't hear me bitching.

He circled me slowly. "I am shocked that you faced down daimons and still stand before me. Some may think you have potential, Miss Andros. I have yet to see it."

Out of the corner of my eye, I saw Aiden. He'd stiffened, gaze narrowed upon us. He also knew what was coming, and there was nothing he could do, even if he wanted to.

"Prove to me that you belong here," Romvi said. "Prove to me that you have gained reentry to the Covenant based on merit and not familial ties."

Instructor Romvi was a bigger jerk than most Instructors. He was one of the pure-bloods who'd chosen to become a Sentinel instead of coasting through life living off old money. Like Aiden, pures who chose this kind of life were a rare breed, but that was where the commonalities between the two ended. Romvi had hated me from the first day of class, and I liked to believe Aiden felt quite the opposite.

Romvi attacked.

For someone so old, Romvi sure could move fast. I backed across the mats, trying to remember everything Aiden had taught me over the summer. Romvi swung around, his booted heel aiming for my midsection. I swiped his leg away and threw a punch I really, *really* meant. He blocked that. On and on we went, exchanging and receiving blows. He was landing more on me, continuously edging me toward the edge of the mat.

With each swing and each kick, Romvi's blows became more brutal. It *was* like fighting a daimon, because I seriously believed Romvi wanted to do me real harm. I was holding my own until my sneaker slipped off the edge of the mat. I made a tactical mistake.

I allowed myself to be distracted.

Romvi took it. Reaching out and grabbing a fistful of my ponytail, he yanked me forward. "You should be less worried about your vanity," he said, twisting me so my back faced the doors. "And cut your hair."

I struck out, catching Romvi in the stomach, but it didn't faze him. Using my own momentum—and my hair—he slammed me onto the mat. I rolled into the fall, half grateful that it was over. I didn't even care that he'd kicked my ass in front of the entire class. Just as long as this—

Romvi grabbed my arm and pulled it high above me, yanking me to my knees. "Listen to me, half-bloods. Dying in battle is not your worst nightmare anymore."

My eyes popped wide. *Oh, no. No, no, no. He wouldn't dare...*

He pushed the sleeve of the Under Armour shirt back until my skin was exposed to the elbow. "This is what happens to you. Take a good, long look at what happens when you fail. They will turn you into a monster."

Fire coursed across my cheeks and my brain sort of emptied. I tried, really tried, to keep the scars hidden from my classmates. I focused on anything other than the faces of the students as he continued to show the world my tags. My gaze fell over his rough, aged hand, then up his own battle-scarred arm. The sleeve of his shirt had fallen back, revealing a tattoo of a torch turned downward.

Instructor Romvi hadn't struck me as the type to be into tattoos.

Romvi dropped my arm then, allowing me to pull my sleeve down. I hoped he got eaten by hungry daimons. I might look like a scarred-up freak, but I hadn't failed a damn thing. I'd killed the daimon ultimately responsible for leaving me this way—my mother.

"None of you are ready to become Sentinels, to face a daimon half-blood trained just like you." Romvi's voice carried through the room. "I don't expect most of you to show any improvement by tomorrow. Class is over."

I fought the urge to jump on Romvi's back like a monkey and snap his neck. That wouldn't win me any fans, but the sick sense of satisfaction would almost be worth it.

On his way out, Jackson bumped into me. "Your arm looks like a checkerboard. That's real hot."

"Yeah, that's what your girlfriend said about your di—"

Instructor Romvi's hand snapped out, catching my chin. "Your mouth, Miss Andros, could also use improvement."

"But Jackson—"

"I do not care." He dropped his hand, glaring down at me. "I do not tolerate such foul words in my class. This is your last warning. Next time you will find yourself in the Dean's office."

Unbe-freaking-lievable. I watched Romvi stalk out of the room.

Caleb approached me, handing Olivia her gym bag. His eyes, the color of the clearest sky, shone with sympathy. "He's a prick, Alex."

I waved my hand dismissively, not sure if he was talking about Romvi or Jackson. They were both pricks in my book.

"One of these days, you're so gonna snap and kill him." Luke dragged his fingers through bronze-colored locks.

"Which one?" I asked.

"Both." Luke grinned as he tapped my arm. "I just hope I'm here to see it."

"I second that." Olivia wrapped her arm around Caleb's. They pretended whatever was going on between them was a casual thing, but I knew different. Whenever Olivia touched Caleb, which was often, he completely forgot about whatever was going on and got this stupid smile on his face.

Then again, a lot of the male halfs got that look on their faces around her. Olivia was stunning. Her caramel-colored skin was envied by most of the halfs. So was her closet. I'd kill to get my hands on her clothes.

A shadow fell over our little group, quickly dispersing them. I didn't have to look up to know it was Aiden. Only he had the kind of power to send just about anyone running in the opposite direction. Respect and fear did that.

"See you later," Caleb called out.

I nodded vaguely, staring at Aiden's sneakers. Shame over Romvi's little display made it hard to look at him. I worked hard for Aiden's respect, to prove I did have the potential he and Leon had believed I had the day Marcus had tried to toss me out of the Covenant.

Funny how one person could ruin that in a matter of seconds.

"Alex, look at me."

Against my will, I obeyed. When he spoke that way, I couldn't help it. He stood in front of me, his long and lean body coiled. We currently were pretending I hadn't tried to hand my virginity over to him the night I'd found out I was going to be the second coming of the Apollyon. Aiden seemed to be doing really well with it. I, on the other hand, couldn't stop obsessing over it.

"You didn't fail."

I shrugged. "Doesn't seem that way, does it?"

"The Instructors are tougher on you because of the time you've missed and because your uncle is the Dean. People look at what you do. They pay attention."

"And my stepfather is the Minister of Council. I get it, Aiden. Look, let's get this over with." My voice was a little sharper than I intended, but Aiden had seen how mortifying this class had turned out. Not like I needed to discuss it with him.

Aiden caught my arm and pushed up the sleeve of my shirt. It had a whole different effect on me. A flutter formed in my chest, spreading a warm flush all over me. Pure-bloods were off-limits to us halfs, which meant what had gone down between us was tantamount to feeling up the Pope or offering Gandhi a roast beef sandwich.

"You should never be ashamed of these scars, Alex. Never." Aiden dropped my arm and motioned me to the center of the floor. "Let's get this going so you can rest."

I trailed behind him. "What about your rest? Don't you have a patrol tonight?" Aiden was pulling double duty between training me and his Sentinel duties.

Aiden was special. He'd chosen to be a Sentinel, and he'd also chosen to work with me so I wouldn't be so far behind the other students. He didn't have to do either, but a sense of justice had propelled him to become a Sentinel. We shared that desire. What made him want to help me? I liked to think he was undeniably attracted to me—like I was when it came to him.

He circled me, stopping to position my arms at mid-level. "You're holding your arms wrong. That's why Jackson's hits kept getting through."

"What about your rest?" I persisted.

"Don't worry about me." He squared off, motioning me forward with one hand. "Worry more about yourself, Alex. This is going to be a tough year for you, and you're doing triple time in training."

"I'd have more free time if I didn't have to practice with Seth."

Aiden swung forward so fast I barely blocked the blow. "Alex, we've been over this."

"I know." I stopped his chop. I alternated days between Aiden and Seth, as well as every other weekend. It was like they shared joint custody of me, but I hadn't seen my *other half* yet today. Strange—he usually lurked around nearby.

"Alex." Aiden moved out of the offensive stance, studying me closely.

"What?" I dropped my arms.

He opened his mouth, seeming to rethink his words. "You've been looking a little tired lately. Are you getting enough rest?"

I felt my cheeks burst with color. "Gods, do I look that bad or something?"

He drew in a deep breath and let it out slowly. Softness crept across his features. "Alex, you don't look bad at all. It's just that… you've been through a lot and you seem tired."

"I'm okay."

Aiden placed his hand on my shoulder. "Alex?"

My heart thundered in response to his touch. "I'm fine."

"You keep saying that." His gaze flickered across my face. "You always say that."

"I say it because there isn't anything wrong with me!" I swatted at his hand, but he dropped his other one on my shoulder, effectively trapping me in front of him. "There's nothing wrong with me," I said again, but much quieter. "I'm okay. Completely a hundred percent fine with everything."

Aiden opened his mouth, probably to say something ridiculously supportive, but he didn't say anything. He just stared at me and then his grip on my shoulders tightened. He knew I was lying.

Everything wasn't fine.

Nightmares of those horrifying hours in Gatlinburg kept me up at night. Nearly everyone at school hated me, believing I'd been the reason for the daimon attack at Lake Lure during the summer. Seth's constant stalking only added to their suspicions. Out of all the halfs, only Caleb knew I was fated to be the second Apollyon—and fated to *complete* Seth as his supernatural supercharger or something. His continuing attentions didn't win me any fans among the female halfs. All the girls wanted Seth, while I just wanted to be rid of him.

But when Aiden looked at me like he did now, I forgot about the world. I couldn't read much of anything from Aiden's expression, but his eyes… well, his eyes told me he wasn't doing so great with the whole pretending-we-hadn't-almost-hooked-up charade. Aiden still thought about it; hell, he was thinking about it right now. Maybe he imagined what would've happened if Leon hadn't interrupted—maybe even as much as I did. Maybe he'd lie awake and remember how our bodies had felt together.

I know I did.

The tension racked up several degrees and my body warmed deliciously. These were the kind of moments I lived for. I wondered what he'd do if I stepped forward and closed the distance between us. It wouldn't take much for me to do it. Would he think I just wanted comfort? Because he would comfort me—he was that kind of guy. And then, if I tipped my head back, would he kiss me? Because he looked like he wanted to do both. Hold me, kiss me, and do all sorts of wonderful, forbidden things.

I stepped forward.

His hands jerked against my shoulders, indecision crawled over his features. For a second—just as second—I think he seriously considered it. Then his hands flattened, like a barrier meant to keep me back.

The doors opened behind us, and Aiden dropped his hands. I twisted around, wanting to punch whoever it was in the face. I'd come *this* close to getting what I'd wanted.

Leon's bulky mass filled the door, dressed in his typical, all-black Sentinel garb. "I'm sorry to interrupt, but this cannot wait."

Leon always had something important to tell Aiden. The last time he'd interrupted us had been two seconds after I'd given Aiden the green light to go all the way.

Leon had the worst timing ever.

Of course, the last time he'd interrupted, things had been pretty serious. They'd found Kain alive. Once a half-blood Sentinel, Kain had helped Aiden train me. A weekend trip to nearby Lake Lure had proved fatal for everyone involved. He'd survived the daimon attack but had come back to the Covenant as something we'd thought was impossible—a half-blood daimon.

Now Kain was dead, and I'd seen it happen. I'd liked and missed Kain, even after he'd killed a bunch of pures and knocked me around the room. That hadn't been the Kain I'd known. Like Mom, he'd turned into a terrible version of who he'd really been.

Leon moved his massive body forward, looking like the poster child for steroids. "There's been a daimon attack."

Aiden tensed. "Where?"

"Here at the Covenant."

CHAPTER 2

PRACTICE WAS OFFICIALLY CANCELLED.

"Go straight to your dorm, Alex, and stay there," Aiden said before leaving the training arena.

I went to the cafeteria instead.

There was no way I was going to hang out in my dorm while there was a daimon running amuck. I'd considered following the two for a moment, but my ninja stealth skills were subpar.

By the time I'd cut across the quad, the sky had darkened and turned ominous. I picked up my pace, because when the sky got this way, one had to pay attention. September was hurricane season around this place. Or it could just mean Seth was pissed off somewhere nearby; his moodiness had a startling effect on the weather.

In the cafeteria, everyone huddled together in little groups, their faces animated. I grabbed an apple and a soda, noting there wasn't a single pure in the lunchroom. I dropped into the seat beside Caleb.

He looked up, eyes bright. "You heard?"

"Yeah, I was practicing when Leon came to get Aiden." I glanced at Olivia. "Do you have any details?"

"All I've heard is one of the younger students—Melissa Callao—didn't show up for classes today. Her friends were concerned and checked her dorm. They found her in bed, the window open."

I sat back, squelching the unease shifting through me. "Is she alive?"

Olivia stabbed a fork into her pizza. Her pure-blood mother worked closely with the Council. Lucky for us, she kept her daughter well informed. "She was practically drained, but she's alive. I don't know how her roommate didn't know, or why she wasn't attacked, too."

"How in Hades is a daimon running around here?" Luke held up a hand, a puzzled frown on his face. "How could one get past the Guards?"

"It had to be a half," Elena said from further down the table. She looked like an extraordinarily tall Tinkerbell with her short hair and wide, green eyes.

Up until this summer, we'd believed that half-bloods couldn't be turned into daimons. A pure was chock full of aether, and a daimon would chew, gnaw, and kill to get at that essence like a psychotic drug addict. Once drained of their aether, the daimon could let the pure die or turn them, adding to the daimon horde. No one thought half-bloods had enough aether inside of them to make the switch over to the dark side, but for a patient daimon more interested in building an army than getting a meal, we were as good as a pure.

It sucked that the only place we were equal to pures was in a fate worse than death.

"Halfs who've turned don't change like the pures." Olivia flicked the fork between her long fingers. "They're immune to titanium, right?" Her gaze landed on me.

I nodded. "Yep, gotta cut off their head. Gross, I know." Or Seth could use his Apollyon mojo. He'd zapped Kain with *akasha*—the fifth and final element—and that'd done the job.

Caleb rubbed a spot on his arm where I knew he'd been tagged. He stopped as his eyes caught mine. I forced a smile.

"If it's a half, it could be anyone." Luke leaned back, folding his arms. "I mean, think about it. They don't need elemental magic to conceal what they really look like. It could be *anyone*."

When pures turned all evil and what-not, they were noticeable to half-bloods—like, really noticeable. Empty black eye sockets, pale skin, and mouths full of razor sharp teeth doesn't make for a look that blends into the crowd. Halfs had the wacky ability to see through the elemental magic pure-blood daimons used, but daimon half-bloods just looked the same after they turned. At least Kain had.

"Well, it would have to be a half-blood who'd been attacked by a daimon," a throaty, husky voice intruded. "Hmm, wonder who that could be? It's not like they grow on trees around here."

Lifting my head, I found Lea Samos and Jackson. It was the middle of September and the chick still sported a super tan—still so beautiful that I wanted to stab her in the eye with a plastic fork. "Yeah, that would make sense." I kept my voice even.

Those amethyst eyes settled on me. "How many half-bloods do we know who've been attacked recently?"

I stared at her, stuck between disbelief and wanting to throw something. "Knock it off, Lea. I don't want to hear your crap today."

She pulled those full lips into a cruel smile. "I know of two."

Caleb shot to his feet, knocking his chair over. "What are you saying, Lea?"

Two Guards by the door stepped forward, eyeing the situation with interest. Olivia grabbed Caleb's hand, but he ignored her. "Come on, Lea. Just say it."

She tossed a mane of coppery hair over her shoulder. "Chill out, Caleb. You got tagged how many times? Two? Three? It takes a hell of a lot more to turn a half-blood than that." She looked at me pointedly. "Isn't that right? That's what I heard the Guards say. That the halfs have to be drained slowly, and then the daimon gives them the kiss of death."

I took a deep breath. Lea and I were enemies. There'd been a time when my heart had sort of bled for her after her parents had been murdered, but that seemed like ages ago. "I'm not a daimon, you skank."

Lea tipped her head to the side. "If it looks like a daimon, then…"

"Lea, go screw someone and tan, in whatever order." Caleb sat back down. "No one wants to hear your crap. And that's the funny thing about you, Lea. You think everyone cares what you have to say, when all they care about is how easy it is to get you on your back."

"Or how the Instructors found a bottle of Brew in your room last week," Olivia added, her lips curving into a half smile. "Didn't know you were into such freaky stuff, or maybe that's how you get guys into you."

I snorted. I hadn't heard *that*. "Wow. Drugging guys to sleep with you? Nice. I guess that's why Jackson practically humped my leg in class today."

Lea's cheeks flamed an odd shade of brown and red. "You stupid, daimon-loving bitch, you're the reason why my father's dead! You should have—"

Several people moved at once. Olivia and Caleb darted across the table, trying to get a hold on me, but I was fast when I wanted to be.

I didn't think; I just launched my shiny red apple right at her face. A throw like that from a half-blood turned an apple into a serious weapon. It struck home with a loud cracking sound.

Lea stumbled back, clasping the front of her face. Blood gushed between her fingers, matching the color of her nails. "You broke my nose!"

Everyone in the cafeteria stilled. Even the drab-looking half-blood servants stopped cleaning tables to watch. No one screamed or seemed overtly startled. After all, we were half-bloods—a violent bunch. The servants were usually too doped up to be concerned.

Somehow I'd forgotten about the Guards as I'd gone for Lea. I squeaked when one of them got an arm around my waist and hauled me across the table. Drinks spilled; food fell to the floor, and mystery meat smeared itself all over my gym pants.

"Knock it off, right now!"

"She broke my nose again!" Lea dropped her hands from her face. "You can't let her get away with this!"

"Oh, shut up. The docs will fix it. Half your face is plastic anyway." I struggled against the Guard until he twisted my arm back so far that any movement caused my shoulder to scream.

"She wanted to get at my aether." Lea pointed a bloodstained hand at me. "Her mother killed my parents, and now she wants to kill me!"

I laughed. "Oh, for the love—"

"Shut up," the Guard hissed in my ear. "Shut up before I make you shut up."

Threats made by half-blood Guards weren't meant to be taken lightly. I quieted down while the other Guard grabbed ahold of Lea.

Blood pounded in my ears and my chest still heaved with fury, but I realized that I may've overreacted a tiny bit.

And I was going to be in *so* much trouble.

Half-bloods fighting amongst themselves wasn't a big deal. The aggression and controlled violence sometimes rolled out of the training rooms into places like the cafeteria. Whenever halfs did get in trouble for fighting, they ended up with one of the Instructors who handled disciplinary issues.

Each dorm floor had one assigned. My floor had Instructor Gaia Telis, a pretty cool chick who wasn't overly strict or annoying. But I didn't end up with Instructor Telis. Five minutes after breaking Lea's nose for the second time, I ended up in Dean Andros's office.

This was only one of many drawbacks of my uncle being the Dean.

I stared at the vibrant fish zooming across the aquarium and fidgeted with the string on my pants while I waited for Marcus. Sometimes I felt like one of those fish—trapped by invisible walls.

The doors swinging open behind me made me cringe. This was going to suck daimon butt.

"If you discover anything else, notify me immediately. That is all." Marcus's deep voice filled the room. The Guards adorned the outside of his office doors like Greek warrior statues. Then he slammed the door shut.

I jumped.

Marcus stalked across the room, dressed like he'd spent the majority of the day on a golf course. I expected him to sit behind his desk like a dean should, so when he ended up directly in front of me, grasping the arms of my chair, I was a bit shocked.

"I am sure you're aware of what has happened today." The tone of Marcus's voice was both cold and distinctively cultured. Most pures sounded that way—classy, refined. "A pure-blood was attacked at some point last night."

I strained back as far as I could go, focusing on the aquarium. "Yeah—"

"Do not look away from me, Alexandria."

Sucking in my lower lip, I faced him. His eyes were the same as my mother's had been before she'd turned into a daimon—a vibrant shade of green, like glittering emeralds. "Yes, I heard."

"Then you understand what I'm dealing with right now." Marcus lowered his head so we were at eye level. "I have a daimon half-blood on my campus, hunting my students."

"So it's a half who's been turned?"

"I think you already know that, Alexandria. You are a lot of things—impulsive, irresponsible, and ill-mannered—but stupid is not one of them."

I wanted to hear more about this daimon half than my character flaws. "Who was the half? You've caught him, right?"

Marcus ignored my question. "Now, I'm pulled out of an investigation that will make or break my career here, all because my half-blood niece broke a girl's nose in the cafeteria… with an apple, of all things."

"She accused me of being a daimon!"

"So your natural response is to throw an apple at her face hard enough to break a bone?" His voice dropped, deceptively soft. Marcus was Chuck Norris in an off-pink polo shirt. I'd learned not to underestimate him.

"She said I was the reason her parents were killed."

"I'll ask you one more time: So you decided to throw an apple hard enough to break a bone?"

I wiggled uncomfortably. "Yeah, I guess so."

He exhaled slowly. "Is that all you have to say?"

I glanced around the room, my brain emptying out. I said the first thing that came to mind, "I didn't think the apple would break her nose."

Pushing off the chair, he towered over me. "I expect more from you. Not because you're my niece, Alexandria. Not even because you have more experience with daimons than any other student here."

I rubbed my forehead.

"Everyone will be watching you—everyone of importance. You will give Seth unprecedented power. We cannot afford any misguided behavior from you, Alexandria. Neither can Seth."

Irritation flared deep inside me. At eighteen, something called palingenesis would hit me like some kind of instant supernatural puberty. I'd Awaken and my power would shift to Seth. What power, I had no clue, but he'd become the God Killer. Everyone cared about Seth, but me? They didn't seem so concerned with what would happen to me.

"People expect more from you. They will watch you because of what you will become, Alexandria."

I disagreed. They watched because they feared history would repeat itself. The only time there'd ever been two Apollyons in the same generation, the First had turned on the Council. Both Apollyons had been executed. Two Apollyons at one time was considered dangerous by the Council and the gods. It was why Mom had taken me from the Covenant three years ago. She'd thought she could keep me safe, hide me among the mortals.

"At Council, you cannot behave like this. You can't run around starting fights and mouthing off at people," he continued. "There are rules—rules of our society that you must follow! They will not think twice about throwing you into servitude, and it won't matter who you're related to. Do you understand?"

Exhaling slowly, I lifted my head and found Marcus by the aquarium. His back was to me. "Yes, I understand."

He ran a hand over his head. "You will leave your dorm for school, training, and dinner—dinner at the assigned time—and that is all. As of now, you have no friends."

My gaze narrowed on his back. "Am I, like, grounded or something?"

He looked over his shoulder at me, lips thinning. "Until further notice, and do not even think of arguing with me. You cannot go unpunished for this."

"But how can you ground me?"

Marcus turned around slowly. "You broke a girl's nose with an apple."

Suddenly, I didn't want to argue. I *was* getting off light. Being grounded also didn't mean anything. It wasn't like my social calendar was full. "All right, but are you going to tell me if you found the daimon?"

He stared at me a moment longer. "No. We haven't found the daimon yet."

I gripped the chair. "So… it's still around?"

"Yes." Marcus motioned me up, and I followed him to the door. He addressed one of the Guards. "Clive, escort Miss Andros back to her room."

I groaned inwardly. Clive was one of the Guards I seriously suspected of hooking up with Lea. Every single conversation spoken inside Marcus's office somehow got back to Lea. Considering Clive had a thing for young girls who wore fake Prada shoes, he was the likeliest suspect.

"Yes, sir." Clive bowed.

"Remember our conversation," Marcus said.

"But what about—"

Marcus shut the door.

Which part should I remember? The fact I was a disgrace to him or the fact there was a daimon running around? Clive grabbed my arm, fingers biting deep. I winced, trying to jerk my arm back, but he increased the pressure. The daimon tags still felt oddly sensitive.

"I guess you're enjoying this." I clenched my jaw.

"That would be a good guess." Clive shoved me into the stairwell. The pures were wealthy, and I mean, more money than anyone could comprehend. Yet there wasn't a single elevator in the entire campus.

"You think you can get away with anything, don't you? You're the dean's niece, the Minister's stepdaughter, and the next Apollyon. You're just so damn special, aren't you?"

There was a very good chance I might hit him, but with my fist instead of an apple. I jerked my arm free. "Yeah, I'm that damn special."

"Just remember you're still a half-blood, Alex."

"Just remember I *am* the dean's niece, the Minister's stepdaughter, and the next Apollyon."

Clive stepped up, his nose almost touching mine. "Are you threatening me?"

I refused to back down. "No. I'm just reminding you of how special I really am."

He stared a moment, then gave a short, harsh laugh. "Maybe we'll all get lucky and you'll be a daimon snack on the way back to your dorm *alone*. Have a good night."

I laughed as loud as I could and was rewarded with the door slamming shut. Hurrying down the stairs, I forgot about Clive. There was a daimon on campus and it'd already attacked one pure-blood, almost killing her. Who knew how long it would take before the daimon half needed its next fix? Mom had said a pure would keep a normal daimon going for days, but was it the same for a daimon half?

She hadn't said anything about that, but she'd talked a lot about their plans to overthrow the Council and the pures while I'd been captive in Gatlinburg. Mom and Eric, the only surviving daimon from Gatlinburg, had plotted to turn the halfs first, and then send them back to infiltrate the Covenants. Sounded like that was already well underway… or could it just be a random attack?

Yeah, I doubted that.

What I'd learned in Gatlinburg was the whole reason I'd be attending the November Council session, but my testimony seemed pointless now.

I rounded the second floor level and came to an abrupt standstill. Apprehension trailed icy fingers down my spine, awakening the uncanny sense we half-bloods carried in our blood. I glanced over my shoulder, practically expecting a half-blood serial killer to be standing behind me… or at least Clive, about to push me down the steps.

But there was nothing.

Trained not to ignore the freaky sixth sense that alerted us to all kinds of messed-up things, I admitted that maybe I shouldn't have pissed off Clive. After all, there was a daimon roaming around. I took the steps two at a time and flung open the door to the main level.

Dread still trailed along with me, coiling around my fingers. It didn't help that the long hallway was lit only by flickering overhead lights, adding to the creepy feeling. Where were all the Instructors and Guards? It was tomb-quiet.

"Clive?" My eyes devoured every vacant inch of the hallway. "If you're messing with me, I'm seriously going to break *your* nose."

Silence was my answer.

Tiny hairs on my body stood up in warning. Up ahead, the statues of the muses cast harsh shadows over the front lobby. Scanning every nook and cranny for a possible threat, I made my way down the hall. My footsteps echoed madly, almost as if the sound was laughing at me. I came to a sudden halt, mouth dropping open. There was a new addition to the Academy lobby, one that hadn't been there when I'd been escorted to Marcus's office.

Three new marble statues had been erected in the center of the lobby. The angelic, beautiful women clustered close to one another, their arms folded close to their bodies and their wings arched high above their tilted heads.

Oh, my gods.

There were *furies* in the Covenant.

Entombed for now, their arrival was a sign from some very unhappy gods. I walked around them slowly, as if they'd break free from their shells and rip me from limb to limb at any moment. I imagined they were waiting, sharpening the claws that would appear in their true form.

Furies were ancient, horrific goddesses once used to capture those who had committed evil but had not been punished. Now they appeared whenever there was a threat to the pures as a whole… or to humankind in general.

Something was about to go down, or already had.

Tearing my eyes away from their serene expressions, I pushed open the heavy doors. A hand clamped down on my arm. My gasp of surprise came out as a shriek as I leaned back and brought my leg up to deliver a vicious kick. My eyes flicked up an instant before I made contact.

"Crap!" I yelped.

Aiden blocked my knee, brows raised. "Well, your reflexes are definitely getting better."

Heart racing, I closed my eyes. "Oh, my gods, you scared the crap out of me."

"I can tell." He dropped my arm, his eyes falling to my pants. "So it's true."

"So what's true?" I still couldn't get control over my heart. For crying out loud, I'd thought he was a daimon about to chomp down on what's left of my arm.

"You got into a fight with Lea Samos and broke her nose."

"Oh." I straightened, pursing my lips. "She called me a daimon loving—"

"Words, Alex, just words." Aiden tipped his head to the side. "Haven't we had this conversation before?"

"You don't know Lea. You don't know how she is."

"Does it matter how she is? You can't fight everyone who says something negative about you. If I approached people the way you do, I'd be fighting all the time."

I rolled my eyes. "People don't talk bad about you, Aiden. Everyone respects you. You're perfect. They don't think *you're* a daimon. Anyway, there's a new happy family entombed in the lobby back there."

He frowned.

"There're furies in the lobby—statues of them."

Aiden dragged a hand over his head, sighing. "We were afraid that might happen."

"Why are they here?"

"The Covenant has been breached, which is something the Council assured would never happen. It was part of their agreement with the gods ages ago, when the first Covenant was established. The gods see this breach as the Council not able to handle the daimon problem."

My stomach flopped. "And what does that mean, exactly?"

He grimaced. "It means, if the gods believe the pure-bloods have lost control, they will release the furies. It's not something anyone wants. The furies will go after anything they perceive as a threat—daimon, half-blood, or…"

"Apollyon?" I whispered. Aiden didn't respond, which confirmed I was correct. I groaned. "Awesome. Well, hopefully that doesn't happen."

"Agreed."

I shifted uncomfortably, my brain unable to really process the new threat. "What are you doing over here, anyway?"

Aiden pinned me with a dark look. "I was going to see Marcus. What are you doing roaming around by yourself?"

"Clive was supposed to escort me back to the dorm, but that kind of fell through."

His eyes narrowed and then he sighed. Tipping his head toward the dorms, he shoved his hands into the pockets of his dark cargos. "Come on, I'll walk you back. You shouldn't be out here alone."

I pushed away from the doors. "Cuz there's a daimon still on campus? And furies ready to attack?"

He glanced down at me, frowning. "I know your flippant attitude is an act. It's probably what made you turn an apple into a deadly weapon. You of all people know how serious this is."

My cheeks flushed at his reprimand. Guilt twisted my stomach into raw knots. I stared down at the markings on the pathway. "I'm sorry."

"I'm not the person you should be apologizing to."

"Well, I'm sure as hell not apologizing to Lea. So you can forget that."

Aiden shook his head. "I know what Lea said upset you. I can even… understand your reaction, but you have to be careful. People are—"

"Yeah, I know. People are watching me, blah and blah some more." I squinted at the shadows of the patrolling Guards. It was the time between dusk and nightfall, but the lamps hadn't kicked on yet. The largest buildings—the ones housing the school, training facilities, and dorms—slipped dark shadows over the pathway. "Anyway, do you guys have any idea where the daimon could be?"

"No. We've searched everywhere and are still searching. Right now we're focused on keeping the students safe."

We stopped at the bottom of the steps outside my dorm. The porch was empty, a sign of everyone's unease. Girls usually hung out here, hoping to get some guy time in. "Did Melissa see the daimon? Was she able to give some sort of description?"

Aiden ran a hand over his forehead. "She barely remembers anything from the attack right now. The doctors… well, they think it's the trauma. A way of protecting herself, I guess."

I looked away, grateful it was dark outside. Why couldn't I forget what'd happened in Gatlinburg? "It's probably more than just that. She's a pure. Where one of us would be trained to pay attention to details, to gain as much information as possible, she wasn't. She's just like a… normal girl. And if the attack happened at night, she probably thought it was a nightmare. Waking up to something like that? I couldn't even imagine." I stopped. He was staring at me strangely. "What?"

"It's just that you're thinking along the right lines."

I couldn't keep the goofy grin off my face. "I'm that awesome. I know."

His lips twitched as if he wished to smile. "So, how much trouble are you in?"

"Grounded basically, but I guess I got off light." I was still smiling like an idiot.

"Yeah, you did." He looked relieved. "Try to stay out of trouble and *please* don't sneak around the grounds. I doubt the daimon is still here, but you never know."

Drawing in a deep breath, I folded my arms over my chest. "Aiden?"

"Hmm?"

I stared at Aiden's boots. They were shiny, never scuffed. "It's starting, isn't it?"

"You're talking about what your mother told you, aren't you?"

"She said this is what they would do. And Eric's still out there. What if he's behind this and—?"

"Alex." He leaned toward me. We were close, but not as close as we'd been in the gym. "It doesn't matter if it's Eric or not. We'll make sure this doesn't happen again. You have nothing to worry about."

"I'm not scared."

Aiden reached out, brushing his fingers over mine. It was a brief touch, but my body tingled nonetheless. "I didn't say you were scared. If anything, you're too brave."

Our gazes met. "Everything is changing."

"Everything already has."

Later that night, I tossed and turned. My mind wouldn't shut down. The daimon attack, the apple assault, bitchy furies, the impending Council session, and everything else kept cycling in one giant, endless cluster. Each time I flipped over, I grew more irritated at the prospect of another sleepless night.

The trouble sleeping had started about a week after returning from Gatlinburg. I'd fall asleep for an hour or so before a nightmare crept into my dreams. Mom was usually in those nightmares. Sometimes I relived fighting her in the woods; sometimes I didn't kill her, and other times it was just me and Daniel, the daimon with the too-friendly hands.

Then there were the dreams where I *wanted* to be turned into a daimon.

I'd flipped onto my stomach and shoved my face into the pillow when I felt a strange tingling in the pit of my stomach—like the butterflies right before a first kiss, only much, much stronger.

I pushed up and squinted at the clock. Past one in the morning, and I felt wide awake. And hot—really hot. Thinking the temperature controls may've gone all wacky again, I got up and opened the window by the bed. Cool, damp air rolled in from the ocean, providing some relief. I didn't feel like I'd crawl out of my skin at any moment, but I still burned—like all over. I ran my hands over my face, aching in a way that reminded me of the time I'd spent with Aiden. Not our training sessions, oh no—but the night before I'd found Kain, the night I'd lain naked in Aiden's bed.

But I remembered more than the physical stuff. Words I'd never ever forget in a trillion years—*you got inside me, became a part of me.* No one had ever said anything like that to me—no one.

I glanced at the clock again, sighing. Fifteen minutes went by, then twenty minutes, then half an hour. Finally, I stopped paying attention to the time. My heart pounded until I squeezed my eyes shut. I could almost see Aiden now, feel the soft brush of fingertips and hear those words again. Then, without any warning, the itchy feeling vanished. The cool air coming in from the window suddenly felt brutal.

"What the hell?" I flopped onto my back. "Hot flashes? Really?"

It was a long, long time before I fell asleep.

CHAPTER 3

EVERYTHING DID CHANGE THE NEXT DAY.

Olivia and I shared a trig textbook in class, trying to figure out the difference between a sine and cosine. Considering we'd be spending the bulk of our adult lives hunting and killing daimons, learning trigonometry seemed pretty pointless, so we really didn't apply ourselves.

I drew a pair of humongous boobs on the free space above the formula and labeled them "Olivia." She immediately scratched her name out and scribbled "Alex."

I snorted, looking up just in time to see Mrs. Kateris, a pure-blood with enough degrees to be teaching at Yale, twist around and frown at us.

"Great," Olivia muttered from behind her hand. "If she picks up this textbook and asks what we're doing again, I'm going to die. Seriously."

I yawned loudly. "Whatever."

Mrs. Kateris placed the chalk down and clapped her hands. "Miss Andros and Miss Panagopoulos." She paused long enough for the entire front of the class to twist around in their seats and look at us. "Would you like to share—?"

"I like how she says your last name," I murmured to Olivia at the exact moment our classroom door swung open and a small fleet of Guards entered the room.

"What the hell?" Olivia sat up straighter.

Mrs. Kateris stepped back, smoothing her hands over the front of her skirt.

The Guards bowed in her direction, the custom when addressing pures of status, which in our world was pretty much every pure. "We apologize for interrupting your class, Mrs. Kateris," said the first Guard. I almost didn't recognize him. He was the Guard from the bridge, the one who'd followed me around the island—Crede Linard. Well, he must've been promoted.

Mrs. Kateris gave him an uneasy smiled. "No need to apologize. How can we help you?"

"Dean Andros wishes the presence of the half-bloods. We are here to escort them."

The halfs in the class glanced around the room, confusion and wariness on our faces. Had there been another attack?

Stepping back, Mrs. Kateris clasped her hands. Guard Linard faced the class, expression impressively blank. "Please follow us."

Olivia snapped the textbook closed as her face lost its color. "What's going on?"

I grabbed my backpack off the floor, thinking of the furies. Everyone had been talking about them this morning, thinking they looked pretty cool. No one seemed to get what a big deal they were. "I don't know."

Several halfs started asking questions as we filed out of the classroom, but Guard Linard frowned at them. "No talking."

The same thing was happening in the other classes. Doors opened as Guards led halfs in a single file down the corridor. Upstairs, the sound of herded footsteps followed our group. I glanced behind us, spotting Caleb and Luke.

Turning back around, I drew in a shallow breath. This was something serious, and we all recognized it. Tension rippled through the air, itching at our skin as we continued to the first floor. Getting down the stairwell took a ridiculous amount of time. Once again, I felt the desire to mention the fact we needed elevators.

We ended up being ushered through the lobby of the school, past the administrative offices, then into the middle of the Covenant—to the indoor coliseum. It was the only place big enough to hold all of us.

Once inside the room we students referred to simply as the "gymnasium," we were ordered to take our seats and to stay with our classes. Olivia and I ended up in the third row. Caleb and Luke were at least in the eleventh, which sucked. I'd rather be sitting near Caleb when they dropped whatever bomb they were about to drop on us, and I knew Olivia felt that way, too.

I bounced my knee, scowling. The seats in here had been made out of some kind of sandstone, and they were the most uncomfortable things to sit on.

Olivia squirmed. "Do you—"

From the gymnasium floor below us, Guard Linard whipped around. "No talking."

Olivia's brows flew up, and I wondered if Linard would stroke out if I asked who was guarding the bridge. I exhaled loudly as I scanned the sea of half-bloods in green training clothes. A bunch of blue-uniformed Guards stood watch. But I didn't see many people in the black uniforms of the Sentinels, the hunters of daimons.

Then my gaze settled on a tall blond leaning against the wall, and I recognized the well-muscled arms and narrow hips. He had one long leg bent at the knee, his booted foot planted on a mosaic of a seminude Zeus.

Seth.

His hair was pulled back in a leather tie, but like always, shorter strands slipped free and curled around his chin. He had this golden complexion uniquely his own and a face perfectly pieced together, with those odd amber eyes holding an exotic curve. Sometimes I wondered if the gods had specially crafted those cheekbones and smug-looking lips, if they'd put the faint cleft in his chin and carved his jaw out of granite. No one else quite looked like him.

He was, after all, the First Apollyon of our generation. According to my stepfather, Seth and I were fated to be together in some weird, energy transfer way. According to me, Seth was a pain in my—

Seth inclined his head in my direction and winked. I leaned back and focused on the Guards below. Seth and I weren't getting along at the moment. In our last training session, he'd "accidentally" hit me with a blast of pure energy and I'd "accidentally" thrown a rock at his head.

Perhaps I did have a problem with throwing things.

After what seemed like forever, Marcus entered the gymnasium, and the entire student assembly shifted forward. Around two hundred of us sat together, ranging from seven to eighteen years old. The wee ones sat on the floor, knee to knee. They probably had no clue what was going on.

Marcus wasn't alone. Council Guards dressed in all white followed behind him. The Council resembled the Olympian Court, eight pures and two Ministers—one male and one female. Only the Covenant locations held a Council—here in North Carolina, upstate New York, South Dakota, and the wilds of Tennessee. The Council acted as our ruling government, establishing laws and carrying out punishments. The Ministers were the only ones who communicated with the gods, but if what Lucian had said during the summer was true, the gods hadn't spoken to the Ministers in ages.

This was a lot of pomp for just one Minister. It wasn't like the entire Council was swarming the gymnasium—just Lucian and his awesome hair. Jet black, it flowed to his waist, pin straight. Complimenting his hair was the only really good thing I could say about my stepfather. Well, that and he sent me lots of money.

The Guards bowed, straightening slowly. I noted that Seth hadn't moved an inch. Lucian stepped forward, clasping his hands together. He wore an all white, tunic-type dress. I thought he looked ridiculous.

"A daimon attack occurred within the grounds of the Covenant yesterday." Lucian's clear voice rang through the silent room. "Such an attack is unprecedented and must be dealt with swiftly. At this time, we believe there will be no further… breaches of security."

Yeah, he must've seen the furies. I bet he hoped there wouldn't be any more breaches.

"But," he continued, "we must move forward and focus on prevention."

Like a violent tide rolling in from the ocean, apprehension swept through us. I held my breath.

"The Council and the Covenant have agreed that measures must be taken to ensure another attack does not occur."

Marcus stepped forward then, smiling in a way that sent shivers down my arms. "Several things are going to happen over the course of the next week. New rules are being put into place and these rules will be unconditional and effective immediately."

And here it starts, I thought angrily. One half-blood turned bad, so all half-bloods will be punished. I recognized the severity of the issue, but it didn't make it any easier to swallow.

Marcus scanned the crowd, meeting the gazes of the halfs. His steady eyes held mine a moment, then glided past. "A curfew of seven p.m. will begin tonight for all half-bloods—" Gasps could be heard echoing through the room. My jaw hit the floor. "—unless the half-blood is accompanied by a Guard and is participating in an activity related to schoolwork. There will be no other exceptions. At no time will half-bloods be allowed into the rooms of pure-bloods unless accompanied by an Instructor or Guard. No half-blood will be able to leave the Covenant-controlled island without permission, and then must be accompanied by a Guard or Sentinel."

"Oh, my gods," Olivia murmured, rubbing the palms of her hands over her thighs. "Can they do this?"

I didn't respond. The pures could do whatever they wanted. I had a feeling it was about to get a lot worse.

"Sentinels will be posted outside the dorms, along with the Covenant Guards. In addition to these measures, all half-bloods will be required to submit to a physical exam. These—" His cut a strong look toward the upper level, where several muffled curses sounded. "—*these* exams will be mandatory. After every half-blood has been examined, then the exams will continue based on need."

Ice rushed through my veins, settling in the pit of my stomach. Of course there would be physical exams. How else could they tell if any halfs had been turned? Their bodies, much like mine, would show the evidence of multiple daimon tags. It was the only sign of a half being turned.

I wanted to puke.

"Exams will begin tomorrow and will be done so alphabetically." Marcus stepped back, allowing Lucian to take center stage once more.

"None of us enjoy the idea of limiting your freedom or imposing potentially uncomfortable situations upon you." Lucian splayed his hands open in front of him. "We care for our half-bloods, and this is as much for your benefit as it is for the pure-blooded students."

I covered my mouth, afraid I'd say something. Benefit us? Restricting our comings and goings, forcing us to submit to *physical exams*? There was no difference between us and the halfs who served them—except we wouldn't have the pleasure of being doped up and unaware of what was happening to us.

I looked away from Lucian and caught sight of Seth again. Every line of his face had hardened in disapproval and his eyes flared like the sun. I could feel his anger as if it were my own.

After going over a couple of more rules regarding where we were allowed to enter and something about random dorm checks, the assembly drew to a close. I had a hard time focusing on what Marcus and Lucian had gone over. My own anger roiled inside me, and the brewing storm against the wall kept my attention.

We were ordered to exit the gymnasium the same way we'd entered: a silent, single-file line of half-bloods. Briefly, I caught a glimpse of Caleb's face. Disbelief and anger warred across his boyish features, making him seem so much older. No one had considered what this could mean for Caleb and me. They would find evidence of recent daimon attacks on both of us. Then what? Shove a bleeding pure in our face and see if we attacked? I glanced over my shoulder, searching for Seth. He stood with Lucian, off from the white-robed Guards, and they appeared to be… arguing.

At lunch, we went over the new rules quietly. More Guards than normal hovered around the perimeter of the cafeteria, and even a few Sentinels stood post, limiting what we could say. I wondered what those half-blood Sentinels thought, knowing that they'd be subject to the exams, too.

Pures usually mingled with the halfs during this time, but today was different. Halfs took up one side of the cafeteria while the pures sat at the farthest tables possible. My gaze landed on Cody Hale and his cronies. Cody hung out with halfs sometimes, like when he had nothing better to do. There were many times during the summer when I'd wanted to hit him, but hitting a pure meant expulsion, and that meant servitude.

Right now his group had their heads bent together. Every so often, Cody would run a hand over his neatly-cropped, brown hair, look at our table, and snicker. I wasn't the only one who noticed this.

Caleb's silent anger simmered around our table. Since the whole incident in Gatlinburg, I hadn't seen much of Caleb. My spare time consisted of training sessions while his revolved around Olivia. Looking back, I kind of wished I'd made time for him. Maybe then I would've noticed the subtle changes in him, the shade of darkness that seemed to surround him, how quickly he reacted with anger.

"Just ignore them, babe." Olivia nodded toward Cody's table, forcing a causal smile. "Cody's an idiot."

"It's not just Cody." He gave a tight laugh. "Haven't you seen how the other pures have been looking at us? Like we're all about to jump them?"

"They're just scared." Olivia squeezed his hand. "Don't take it personally."

"Caleb's right." Luke leaned forward and lowered his voice. "Today in class, a pure I've known for years requested his seat to be changed. Sam didn't want to sit next to me—or any half. Hades, he looked like he didn't want to be in the same room as us."

I rubbed my fingers over my temple as my appetite vanished. "They're all scared. There's never been a daimon on campus before."

"It's not our fault." Luke's eyes met mine. "And what do they have to be afraid of? The way the Minister talked today, it sounded like the daimon wasn't here anymore."

"No one really knows that for sure." I picked up my soda, watching Caleb. He didn't speak for the rest of lunch. As we filed out of the cafeteria, I pulled Caleb aside. "You doing okay?"

He nodded. "Yeah, I'm fine."

I wrapped my arm around him, ignoring the way he stiffened. "You don't seem like it. I get—"

"You get that we're already top suspects, Alex?" Caleb pulled away. "That none of this is right or fair? I don't want them stripping you down, or Olivia, looking for some sign that we're chomping on pures during our spare time. And with you…" He paused, glancing around the hallway outside the cafeteria. Luke and Olivia went on, but two Guards eyed us—the same two from yesterday. "Lea was being a bitch yesterday, but people…"

"People have been talking? Caleb, people have been talking about me since they found out my mom was a daimon. So what? Who cares?" I squeezed his hand, just like Olivia had. "Why don't you sneak over tonight and bring a movie?"

Caleb pulled away again, shaking his head. "I got things I need to do."

"Like Olivia?" I joked.

That brought a hint of a smile. "Come on, you're going to be late for class. You have practice with Seth—"

I groaned loudly. "Please don't say his name. He throws balls of energy at my head like it's some kind of game."

"He looked pretty pissed off during the assembly."

"Yeah, he did." I thought about him arguing with Lucian. Only gods know about what. "Anyway, sure you don't want to come by?"

"Not feeling it tonight. Besides, dodging the normal Guards is bad enough, but double the amount? Even I may have problems with that."

I pouted but relented as we parted ways. The rest of the afternoon crawled by, but I perked up when I saw Aiden enter the gym toward the end of Gutter Fighting. I tried and failed to contain my excitement.

"Where's Seth?" I bounced up to Aiden.

Aiden's eyes glittered with amusement. "He's with the Minister. Would you prefer him?"

"No!" I said a bit too eagerly. "What's he doing with Lucian?"

Shrugging, Aiden led me out to the center of the mats. "Didn't ask. You ready?"

I nodded, and Aiden handed me the dummy blades. He'd allowed me to practice with the real ones a week ago. Sadly, the thrill of finally getting to practice with them ended up overshadowed by the fact I'd already used them for real. I knew the weight of the slender daggers in my palms, the feeling of them slicing through daimon flesh. Using them in battle had killed that naïve appeal.

Aiden coached me through several techniques we'd learned in Silat training. We broke apart while he pulled out the dummies for me to stab. I twirled the plastic daggers like they were batons. "The new rules they set up for us suck. You know that, right? Physical exams and dorm searches?"

Aiden reached out, carefully tucking a strand of hair back behind my ear. He was always doing little things like that, things he shouldn't be doing. "I don't agree with all of them, but something has to be done. We can't continue as if nothing has happened."

"I know we can't continue as if nothing has happened, but that doesn't mean the pures have a right to punish every single half-blood."

"We aren't punishing the half-bloods. These rules were put into place to protect the half-bloods also."

"To protect us?" I gaped at him. "Because all I heard today were rules limiting what we can do. I didn't hear anything about the pures having to submit to embarrassing exams or being told they couldn't even visit the main island."

"You weren't in the assembly when they laid down the new rules for the pures, were you?" A bit of frustration began to seep through, furrowing his dark brows.

"Well no, but I haven't heard any pures bitching about anything."

Aiden took a deep breath. "Then you haven't been listening. They aren't allowed to go anywhere unless they're in groups. They can't leave the island unless they're with a Guard or a Sentinel—"

"Whoa." I laughed harshly. "Those poor pures have to have babysitters? At least they don't need to get permission to leave. We don't even have that option."

"Aren't you grounded from doing anything anyway? And preventing the halfs from leaving the island is to keep them safe."

I clenched the dagger, squeezing it so hard I thought it would shatter. "The new rules aren't fair, Aiden. You have to see that. I know you're a pure, but you can drop the act around me. You don't have to say you agree with it because you're expected to."

"This isn't an act, Alex. And this has nothing to do with me being a pure. I agree that drastic measures need to be taken. If the half-bloods have to sacrifice a couple of weeks of partying and jumping dorms to ensure—"

"Sacrifice a couple of weeks of partying? Are you serious? Do you think that's why we're upset?"

Aiden stalked toward me. "You're upset because you're being irrational and stubborn. You're letting your emotions rule your logic, Alex. If you'd stop and *think* for five seconds, you'd see that these rules need to be in place."

I jerked back a step, unable to remember the last time he'd spoken to me like that. An icky feeling started in my chest and spread.

"So let me get this straight." My voice shook. "You think it's okay for them to restrict where we can go and what we can do? That they can search our rooms at any time? You think it's acceptable for them to subject us to *full body* searches? And it's just okay for them to launch a witch hunt the moment they think there's another daimon?"

"No one's starting a witch hunt, Alex! I agree that certain measures have to be taken, but I don't agree with—"

Anger pounded through my blood. I threw the practice blade to the floor. "My gods, you're just another pure, Aiden! You're no different than the rest of them. How *irrational* of me to think otherwise."

Aiden flinched as if I'd hit him. "I'm no different than the rest? Do you hear yourself?"

"Whatever. Who cares, right? I'm just a half-blood." I pushed past him before I did do something irrational, like cry in front of him. Turns out, I didn't make it very far. I kept forgetting how fast Aiden could move.

He blocked me, eyes flashing silver. "How can you even say I'm like the other pures? Answer me, Alex."

"Because… because you should know that those rules aren't fair to us!"

"This isn't about the damn rules, Alex. I'm like the other pures?" He gave a low, sharp laugh. "You really believe that?"

"But you think—"

Aiden grabbed my arm, pulling me right against his chest. The unexpected contact fried my brain. "If I was like every other pure-blood, I would have had you by now, without even thinking about the consequences for you. Every day is a struggle not to be like them."

I stared up at him, shocked to hear him put it out there so bluntly. Words—and I always had words—totally escaped me. *I would have had you by now.* I was pretty sure I knew what he meant.

"So don't tell me I'm like other pures."

"Aiden—I'm—"

"Forget it." He released me, a cool mask slipping onto his face. "Practice is over."

Aiden left the room, and I stood there for several minutes. I'd never really argued with him before. Not like that. Sure, we disagreed on things all the time—like favorite TV shows. He liked the golden oldies—the kind they showed in black and white. I hated them. We'd come close to knocking each other out over that, but we'd never argued over *who* we were.

To add insult to injury, Guards were searching my room when I returned to the dorm. I don't know what they were looking for. Did I have a daimon hidden in my sock drawer, or evidence I was going to pounce on the next pure and suck up their aether stashed away with my undies? I stood by—powerless to stop them—and when they were done my stuff was a mess. It took me a better part of the evening to clean my room.

After I'd showered and slipped on my pajamas, I paced the room. I kept revisiting the lovely conversation I'd had with Aiden, and my stomach did the twisting thing again. I needed to apologize, because I'd been out of line. And to hear him say what he had? That if he'd wanted to be like other pures—he would have *had* me?

So caught up in my thoughts, I banged the sensitive part of my elbow into the doorframe. I cursed and bent over, gasping. Standing there, with sharp pain shooting through my arm, I thought of Mom. About whether or not she really did look relieved the instant before she simply crumbled away. Had I seen the glimmer of relief in her eyes because I'd wanted to see it? Because I'd wanted to believe I'd done the right thing by killing her?

Aiden believed that I'd done the right thing. And I… well, I wasn't so sure anymore.

A soft knock sounded, then it came again, and there was no denying that someone had knocked on the window in my bedroom.

Caleb? Maybe he'd changed his mind and brought some movies over. Thrilled over the prospect of hanging out with him, I went to the window and drew the blind up.

"Crap." I recognized the back of the blond head. "Seth."

CHAPTER 4

SETH SPUN, POINTING TO THE LOCK ON THE WINDOW. "Open," he mouthed.

I planted my hands on my hips. "Why?"

His stare became dangerous. "Now."

Against my better judgment, I unlocked the window and pushed it up. I had about a second to step back before he jumped through the window like a damn alley cat. My room was dark, but I could make out the eerie glow to his eyes.

"What do you want? Hey! Don't shut that window. You're not staying."

"Do you want me to leave it open so the next Guard who makes his rounds looks in here and sees me in your bedroom?" He shut the window and pulled the rope on the blinds. They clattered against the windowsill.

"I'll tell them you forced your way in here." I walked over to the lamp and switched it on. Hanging out in a dark bedroom with Seth wasn't on my list of things to do at the moment.

Seth smiled. "I wanted to apologize for not being at training today."

I watched him with a general sense of wariness. He tossed a few loose strands out of his eyes as he surveyed me with almost the same look. "Apology accepted. You can now leave."

"Do something to your arm?"

"Huh?"

He leaned over, brushing his fingers over the elbow I'd just cracked. "This."

There was a small, barely visible red spot. "How in the world can you see that? I hit it on the door a few minutes ago."

A grin slipped over Seth's lips. "You're so unbelievably graceful. Should I kiss it and make it better for you?"

I could tell he was only half joking. His presence around the Covenant had created quite the stir. So had his… extracurricular activities. If bed-hopping ever became a major sport, Seth would go pro. Or so I'd heard. I stepped around him. "Thanks, but I'll pass."

He followed me around the edge of the bed. "I've been told my lips can make a girl forget just about anything. You should try it out."

I wrinkled my nose. "Anyway, why were you with Lucian instead of at practice?"

"Alex, that's none of your business."

Somehow I'd cornered myself between the wall and the bed. "He's my stepfather. It's my business."

"What crazy logic you have."

My hands curled into fists. "Look, you can leave now. You apologized. Bye."

His smile increased as he looked around my room. "I think I'll stay. I kind of like it here."

"What?" I sputtered. "You can't stay. It's against the rules."

Seth laughed deeply. "Since when do you care about rules?"

"I'm a changed person."

"When did you change? Just right now? 'Cuz I heard about your smackdown in the cafeteria yesterday." A mischievous grin played across his lips. "By the way, that was made of awesome."

"Really? No one else thinks it was awesome. They said I was being… irrational." I pushed away from the wall and dropped on the bed. "Do you think I'm irrational?"

Seth sat down beside me, his left leg pressing against mine. "Is that a trick question?"

I scooted to the top of the bed. "So I'm irrational?"

He twisted at the waist and stretched out on his side. "You're a bit crazy. You throw apples in people's faces when you're angry. You go off half-cocked half the time. It entertains me to no end. So if you are irrational, I hope you stay that way. I love it."

I frowned. "All of that sounds really good. Thanks."

"Rational is mundane and uninteresting. Why would you want to be that?" He reached out, tugging lightly on the hem of my PJ bottoms. "You don't even have it in you."

"Have what in me?" I pushed his hand away. Of course Seth would be drawn to the unstable part of my personality. He was a bit crazy himself. I wasn't sure if it was all the aether in him that made him that way, or if he was just plain old crazy.

"You're too wild to be balanced and normal. Or logical," he added as an afterthought.

"I'm completely logical—totally. You don't know what you're talking about."

He sent me a knowing look before rolling onto his back. "I think I'll stay here tonight."

"What?" I shot to my knees. "Absolutely not, Seth. You aren't staying here."

He chuckled, resting his hands on his flat stomach. "I haven't been sleeping well. Have you?"

"I've been sleeping great." I pushed at his shoulders, but he didn't budge. "Seth, you're not staying here, so don't change the subject."

He rolled slightly, catching my hands with his. "Look, we didn't have training tonight. I'm owed an hour of your time."

I tried to pull my arms free. "That's ridiculous."

Seth sat up in one clean motion. "And it starts now."

"What?" My fingers curled helplessly. "It's late. I have class tomorrow."

He grinned, letting go of my arms. "You'd still be up even if I wasn't here."

Scooting back once more, I kicked him in the thigh. "You're a pain in my—"

"I think we'll work on how to control your anger."

I moved to kick him again, but he caught my calf. "Let go."

Seth leaned over, voice low. "Don't kick me again."

Our eyes locked. "Let. Go."

Slowly, he released his grip and sat back. "I want all of your attention for a moment." He paused, brows lowering. "That is, if you're capable."

"Whatever."

"What do you think about the daimon attack?"

I glanced at him. Everything about him had changed in an instant. "Honestly? I think it's just the beginning. I mean, for all we know, this could have been going on long before."

Seth swiveled around and sat beside me. Once situated, he nodded approvingly. "There's something you don't know, but I don't think it would hurt if you did."

I shot forward. "What?"

"The Council has been tracking incidents that look like daimon half attacks. They've been picking up over the last three weeks, discovering two to three attacks a week. And it's happening all over."

"But… they haven't said anything." Mainly, Aiden hadn't said anything, and I'd thought he told me everything. "How do you know about this?"

"I have my ways. The Ministers don't want the pures or halfs knowing right now. They're afraid it would cause a panic."

"So that's why you were with Lucian? He's feeding you this information?"

Seth just raised his brows.

I fell back against the headboard, sighing. "But not knowing is stupid. People need to know what's happening. Look at what my mother told me. It's happening."

"I know." He tipped his chin toward me, but his heavy lashes concealed his eyes. "I don't think the Council wants to believe that."

"That's so stupid, Seth. They need to focus on that instead of trying to control us."

"I agree. These rules are wrong." He lifted his eyes, meeting mine. "But you won't have to submit to them."

"Uh… it doesn't sound like I have a choice."

"The half-bloods won't have a choice, but you're different."

I stared at him in amazement. "I'm not any different, Seth."

He held my stare. "Yes, you are. You will become an Apollyon, which makes you very different from the other half-bloods. You won't submit to those exams."

"Is that what you and Lucian were arguing about after the assembly?"

His stare was intense, calculating. "Among other things, but it's not anything for you to worry about."

"It's not? That's pretty ballsy of you to argue with the Minister, Seth."

The look on his face faded, replaced once again with the smug amusement. "Lucian has promised me that you… will not be searched."

I slouched to the side, eyeing him suspiciously. "I didn't know you had the kind of influence to make Lucian promise anything."

"You don't need to worry about the exams. So don't."

"What about the other halfs? They shouldn't have to go through that."

He looked away, letting out a soft breath. "Can I ask you a question—a serious question?"

"Sure." I stared down at my scuffed hands. I doubted Lucian cared enough to honor that promise.

"Why do you want to become a Sentinel? Is it a sense of obligation or…?"

That question took me a few moments to respond to. "It's not about protecting pures, if that's what you're getting at. That's what the Guards are for."

"Of course you wouldn't settle on being a Guard," Seth said mostly to himself.

"Daimons kill for no reason—even mortals. What kind of creature just kills for the fun of it? Anyway, I'd rather do something about it than sit around and wait for them to attack."

"What if you had a different choice?"

"Servitude?" I stared at him. "Are you serious?"

He rolled his eyes. "I mean, what if you had other choices not given to half-bloods? To live a normal life?"

"I already did that," I reminded him, "for three years."

"Would you do it again?"

Why he was asking this? "Would you?"

Seth snorted. "I wouldn't give up being a Sentinel for the world. Or being the Apollyon. I rock."

Laughing, I rolled my eyes. "Wow. You're so humble."

"Why should I be humble? I'm great."

I didn't even bother responding, because I felt confident he was being serious. We sat in silence for a little while. I knew he caught I hadn't answered his question, but in not-so-typical Seth fashion, he didn't push it. "Did you see the furies in the lobby?"

He nodded.

"Aiden said they're here because the gods feel the Council isn't doing an adequate job." I toyed with the hem of my shirt. "Do you think… we need to be worried about them?"

"Ah… if they get loose, then it could be a… potential problem."

"Oh." I don't know what made me say the next thing that came out of mouth. "I yelled at Aiden in training."

Seth nudged my arm with his shoulder. "I'm afraid to ask."

"He agrees with the new rules." I yawned. "So I yelled at him."

"And he said you were being irrational, huh?"

"Yeah, so I yelled at him some more. I told him he was just like all the other pures."

"Well, he is like other pures."

I shifted down, trying to ease the ache in my side. "Not really."

Seth frowned down at me. "Alex, he's a pure-blood. Just because he chose to become a Sentinel doesn't make him any different. Ultimately, Aiden will always side with the gods. Not us."

"You mean the pures, not the gods." Weary, I lay my head down on the pillow and closed my eyes. Our hour was almost up. Maybe I'd get some sleep tonight. "You don't know him, Seth."

"I don't need to know him to know what he's capable of."

My brows rose, but I ignored that. "I need to apologize to him."

"You don't need to apologize to him." He bent down, brushing my hair off my cheek. "I'm being serious. You'll be the next Apollyon,

Alex. You won't apologize to him, to any pure, or even to a god."

After a few moments of silence I said, "You know you need to leave, right? Even if I fall asleep, you're going to leave?"

"Of course." I couldn't see him, but I heard the smile in his voice. Seth kept talking, bombarding me with questions, but I gave up answering them as sleep pawed at me, the kind of sleep I was almost sure I wouldn't wake up from in an hour or two. I finally gave into it, confident that when I awoke in the morning, Seth would be gone.

†

It felt like someone had trapped me face down on the bed. I thought I was having one of those dream paralysis things I'd read about once, but then I realized what pinned me to the bed was an arm.

And that arm belonged to Seth.

He hadn't left, and apparently, Seth was a cuddler.

His arm curled around my back, fingers balled into the comforter. His steady breath blew across my neck, almost as if he had moved my hair out of the way. Under a different circumstance, I would have enjoyed the feeling of having someone wrapped around me so closely. Because the warmth Seth exuded was nice—very nice. It was Seth, yet for a moment—a really tiny moment—I closed my eyes and drank in the warmth.

Then I wriggled out from underneath him, beat him on the chest until he woke up, and yelled at him for staying. All of this made me late for my first class, and the whole episode left me in a weird funk, which wasn't helped when I passed Lea in the hallway.

Even with the black eye and bandaged nose, Lea looked good. No one could sneer like her. I ignored her for the most part, feeling ambivalent for doing so.

In Technical Truth and Legends, which was a cross between history and English, I usually sat beside Thea, a quiet pure I'd met over the summer, but today Deacon St. Delphi slid into the seat beside me.

I liked Deacon for a lot of reasons—none of them being the fact he was Aiden's younger brother. He tended to drink a bit too much, but he was fun—lots of it.

"Hey there." Deacon dropped his book on the desk.

"Why isn't Thea sitting here?"

He shrugged and several blond curls fell across his gray eyes, the only physical trait he and his brother shared. "Some of the pures are scared of you. Thea knows we're friends. She asked to switch."

"Thea's scared of me? Since when? What did I do to her?"

"It's not you personally. A lot of us are freaked out right now."

"That's nice to know." I focused on the chalkboard. Our teacher hadn't showed yet.

"You asked."

"I did."

"Besides, you should be nice to me."

I cracked a half smile for him. "I'm always nice to you, Deacon."

"Yeah, but you need to be nicer. I'm losing a lot of cool points being seen talking to you."

I glared at him.

Deacon grinned. One dimple in his right cheek appeared. "Not just you, but any half at this moment. We pures don't trust a single one of you. Every half is suspect. We're just waiting for one of you to pounce on us and suck away at our aether."

"Then why are you talking to me?"

"Have I ever cared for what the other pures think?" His voice was loud enough for several of the pures seated around us to hear. I cringed inwardly. "Anyway, my brother thinks I need a babysitter while he goes to Council. Probably thinks I'm going to overdose or something without him being up my ass."

"That's not what he thinks. He's probably worried someone *will* suck up all your aether."

Deacon arched an eyebrow at me. "Defensive, aren't you, when it comes to my brother?"

Looking away, I felt my cheeks flush. "No. You give him a hard time when all he does is care about you."

"I don't know. He just thinks I'm a drunk little shit, which I am." He grinned, but it rang sort of false. "Anyway, his birthday is coming up. He's going to be twenty-one, yet he acts like he's thirty."

"'Cuz thirty is real old," I said. Of course I hadn't forgotten Aiden's birthday. It was the day before Halloween, and a week or so before we left for the Council.

"Anyway, I thought about throwing him a party. You should come."

I shook my head, grinning. "Deacon, I'm not allowed to go anywhere. None of the halfs are." I also doubted Aiden would be down with a party, but I didn't say that. I think Deacon was serious in wanting to do something for Aiden, and I didn't want to hurt his feelings.

"So you excited about going to Council? I hear they know how to party up there."

Edginess turned my tummy upside down. "Excited isn't the word I'd use."

Our teacher finally showed up and launched into a long-winded, dry lecture about archetypes and the first creation of the Council. Other than wanting to bang my head against the desk, the class was a breeze. So was the rest of the morning, once I got used to the suspicious looks. They weren't directed just at me, but at any and all half-bloods.

The pures were a paranoid bunch.

Halfway through Silat training, several Guards entered the room, bringing everyone to a halt. I sent Caleb and Luke a nervous look as the first Guard started reading out names in a flat, emotionless tone. My name was among the ten called out.

My stomach turned over as I grabbed my bag and followed the other halfs out. Their faces were pale, eyes sharp with distrust. Quietly, we trailed behind the three Guards to the med center. The sickening feeling expanded when I saw we were going to the same room Kain had been kept in. That alone was enough to make me want to flee.

One of the male nurses, a pure with salt and pepper hair, faced our group. Part of me hoped Lucian really had promised Seth that I wouldn't have to go through with the exams, but I should've known better. There was no bond between us, nothing to make him care about me.

The pure smiled, showing off a row of straight teeth. Something about his smile clenched my lungs. There were three female halfs in the group, and his mouth twisted into a greasy grin. Nausea rose sharply.

"We will take you in one at a time. We will make this as fast as possible for you," the pure said. "Any questions?"

I raised my hand, heart tumbling over itself.

"Yes?" He sounded surprised.

"What if we don't agree to this?"

The pure's gaze darted to the Guards behind me, and then bounced back to me. "There's nothing to be worried about. It will be over within a couple of minutes."

I nodded slowly, feeling the eyes of the other halfs on me and the Guards shifting uncomfortably. "Yeah, I'm not down with this."

"But… you have no choice," he said slowly.

"But I do and I'm choosing no. And if you don't like that, then I'd like to see you try to make me do this."

That was pretty much when the Guards behind me decided they were going to try to make me do this. And that is when I decided I was going to be hitting someone again.

CHAPTER 5

I ELBOWED THE FIRST GUARD IN HIS STOMACH. THE second Guard tried to force me into a corner, but my spin kick sent her flying into a gurney. The third and final Guard took a swing at me, and I'm not sure what happened, but I do know I kind of lost it.

A deep and terrible rage flowed through me. Time sped up incredibly fast. I caught the Guard's hand and twisted his arm backwards, spinning him around. Planting my foot in his back, I knocked him into a table. The first Guard came at me again. He dodged my kick, but I spun around before he could anticipate my next move and my foot connected with his chin. The impact sent him staggering back.

The female half rushed me. I jumped the table of medical gloves and cotton swabs with startling grace. There was a second when I acknowledged that I *shouldn't* have been able to do that. Not clear a five-foot table with one jump. Especially when I hadn't even looked behind me, but then the heel of my shoe slammed into the cart, crashing it into the female's chest. The three Guards struggled on the floor in various degrees of pain.

The white walls of the med office spun as I turned around, facing the cowering pure.

"I still don't have a choice?"

He edged along the wall, his face as white as his coat, hands held out in front of him as if *that* could stop me. I took a step toward him out of maliciousness. Not like I'd actually hit a pure… again. He bolted for the door yelling, "Guards! Guards!"

Several of the halfs looked shocked, like they too couldn't believe what I'd just done. Two of them looked like they wanted to join the melee.

"You don't have to do this," I said earnestly. "They can't make you if you don't—"

My words were cut off by the first Guard. Recovering, he jumped to his feet. "Miss Andros, you have made a very unwise decision. No one would have hurt you."

I wheeled around. They weren't going to come at me one at a time now. Some of the rage ebbed as I stumbled backward. Time stopped moving so fast. The three of them rushed me at once. I managed to knock one of the Guards aside, but another grabbed hold of my arm. I would have had him too, I swear, but the swarm of Guards entering the room distracted me.

So did the two halfs blocking their entrance, putting up a decent fight. I almost smiled, but a heartbeat later, I was pinned to the cold tile. Two of the male Guards held my arms down, and the female half literally sat on top of me. I bucked, trying to free myself.

"Stop." She grabbed the sides of my head and forced it back. Blood trickled from her nose. "Stop fighting us. No one wants to hurt you."

I could hear the scuffle by the door. "You're hurting me now," I gasped out. "You're busting my spleen."

The commotion caused by the fighting quickly ceased, and for a moment, all I could hear was the sound of my heartbeat slamming against my ribs painfully. "Okay. I'm done."

She glared down at me. "We'll decide when you're done."

"No. I will decide when you are done. And you are done with her," came a new voice—one that was both as cold and as hard as it was oddly musical.

The weight on my chest suddenly vanished, along with the Guard. She flew across the med room, slamming into one of the many carts lining the walls. I rolled onto my knees, drawing in air.

Seth took one step into the room, eyes simmering with anger. "You. Help her up now."

"But… we have our orders. She refused to comply." said the Guard.

"You must not have paid close attention. The Minister gave orders for all halfs to be searched, but not his *stepdaughter*. I doubt he will be pleased to know you three disobeyed him." Seth's gaze fell over me. "Why have you not helped her up yet?"

The Guard who had spoken darted forward and gently placed me on my feet.

"Apologize to her. All of you."

Surprised, I looked at Seth. He was being serious. He actually wanted them to apologize for doing their jobs. And the way he looked, well, he looked like he wanted to physically make them sorry. There was something unstable in his eyes. "Seth, that's not—"

"Be quiet, Alex. I want to hear them apologize."

My brows shot up. "Excuse—"

"I'm sorry, Miss Andros," the male Guard interrupted, as pale as a daimon. "I beg your pardon."

Seth looked pointedly at the other Guards. The female Guard limped forward, apologizing profusely. When I nodded, they filed out of the room, leaving Seth and me alone for a few moments.

"You didn't have to make them apologize, Seth. They were just doing their jobs. You didn't—"

He stood directly in front of me, moving so fast I hadn't even registered it. He caught the edge of my chin with the tips of his fingers, looking me over. My cheek felt a little tender, but I doubted it would bruise. "A 'thank you' would be nice. I did stop them, you know."

I shifted uncomfortably. "Thanks."

Seth arched a brow as he tipped my head back. "You could also sound like you mean it."

"I do mean it, but you embarrassed them."

He dropped my chin, seeming pleased that I didn't screw up my face. "You beat the Guards up when they were just doing their jobs. I guess we're even."

Dammit. Seth had a point. I sighed. "Did… Lucian really order them not to search me?"

"Yes, but apparently he wasn't clear enough."

"But what about the other halfs? They shouldn't have to go through that." Instead of answering, he reached out and straightened the collar of my shirt. It must have come down during my fight, exposing the tags covering my neck. "Seth, what about them?"

Dropping his hand, he shrugged. "I don't know. I only have enough room in my head to be concerned about myself and you."

I snickered. "I'm surprised you have any room to think about anyone but yourself."

The smug grin was back. "Me too. I don't think I like it, actually." He dropped his arm over my shoulders and steered me toward the exit, pass the halfs waiting outside and the cold looks of anger from the pures.

†

Aiden ended practice early that evening. We didn't speak much, but I could tell he had heard about what'd happened earlier. The only bright spot of the evening was when I ended up getting to eat dinner with Caleb. The news had already traveled to him and probably the rest of the Covenant.

"How much trouble did you get in?" Caleb asked.

I shrugged and dipped a fry into a glob of mayo. "None, actually. Lucian had ordered them not to search me."

Caleb cringed as I stuck the mayo-covered fry in my mouth. "You've been touched by the gods. I swear."

"Touched in more ways than one," I cracked. "Where's Olivia?"

"Can you dip your fries in something normal, like ketchup?"

I swirled my fry in the mayo gleefully. "And where's Olivia?"

Caleb leaned the chair back on two legs, sighing. "She's mad at me about yesterday. We got into an argument this morning."

"Oh. You guys fighting?"

"I guess so. It's stupid. Anyway, any news about the daimon?"

I told him what Seth had said about more half-bloods being attacked and turned. Caleb had the same reaction as I did: disbelief and anger. Sometimes I really, truly believed that the Councils would run better if half-bloods had control. We seemed to have better critical thinking skills and more common sense.

After a few moments, Caleb spoke. “You know, I think what you did was pretty awesome.”

I shrugged, thinking about how embarrassed the Guards had seemed. “Thanks. But it doesn’t feel pretty awesome now.”

Caleb raised his brows. “Well, it’s got everyone talking and thinking. None of us want to go through with this. We think it was brave.”

“It wasn’t brave. Stupid maybe, but not brave.”

“No,” he insisted. “It was brave.”

“Caleb, you know the pures will go crazy if we start really, really pushing them. One half refusing a strip search is one thing, but dozens? That’s treason to them. You know what they do when you’re suspected of treason.”

The determined look gave his blue eyes an unfamiliar edge. “Like I said, I think things have to change around here.”

I leaned forward. “Caleb, don’t get in trouble.”

“Why are you arguing with me about this, Alex? You stood up to them today, but you sound like you don’t think any of us should. Why? Only you’re allowed to, and the rest of us should just go along with whatever they want?”

“No. That’s not what I’m saying at all. It’s just that this is serious, Caleb. It’s not about sneaking into rooms or leaving the Island. People could get expelled or worse.”

“You didn’t.”

“Yeah, well… I’m different. And—*and* I’m not saying that to be like I’m super cool, either. The only reason I’m not in trouble is because Lucian stepped in—why, I don’t know. But you guys will get in trouble.”

Incredulous, he threw up his hands, shaking his head. “You’re being way too… ”

“Way too what?”

Caleb frowned. “I don’t know, too rational about this or something.”

For a moment I did nothing but stare at him, and then I busted out laughing. “Do you know you’re the only person to accuse me of being *too* rational?”

A smile broke out across his face, reminding me of the younger, more carefree Caleb—the Caleb who didn't get excited about taking a stance against the pure-blooded Council. "Well, I guess there's a first time for everything."

We grinned at each other, but then my smile faded. "Caleb, you've changed."

His smile disappeared. "What do you mean?"

"I don't know. You're just different now." I didn't think he was really going to respond, especially when he stood up.

He walked around the table to sit next to me, and his lips pursed for a thoughtful moment. "I am different."

"I know," I whispered.

A brief smile appeared. "You know, I keep thinking about when we were… in that cabin and I couldn't do anything to help you. I don't know what I'd thought it would be like to face a daimon. I guess I really had no idea." A muscle along his jaw ticked as he rubbed his fingers over a scuff mark on the table. "All I keep thinking is there had to be something I could've done to make them stop hurting you. I should've fought through the pain or something."

"Caleb—no." I grabbed his cool hands. "There was nothing you could do. And that whole, messed-up situation was my fault."

He faced me, lips twisting into a cynical smile. "I just never felt more… powerless in my life. I don't want to feel that way again."

"You're not powerless. You never were." I scooted over and wrapped my arms around his stiff shoulders.

Caleb responded a little awkwardly at first, but then he rested his chin atop my head. We stayed like that for a little while. "You have mayo in your hair," he murmured.

Giggling, I pulled back. "Where?"

He pointed. "You're such a messy eater."

After I got the mayo out of my hair, he studied me. "What? Do I have more mayo in my hair?"

"No." He glanced around the empty cafeteria. "How are things between … you and Aiden?"

I dropped the napkin. Usually Caleb sensed Aiden wasn't something I wanted to talk about. "I don't know. Everything is the same, I guess."

He rested his chin on my shoulder. The edges of his soft hair tickled my cheek. "Was he mad about the Guard thing?"

"He didn't say anything about it, but I'd go with a yes."

"Have you guys, you know, done—?"

"No!" I jerked back, hitting his arm lightly.

Caleb shot me a knowing look.

"Nothing can happen between us, you know that. So stop looking at me like that."

"Like not being allowed has ever stopped you before, Alex. Just… just be careful. I'm not going to lecture you—"

"Good."

He flashed a grin. "But if anyone finds out about what almost happened between you two…"

"I know." I glowered at the rest of my fries. "It's nothing to worry about, all right?"

The topic thankfully switched to less serious subjects. Way too soon, we had to head back to our dorms, and I was feeling a little bit better about things by the time I showered. But I still worried about Caleb, feared that the events in Gatlinburg had damaged him.

After I'd changed I was hit again by that weird tingly sensation. Heat crept over my skin right before the intense ache started in my belly. Really, I tried to ignore it. I even picked up my trig book, but I couldn't focus. I turned on the television, but the force of whatever affected me made it nearly impossible to think about anything other than not having a boyfriend. Maybe this was the way my body was telling me I needed to find someone—someone who was actually available and wasn't a pure-blood.

When it finally did ease off, I fell into a restless sleep that lasted only hours before I shot straight up in bed, heart racing. I scanned the dark bedroom, trying desperately to rid the image of Daniel's face from my mind, his touch from my memories.

I rolled over and looked at the window. A second passed before my brain processed the dark shadow behind the blinds. My heart leapt into my throat. Jerking up, I threw the covers off and crept over to the window. The shadow was still there, sending shivers over me. Was it Seth trying to peep into my window?

If so, I was going to beat him over the head.

Or it could be the daimon—since they hadn't caught it yet. Hell, if it was, it wasn't going to sneak into my room.

I drew the blinds up and jumped back. A pale face—clearly not Seth's—stared back at me. In the pale light of the moon, I almost thought it was a freaking daimon.

But it was a Sentinel. I think the icy blonde was named Sandra. Still, what was she doing staring into my bedroom window? Something about that creeped me out majorly. Without further ado, I unlocked the window and pushed it open. "Is everything okay?"

Sandra's eyes dropped to the tags on my bare arms before she dragged them back to my face. "I thought I heard screaming coming from this room."

I flushed as I realized I must've been dream-screaming. "I'm sorry. Everything's fine."

"Make sure this window is locked." She smiled. "Good night."

Nodding, I closed the window and threw the lock. My cheeks still felt bright red as I climbed back into bed and pulled the covers over my head. Although my childish screams had brought a Sentinel and not a daimon to my bedroom, the creeped-out feeling lingered all night.

†

I stumbled through the day, feeling out of it and sick. Not throwing up sick, but nervous sick. I dozed off beside Deacon in class. He woke me up before the teacher spotted me sleeping. My hands trembled when I picked up my soda at lunch, which earned me a slew of concerned questions from Caleb and Olivia.

Maybe I was coming down with something. Or maybe it was the nightmares I'd had for the last two nights. I really didn't know, but all I wanted to do was crawl back into bed and sleep.

In Gutter Fighting, it was hard for me to follow the movements of my sparring partner. Luke took it easy on me, only knocking me to the floor a couple of times. And my day wasn't anywhere near over.

Practice with Aiden immediately followed, and I sucked at that, too.

I feinted to the left, but my movements felt jerky and too slow. Aiden's leg came around viciously, striking me in the calf. The impact knocked me forward, face-first into the mats. Dropping very real blades, I caught myself awkwardly. All my weight landed on my wrists and I let out a sharp gasp.

"Alex! Are you okay?" Aiden came to my side and reached down.

Ignoring the pain, I pushed myself up. "I'm fine."

Aiden's arm was still extended, as if he'd forgotten he had been reaching for me. He just stood there, staring at me. "What's up with you today? You're going to break your neck at this rate."

Fire scorched my cheeks as I grabbed the blades off the mats. "I'm okay."

I wanted to apologize for accusing him of being like other pures while we had a few moments of downtime, but the words "I'm sorry" just wouldn't move past my lips, and then Aiden was falling back into an attack stance.

He flipped the blades over in his hands. "Again."

I attacked. Aiden brought his blades down on mine, the sound of metal clashing rung through the training room. He pushed me back, jabbing one blade at my midsection. I caught his arm with my forearm, knocking his aim off.

"Good," he said. "Keep moving. Never stay still."

I darted under his arm, staying out of his range while I studied his moves. There was always something that gave away the move, the technique. Sometimes it was just a fine tremor of the muscle or eye movement, but it was always there.

Aiden jabbed, but it was a ploy. I saw it an instant before he dropped down, going for my legs with a low kick. I jumped out of way and then went for the kill shot. This game would have been over for an untrained half, being caught on the mats like that. But Aiden wasn't untrained and he was incredibly fast. He jumped to his feet in one swift movement, simultaneously tucking both blades into one hand.

I leapt, bringing the blades down. Aiden met me midflight, catching my arm. Within a second, he had my back pinned against him and two daggers pointed at my throat.

He bent his head down, his breath dancing over my cheek. "What did you do wrong?"

I felt his heart slamming against his chest. We were *that* close. "Um…?"

"You saw me moving the blades to one hand as a vulnerable move. You should have gone for the hand that held the blades. One clean swipe and you would have disarmed me."

Mulling that over, I saw he was right. "Well, hell's bells."

He leaned his head down further, the longer strands of his hair brushing my cheek. Neither of us moved. I let my eyes fall shut as his warmth surrounded me. I think I could've fallen asleep standing against him. "Now you know." He released me. "Go again."

And I did. Again and again, we squared off. I blocked a series of his jabs and he blocked all of mine. After a few rounds, I was slick with cold sweat and exhausted. All I wanted to do was sit down.

Aiden rushed me, and I pushed him back. With distance between us, I launched to the right, fingers spasming around the hilt of the blade. *Kick. Use a kick,* I ordered myself. Aiden dodged my jab, but not my kick. He lost his grip on one of the blades, and it clattered to the mat. Surprise and pride flickered across his face before he charged me with one blade. I blocked his attack, arms trembling. He dropped down, moving into position to sweep my legs out from underneath me. I saw it coming a mile away.

I just didn't—couldn't will my legs to move fast enough.

Everything slowed down, ensuring that the lameness of what was about to occur would be perfectly captured. I jerked back toward the edge of the mat. His long leg swept around, catching both of my legs. I lost my grip on the blades and fell backward. A second later my head cracked off the floor.

I lay still, stunned and queasy.

Aiden's face popped into my vision, but his features were a bit muddled. "Alex, are you okay?"

I blinked slowly. My head hurt so bad my teeth ached. "I… think so."

"Can you sit up?"

Every part of me protested the movement, but I sat up. Aiden immediately checked the back of my head for damage with swift and gentle fingers. "That… was kind of lame of me."

"It's not a big deal. You were doing really well. You even disarmed me." He sat back; his hands cupped my cheeks and tilted my head back. He smiled. "I don't think there's any permanent damage."

I tried to smile, but failed. "I'm sorry."

A frown creased his brow. "Alex, don't apologize. It happens. You can't always be the fastest—"

"I saw your move, Aiden. I had more than enough time to get out of the way." I lowered my eyes. "I'm just so freaking tired."

Aiden scooted forward, his knees pressing against my thigh. "Alex, look at me." Sighing, I lifted my eyes. He smoothed my hair back with a little smile. "Are these practices too much?"

"No—"

"Alex, be honest with me. You're training all the time. Is it too much?"

If he kept touching my hair I'd admit to anything. "It's not too much, Aiden. Really, it's not. I'm… just not getting a lot of sleep."

He shifted so that he was right beside me, his other hand falling to my shoulder. I inhaled his unique scent of sea and burning leaves. With him this close, with one hand curving over my shoulder and the other continuingly smoothing back my hair, I was putty in his hands. I think he knew that.

"Why are you not sleeping, Alex?" he asked, voice low and soft.

The words just kind of spilled out of me. "I have nightmares—every night and all night."

"Nightmares?" he repeated. He didn't sound like he thought it was funny, but that he just didn't understand.

I closed my eyes, taking a shallow breath. “You don’t know what it was like all those hours… in Gatlinburg, not able to really do anything. And all those tags—it felt like they were breaking off pieces of *me*. You don’t know what I would’ve done to make them stop—*just stop*.”

Aiden stiffened, his fingers curling around the nape of my neck. “You’re right, Alex. I don’t know, but I wish I did.”

“You don’t mean that,” I whispered.

“I do.” He went back to moving his fingers through my hair. “Then maybe I’d be able to help you somehow. Is that what you’re having nightmares about?”

“Sometimes they’re about Mom and other times it’s the other two—Eric and Daniel. They’re so vivid, you know? Like it’s happening again.” I pressed my lips together, stopping the ball of emotion from making it past my throat. Talking about that night, about what they’d done, curdled my stomach like sour milk. “So yeah, I don’t get much sleep.”

“How… how long has this been going on?”

I shrugged. “Since a week or so after everything happened.”

“Why haven’t you said anything? That’s too long for you to deal with this alone, Alex.”

“What was I supposed to say? It’s pretty damn childish to be having night terrors—”

“They’re not night terrors. It’s stress, Alex. What you’ve had to deal with…” He looked away, a muscle working in his jaw. “No wonder you’re having nightmares. She was a daimon, Alex, but she was also your mother.”

I pulled back, looking into his face. Concern etched across Aiden’s features, shifting his eyes to a thunderous gray. “I know.”

He shook his head. “And then you’ve been running nonstop. You haven’t had a moment to just… shut down. The daimon attack probably added to it. I don’t know why I didn’t think about that—why no one did. This is all too much. We have to—”

“Please don’t tell Marcus. *Please*.” I started to climb to my feet, but he kept me on the mat. “If he thinks something’s wrong with me, he’ll take me out of the Covenant.” And he would, too. If Marcus thought I was damaged, I'd be in servitude. Halfs didn't go to counseling. They didn't get posttraumatic stress. They *dealt* with things. They didn't lose sleep and screw up in practice. "Oh, gods, Marcus is going to kick me out."

Aiden caught my chin again. "That's not what I was going to say. You worry too much, *Agapi.* I'm not going to say anything to anyone. Not a single word of this, but that doesn't mean I'm going to forget."

"What does that mean?"

He smiled, but it seemed off and a little sad. "Well, you need to get some rest, and you need time to just chill out. I don't know. I'll think of something."

I covered his hand with mine. At once, he let go of my chin and threaded his fingers through mine. My little heart just got all kinds of happy. "What does *Agapi* mean?"

Aiden sucked in air. "What?"

"You've called me *Agapi*… a couple of times. It sounds beautiful."

"Oh. I… I didn't realize I had." He pulled his hand free. "It's the old language. It doesn't really mean anything."

That was kind of disappointing. Reluctantly, I climbed to my feet. I drew in a deep breath and watched Aiden stand. "I feel okay—"

The gym doors flew open, banging against the wall. Seth strode in like he owned the place. "What's going on?"

I glared at him. "What does it look like?"

Aiden swiped the blades off the mats. "I really need to find a way to bar those doors."

Seth shot Aiden a look. "I really wish you'd try."

Aiden lowered his arms, his fingers inching over the hilt of the blades. "Don't you have something you should be doing? I cannot believe your sole purpose of being here is to help Alex a few days a week and prowl the halls of the female dorm."

"Actually, that is my sole purpose. Didn't you know? I'm here—"

"Uh, is practice over, Aiden?" I cut in before the two choke-slammed one another.

"Yeah." His eyes stayed on Seth.

I felt there was a good chance he might stab Seth. There was also a good possibility Seth might zap Aiden. "Okay. Thanks for the practice… and everything."

Seth smirked and raised his brows at Aiden.

"No problem," replied Aiden.

Groaning inwardly, I hurried over to my bag. On the way out, I grabbed a fistful of Seth's shirt. "Come on."

"What?" Seth protested. "I think Aiden wants to hang out with me."

"Seth!"

"All right." He spun around, straightening his shirt.

I didn't look back. Once outside the building, I dared a glance at Seth. "Did you need something?"

He grinned. "Nope."

"So, you busted up my training for no apparent reason? I call bullshit on that."

Seth dropped his arm over my shoulder. "You can call whatever you want. Let's go get something to eat. You can still do that, right? Or are you grounded from showing your face in the cafeteria?"

"I'm not supposed to be hanging out with friends."

"Then I guess it's a good thing that you and I aren't really friends."

CHAPTER 6

AFTER ANOTHER LONG AND BORING DAY OF CLASSES, I waited for my turn with Seth, praying I didn't crack my head again. Last night, I'd gotten another decent night's sleep after Seth had shown up and popped in a DVD. I was feeling pretty rejuvenated.

Since I was alone for a few moments before training, I approached the wall of mass destruction. I was about to pick up the dagger Aiden favored when I realized something was off about the wall.

The weapons hung from little black hooks, and now several spots were empty. Of all the times I'd practiced in this room, I'd never seen any spot open. Daggers and blades were kept in this room for training purposes only. Each blade required a different handling technique and were used at different times throughout the day. Did they remove the blades for cleaning? It wasn't like they gathered much dust in this room.

"Ready, my little Apollyon-in-training?"

I dropped my bag and turned around. Seth strolled across the mats, a cocky grin smeared across his face. Rain dripped from his hair and ran down his neck, giving him a wild look. I forgot about the missing blades at the sight of the wicked look on his face. He was *so* up to something. "Not really."

Seth cracked his knuckles. "Since it's pouring outside, I figured we could work on your grappling skills—since they are terrible. I know, I know—you're devastated by the knowledge of not being able to practice with the elements today, but look on the bright side. We get to roll around on the mats. Together."

I arched an eyebrow. "Sounds like fun."

He stopped behind me and placed his hands on my shoulders. "You up for it?"

I shrugged off his hands and ripped the hair tie off my wrist. "Yeah, I'm not damaged."

"I didn't say you were."

"Can we do this without you talking?"

Seth pouted. "But I have something you may want to know."

"Doubtful."

"Let me ask you a question: Do you feel bad about getting the halfs to refuse to submit to the exams being done? I saw five more halfs all bruised up today."

Caleb hadn't been joking when he'd said several halfs had been planning on refusing the exams. I could pick them out easily. Though there hadn't been a sign indicating that the daimon was still on campus, the pures kept up with the rules and exams. I think it had something to do with the fact no one knew how long a daimon half could go without aether.

"I didn't make them do anything," I grumbled.

"They're following your lead, and if I remember correctly, didn't you tell the ones with you that they didn't have to do it?"

My cheeks flushed with frustration. "Whatever. Shut up."

"Then let's play, Alex."

He considered grappling "playing" only because it really did involve a lot of rolling around… and at times, hair pulling. And I think Seth used it as an excuse to cop a feel. Like right now. I knocked his hand off my butt. "You're such a dog."

"And your grappling skills suck." He pinned me for the third time. Most of his hair had come loose, hanging over his face. "Most females suck at it. It's basic body strength. Males have more mass. So you need to stay on your feet."

Rolling my hips, I managed to knock Seth off. I scrambled back to standing. "Yeah, I think I grasped that already."

Lounging on his side, he tipped his head back. "So, you slept like a little baby Apollyon last night. I wonder why."

I glared at him. Seth had stayed the night again. "I loathe you."

He chuckled. "You reluctantly like me."

"Whatever. So are you going to tell me why you're always with Lucian? Is he a part of your little fan club now?"

"My *fans* love to hear my war stories." He jumped to his feet, swinging at me. "They're obsessed with me. What can I say? I'm that cool. And I'm not always with Lucian."

I grabbed his arm, twisting it back in a submissive hold. "I seriously doubt that."

Seth stilled. "You know what, Alex?"

Straightening, I relaxed my hold on his arm. "What?"

He glanced back over his shoulder at me. "You really need to start resting more. The lack of sleep is clouding your judgment. I am that cool, and you just made a fatal mistake."

"Huh?"

"You should never relax your hold." Then he flipped me off his shoulder. I hit the mat with a loud grunt. "Aw, did you just fall?"

"No." I rolled onto my back, wincing. "I attacked the floor."

He dropped down, planting one leg on either side of mine. He caught my chin. "What were you and Aiden doing in practice yesterday?"

I grabbed Seth's wrist, intending on snapping it. Seth appeared to guess my intentions, because his eyes narrowed into thin slits before he slipped his hands away from my chin. "We were practicing, and why do you need to sit on me to talk to me?"

"Because I can and I like it."

I wanted to hit him. "Well, I don't like it. So get off me."

He leaned forward instead, his face only inches from mine. "I don't like your practices with Aiden. So no, I won't get off."

My throat felt dry. "You just don't like Aiden."

"You're right. I don't like him. I don't like the way he looks at you, and I really don't like the way he looks at me."

I tried to keep my expression blank, but I felt my cheeks burn. "Aiden doesn't look at me weird. And he looks at you that way because you *are* weird."

He laughed. "Yeah, I don't think so."

Could Seth be picking up on my feelings for Aiden like he'd picked up on my fear while I was in Gatlinburg? If so, that would be really, really bad. "What are you getting at?"

Seth rolled off and sat cross-legged beside me. "I'm not getting at anything. By the way, I do have something to tell you."

As long as I lived, I'd never get used to the way Seth switched topics so frequently. He made my brain hurt. "What?"

"There was an attack at the Tennessee Covenant last night. It was a half who'd been turned. He cut up a pure, drained him of aether, and tossed him out of a seventh-story dorm window."

Horrified, I jackknifed up. "Oh, my gods! Why didn't you say something at the beginning of practice?"

He stared at me. "I clearly remember telling you I had something you'd be interested in knowing and you said it was doubtful."

"Well, you could have explained it a little better." I fell back against the mats. "Holy crap, what are they doing about it?"

"The same thing they are doing here, but they caught the daimon—it was a Guard once upon a time, and since the pure died, they're taking more extreme measures."

"Like what?"

"There's talk of segregating the pures from the halfs."

"What?" I shrieked.

Seth flinched and scooted away. "Ouch. Damn, Alex, I can only imagine what you sound like in the throes of—"

"Are you serious?" I sat up again, folding my legs under me. "How can they do that? We share dorms with the pures. And classes. It's the same everywhere!"

"From what I hear, they're going to put all the pures in one dorm and all the halfs in the other. And change the class schedules."

I rolled my eyes. "Oh, so they're going to make the dorms co-ed? Yeah, that is going to go over well. Everyone's going to be having sex."

"Sounds like my kind of place." Seth grinned. "Maybe I can get a transfer."

"Do you ever take anything seriously?" I pushed to my feet.

Seth shot to his feet, towering over me. "I take you seriously."

Eyeing him, I stepped back. "This is serious, Seth. What if they do something like that here? What if this is the beginning of everything changing?"

The ever-present—and annoying—mix of smugness and amusement faded from those eerie, golden eyes, revealing a level of gravity I didn't think Seth was capable of. "Alex, everything has already changed. Don't you see that?"

I swallowed and folded my arms around me, but it didn't stop the sudden coldness from washing over my body like I'd stepped into the freezing downpour outside.

Aiden had said the same thing.

"There are two of us," Seth said quietly. "Everything changed the moment you were born."

I tapped my finger along the edge of the keyboard. I was having one of those nights where I questioned everything that ever was, and I was getting on my own nerves.

I blamed Seth.

Everything changed the moment you were born.

I tried not to think about how the whole Apollyon business worked most of the time. Usually I pretended like it wasn't a big deal. But that didn't mean I wasn't dealing with it, I just knew there was nothing I could do about it. It's like not crying over spilled vodka and cranberry juice or whatever. But there were times—like earlier with Seth—when the idea of becoming this *thing* that people expected something miraculous from, and were also scared to death of, terrified me.

I stared at my computer screen, forcing myself to stop worrying about the Apollyon stuff and what was happening at the Covenants. I then played about a dozen rounds of minesweeper and solitaire—anything to keep my brain nicely blank. It worked beautifully for a short while.

Another question poked at me. Why had Lucian intervened on my behalf? And why was Lucian handing over so much information to

Seth? Yes, he was the Apollyon, but Lucian was the Minister and Seth was just a half-blood. Why would Lucian allow Seth to be privy to such information?

Then there was the business with the Council. I had this feeling I didn't have many fans on the Council and my time with them was going to suck daimon butt.

All of this made my brain sore.

Groaning in frustration, I dropped my head on the keyboard. An immediate, shrill buzzing filled the otherwise quiet room, but I ignored it until I had a streak of brilliance. And it had nothing to do with the Apollyon, the Covenant, or Lucian.

It had to do with Aiden.

Lifting my head, I bit my lip and opened up an internet page. For the last week, I'd been scouring the internet for the perfect gift for Aiden's birthday. Not just a birthday gift, but a peace offering, too. I figured I could get him something—I don't know—special. I'd come up empty-handed for the most part, but tonight, I had an idea.

It had to do with what I'd seen in his cottage that night—a ridiculous number of books, comics, and a colorful assortment of guitar picks. I'd thought then it'd been a strange thing to collect, but at least he didn't collect something gross like body lint. Anyway, I knew there was one color he didn't have—black. But I didn't want to get him just some crappy, old plastic pick. I wanted—needed—something special.

An hour later, I came across an online store dedicated to rare picks and I knew I'd found the perfect gift. They had one made out of onyx gemstone, and apparently it was a super extraordinary guitar pick. I had no idea why. Buying the thing would be hard, though. I hadn't been trusted with a bank account for some reason.

The next day I cornered Deacon before class started. "Can you do something for me?"

"Anything for my favorite halfy." He gave me a little nod as he eyed Luke, who was gesturing wildly at the front of the class.

"Halfy? Never mind. Forget it. You have credit cards, right?"

He flicked a wayward curl out of his eyes and smiled. "Loads of them."

I shoved a piece of paper in his face. I'd scribbled the name of the website and the stock number of the pick on it. "Can you order this for me? I'll give you cash."

Deacon glanced down at the paper and then lifted his head, looking at me. "Do I even want to know?"

"Nope."

"This is for my brother, isn't it?"

I felt my cheeks flush. "I thought you didn't want to know."

He folded up the paper and stuck it in his pocket, shaking his head. "I don't. I'll order it tonight."

"Thanks," I murmured, feeling overexposed.

Staring at the front of the classroom while not really seeing anything the teacher wrote on the board, I hoped Aiden liked the pick—*loved* it. My muscles locked up at the idea of love and Aiden in the same sentence.

Just because I was buying him a stupid little guitar pick didn't mean anything. And just because I wanted to jump his bones didn't mean I… loved him. Halfs didn't love pures. So where had that thought even come from?

I ignored Deacon for the rest of the class and slipped into a weird mood that lasted all day long. Not even Caleb and Olivia's hilarious bickering at lunch snapped me out. Not even when Lea tripped in the hallway. Practice with Aiden couldn't shake me out of the funk.

Aiden's tense and concerned gaze followed every one of my movements. I imagined he was waiting for me to fall asleep and crack my head or something.

But I didn't.

By the end of practice, some of the tension had eased off his face and a lopsided grin appeared as he picked up my gym bag. "I want to do something different tomorrow."

"Are you going to let me off my Saturday training?" I was only half-joking. The idea of lying around in bed all day did sound really nice.

"No. That's not what I was thinking. Not really."

I reached out for my bag, but he held it back. I grinned. "What were you thinking?"

"It's kind of a surprise."

"Oh." I perked up. "What is it?"

Aiden chuckled. "It wouldn't be a surprise if I told you, Alex."

"I can act surprised tomorrow."

"No." He laughed again. "That would kind of ruin it."

"All right, but it better be good." I reached for the bag again, but Aiden caught my hand. His fingers wrapped around mine. Our hands fit perfectly together. Well, at least I thought so. A swarm of butterflies stirred in my stomach. My eyes flicked up, and I was immediately snared. I could always tell what Aiden was thinking by the color of his eyes.

Generally, they were the palest shade of cool gray, but when they shifted, becoming an intense silver, I knew he was on the verge of doing something—something he probably shouldn't, but something I really wanted him to do. Like right now they'd heated to a bright quicksilver.

"It's going to be good." Aiden's gaze dropped to my lips. "I promise."

"Okay," I whispered.

"Wear something warm tomorrow, but no workout clothes."

"No workout clothes?" I echoed dumbly.

"Meet me here at nine." He carefully placed the strap of my bag over my shoulder. His fingers lingered long enough to making breathing difficult. My skin still tingled from the brief, wonderful contact long after he'd left the room.

†

After grabbing some food from the dining hall, Olivia and I walked back to our dorm. Neither of us had made it to the cafeteria in time to eat there. Apparently she and Caleb had had another fight.

"I don't know what else to do." She clutched a can of soda in her hand so tightly I thought she'd crush it at any second. "One minute he's hot and the next he's cold."

I didn't know how much Caleb had told Olivia about what'd happened to him in Gatlinburg, so I was fairly limited on what I could tell her. "I know he really likes you." I decided that was the best tactic. "During the summer he totally obsessed over you."

A light breeze played with her tight curls, tossing them across her face. "I know he likes me, but he's just been so… I don't know, off lately. All he cares about is what Seth is doing. Gods, it's like he loves him."

I focused on how the horizon and the sky blended seamlessly together, trying not to laugh. "Unfortunately, I think Caleb looks up to Seth."

Olivia stopped walking. "I don't get why everyone is so infatuated with Seth."

"I'm not."

"Then we're the only halfs in the world that don't think he's awesome." She suddenly screeched, startling several seagulls. "I just don't understand! Seth's arrogant, rude, and he thinks he's better than everyone else!"

I stared at her, quickly ascertaining I wasn't really good at girl-talk. I had no idea how we'd jumped from Caleb to Seth. "Is Caleb with him now?"

A bit of the anger faded from her face. Olivia sighed, shaking her head. "No. We were hanging out in the rec room before dinner, and I asked him if he thought about where he would take a Sentinel post. You know, not a serious question, but a really important one."

Nodding, I shifted my soda to my other hand, trying and failing to get my hair out of my face.

"I mean, I know we say it's nothing serious between us, but I think it is." She started walking again. "Anyway, we're graduating in the spring, and they give us options. I was hoping Caleb and I could pick the same place or get posted close together so we could still see each other."

"Okay… so what happened?"

"He told me he hadn't thought about it, and I was like, 'What the hell?' If I was important to him, then he would have thought about it. Right? So I told him that." The skin on her cheeks darkened. "And do you know what he said? 'What's the point of picking a place? In the end, the Council will determine where we go.' Well, duh—thanks for the newsbreak, asshat. That's not the point. The point is we can hope that we end up together, right?"

"Olivia, I don't think it has anything to do with you. Right now…" I shifted, suddenly feeling warm even though it was an overcast, chilly day. "He told you about…"

Unable to ignore the swamping heat flooding me, I stopped and drew in a shallow breath. My entire body tensed painfully.

"Alex?" Olivia stepped closer. "Are you okay? You look really flushed."

No. Oh. No. This could not be happening during the day and in front of Olivia. This was so unfair. On top of everything else, I was losing my—

Delighted giggling drifted out of the courtyard. Then a very male and very pleased chuckle followed. There were more sounds, sounds indicating that either someone was in a lot of pain or having a lot of fun.

"Are you kidding me?" Olivia shoved her food into my limp hands. "For the love of the gods, there are empty classrooms and beds for this kind of stuff."

Before I could stop her, she pushed open the gate to the courtyard. I guess if she wasn't getting laid than no one else could? "Olivia—"

"Hey!" she yelled, storming forward. "Hey! You little pervs, go get a room!"

Olivia disappeared around a thick rosebush. Rolling my eyes, I trailed behind her. Walking inside the courtyard was like being in a different world. The wild mixture of flowers and plants, all sweet and tangy, mixed with the bitterness of herbs and assaulted my senses. There was also something unique about the plants in here. Come summer or winter, the foliage never died. God mojo juice, I guessed.

Greek statues lined the walkway, serving as a reminder that the gods were always watching. Runes were etched into the pathway, as were various symbols that signified the gods. Whoever had done the drawings seriously could have benefited from art lessons. But the place was kind of like the Garden of Eden.

And someone was partaking in its forbidden fruit.

"You guys need to—*oh*."

Olivia stopped so unexpectedly I nearly crashed into her. She stood beside the nightshade—the plant the oracle had compared to "kisses from those who walk among the gods" or something crazy like that. I don't know why I noticed the purple hue of the petals first. Perhaps it was some kind of natural preservation instinct.

But then I saw Elena.

I'd never seen her quite so undressed before, however. Her skirt was hiked up, shirt gaping wide open, and… that was pretty much all I wanted to see. Then my gaze fell on her partner.

"Oh. My. Gods!" I shrieked, wishing my hands were empty so I could cover my eyes—or claw them out.

Golden eyes, full of amusement, met mine. "Is there something we can help you two with?" Seth asked, clearly unfazed by the intrusion.

I whirled around, squeezing my eyes shut. My face felt like a thousand shades of red.

"No. Nothing at all." Olivia backed up. "Sorry to interrupt."

"You sure? There's always room for one—or two—more."

"Seth!" Elena shrieked, not sounding entirely dismayed by the prospect.

I headed back up the path, Olivia snapping at my heel. Seth's deep laughter followed us all the way out of the courtyard. We didn't speak again until we stood in front of our dorm. Shock must have dampened the weird hot flash, because it was no longer there. For a multitude of reasons, I felt grateful.

"Well," Olivia said a bit unsteadily.

"Yeah…"

Her lips pursed. "I hate Seth. I think he's an ass, but he does have a really nice butt."

"Yeah…"

Olivia's eyes were wide. "You know what? I think I'm going to go see Caleb. Like right now."

I snickered. "Yeah, you go do that."

CHAPTER 7

NOT SURPRISINGLY, SETH KNOCKED ON MY BEDROOM window that night. Honestly, the curfew thing sucked—being confined to my room and not being able to really sleep usually left me with a mad case of boredom—so I kind of welcomed his little visits. Especially when he just wanted to watch a movie and I'd fall asleep.

But tonight was different.

I still hadn't decided what to wear tomorrow, and that was a major deal. Aiden only ever saw me in boring gym clothes. I needed something cute—a little sexy—but I couldn't look like I was trying too hard. My entire closet was on my bed. And of course, I'd just seen some of Seth's—uh, more private parts. I kind of didn't want to see his face tonight.

The knock came again, more urgent. Groaning, I went to the window and opened it. Thankfully he was fully dressed. "What?"

Seth loped over the windowsill, inviting himself in. "Nice jammies."

"Shut up." I grabbed a sweater off the bed and slipped it on, wishing I'd put on long PJ bottoms instead of shorts and a thin tank.

"You know, I don't care about the tag marks. Makes you look dangerous in an extremely hot way."

"It's not the marks I'm covering up, and you know that."

"Partly true and partly a lie. The scars embarrass you, because you're incredibly vain for a chick who wants to be a Sentinel. And you're uncomfortable being half-naked around me—"

"I'm not half-naked! And I'm not uncomfortable around you. *And* I'm not vain."

"You're a terrible liar." He sat down on my bed.

Okay. I was lying. Vanity wasn't the worst sin and yeah, Seth made me uncomfortable for a lot of reasons, but that wasn't the point. "Why are you here?"

"I wanted to check on you."

My brows furrowed. "Why?"

His glanced around the room, his gaze settling on the clothes scattered around. "Can't find what to wear?"

"Uh… I was just going through my closet."

"I can tell."

I sighed, rubbing my forehead wearily. "What do you want? As you can see I'm kind of busy."

A brow arched. "I know. What an exciting life you live, going through your closet on a Friday night and all."

"Yeah, not all of us have the exciting life you do, Seth."

His lips split into a satisfied grin. "I knew it."

"Knew what?"

"You're mad at me."

I stared at him and lifted my arms, waiting for a better explanation.

"You're upset over this afternoon." He pushed aside several potential choices for tomorrow as he leaned back. "Were you jealous, Alex?"

My jaw almost hit the floor. It took me a moment to respond. "I'm confused to why you think I'd be jealous."

Seth gave me a knowing look. "Perhaps you're jealous of Elena?"

"What?" I picked up a cute sweater I'd bought before we'd gone into lockdown. "Me, jealous of Elena and her Tinkerbell hair—don't think so."

He stretched over and tugged the sweater out of my hand. "Oh. Catty, aren't you?"

"Not at all. If I'd only known about your Peter Pan complex, I would've introduced you two sooner." I reached for it, but he rolled it up into a ball and tossed the sweater across the room. "Ugh! You are so annoying!"

"Just admit you're jealous. That's the first step, and the second step is doing something about it."

I glared at Seth. "I could care less what—or who—you do in your spare time." Then something struck me. "Wait. You know what? This is messed up."

"Do tell."

"Everyone jumps me about how every single thing I do is a reflection upon you, but you're *doing* people in the garden! How is that okay?"

"You make it sound so distasteful." He smiled much like a cat. "Don't knock it until you try it. Oh. Wait. You haven't tried *anything*, have you, my little virgin Apollyon?"

I swung out at him as hard as I possibly could. Anticipating my reaction, Seth caught my hand. His eyes flashed dangerously as he tugged me forward. My own momentum caused me to stumble. I ended up falling forward.

Seth twisted onto his side and circled his arms around me. "Always hitting," he said cheerfully. "I think we should work on your manners."

The side of my face was smashed into a pile of shirts that had gone into the "maybe" pile. "Oh, come on. You're wrinkling all my clothes, you jerk-face."

"Your clothes are fine. I want to chat."

I tried to elbow him, but his arms clamped down. "Really, you want to talk right now?"

He wriggled closer. "Yes."

"And we have to be lying like this for what reason?"

"I don't know. It makes me feel good. I know it makes you feel good. And I don't mean the way I'm sure you think I mean." He paused, and I could feel his chest rise and fall against my back. "Our bodies relax around each other."

I scrunched up my face, not buying his reason at all. "Can we talk about something else?"

"Sure." I could hear the smile in his voice. "Let's talk about the fact you haven't been sleeping."

"What?" I managed to squirm enough to get one of my arms loose and flip onto my back. "I… I sleep fine."

"You sleep for a few hours. Then you wake up. Nightmares, huh?"

I stared at him. "Why do you always have to be so creepy?"

His lips twitched. A flicker of amusement, then his expression returned to a customary smug mask. "Whenever you're upset you suck me right in. Wakes me up every single night, and now I'm not getting any sleep unless I stay with you."

I scooted over, but his arm caught me. "Well, sorry. I don't know how to stop it. If I did, I wouldn't interrupt your precious beauty sleep."

Seth chuckled low in his throat. "I guess it's because the connection between us is getting stronger since we're spending more time together. With you being an emotional wreck these days, I spend half my time wanting a Valium."

The urge to kick him off the bed hit me hard. "I'm not an emotional wreck."

He didn't bother responding to that. "Doesn't it strike you as odd that the only times you sleep all the way through the night are when I stay with you?"

It did strike me as odd—and annoying. "So?"

Seth leaned over. "Your body relaxes around me and you can rest. All thanks to your favorite thing—the connection we share. If you get too upset, you just need me. It will work both ways once you Awaken."

I jerked as far away from him as I could, which wasn't very far at all. "Oh, for the love of the gods, you have got to be kidding me."

"Alex, I'm as serious as a daimon attack."

And I knew he was being serious. I just didn't want to admit it. The idea of him sensing my emotions made me what to hurl. If I wanted to cry, he'd know. The same went for needing to punch someone or if I was in the middle of a hot make-out session, he'd know and—

My eyes widened in realization and a strange feeling unfurled in the pit of my stomach. "Wait. Wait one second, Seth. If you can feel my emotions or whatever when I'm spazzing out, then I should be able to feel yours."

"Right, but not—"

I moved so fast I broke free of his embrace and shot to my feet. He stayed on the bed, half-reclined. "Oh. My. Gods. I *have* felt you."

Seth's brows rose slowly. "No way, I know how to shield myself so that I'm not broadcasting my every wish and desire like you."

"Oh. No. You are so wrong." My cheeks burned just thinking about it. The nights I'd felt all hot and tingling—and right before I'd walked in on him and Elena—it wasn't just my overactive hormones. "Oh, this sucks."

Interest sparked in his eyes and he sat up, resting his hands on his knees. "What are you talking about?"

"I've felt you a couple of times—at night. Like when you're doing… your thing."

He gave a short laugh, and then it seemed to hit him. His mouth dropped open. "Doing my *thing*?"

"Yeah," I said, growing frustrated. Did I have to spell it out for him? "Just forget I said anything."

"No. Not likely. What did you feel?"

This really did suck. It was also mortifying and beyond freaky. "You know, fooling around. I've felt… you then."

Seth stared at me so long I thought he lost the ability to speak. Then, when I was just starting to get worried, he threw his head back and laughed. Really loudly—and he didn't stop.

I gaped at him. "It's not funny!"

"Oh, it's probably the funniest damn thing I've heard in a long time." He stopped long enough to draw in a deep breath. "This is great."

"It's not great. What kind of connection is this? A one-way hotline to Pervyville?" I took a step forward, on a roll now. "It's disgusting. Freaky—stop laughing, Seth!"

"I can't," he gasped. "Of all the times for you to connect with me, and it had to be then? Damn Alex, I didn't know you're such a peeping—"

I hit him hard on the arm. It wasn't a playful tap. It would bruise. I wanted to do more—like kick him in the head.

"Jeez. And you're so violent. Do you know how hot—"

I swung at him again, but this time Seth was prepared. He dodged my fist and caught me around the waist. Before I could even break his hold, he flipped me onto my back. This time he hovered above me, arms planted on either side of my head. A wild and beautiful smile chipped away at some of the coldness in his face. Not all of it, but some. "This is priceless."

"You are so annoying."

That seemed to amuse him even more. He laughed so hard I felt it rumble through me. Not in the way Aiden's laugh usually did. Aiden's laugh made me feel all light and fluttery. Seth's made me feel weird—flushed and weird. And a part of me wanted to hear it again—or feel it again. Which was wrong—all kinds of wrong—because I didn't think of him that way. At least my brain didn't. My body, on the other hand, had a totally different viewpoint on these things.

My body must be a sad, lonely thing.

"You know," Seth grinned, "you probably shouldn't have told me this. I'm going to take advantage—Alex, what are you *doing*?"

I didn't get what he was talking about at first. Then my eyes dropped and I saw my hand pressed against his stomach, my fingers curling around his shirt. How in the world did my hand get there, because surely—*surely*, I didn't do that?

Seth appeared on the verge of saying something ignorant, like always, but he became very, very still. I don't even think he breathed. Slowly, I lifted my gaze and found what I expected. Swirling glyphs spread across the left side of his face. The intricate markings etched down his neck and disappeared under the hem of his black shirt, reappearing on his left arm and coming to stop over his hand.

And Seth, well, Seth was no longer laughing. Those odd eyes caught mine and flared a heated tawny. He lowered his head; the loose strands of hair brushed my cheeks. I jerked my hand back, but he was still close, way too close. So I did the only thing suitable in situations like these. I shoved my knee into his stomach—hard.

He rolled off me, onto his back, laughing once more. "Crap, Alex, why did you go and do that? Actually kind of hurt, you know?"

I scrambled off the bed, putting as much distance between us as possible. "I hate you."

"No you don't." He tipped his head back, his gaze finding me. "I guess this was bound to happen. The more time we spend together, the more we'll start connecting. It is the way of the Apollyons."

"Just go somewhere, why don't you?"

Seth flipped onto his stomach and rested his chin in his hands. "I'd love to. I could go for seconds with Elena right about now."

I let out a groan and rolled my eyes. "No one is stopping you."

"True, but then you'd fall asleep after pacing or reading some incredibly boring textbook and have another nightmare about Mommy, and then I'll be awake all night long." He arched one blond brow at me. "I do need my beauty sleep."

I glared at him. "You're not staying here again, Seth. You have a bed—several, actually. Go."

"You didn't care the last couple of times."

"Because … well, those times were different," I sputtered, running a hand over my hair. Turning around, I started grabbing clothes off the floor. "I didn't know you were staying. You just helped yourself."

Seth sighed. "You don't like any of this, do you?"

"No. I don't like not being in control. You know that." I grabbed another shirt. I also didn't like the fact that my body reacted to him even though my heart didn't. "It's about having control over—" I dropped the clothes and straightened. "Remember what you said to me during the summer, the night you were in my room?"

He looked confused. "Not really."

I took a deep breath, searching for patience I didn't have. "You promised me that you would leave if things got out of hand. Do you remember that?"

Seth's lips pursed. "Yes, I do."

"Do you still mean it?" I stepped forward, standing in front of him. "Do you?"

"Yes. I still mean that. I made you a promise. I keep my promises." Seth reached out and grabbed my hand. With a gentle tug, he pulled me down beside him. Whatever relief I felt was short-lived. "Do you know what I find interesting?"

I watched him wearily. "What?"

He turned his head toward me. "You've never shown any interest in getting to know me better. You don't know a thing about me."

"That's not true."

His lips curled into a sardonic grin as he let go of my hand. "You don't even know my last name, Alex."

Well, he didn't need a last name. Seth was just *Seth* to me.

"You don't even know where I'm from, if my mom was a pure or my dad," he continued. "I bet you don't even know how old I am."

I started to protest, but Seth was right. We've known each other for about four months, give or take a week or two, and I didn't know anything about him. In all of the time we'd spent together, in training or when he showed up in my room, we never talked about anything personal. And I never cared to even ask. I frowned. Was I truly that self-centered?

Seth sighed. "You have this one-track mind thing going on."

I looked at him sharply. "You can't read my thoughts, right?"

"No. But that doesn't mean some of what you think isn't as obvious as reading your thoughts." He turned to me. "Everything you think, everything you feel is always right on your face. You're terrible at hiding your emotions. Or what you're thinking. Like I said: one track mind. Whether it's getting back into the Covenant, fighting your Mom or fighting your fate or that… *special* person in your life."

"I don't have a special person in my life!" I felt my cheeks start to burn again. "I have no idea where you come up with these things."

One side of his lips curled upward as he met my stare. "I'm nineteen."

I blinked. "Huh?"

Seth's eyes rolled. "I'm nineteen years old."

"Oh. *Oh*. Only nineteen—wow. I thought you were older than that."

"Well, I don't know if I should be offended or flattered."

"Flattered, I guess."

A few moments passed before he spoke again. "I'm from a tiny island near Greece."

"Ah, that explains your voice—the accent. What island?"

Seth shrugged and didn't respond. Sharing and caring time seemed to be over. Why had I never thought to try to get to know Seth any better? After all, I was going to be stuck with him for a while.

I bit my lip. "Do you think I'm self-centered?"

A surprised laugh escaped him. "Why are you asking?"

"Because you said I have a one track mind. And everything you listed had to do with me, like I don't think about anything or anyone other than me."

Seth let out a ragged sound and came to his feet. "Do you want me to be honest?"

"Yes."

Several seconds passed as he stared down at me. "Sometimes, Alex, you have more pure in you than you do half."

My mouth dropped open, shocked that he would say that about *me*.

He ran a hand over his head. "Look, I've got some stuff I need to do. I'll see you later."

I didn't say anything as he climbed back out the window. I sat on the bed; the fun of finding something pretty to wear tomorrow had lost most of its appeal.

You have more pure in you than you do half.

It was a terrible thing to say to a half-blood, like I was a disgrace who couldn't be trusted—a sellout, phony, and fake. That if it came down to choosing between a half and a pure, I'd choose the pure.

†

I think something crawled into my hair and made a nest during the night, because nothing I did—no curling iron, no flat iron—seemed to make it do what I wanted. One side wanted to settle in waves, while the other looked like limp spaghetti.

Maybe I was being overly critical of myself, but I truly believed that the dark smudges under my eyes made me look like I'd entered the first stage of a zombie infection. I'd put on too much lip gloss, and then rubbed my lips raw getting it off and reapplying. The mountain of concealer I'd put on the disgustingly huge zit on my temple made it seem even bigger.

I finally tore myself away from the bathroom mirror when I made a grab for the lip gloss again. I settled on a pair of skinny jeans—not the designer kind Olivia wore, more like the Target brand. I chose a deep red sweater that dipped a little low in the neckline area, and these killer heels I'd stolen from Olivia's closet.

But before I ran out to meet up with Aiden, I was struck dumb by the cold possibility that this could be some sort of field experience. It definitely wasn't a date, so what the hell was I doing?

And if I would be training, then I'd look stupid in heels and my boobs would fall out. While that sounded pretty entertaining for the masses, somehow I doubted Aiden would appreciate it. So with no time to spare, I slipped on a pair of checkered flats and a more sensible top—a black, cable knit sweater.

I made it to the training room late, of course.

"Sorry," I said as soon as I spotted Aiden's dark head by the wall of things that stabbed, out of breath from running across the quad. "I… I had to do something…"

Every single excuse I'd practiced on the way over leaked out of my mouth when I got a really good look at Aiden. He wore a pair of worn jeans, the kind that looked so comfy you wanted to climb into them. He also had on this gray sweater, and gods, *oh, gods*, did it look good on him—like it'd been crafted to just fit the strong expanse of his shoulders, his chest, his arms, and so on.

I needed to get a grip.

I knew this, but I rarely saw Aiden in anything other than workout clothes or a uniform. He'd been wearing something different the night I'd sent those spirit boats into the sea, but I hadn't been paying attention. My mind had been occupied.

It was sure as hell occupied in a totally different way now.

"It's no problem," he said. "You ready?"

I nodded in a jerky motion. Suddenly, I felt as adept as a cow in a china shop. "So what are we doing?" I asked, humiliated to hear my voice crack halfway through the question.

Either Aiden hadn't noticed or he pretended otherwise. "It's a surprise, Alex." He started walking. "Are you coming, or what?"

I hurried behind him, my suspicions were confirmed when he led me out the back way. "We're leaving the Covenant, aren't we?"

He pushed the hair off his forehead, clearly trying not to smile. Aiden reached into his pocket and dangled keys in front of my face. "Yes."

"Field experience! I knew it." Silently, I thanked every god there was that I'd developed enough common sense to change shoes.

Aiden looked at me strangely. "I guess you can consider this field experience."

I followed him to one of the black Hummers, feeling rather smug for figuring out his surprise. "So what are we going to do? Trail some daimons back to their hive?" I climbed into the passenger side and waited until he got behind the wheel. "I have to admit, I'm not really good at the whole tailing thing. I'm more—"

"I know." He turned on the engine and eased the dinosaur-sized vehicle out of the fleet of cars. "You're more of an action girl instead of a sit-and-be-quiet girl."

I smiled in spite of the fact I doubted that was a compliment. "Well, my quiet-as-a-ninja skill could definitely use some practice."

Another quick smile appeared. "But the other skills? Not so much. I really don't think you need much more of the additional practices. You'd definitely have more time to yourself—time to rest."

Now I really beamed... for about three seconds. No extra practices also meant no Aiden. My smiled faded as I stared at him. Suddenly, a giant clock appeared between us, quickly counting down to when there would be no more Aiden in my life.

A rather depressing thought.

"What?"

I faced straight ahead, swallowing down the lump in my throat. "Nothing."

When we were stopped by the first set of Guards, I expected them to demand what Aiden was doing with a half-blood. But they let us pass without so much as asking for an explanation. The same thing happened at the second bridge, the one leading off of Deity Island and onto Bald Head Island.

"I can't believe they just let you take me off the island without a single question," I said as Aiden navigated the streets of the mortal island. "What happened to the rules?"

"I'm a pure-blood."

"And I'm a half-blood—a half-blood who's not supposed to step one foot off the Covenant, let alone Deity Island. Not that I'm complaining or anything. I'm just a little surprised."

"They assume we're doing field training."

I glanced at him. "Aren't we?"

Smiling, Aiden leaned over and turned on the radio. He settled on a rock station, and I stared at him. The early smugness started to flake away. He didn't give any further explanation when I asked again, and finally, I decided to stop asking and we started talking about normal things. My classes, an episode of some TV show called *Sanford and Son*—never heard of it—but some guy apparently pretended to have a heart attack every episode, and Aiden found it hilarious. I wasn't convinced of the hilarity.

We talked about how I'd almost beaten him in practice yesterday, and how he was considering buying a motorcycle. Which I was strongly behind, because really, what could make Aiden hotter than he already was?

A motorcycle.

"What kind of bike are you looking at?"

He got this dreamy, far-off look on his face—almost like the kind of look I got when I saw chocolate… or him. "A Hayabusa." He passed a string of cars without missing a beat.

"A crotch rocket?" I reached for the radio, flipping the stations. Aiden had the same thought in mind, because his fingers brushed over mine. I jerked back, flushed.

Aiden cleared his throat. "It's more than a crotch rocket. It's, well, let me put it this way. If it came down between me saving a Hayabusa or the Minister, it would be a difficult decision."

I busted out laughing. "Oh, my gods, I can't believe you admitted that."

He started to smile. "Well."

"It's awesome," I gasped.

The smile grew, exposing the deep dimples in his cheeks. For a moment, I stopped laughing, stop smiling—hell, I stopped breathing.

Then I saw the sign along the interstate for Asheboro, and I really did stop breathing for a couple of seconds.

We were thirty miles from Asheboro. "I know Asheboro," I whispered.

"I know."

I could feel his eyes on me, but I couldn't pull my gaze from the window. The trees lining the road formed an array of browns, reds, and yellows. The last time I'd been near Asheboro it had been summer, and the rolling hills had been green.

Seven years ago.

Tearing myself away from the window, I stared at Aiden. He focused on the road. "I know where we're going."

"You do?"

Excitement bubbled through me. So did disbelief. I bounced forward in my seat. "This isn't field experience."

Aiden's lips twitched. "Consider it an experience in taking a day off—a day being normal."

"You're taking me to the zoo!" I screeched, bouncing again. The seatbelt choked me back.

He couldn't keep the smile back. It covered his face, filled his eyes. "Yes, we're going to the zoo."

"But—but why?" I swiveled around in the seat, pressing my face against the window. The smile on *my* face was absurdly huge. "I don't deserve this."

Several moments passed. "Yes, you do. I think you deserve a break from everything. You've been working so hard, pulling double—triple—duty. And you really don't complain—"

I shot around, facing him. "I complain. I complain all the time."

Shaking his head, Aiden laughed. "I stand corrected."

Shock kept pushing more stupid statements out of my mouth. "But I've been in so much trouble. I threw an apple at Lea's face. I fought Guards. I cheated on my trig exam."

Aiden looked at me, frowning. "You cheated on your math exam?"

"Uh, forget that. Anyway, wow, I'm just surprised."

"Alex, you need to get away from it all every once in a while. You need a break—a real one. Just like I do," he paused, concentrating on the road. "I figured we could get away together."

I think my heart may have exploded, right then and there. The importance of what he was doing—the implication of it—didn't pass me by unnoticed. This was huge—huge to us. Pures and halfs didn't get away together for a relaxing day. We may coexist together, but we lived in different worlds. We had to. It was the rules, the way of our society. Aiden risked a lot by doing this. If by random chance we were spotted, he'd be in a lot of trouble. Maybe not as much as me, but hell, I didn't care. I cared that he wanted to do this *for me*.

That had to mean something—something really wonderful.

Aiden glanced at me, his eyes shining—with what? I didn't know, but in that instant, I could only think about what I felt for Aiden. Until then, I hadn't been willing to admit that it was anything more than a crush or lust, because really, who didn't lust after him? But what expanded in my chest, swelled my heart until I felt sure it would burst from my chest, wasn't a silly crush. It wasn't just a physical attraction.

It was love.

I loved Aiden—I loved a pure-blood.

CHAPTER 8

I STARED AT HIM, CAUGHT UP IN MY REALIZATION. *I loved Aiden.* I loved him, really loved him.

Oh, gods, I was so totally screwed.

Aiden's cheeks flushed under his natural tan. "I mean, all of us need a day away from our world. We need moments to take a breather and let it all go." He glanced at me, a wry grin replacing the one I'd throw pretty much anyone in front of a daimon to see. "Anyway, today is just a normal day. We aren't going to talk about training or the daimon attack."

"Okay." I took a deep, calming breath and ordered myself to pull it together. Then I saw the sign for the zoo and I face-planted the window again.

"We can't stay for long—only a couple of hours—or the Guards will suspect something. We also need to keep this a secret. We can't let anyone find out."

I nodded. "Of course. I won't say a single word. I just can't believe you remembered this." I also couldn't believe I was in love with a pure-blood.

He merged toward the exit ramp, expression suddenly serious. "I remember everything you say."

I peeled myself off the window. It was all too easy for me to recall the day I'd told him about my love of animals and zoos. It'd been in the small med office, when he'd rubbed that gunk over my bruises. But I didn't expect him to actually remember that day, or any day for that matter. And if he really did remember everything I said, then…

My fingers curled in my lap. I was a big douchebag. I said mean things. A lot. I took a deep breath. "I'm sorry."

Aiden looked at me sharply. "For what?"

I stared down at my hands, guilt gnawing at my insides. How could I not have apologized sooner? "I'm sorry about saying you're like other pure-bloods. I shouldn't have said that. Because you're not—you're nothing like them."

"Alex, don't apologize. You were angry. So was I. It's in the past. Over."

The guilt eased off a little bit as I gazed out the window, but an old yearning pulled at my heart. Mom had loved it here. The sights brought forth a mix of sorrow and happiness. I sighed, wanting to be happy but feeling bad about it.

Trees dotted the winding road leading up to the entrance. Mom had known the names of the trees. I didn't. Off in the distance, I could make out the top of the main building.

"It bothered you though," I said as Aiden coasted the Hummer to a stop. The lot was full for this time of year, but the weather was still warm enough. The zoo would be packed. I undid the seatbelt and twisted toward him. "I know it did."

Aiden cut the engine and pulled the keys out. Lifting his gaze from his hands, those eyes pierced me. "Yeah, it did."

I bit my lip, wanting to apologize again.

"I don't want you to see me like that." A short, harsh laugh escaped him and he focused on the steering wheel as he held the keys in a tight grip. "The funny thing is that what you said shouldn't have bothered me. I'm a pure. So I should be like all the others. I really shouldn't care if you saw me like that. I should care how the other pure-bloods view me."

"I'm sure they think you're wonderful, too." I flushed after saying that, because it sounded stupid. "Anyway, screw what anyone thinks. Who cares, right?"

Grinning, he glanced over at me, and I felt my heart skip a beat. "Yeah, who cares? We're at the zoo. Screw them."

"Yeah, screw them."

Aiden tilted his head back, letting out a relieved sigh. "Does the place have funnel cakes?"

"I think so. I want a hamburger and a hot dog." I paused. "And ice cream in one of those waffle cones. And—and I want to see the big kitties."

"So demanding," he murmured, grinning. "Well, we better get started, then."

†

First stop honors went to a portly, balding man who had more grease on his shirt than he did in his pan. He made funnel cakes. Aiden liked him a lot. While I waited in line beside him, I spotted a vendor flipping burgers. I darted in that direction, after which Aiden commented that he'd never seen me run that fast before.

When we finally made it past the food and into the actual park, I was overflowing with giddiness. The slight breeze carried the oddly alluring scent of animals and people. Sunlight broke through the park's dense canopy of trees, casting slivers of warmth as we made our way deeper into the attractions.

I probably looked goofy with the extra bounce in my step and the way I kept grinning at everyone we passed. I was just so happy to be out in the world again—and with Aiden of all people. And watching how the mortals responded to him was highly entertaining. It could have been his alarming height or godly looks that stopped women *and* men in their tracks. Or it could be the way he laughed, tipping his head back and letting loose that rich, deep sound. Either way, I got a thrill seeing him do his best to ignore them.

"You don't mingle with the natives a lot, do you?" I asked as we stepped into the Forest Glade and watched a gorilla sitting on a rock, picking fleas. Stimulating stuff here.

Aiden chuckled. "Is it that obvious?"

"A little bit."

He shifted closer, lowering his voice. "Mortals scare me."

"What?" I laughed in disbelief.

Smiling at my expression, he nudged me with his hip. "They do. They're unpredictable creatures. You don't know if they're going to hug you or stab you. They're ruled by emotions."

"And we're not?"

Aiden appeared to consider that. "No. They—I mean, we're taught to control our emotions. To not let them be what guides our decisions. Everything in our world—both of our worlds—is about logic and continuing our races. You know that."

I glanced over at him, noticing the way the proud lines of his face were relaxed. In these moments, he did look younger and carefree. I liked him this way—with his eyes full of light and laughter, his expressive mouth curved upward. Seeing him now, it was almost hard to believe he was far more deadly than any animal in the park.

"But you seem to be at ease around all of them." He nodded at a group at the other end of the pen. A mother and a father stood with two young kids. The little girl handed her brother a half-eaten ice cream cone. "You have more experience dealing with them than I do."

I nodded, turning back to the cage. Another hairy beast made its way to the one on the rock. Maybe something interesting would happen. "I blended in, but I never fit in. They can sense something off about us. That's why no one will get too close to us."

"I cannot possibly imagine you blending in."

"Why? I think I did a damn good job of going unnoticed for three years."

"I just can't. No one is like you, Alex."

I grinned. "I'll take that as a compliment."

"It is." He nudged me again, and my grin grew into another ludicrous smile—the kind Caleb gave Olivia when they weren't tearing each other's heads off. "You're incredibly intelligent, Alex. Funny and…"

"Pretty?" I supplied, only half-serious.

"No, not pretty."

"Cute?"

"No."

I frowned. "Well, then."

Aiden's laugh sent shivers through me. "I was going to say 'stunning.' You're stunningly beautiful."

I sucked in air sharply, cheeks flushing. I tipped my head back and our gazes locked. Somehow I hadn't known we stood so close. And Aiden was close. Close enough that I could feel his warm breath against my cheek, speeding up my pulse.

"Oh," I whispered. Not the most eloquent of responses, but it was the best I had.

"Anyway, what is it with you and zoos?" Aiden stretched his arms above his head.

A shaky sigh escaped me, my gaze drifting over the family, settling on the little girl. She had the cutest pigtails ever, and she was smiling at me. I smiled back.

"I like animals," I said finally.

Aiden glanced down at me, eyes full of… well, full of yearning. "That's why you practically choked yourself in the car?"

I cringed. "You noticed that, huh? My mom loved animals, too. She said once that we were a lot like the ones in the cages. Well fed and taken care of, but caged nonetheless. I never agreed with that."

"You don't?"

"Nope. Here the animals are safe. Out in the wild, they'd be killing one another or being poached. I know they've lost their freedom, but sometimes things have to be sacrificed."

"That's a strange perspective for you to have."

"You mean it's a strange perspective for a *half-blood* to have. I know. But we all have to sacrifice something to gain something else."

Aiden reached out and grabbed my hand, pulling me out of the path of a woman on a mission of pushing a stroller. I'd been so caught up in watching him I hadn't seen the woman—or heard her screaming baby. I glanced down between us. His hand was still wrapped around mine. The simple, unexpected gesture sent a crazy amount of heat through me.

Aiden guided me through the ever-increasing throng of visitors. He parted the crowd like the Red Sea. People just got out of the way for him as we left the Kitera Forest and entered the Forest Edge.

"Can I ask you a question?" I asked.

"Sure."

"If you weren't a pure, what would you be doing right now? Like, what would you want to do with your life?"

Aiden glanced down at our hands and then his gaze flicked to mine. "Right this instant? I'd be doing a hell of a lot more than what I'm allowed to do."

Heat infused my entire body, swirling my thoughts into a heady mess. I almost convinced myself I totally made up that response and that lack of sleep had finally driven me crazy. Auditory hallucinations were a bitch.

His fingers tightened around mine. "But I'm sure you were wondering more than that. What would I be doing if I was just a mortal? I don't really know. It's not something I've really thought about."

I had to mentally kick myself to find my voice again. "You've never thought about it? For real?"

Aiden sidestepped a couple taking pictures, shrugging. "I never had to. When I was younger, I knew I would follow in my parents' footsteps. The Covenant groomed me to do so. I took all the right classes: politics, customs, and negotiations. Basically, the most boring classes you could imagine. Then after the daimon attack, everything changed. I went from wanting to follow my parents to wanting to do something to ensure another family didn't go through what Deacon had to."

"And what you had to," I added quietly.

He nodded. "I don't know what I would do if I woke up tomorrow and had a choice. Well, I can think of a few things, but a career?"

"You do have a choice. Pures have all the choices."

He glanced down at me, frowning. "No, we don't. That's the biggest misconception between our races. Halfs think we have all the choices, but we are just as limited as your kind is, but in different ways."

I really didn't believe that, but I didn't want to argue and ruin the moment. "So… you really don't know what you'd do?" He shook his head, so I offered my suggestion. "A police officer."

Aiden brows rose up. "You think I'd be a police officer?"

I nodded. "You want to help people. I don't think you're corruptible.

Being a Sentinel and a police officer are kind of the same thing. Fighting the bad guys, keeping the peace, and all that good stuff."

"I guess you're right." He smiled then. A mortal girl about my age stumbled as she passed us on the trail. Aiden seemed oblivious to her. "Hey, I'd get a badge. I don't have one of those now."

"I want a badge, too."

Aiden cocked his to the side, laughing. "Of course, you'd want a badge. Hey—look what I see." He pointed around the bend.

"Cats!"

His hand curved around mine more fully, almost like some unconscious part of him was responding to me.

Several yards of empty space and fencing separated the lion pen from the visitors. At first, I didn't see him, and then he prowled up from behind a rock, tossing his mane from side to side. His orange-yellow coat reminded me of Seth's eyes. Actually, the way the lion stopped in front of the gathering crowd and yawned—flashing a row of razor sharp teeth—also reminded me of Seth.

"He's beautiful," I whispered, wishing I could somehow get closer. I wasn't one of those lunatics who climbed into a lion's den, but I also wanted to touch one—a people-raised, totally tame one not likely to rip off my hand.

"He looks bored out of his mind."

We stayed there a while, watching the feline stroll around the grassy knoll before climbing atop a large rock and lying down, tail swishing back and forth. Finally, some of the female lions decided to show up. I told Aiden they were the real deal, recalling something I heard on *Animal Planet* about the females actually being more badass than the males. Within a couple of minutes, two of them joined the male on the rock.

I groaned as they lay down beside the male. "Ah, come on. Knock him off the rock."

Aiden chuckled. "I think he's got two girlfriends."

"Dog," I muttered.

We left the Bushlands, wandering into the North American section. This part seemed virtually empty compared to the other. I guess the mortals were bored by the bears and other familiar critters. Aiden seemed fascinated with them, and I spotted a bobcat. I let go of Aiden's hand and went up to the outer fence. A slight breeze rolled in. We were much closer than any of the other exhibits. Close enough that the bobcat appeared to catch our scent.

It'd been stalking some unseen prey up until that moment. She stopped, though, inclining her head in our direction. A second or two passed, and I swear our eyes met. Long, thin whiskers twitched as she smelled the air.

"Do you think she knows what we are?" I asked.

Aiden propped himself against the guardrail. "I don't know."

We weren't allowed to have pets on the island. Some pures could use compulsion to control their actions, which meant so could a daimon. It was rare and took an extremely powerful pure to do so, but it was a risk no one ever took. I'd always wanted a pet growing up—a cat.

"Mom believed they did," I said. "She said animals could sense we were different from the mortals, especially cats."

He was silent for a few moments, and I was sure his brain was turning. Putting together some sort of puzzle. "Did your mother like cats?"

I shrugged. "I think it had something to do with my father. Whenever we'd come here, we'd always ended up here right before we left." I glanced over my shoulders, nodding at the weathered benches. "We'd sit over there and watch the cats."

Aiden shifted closer, but didn't speak.

I turned back to the pen, smiling. "It was the only time Mom would talk about my father. She never really said much about him. Except that he had the warmest brown eyes. I wonder if he had something to do with animals, you know?" I curled my fingers around the wire mesh of the fence. "Anyway, the last time we were here was when she told me he was dead and told me his name. She named me after him, did you know that? I guess that's why Lucian hated it when Mom called me Alex. After a while, she started calling me Lexie instead. My father's name was Alexander."

Several moments passed where neither of us said anything. Aiden spoke first. "That's why you like the zoo so much."

"Yeah, you got me." I laughed self-consciously.

"It's nothing to be ashamed of, to want to be close to something that reminds you of your loved ones."

"I didn't even know him, Aiden."

"Still," he said. "He was your father."

I watched the bobcat for a few more seconds. It prowled the edge of its pen, no longer curious about our presence. Its powerful muscles flexed under the spotted coat. There was something amazingly graceful about the way it moved.

"I hate to do this, but we need to head back, Alex."

"I know."

We started walking back through the park. Aiden was a lot quieter this time around—lost in thought. It didn't take nearly long enough to reach the front gates. Thick trees gave it an almost surreal quality as we strolled back to the Hummer.

Before I knew it, I was sitting in the passenger seat, and Aiden had just put the keys into the ignition, but he hadn't turned the car on. He twisted in his seat, facing me, and the expression on his face caused my heart to falter in my chest.

"I know how brave you are, Alex. But you don't always have to be. It's okay every once in a while to let someone else be brave for you. There's no loss of dignity in that. Not for you. You've already proven that you have more dignity than even a pure-blood can muster."

I kind of wondered where that had come from. "You must be high off sugar or something."

Aiden laughed. "You just don't see what we see, Alex. Even the times you're being utterly ridiculous about something or when you're just standing around, doing nothing, it's hard to not notice. As a pure-blood it's the last thing I should notice." His eyes flickered shut, long lashes fanned his cheeks before his eyes reopened to reveal intense silver. "I don't think you have a clue."

The world outside the car ceased to exist. "What don't I have a clue about?"

"Ever since I've met you, I've wanted to break every rule." Aiden turned away, the muscles in his neck tensing. He sighed. "You'll become the center of someone's world one day. And he'll be the luckiest son of a bitch on this earth."

His words created a mad rush of strong emotions. I was hot—so incredibly hot. I really did think the world ended right then. Aiden glanced over at me, his lips parting. The intensity in his gaze, the hunger in his eyes left me dizzy. His chest rose sharply.

"Thank you." My voice sounded thick. "Thanks for doing all of this for me."

"You don't need to thank me."

"When am I ever supposed to thank you?"

"When I do something that is truly worth thanking me for."

Those words struck a deep chord in me, and I don't know who moved first. Who leaned over the center console—who was the first to cross the invisible line between us? Who broke the rules first? Aiden? Me? All I did know was that we both moved. Aiden's hands were around my face, and mine fell to his chest, to where his heart beat just as fast as mine. In an instant, our lips met.

This kiss was nothing like the first one we'd shared. Its rawness left us both breathless. There wasn't a moment of hesitation or indecision. There was just want and need and a thousand other powerful, crazy things. His lips scorched mine, his hands dropping to my shoulders, sliding down my arms. My skin burned under my sweater, but oh, this was so much more than just a kiss. It was the way he touched the deepest parts of me. My heart and soul would never be the same. It was nearly overwhelming to realize something as powerful as that and it brought a sense of urgency that pushed me into the unknown.

Aiden pulled back, resting his forehead against mine. He was breathing heavily. What came out of my mouth next was not something I'd planned. The three words just bubbled up my throat, barely even audible.

"I love you."

Aiden jerked back, eyes wide. "No. Alex. Don't say that. You can't... *you can't* love me."

I started to reach for him, but then pulled my hands back to my chest. "But I do."

His face was tight, as if he was experiencing some terrible pain. Then he closed his eyes and leaned in, pressing his lips against my forehead. He lingered there a few moments before pulling back. His chest rose and fell as I stared at him.

Aiden scrubbed the palms of his hands over his eyes and let out another ragged breath. "Alex..."

"Oh, gods," I whispered, facing the front of the car. "I never should have said that."

"It's okay." Aiden cleared his throat. "It's all right."

Okay? It didn't seem okay. And *okay* and *all right* weren't what I wanted to hear. I wanted him to say he loved me, too. Wasn't that what was said after a declaration of love? Not *okay*. I knew he cared about me and he wanted me in the physical sense, but he wasn't saying those three little words.

And those three words were so important. They changed everything.

I willed my heart to stop the aching it was doing. Maybe he was just shocked into silence. Maybe he didn't know how to say it. Maybe he felt it but thought he couldn't say it.

Maybe I should've kept my big mouth shut.

I fell asleep during the ride back, which served several purposes. I got one hell of a power nap, and I avoided what probably would've been the most awkward car ride of my life. I pretended to still be asleep while we crossed the bridges.

Aiden kept it cool, like he hadn't kissed me and I hadn't professed my undying love for him. He even hopped out and opened the door for me before I'd even gotten the seatbelt off. He was such a gentleman—or he was just that eager to get rid of me.

After a half-assed goodbye, I headed back to my dorm. I cut through the courtyard, hoping to avoid the more heavily populated areas of the quad. I kept replaying everything Aiden had done and said.

Those kisses still sent shockwaves through my belly. The way he'd kissed me had to mean something, because people didn't *kiss* like that. He had wanted to get away with me, and planned the whole zoo thing. He had to feel something—something powerful for me.

But he hadn't said he loved me. He hadn't really said anything after I'd said it.

I kicked a loose pebble, sending it flying into a nearby lilac bush. There was a good chance I was overreacting. I tended to do that a lot. Tallying up everything Aiden had done in the last few hours, his actions proved he cared and totally outweighed the fact that he hadn't said he loved me.

I moved on to the rose bush and broke off one bloom by the stem. Somehow the roses were thornless here. I had no clue how they grew that way, but hell, I hadn't a clue about anything. I closed my eyes, inhaling its clean scent. Mom had loved hibiscuses, but I loved roses. They reminded me of spring and all things new.

"Child, that rose ain't going to ease your heart. Move on? Let go? Stay on the path your heart has chosen? Ain't nothing easy when the heart has laid claim."

My eyes popped open. "You have got to be kidding me."

A dry, rasping cackle that sounded like it was one step away from death confirmed who stood behind me. I wheeled around. Standing in the middle of the walkway, bent over a gnarly cane, was Grandma Piperi—oracle extraordinaire. Her hair looked like it had the last time I'd seen her, like its enormous weight would topple her over.

She smiled, stretching her way-too-thin skin. It looked a bit grotesque and crazy. "Do you know why a heart lays claim? Survival. That heart lays its claim to ensure survival of its kind."

Once again, I was standing in front of the oracle and she was sprouting the craziest crap I'd ever heard. "Why didn't you tell me my mother was a daimon?" I clenched the fragile stem of the rose in my fist. "Why didn't you tell me the truth?"

Piperi cocked her head to the side. "Child, I only speak in truths. I gave you the truths."

"You told me nothing!"

"No. No." She shook her head. "I told you everything."

I gaped at her. "You told me a bunch of crazy crap that didn't make any sense! You could have just said 'Hey, you're the second coming of the Apollyon. You're mother is a daimon and she's going to try to turn you. And oh, by the way, she's going to try to kill your friend!'"

"Isn't that what I told you, child?"

"No!" I screamed, throwing the rose to the ground. "That's not what you told me."

Piperi clucked her tongue. "Then you didn't listen with those ears. People never do. Only ever hear what they want to hear."

"Oh. My. Gods. Woman, you're the reason my mom left here in the first place. She was turned into a damn daimon. If you hadn't told her about me—"

"Your momma wanted to save you—save you from your fate. If she hadn't, you'd be nothing but a memory and a fear long forgotten. Just like all you who mix the breeds. What they want you two for, what they planned." She shook her head again and when she looked at me, sorrow etched across his face. "They fear you, fear what comes from you. I told you, child. I told you that your path was filled with dark things that must be done."

I blinked. "Uh… okay."

Piperi hobbled forward, stopping in front of me. She only came up to my shoulders, but I remembered how strong she was. I took a step back. She cackled, but this time the laugh ended in a wretched wheezing sound. Gods, I hoped she didn't keel over right here. She lifted her head, giving me a big, toothless smile. "Do you want to know about love, child?"

"Oh, come on." I groaned. "You make me want to hurt myself."

"But love, child, love is the root of all that is good, and the root of all things that are evil. Love is the root of the Apollyon."

I shifted to my other foot. "Yeah, I think this is around the time I say goodbye. I hope you have a nice trip back to whatever hut you crawled out of."

Her free hand snaked out, covering mine. Her skin felt papery thin, dry, and so gross. I tried to jerk my hand back, but she held on. Her strength was unnatural. Her eyes fastened on me. "Listen to me, child. Fate is afoot. Things cannot be undone. Fate has looked into the past and into the future. History is on repeat, but this is the time to press 'stop.' To change everything."

"I don't know what you're talking about. I'm sorry. You're not making—"

"Listen to me!"

"I'm listening! But could you speak a coherent sentence for once?"

Piperi's fingers slid over mine, and then she let go, wheezing. "I ain't nothing no more. You must see what I've shown you. Hear what I have spoken. Nothing is what it seems. Evil hides in the shadows, plotting its plans while you fear the daimons."

I scowled. "I don't fear daimons."

Her black eyes pierced me. "You should fear those who follow the old ways. Those who do not seek change and cannot allow things to continue as they are. And what a path, what a path the Powers have chosen. The end, the end is near. He," she japed at the sky, "will see to it."

I rolled my eyes. "Oh, for the love of the gods, this makes no sense."

She shook her head again. "You don't get it. Listen to me." Piperi poked me in the chest with one bony finger. "You must make a choice between what is fated and what is unknown."

"Ow!" I stepped back. She jabbed me again. "Hey! Knock it off!"

"Take the risk or suffer the consequences!" She stopped suddenly, her eyes growing wide as her gaze darted around the otherwise silent garden. "You must not accept gifts from those who seek to destroy you."

"Or candy," I muttered.

Piperi ignored my sarcasm. "You must stay away from the one who brings nothing but heartache and death. Do you hear me? He brings nothing but death. Always has. Know the difference between need and love, fate and future. If you don't, everything your momma sacrificed will be for naught."

That caught my attention—perhaps because it was the clearest thing she'd ever said to me. "Who is *he*?"

"He is not what he seems. He has them all fooled—has *him* fooled. Poor child doesn't see it. He doesn't see it, and it has sealed his fate." She sighed. "That one plays both sides. You don't know—you wouldn't know. He—" She jerked backward, the cane slipping from her grasp. The thing hit the marble sidewalk, shattering into a dozen thick pieces.

I grabbed for her, expecting her to fall flat on her face. So I was surprised when she didn't fall over… and utterly shocked when she folded in on herself, flaking away until nothing remained but a pile of dust.

CHAPTER 9

"THE ORACLE HAS PASSED." LUCIAN WHIRLED AROUND, addressing each of us. He looked ridiculous as the white robes twirled around his slender body. "Another has come into power."

I had a headache.

Apparently, the oracle dying wasn't a big deal. Grandma Piperi was ancient. I just happened to stumble upon her on her dying day or something—lucky me.

Woo.

Leon raised one massive arm and pinched the bridge of his nose. This impromptu gathering of the minds had not been going well. I'd come straight to Marcus after Grandma Piperi *poofed*, and from there, Marcus had called everyone to his office. Unfortunately, Lucian had brought a very contrary Seth. And worse yet, Aiden had *already* been in Marcus's office for whatever reason.

Marcus took a deep breath. "Alex, what happened exactly?"

"I've already told you everything. I ran into her in the garden. She was talking one second and the next, she just sort of poofed—"

"She poofed?" Seth laughed. He lounged in the corner, arms folded across his chest, and that damn smile plastered across his face. "Seriously?"

"Yes, she poofed. Like she was there one second and the next she was a pile of dust."

"We just don't *poof*, Alex. That doesn't happen."

"Well, it did. She poked me in my chest with her bony fingers and said some crazy stuff. Then she poofed!"

Seth's brows flew up and he laughed again. "What have you been doing today? Smoking something?"

Addressing Marcus, I threw up my hands. I had no idea why Seth was being such a jerk to me. He'd started in the moment he'd stepped into this room, and now I wanted to kill him. "Does he have to be here?"

"He is where I need him to be," Lucian answered instead. "And I need him here."

"Can he shut up, at least?" I missed the more charming version of Seth. This version sucked. "There's no valuable need for him to comment on everything that comes out of my mouth!"

"I'm commenting on everything, because it sounds like you've smoked some crack," Seth countered. "Where have you been all day?"

"Seth," Aiden warned. It was the first he'd spoken since the meeting began. He had changed into his Sentinel garb, and I was having one hell of a time not looking at him. "Can you be quiet for five seconds?"

Seth's yellow eyes snapped fire. "Does he have to be here? He's *just* a Sentinel."

"He was here before any of you were," Marcus responded with a tight smile. "And Seth, please try to contain the comments."

Seth slouched against the wall, raising his hands in surrender. "Sure. Sure. Go on, *Alexandria*. Tell us how she *poofed* again."

"I've already explained it," I said. "It's pretty easy to understand. Even for you. Or did you wake up on the wrong side of stupid this morning?"

"Alex," Aiden sighed. "Just talk to Marcus."

I stiffened. "Sorry. If he says one more word to me, I'm going to take that dagger off that wall and shove it through his eye."

Seth straightened, every cell in his body rising to the occasion. "Well, that's brave for a little Apollyon in training. If you want to try it, I'm game."

"Seth!" Marcus yelled, slamming his palms down on the table. Several ledgers and books shuddered.

My hold on my temper stretched to the breaking point. "You know what? I bet your mother wanted to drown you after you were born."

"Alexandria!" Marcus started around the desk. "Would you two—"

"And there's a reason why mothers turn daimon and try to kill their daughters."

I shot across the room, aiming right for the dagger behind Marcus's desk. Aiden cut me off. I considered barreling through him, but he looked like he would employ every measure possible to keep me from killing Seth.

"Don't," Aiden ordered in a low voice. "Just ignore him."

"Don't tell me what to do," I seethed. "I want the dagger so I can cut him."

"Cut me?" Seth laughed. "What are you—a street thug Apollyon about to shank me?"

Lucian sat down in one of the leather seats. "So much passion between you two," he murmured. "Can be expected, I imagine. You two are one and the same. Let them go. We can continue this conversation without any more interruptions, entertaining as they are."

I stopped. So did Seth. Actually, everyone in the room who didn't appear to be on drugs stopped and stared at Lucian. "What?"

Smiling like he knew some huge secret, he flicked his wrist elegantly. "Let them go. Alexandria has already told us what has happened. The oracle has passed and another has come into power. Let them work through their lovers' quarrel in private."

Even Seth's eyes widened at that. I had a more vocal response, one that caused Marcus to look like he wanted to shove me in a dark room and never let me out again.

"We have not yet determined what the oracle told Alexandria," Leon interjected from the corner. I'd almost forgotten he was there.

"She's already told us what she could. What was it, dear?" Lucian simpered in my direction. My hand itched to smack him upside his head. "She said that fate can be changed? Is that not great news? The oracle was referencing our two Apollyons."

I scowled at him. "Why does everything in your head automatically go back to the Apollyon?"

Lucian waved his hand again. "Let them go."

Aiden's hard stare bounced between us. "I don't think that's a good idea at the moment. One of them may seriously injure the other."

I wondered if he really thought that or if the idea of us "handling" our "lovers' quarrel" in private bothered him.

Marcus sighed. "I think it is an excellent idea, as we aren't getting anywhere with both of them in the roo—"

"I thought Lucian needed Seth here," Aiden interrupted, eyes like chips of ice.

Something ridiculously stupid sprung alive in my chest. Aiden was jealous? "You know what?" I shot Aiden a defiant look. "Let's go. Come on, Seth. Let's go continue our *lovers' quarrel*."

Pushing off the wall, Seth arched a brow. "Yes, *my love*, that sounds absolutely fantastic. Don't forget to grab a dagger so you can poke my eyeball out. Oh, that's right." He fixed a sympathetic look on his face. "Only a trained Sentinel can carry a dagger."

I shot him a sneer, and then whirled around and stalked out of the room. My head pounded like crazy, and even though I'd agreed to leave, I didn't want to continue talking with Seth. We actually made it to the first floor before all hell broke loose.

Seth grabbed my arm and dragged me into one of the empty offices, slamming the door shut behind him. "You little brat, what the hell have you been doing all day?"

I pulled my arm free and moved to the other side of the office. Seth stalked after me, and I thought of the lion from earlier. All he needed was a swishing tail. I laughed, not able to help it. The image of Seth with a tail was kind of funny.

Seth stopped short, scowling. "What's so funny?"

I sobered up. "Jeez, nothing."

"What have you been doing all day, Alex?"

"What have you been doing?" I sidestepped him, putting some space between us. "And why don't you seem to care that the oracle died?"

"Alex, she was ancient. At least a couple of hundred years old. It was bound to happen. Lucian is right. Another has come into power and blah, blah."

"She died right in front of me! It was a bit unsettling."

Seth cocked his head to the side. "Do you want me to host a pity party for you? I'm sure I can wrangle up a few people who can help you commiserate."

"Gods, would it kill you to be a tiny bit nice? Oh. Wait. It would. So excuse me, I have stuff I need to do." I started for the door, but Seth caught my arm. His skin felt like fire. "Seth, come on. I have a freaking headache and—"

His eyes searched my face. "What have you been doing today?"

I started to get uncomfortable. "I've been training. What the hell else could I be doing?"

"Training?" Seth laughed harshly. "Where?"

"Here," I said immediately.

Seth's eyes narrowed. "You little liar, I checked the training room for you. You weren't there."

Oh, crap.

A smug smile inched across his face. "So I checked all the other training facilities, and the gym, and the beach, and finally your room. You weren't in any of them."

Oh, double crap.

"So don't lie to me." He backed me up until I hit the edge of the desk. "Your cheeks are blood red, your pulse has skyrocketed, and you're a terrible liar."

I clenched the edge of the desk. "I have no idea what you're talking about."

Seth bent down so we were eye level. "You don't?"

"No."

"I'm going to ask you one more time, Alex. What were you doing today?"

"Or what?" I demanded. "What are you going to do? And why do you even care?"

"Because the emotions you were feeling today were outrageous."

"Gods, this day will never end," I muttered. Throbbing temples aside, I was pretty sure I had enough aggression in me to take out Seth at this point. "Who cares?"

"I care because you were supposed to be training with Aiden today, and there is no reason you'd be feeling those kind…" Seth's eyes widened. I swear, I'd never seen his pupils so dilated, and for someone who kept dragging me back to him, he sure let go of me awfully fast. "Oh. No, no, no."

Apprehension blossomed, quickly turning my insides cold. "What?"

"You wouldn't." He ran his hand down the side of his face. "Wait. What am I saying? You *would* do something so incredibly stupid."

I leaned against the desk. "Uh… gee, thanks."

Seth shot forward, grasping my shoulders. I flinched, unable to suppress the natural response. "Please tell me I'm wrong. Tell me that you are not messing around with a godsdamned pure-blood. Damn it, Alex. *Him?* My gods, it explains so much."

Anything and everything in my head sort of emptied out. My brain had this wonderful ability of doing so when I really needed to think fast.

He laughed harshly. "Now I know why he hates me, at least. Why he's always on you. I just figured it was in the figurative sense and not literal. What the hell are you thinking? What is he thinking? You're going to throw everything away! Your future—my future—and for what? To get more pure in you?"

Shrugging his hands off my shoulders for the umpteenth time, I snapped out of it. "You don't have a clue what you're talking about! I'm not messing around with Aiden."

"Don't you dare lie to me about something like this!" He shoved his finger in my face. I had the urge to break it. "You can't do this, Alex. I will not allow this to continue." Seth started for the door.

"No. No! Seth, stop! Please." This time I grabbed him, pulling him back from the door. "Please listen to me. It's not what you think!"

His eyes practically glowed he was so angry. "It's not about what I *think*. It's what I *felt* today!"

"Please. Just listen to me for a second." My fingers dug into his arms. "You can't say anything. They'll—"

"I'm not going to say anything to the Council, you little idiot. They would send you into servitude in a heartbeat." He pushed me off, swearing under his breath. "You know, I actually thought he might be different from the other pures, but he sure as hell doesn't act any different. Screw a half; enslave a half. That's what they say, Alex."

"What are you doing? You can't—"

"I'm going to have a little talk with Aiden."

I flew in front of him, plastering myself to the door. "You are so not going to talk to him! You're going to try to fight him."

"Quite possibly. Now get out of my way."

"No."

"Get out of the way, Alex," he snarled. Edges of the Apollyon marks started creasing his otherwise flawless skin.

"Okay," I breathed, pressing against the door. "I'll tell you the truth. All right—just please don't do anything… stupid."

"I don't think you should be lecturing me on not doing anything stupid."

I counted to ten. Now was not the time for me to lose my patience. "Nothing happened between Aiden and me. Okay? I do care about him, all right? I know it's wrong." I closed my eyes, wishing the words didn't hurt as much as they did. "I know it's stupid, but nothing is going on between us."

"What I felt from you today wasn't *nothing*, Alex. You're still lying to me."

"Okay. We kissed, but—stop!" I pushed Seth back as he tried to pry me away from the door. "Listen to me. We did kiss, but it's nothing. It was stupid—a mistake. It's nothing to get all bent out of shape over. Okay?"

He stared down at me, lips drawn tightly. Then he closed his eyes. Terse silence stretched out between us. "You… you love him, don't you?"

I stared at him, my heart thumping loudly. "No. No, of course I don't."

Seth nodded, running a hand over his face again. "Alex… Alex, you're insane."

Obviously, he didn't believe me. I needed to make Seth understand that nothing needed to be done about this. There was no way he could go after Aiden. Gods only knew what Seth would do, or what Aiden would do. I could see them now, brawling on the beach. One thing would lead to another, and the Council would find out. The pures would dope me up to suppress the Apollyon in me and I'd be scrubbing floors for the rest of my life. Aiden would never forgive himself. I couldn't let that happen. And then there was the idiot standing in front of me. If Seth attacked a pure, that would be it. The Council would move against Seth, and even though I wanted to strangle him, I didn't want… well, I didn't want anything to happen to him.

Call it self-preservation.

"Nothing's going on," I said. "Just promise me you won't do anything."

Seth stared at me so long the silence that enveloped us started to get to me. Then the tattoo started to sink back into his skin and he looked surprisingly calm.

"You're not going to do anything, right?"

"No." Seth reached for me and pried my hand off the doorknob. "I'm not going to say anything."

Relief, sweet and beautiful, flooded through me. I let out my breath. "Thank you."

"You're not going to ask why?"

"No." I shook my head. "I'm not going to look a gifted horse in the mouth."

"Do you even know what that means?"

"Not really," I said, "but it sounds about right."

Seth arched a brow, and then tugged me away from the door. "Come on, let's go."

I spared our joined hands a brief glance. "Where are we going?"

"We're going to do some training, since you apparently didn't do any of *that* today."

"She poofed into nothing? Damn, that's crazy."

I stared at Caleb, wishing he would poof into nothing. "What is everyone's big deal with the terminology? I swear to the gods, if one more person questions that, I'm going to lose it."

"Poof," Olivia whispered, grinning.

I shot her a death glare. "Ha. Funny."

"Sorry." She slid her arm around Caleb. Apparently, they'd made up at some point, again. That made me happy. I liked the way they looked at one another when they weren't fighting. "I bet that was freaky, though."

"Freaky doesn't even begin to describe it."

"She was old as dirt," Caleb said, "but still. The old crone was kind of entertaining."

"Entertaining" wasn't a word I'd use to describe Grandma Piperi. I leaned back in the moon chair and let my eyes drift shut as Olivia and Caleb started talking about the party they'd snuck off to last night. I felt a spark of jealousy and bitterness. I hadn't been invited. Maybe Caleb thought I had more pure than half in me, too. Blech.

I refocused my thoughts on Piperi. Even a few days later, I was still so wrapped up in the almost exposure of Aiden's and my nonexistent relationship to give much thought to what she'd said before she'd died.

The conversation I'd had with her didn't make much sense—no big surprise there. The only thing important I'd picked out was about the guy who wasn't who he appeared, that he had everyone fooled. If only she hadn't poofed into nothing a second later, maybe she would've said his name, which would've helped tremendously. I didn't share this part of the conversation with anyone. It seemed that whoever it was wasn't a friend of mine. Then again, I couldn't be sure. After that thought, I must've drifted off to sleep, because I jerked upright at the sound of my name.

"Miss Andros."

I peeled my eyes open and found Leon standing in the doorway to the rec room. "Yeah?"

"You're not supposed to be in here."

Odd. When had Leon been assigned to be my babysitter? I only saw him around campus when he had terrible and urgent news to deliver. "Come on," I whined.

Caleb peered over the back of the couch. "She's not bothering anyone."

Leon didn't even glance at Caleb. "Up."

Caleb twisted toward me. "One of these days, you'll be able to stay out and play. Then everything will be right in our world."

Pulling myself out the chair, I rolled my eyes at Caleb. "Leon, can I have a playdate with my friends?" That got a giggle out of Olivia.

Leon's expression remained bland. "Perhaps you'd be allowed to have playdates if you stayed out of trouble for a whole week."

"I guess that's a no." Caleb grinned up at me. "So now you know what to do. Stay out of trouble for a whole week, Alex. *A whole week.*"

I smacked the back of Caleb's head as I made my way past the couch. He swung out at me, but Olivia got in the way.

"Bye!" Olivia chirped, already snuggling down beside Caleb.

Giving them a little wave, I followed Leon out of the lounge. I felt a little uncomfortable walking beside him. The man was almost seven feet tall and looked like he belonged on the pro wrestling circuit. Not to mention, I didn't know how much Leon knew. I remembered how unsurprised he'd looked when Marcus had mentioned me being the Apollyon.

I searched for something to say, but came up empty until my gaze fell on a statue of Apollo. "Hey, you kind of look like Apollo. Has anyone told you that? All you need is blond hair and raging hormones. Maybe he's your great-great-great-great grandfather or something."

Leon's gaze flicked over the marble statue. "No. No one has ever said that."

"Huh. Funny. 'Cuz you do. I wonder if you have anything else in common with Apollo."

"Like what?"

"You know. Didn't Apollo have a thing for pretty boys?" I snorted. "Wait, didn't Apollo have a thing for just about everything that walked? Until they got turned into trees or flowers, that is."

"*What?*" Leon came to a complete standstill, gaping down at me. "There are some myths that are true, but most are exaggerated."

I raised my brows quizzically. "Didn't realize you were an Apollo fanboy. Sorry."

"I am *not* a fanboy."

"Okay. Never mind, then."

"Do you know what I find interesting, Alexandria?" he asked after a few moments.

"No. Not really." I shivered in the rapidly cooling air.

"How you happened across the oracle right before she died."

I glanced around the nearly empty campus, spotting only Sentinels and Guards. I hadn't realized it had gotten so late. "I have no clue. I guess I have that kind of luck."

"Twice?"

I looked at him sharply. And there was another thing I hadn't known he was aware of. "I guess so."

Leon nodded, eyes scanning the pathway to the girls' dorm. "Did you know the oracle only seeks out those she wants? That many, many pure-bloods go their entire lives without even seeing the oracle once?"

"No." I wrapped my arms around myself, wondering where summer had gone. It was almost the end of October, but usually it didn't get *this* chilly.

"Then she must have had something very important to tell you," Leon said. "I'd assume something more than just being able to change history."

My steps slowed as the oracle's words rushed through me. *He is not what he seems. He has them all fooled. He plays both sides.* I glanced up at Leon, wary of where this conversation was going. There was nothing I knew about Leon except his wonderful ability to pop up when I didn't want him around—and his fanboy love for Apollo. "That's all she said."

Leon stopped in front of the steps to the dorm, folding those massive arms over his chest. "Seems rather vague."

"Piperi is—was—always vague. Nothing she ever said has made much sense to me."

He cocked his head to the side and a small smile appeared on his face. I think that was the first time I'd ever seen him smile. "That's the thing about oracles. They do tell you the truth, you just have to really hear it."

My brows inched up my forehead. "Well, I guess I didn't hear it."

Leon's gaze fell on me, heavy and hard. "I'm sure in good time you will." Then he twisted around and disappeared down the pathway.

I stood there a few more moments, staring after him. That had been the longest conversation I'd ever held with the guy and it ranked right up there with the conversations I'd held with the oracle. It made no sense.

It also filled me with a decent amount of unease. There was always something about Leon that didn't seem right—a sort of otherworldly trait I couldn't quite put my finger on. But could he be the mystery man the oracle had been talking about?

I shivered and headed up the stairs. I hoped not. There was no way any of us could take that massive hunk of flesh out in a battle.

CHAPTER 10

I WAS A NERVOUS MESS OF FUNK.

It had to do with the little box in my gym bag. Nice of Deacon to gift wrap the guitar pick, but now I felt stupid for giving it to Aiden, especially after everything that had gone down between us at the zoo.

But I had it and I needed to give it to him. If I didn't, there was a chance Deacon could make some passing comment to him about it and then I'd be even more mortified. And it was just a guitar pick. It wasn't like it screamed *I love you* or anything. Not that it mattered since I'd already blabbed that.

I went through practice with Aiden sort of numb and hyperaware. I kept missing chances to say "happy birthday" or give him the damn box. I just couldn't bring myself to do it.

What if he laughed at me? What if he hated it? What if he looked at me and said, "What the hell is this for?" and threw the box on the mat? Then stomped on it?

I couldn't stop thinking about how many ways this could go wrong. Did his reaction really matter? Since our trip to the zoo and my embarrassing declaration of love, he'd kept things perfectly cool between us. There were only a few times I'd caught him watching me with this hawkish level of interest. I always wondered what went through his mind then.

Aiden sent me another weird look, and I felt my face turn red.

I'd never hated myself more.

Unsurprisingly, I ran out of time. While my heart pounded in my chest, I bent down and dug the little white box out of my bag. Deacon had even put a black bow on it. I hadn't known he was such a crafty guy.

"Alex, what are you doing?"

Clenching the box in my hand, I stood. "So are you doing anything… um, special tonight?"

He dropped the mat he'd been rolling up. "Not really. Why?"

I shifted uncomfortably, keeping the box hidden between my hands. "It's your birthday. Shouldn't you be celebrating?"

Surprise flashed across his face. "How did you know it was today? Wait." He gave a rueful smile. "Deacon told you."

"Well, your birthday is the day before Halloween. Kind of hard to forget."

Aiden brushed off his hands. "We're going to have dinner with some people, but it's nothing big."

I smiled, inching closer. "Well, that's doing something."

"Yeah, it's something."

Just give him the stupid box, Alex. "Well… you don't have to work tonight, right?" *Give him the damn box, Alex, and stop talking. Like forever.*

Aiden flashed a quick grin as his gaze drifted toward me. "No. I got the night off. Alex, I need to tell—"

I stepped forward, shoving my hands at his chest. Well, I shoved the box at his chest. "Happy birthday!" I looked and felt like the worst kind of dweeb.

His startled gaze dropped, and then flicked back to mine. He took the little box. "What's this?"

"It's just a small gift. Nothing big," I said in a rush. "It's for your birthday. Well, obviously."

"Alex, you really didn't have to do this." He turned it over, running those graceful fingers over it. "You didn't have to get me anything."

"I know." I pushed a few strands of hair off my face. "But I wanted to."

"Can I shake it?"

"Yeah, it won't break."

Grinning, he shook the box. The pick rattled off the sides. He glanced at me once more and then untied the black bow. Holding my breath, I watched him carefully open up the lid and peer inside. Aiden's eyes narrowed and his lips parted. I didn't know what that expression meant. Slowly, he reached inside and plucked the pick out of the box.

Aiden held the gemstone pick between two long fingers, his expression incredulous. "It's black."

I glanced around the room. "Yeppers. It's black. Um, I saw that you had every color except black." He continued to stare at the pick with this dumbfounded look on his face. I folded my arms, suddenly wanting to cry. "If you don't like it, I'm sure you can return it. I got it at this store online. They do—"

"No." Aiden looked up and his eyes met mine. They were a dark gray, bordering on silver. "No. I don't want to return it." He flipped the pick over, smoothing his thumb over it. "It's perfect."

I flushed, still wanting to cry, but in a totally good way now. "You really think so?"

Aiden took a step forward, his eyes like liquid pools. They took up his face, my entire world. I didn't know what was going to happen next. All I knew was that I was hooked on him, irrevocably so.

"There you are." Marcus stood at the entrance to the training room. "I've been searching everywhere for you."

There was sort of grace to how fast Aiden slid the gift into the pocket of his pants and twisted around. I couldn't see his face, but I knew it was perfectly devoid of any emotion. Only his eyes would give anything away, and Marcus would never be able to tell anything from their colors like I could.

However, I was also sure my face would give everything away. I hurried over to my gym bag and became fascinated with its strap.

"What can I do for you?" Aiden asked casually.

"Practice is running a little late for you two, isn't it?"

"We were just finishing up."

"Alexandria, what are you doing over there?" asked Marcus.

Cursing under my breath, I shouldered the bag and faced my uncle. He wore a three-piece suit. No one on campus dressed as well as he did.

"Nothing, just getting my stuff."

He raised a brow elegantly. "Were you running late from class and held up Aiden? You should have more respect for his time."

I shot my uncle a dirty look, but managed to keep my mouth shut.

"It's fine," Aiden responded quickly. "She wasn't that late."

Marcus nodded. "Well, I'm glad I found you two together."

My brows inched up my forehead, and the urge to laugh hit me hard. Aiden looked less amused.

"I've given what you asked some thought and I do agree with what you've suggested, Aiden."

The lines around Aiden's mouth tightened. "I haven't had a chance to discuss this with Alex."

Marcus frowned. "Don't concern yourself with that. You've done wonderfully with her. I have to admit, I didn't think she'd be able to get caught up, but you were right. We can end the additional practices."

I stepped forward, but I didn't feel the floor under my sneakers. "End my practices?"

"Aiden feels that you no longer require these additional practices, and I happen to agree with him. You'll still be working with Seth, but this will afford you some time off and also allow Aiden to return to his Sentinel duties fully."

I stared at Marcus, hearing him but not really understanding. Then I turned toward Aiden. His face was utterly blank. I knew I should feel good about this, because it was a huge step in the right direction and Marcus had sort of complimented me, but I couldn't get past the hole opening up in my chest. Aiden and I would never see each other if we didn't train together.

"Aiden, you've spoken about this with Seth?" Marcus asked. "Discussed areas for potential improvement?"

"Yes, Seth is aware of things she can use additional work on." Aiden's voice sounded surprisingly empty and flat.

He'd already talked this over with Seth? I inhaled, but the air fled my lungs. My chest seized in a weird way and my brain tried to tell me that I'd known this day was coming. I just hadn't thought it was coming *this soon.*

"Well, I don't want to keep you. Enjoy your dinner tonight." Marcus paused, seeming to remember I still stood there. He turned back, smiling politely. "Good night, Alexandria."

He didn't wait for my response, which was good, because I had none. The moment I felt sure he was out of hearing range, I whirled on Aiden. "We aren't going to train anymore?"

Aiden still wouldn't look at me. "I was going to talk to you about it. I think—"

"You were going to talk to me about it? Why didn't you talk to me before you went to Marcus?"

"I went to Marcus last week, Alex."

"After… we got back from the zoo? That's why you were in Marcus's office when I got there?"

Aiden still hadn't looked at me, not once since Marcus had dropped the bomb. "Yes."

"I... I don't understand." I gripped the bag's shoulder strap like it was some kind of lifeline. "Why don't you want to train me anymore?"

"Alex, you don't need me to train you anymore." His body started to tense, to lock up. "You're caught up with the other students."

"If that's true then why did you have to discuss areas of improvement with Seth? Why can't you just work on them?"

Aiden turned away fully, running a hand through his hair. "You need time off. You're exhausted all the time, and something has to give. You need to work with Seth a lot more than you need to work with me. He can work with you on the elements, prepare you for when you Awaken."

There was a strange buzzing in my ears, adding a surreal element to all of this. "That's not true. I don't need Seth."

Aiden's head snapped in my direction. "You don't need me, Alex."

It took me several tries to get the next words out over the huge lump in my throat. "I do. I won't see you anymore if we don't train."

"You'll see me at Council, Alex, and you'll see me around here. Don't be ridiculous."

I ignored the coldness in his voice. "But after that? I won't see you." My voice cracked. The sound was equally humiliating and sad.

"Well, I think that is… for the best."

It felt like he'd reached inside me and crushed my lungs into lifeless lumps. I drew in a deep breath and tried to calm down, but there was this raw hurt in my chest. It ached, throbbed in a way that felt so real. I could only stare at him. "Is… this because of what I told you at the zoo? Why you don't want to train me anymore?"

Aiden's lean body tensed again, and a muscle in his jaw jumped. "Yes, that has something to do with it."

A crack in my heart started. "Because… because I said I loved you?"

He made a deep sound in his throat. "And because I don't…" He paused, looking away. "I don't feel the same way about you. *I can't.* Okay? I can't let myself love you. If I did, I would take everything from you—*everything*. I can't do that to you. I won't do that to you."

"What? That doesn't—"

"It does matter, Alex."

I reached for his arm, but Aiden moved away from me. Stung, I wrapped my arms around my waist. "You're saying this—"

"Just stop." He ran a hand through his hair again.

The rawness of his words sliced through. "Then why did you tell me that stuff at the zoo? Why did you say you cared for me? That you wanted to break the rules for me? Why would you tell me any of that?"

Aiden turned gunmetal gray eyes on me, and I took a step back. He looked nothing like the Aiden I knew. Aiden never looked at me so coolly, so detached. "I do care for you, Alex. I… don't want to see anything bad happen to you or to see you hurt."

"No." I shook my head. "It's more than that. You… you held my hand." The last bit came out a pitiful whisper.

He flinched. "That was… a silly mistake."

Now I flinched, and I couldn't stop the words from coming out. "No. You want me—"

"Of course I *want* you," he said harshly. "I'm a man, and you're a beautiful girl. I can't help that. Wanting you in the physical sense has nothing to do with how I feel about you."

My mouth opened, but nothing came out. I blinked back hot tears.

Aiden's hands curled into fists. "You're a half-blood, Alex. You can't love me, and pure-bloods don't love halfs."

I staggered back, feeling as if he'd smacked me in the face. I was so embarrassed—humiliated. How had I mistaken how he felt about me so badly? I had *everything* wrong. Letting out a ragged breath, I turned away just as Aiden closed his eyes and lowered his head. Sick to my stomach, I walked back to the dorm in a daze. The worst part was the shame. I couldn't see past it, couldn't think around it. There was a burning in my eyes I desperately fought. Crying wasn't going to solve anything, but damn, that's all I wanted to do. My chest felt like it'd been ripped open, my heart torn apart.

When I opened the door to my room, I wasn't entirely surprised to find Seth sitting on the couch. Not surprised, but angry. I needed to consider barring the window in the bedroom.

He didn't look up. "Hey."

"Please leave." I dropped my bag on the floor.

Seth's lips pursed as he stared straight ahead. "I can't do that."

Fierce emotion swept through me, agonizing and raw. I couldn't—wouldn't lose it in front of Seth. "I'm not screwing with you. Get out."

He looked up, eyes the color of a warm sunset. "I'm sorry… but I can't leave."

I stepped forward, clenching my hands. "I don't care what I'm throwing off right now and how it's affecting you. Please leave."

Seth slowly came to his feet. "I'm not leaving. You could use the company."

I might hate the connection that fed my emotions to Seth more than I hated anything in my life. "Don't push me, Seth. Leave, or I'll make you leave."

He was in my face in a heartbeat. Grasping my arms, he lowered his head so that we were eye level. "Look, I can leave this room. Fine. You're still going to feel like hell, which means I'm still going to feel like hell."

I inhaled roughly, unable to escape him. Tears burned my eyes and clogged the back of my throat, threatening to choke me.

He took a deep breath. "I knew you'd lied to me when you said you didn't… love him. Why are you doing this to yourself? Aiden is like every other pure, Alex. Sure, he may have moments where it doesn't seem that way, but he *is* a pure-blood."

I turned my head away from Seth, biting down on my lip until I tasted blood. An hour ago I would never have agreed with that, but Aiden had just said the very same thing.

"And what if he did love you, Alex? What then? Would you be satisfied with being something he had to *hide*? Satisfied with lying to everyone and watching him pretend like he didn't care for you? Then, when you did get caught, would you be satisfied giving your life up for him?"

All very good questions, ones that I'd asked myself time and time again.

"You're too important, too special to throw everything away for a pure." Seth sighed, dropping his hands to mine. "Now, I brought us a movie to watch, the one that has sparkly vampires in it. I thought you'd be down for that."

I studied him silently. He looked like he always did—a living, breathing statue. Perfection without any humanity, and yet he was here. "I can't figure you out."

He didn't answer as he deposited me on the couch. He put the movie in and then returned to the couch, remote in hand. "I'm moody," he said finally, fiddling with the controls.

I stared at him and a strangled sort of laugh escaped me. Moody? More like borderline personality disorder or something. But who was I to judge? I had to be crazy, didn't I? I'd fallen for a pure-blood. That topped the list of symptoms for possible mental illness.

Thinking about Aiden brought a sharp pang to my chest. And here I'd thought my heart was somewhere in the gym, bleeding on the floor. I tried focusing on the movie, but my brain wasn't into it. Immediately, I rewound my conversation with Aiden—all my conversations with him, actually. How could he go from the guy I could spill my guts to—could trust and rely on, who could make my heart swell with the tiniest of smiles or compliment—to someone just as cold as I believed Seth to be?

Yet Seth sat next to me.

Maybe he wasn't as cold as he appeared, and Aiden wasn't as perfect as I'd believed him to be. Maybe my judgment was just as screwed up as my taste in guys.

Seth sighed again, this time much louder than before. Quietly and rather casually, he reached over and tugged me across the couch. I ended up with the side of my face smooshed against his thigh and his heavy arm draped over my side. "What are you—?"

"Shh," he murmured. "I'm watching the movie."

I tried to sit up, but didn't make it very far. His arm weighed a ton. Several unsuccessful attempts later, I gave up. "So… uh, you're a Team Edward kind of guy?"

He snorted. "No. I'm Team James or Team Tyler's Van, but apparently neither of them won by the look of it. She's still alive."

"Yeah, seems that way."

Seth didn't say anything after that, and eventually, my body relaxed and some of the hurt eased off. It was still there, but muted by Seth's nearly overwhelming presence—the Apollyon connection doing its thing. Perhaps that was why Seth had made himself available. Or maybe he'd just wanted to witness my stupidity.

CHAPTER 11

THE NEXT WEEK OF MY LIFE SUCKED.

It sucked in a way I wasn't entirely accustomed to. I'd had crushes before, even a few cases of mad lusting. But I'd never loved someone other than my Mom and Caleb, and that was a different kind of love.

This kind of love hurt like hell.

Not seeing Aiden after class felt wrong, like something was missing or I'd forgotten something terribly important. On the days I should've practiced with him, I tried spending time with Caleb and Olivia, but I usually retreated to my room and sulked until Seth showed up.

I missed Aiden, missed him so badly. Hurt consumed every waking second, turning me into one of those girls whose world ended when a guy rejected them. I lived in this miserable state of existence—miserable and obnoxious.

"Are you going to get out of this bed at some point today?" Caleb sat with his back against the headboard of my bed. A classics textbook lay unopened in his lap. He'd gotten the humiliating story out of me a few days ago. Just like Seth, he hadn't been surprised by the outcome. However, he'd been pretty pissed that I'd been entertaining the idea of a relationship with Aiden this entire time. And I just felt more stupid.

He nudged me with his knee when I didn't respond. "Alex, it's almost seven and you haven't budged."

"I don't have anything to do."

"Have you even showered?" Caleb asked.

I rolled over, shoving my face into my pillow. "No."

"That's kind of gross."

"Uh-huh," was my muffled response. A second later his cell made this annoyingly shrill sound from the table next to my bed, and the textbook smacked the floor. I didn't move. Caleb climbed over me, shoving his elbow into my back.

"Gods!" I yelled into the pillow. "Ouch."

"Shush," Caleb said, still sprawled over me, his bony elbows digging into my back as he flipped his phone around and checked his messages.

I could turn my head to the side, but that was all. "Jeez, you weigh a ton. Who is it? Olivia?"

Caleb rolled onto his side, cracking my lower back in the process. Kind of felt good. "Yeah, she wants to know what the smell is radiating up to her room."

"Shut up."

"Seriously, she wants to know if you've showered." He shifted onto his stomach. "You know, you're kind of comfortable. You're getting some extra cushion, Alex."

"Am not, you douche."

He laughed. "Olivia wants to know if we want to watch a movie."

"I don't know."

"How can you not know? It's a simple question."

I managed to wiggle out a shrug.

Caleb snorted. "Look, I just sat here for the entire day while you stared up at the ceiling like an idiot. You're getting out of this bed, taking a shower, and we're going to have a movie night in *your* dorm. Then Olivia and I are going to leave and engage in wild animal sex. End of discussion."

"Ew, that's an image I never wanted imbedded in my memory. Thanks."

"Whatever. So what do you think? You game?"

I rolled my eyes. "It's almost curfew time."

"What the hell?" He dropped the phone next to my head, and the next thing I knew, he was sitting on my back with both his hands planted on my shoulders. "We haven't done anything fun in ages, Alex. And you need fun—STAT."

"You're killing me," I squeaked. "Can't… breathe."

"It's not like I'm suggesting we have a threesome. I'm suggesting we sneak over to the cafeteria, grab some drinks and food, and then watch a movie."

I lifted my head off the pillow. "Darn, you're not suggesting a threesome? My life is over."

"Pay attention to the finer points of what I'm saying. With all the rules crap and you being grounded," Caleb continued while his phone buzzed in my ear. "Besides, you're leaving next week for the Council and you're going to be gone for weeks. We need to do this. You need to do this. It's our last hoorah."

"Can you check your phone? It's annoying."

He leaned forward, pressing his head against the back of mine. "Where's the old Alex I know and love, my wild and crazy friend?"

I grunted, unable to push him off. "Caleb, come on."

"Come on, come out and play. What else are you going to do?"

What else? Lie around my room all night and feel sorry for myself, and… and that was just lame. Hanging out with Caleb and Olivia would do me some good. For a little while I could forget about Aiden, about how badly I loved him and how he'd rejected me.

I squeezed my eyes shut. "Do you think… was I being stupid for, you know, the stuff with Aiden?"

Caleb leaned over, pressing his cheek against mine. "Yes, it was and is stupid. But I still love you."

I laughed. "Okay. Fine."

He rolled off me, resting on his side. "You serious?"

"Yeah." I sat up. "But I need to shower first."

"Thank the gods. You stink."

I punched his arm and swung off the bed. "Still smell better than you, but I love you nonetheless."

Caleb fell back. "I know. You'd be lost without me."

Olivia dropped three packs of microwave popcorn, overloaded with butter, a packet of Twizzlers, and a bunch of candy bars on my coffee table.

"Do you hoard food or something?" I grabbed one of the red ropes.

She giggled as she reached into the pocket of her hoodie and pulled out bags of Sour Patch Kids. "I like to be well stocked. Now all we need are some drinks."

"That's where Alex and I come in." Caleb wrapped his arms around Olivia's waist.

I gnawed on my Twizzler, eyeing the candy bars. Gods know I'd assaulted the vending machines this past week. I didn't need more chocolate. "We need a bag." I turned around and went back in to my bedroom. Digging around in my closet, I found a dark blue tote bag that would do. Holding the candy between my lips, I rolled up the bag and went back in the little living room.

It was like Caleb had fallen into Olivia's mouth; they were kissing that deeply. Rolling my eyes, I plucked the Twizzler out of my mouth and threw it at the back of Caleb's head. He turned around, running a hand through his hair. Looking down, he spotted the candy on the floor. "Gross," he said. "That's really gross, Alex."

Laughing, Olivia ducked around Caleb. "You tasted kind of sour and sweet, baby."

"Oh, gods," I moaned, twisting my still-damp hair up in a bun. "That was lame."

She flipped me off as she hopped on the couch. Her hair was one thick braid tonight, falling over her shoulder. I suspected the distressed jeans and gray sweatshirt had cost a pretty penny. "All right. The mission, if you choose to accept it, is to return with a bag of canned liquid goodness. It will be a risky, yet fruitful one. Do you accept this mission?"

I glanced over at Caleb, grinning. "I don't know. It's dangerous. There'll be Guards and Sentinels lurking in the shadows, preventing us from reaching the ark of soda. Are we up for it, Caleb?"

He pulled a band off his wrist and secured the shoulder length blond strands in a ponytail at the nape of his neck. "We must be brave and strong, cunning and quick." He paused dramatically. "We shall not fail this mission."

"Oh, I like it when you're all macho and serious. It's sexy." Olivia leaned over, pressing a kiss to Caleb's cheek, which led to a full-blown make out session.

Standing there awkwardly, I tried to focus on anything but the two of them. It didn't work. "Olivia, I pray to the gods you haven't forgotten your booster shot. 'Cuz you guys are *so* about to make some babies."

Caleb pulled back, his entire face flushing. "All right, any requests?"

"Anything with lots of caffeine," Olivia responded, straightening her shirt. Her eyes gleamed in the light. "Don't take too long and don't get caught."

I laughed. "Us get caught? Ye of little faith."

Olivia waved her hand and sat down, messing with the remote. I motioned Caleb to follow me back into the bedroom. I opened the window Seth used quite frequently and gripped the bag. "You ready?"

Caleb nodded, his cheeks still a pretty shade of pink. "After you."

I swung my legs over the windowsill and hung there for a moment, scanning the area. Finding it empty, I dropped the five feet to the ground, landing in a crouch. I popped up. "All clear, my dear."

He stuck his head out. "That rhymes."

"Well, yes it does. You're so observant." I stepped back as Caleb launched out the window.

Standing beside me, he shook out his shoulders. "Which way should we take?"

I turned around, facing the back of the dorm. "This way. Lots more shadow back there and no lights."

Caleb nodded, and we set off for the cafeteria. Chilly air clung to my damp hair, sending shivers down my neck.

We stayed in the shadows, edging along the building. Both of us knew better than to talk too much as Guards and Sentinels had uncanny hearing abilities when it came to rooting out students sneaking around.

At the edge of the girls' dorm, I peeked around the corner. It was hard to make out much of anything in the darkness. I wondered how the Guards could even see a daimon creeping up on them.

Caleb stopped beside me, giving me a hand motion I couldn't decipher. He looked like a crossing guard. "What's that supposed to mean?" I whispered, dumbfounded.

He grinned. "I don't know. It just seemed like the right moment to do it."

I rolled my eyes, but smiled. "Ready?"

"Yeppers."

We took off, crossing the wide-open space between the girls' dorm and the training facilities. Halfway across, Caleb pushed me into a prickly bush. Cursing under my breath, I flew after him. Caleb was fast, reaching safety a few feet before me. He leaned against the side of the training arena, laughing softly.

I punched him in the stomach. "Douche." I started picking little needles out from my jeans.

After that, we continued to the edge and dashed to the medical building. It was kind of like a weird version of hopscotch. Next, we had to skirt around the building where they stored all the weapons and uniforms and then we'd be at the back of the cafeteria and rec rooms. From there, Caleb knew how to get in the cafeteria even when the main entrance was gated shut. He'd raided the place many times.

A shadow moved up ahead, blending in with the night sky. As the form drew closer, we flattened ourselves against the building and waited until the Guard disappeared around the corner of the med building. Almost getting caught fueled the excitement of doing something we shouldn't. I could tell it got Caleb going, too. His blue eyes seemed to glow and the devilish grin on his face spread.

A sudden sound—much like a muffled gasp—broke the silence. We looked at each other, puzzled. Caleb's grin slipped a little as his eyes met mine. Shrugging at him, I strained to hear anything else, but there was only thick silence. Slowly, I crept to the side and tried to see into the darkness.

"Looks good," I whispered.

We darted across the pathway, slowing down as we made it to the back of the dining hall, keeping an eye out for more Guards. I took a deep breath and immediately regretted doing so. The smell of rotting food filled my nostrils. Black garbage bags lay where several trash cans had toppled over. "Gods, it stinks back here."

"I know." Caleb pressed against my back, looking around. "Or it could just be you I smell."

I shoved my elbow into his stomach. Caleb doubled over, groaning. I started around the corner of the dumpster and froze. The small light at the back door used by servants flickered, casting ghoulish yellow light over the trash cans. We weren't alone in the cramped space. Another shadow moved up ahead, smaller than the Guard we'd spotted before. I held up my hand, silencing Caleb's groans.

He straightened and looked over my shoulder. "Shit," he muttered.

The shadow was moving straight toward us. I backed into Caleb, pushing him against the wall. In the seconds before the shadow reached us, I could easily picture Marcus's face when I got hauled into his office tomorrow morning. Or worse yet, they might notify him now. Oh, gods, it would be epic.

Caleb's breath sawed in and out as his fingers bit into my arm. I looked around desperately for a better hidey hole. Our only option was to climb into the dumpster, and that wasn't happening. I'd rather face down a pissed off uncle than that.

The shadow came into view as it crested the edge of the dumpster. My mouth dropped open. "Lea?"

Lea jumped back, letting out a little shriek. She recovered quickly, whirling on us. Loose gravel crunched under her sneakers. "Seriously," she hissed. "Why am I not surprised to find you two hanging out with the trash?"

Caleb stepped out from behind me. "That's real original, Lea. Come up with that one all on your own?"

"What are you doing out here?" I pushed away from the dumpster and the gods-awful smell.

Her lips curled at the corners. "What are *you* doing?"

"She's probably sneaking back from hooking up with one of the Guards." Caleb craned his neck as he kept a wary eye on the darkness.

"I am not!" she screeched, startling both of us. "I hate when you guys say crap like that! I'm not a whore!"

I raised my brows. "Well, that's totally up for—"

Lea's hands slammed into my chest, knocking me back a few steps. Catching myself before I tumbled into bags of garbage, I dropped the tote bag on the dirty ground, and then threw myself at her. My fingers brushed her silky strands just as Caleb wrapped his arm around my waist and hauled me back.

"Oh, gods, come on." Caleb gritted his teeth. "We don't have time for this."

"You freaking pushed me?" I reached for her again, hands coming up empty. "I'm going to rip out every strand of your hair!"

Lea squinted as she flipped her hair over her shoulder. "What are you going to do about it, you little freak? Break my nose again? Whatever. You get into another fight, you're out of here."

I laughed. "You want to test out that theory?"

She smirked, giving me the middle finger. "That's probably what you want. Then you could go hang out with your daimon friends."

"You're such a *bitch*!" I considered knocking Caleb down just to get my hands around her skinny, tanned neck. He must have suspected as much, because his grip tightened. "I'm sorry about what happened to your parents, okay? I'm sorry that my mom had something to do with it, but you don't have to be such a—"

Footsteps at the mouth of the alley silenced us. Turning in Caleb's arms, my heart sank. A female Sentinel stood there, watching us. Her long blonde hair was pulled back tightly, giving her face a sharp, angular look. In the weak light, her eyes looked like two black, empty sockets. A shiver coursed down my spine, heightening my senses.

Caleb groaned, releasing me. I straightened my shirt while I shot Lea a nasty look. I held her a hundred percent responsible for us getting busted. If she hadn't been out here, slinking around, then we wouldn't have been held up. We'd already be inside, shoving my bag full of soda.

"I know this looks bad, but—"

"They were totally sneaking around," Lea cut Caleb off, planting her hands on her hips.

I looked at her, wanting to smack her upside the head. "And what the hell are you doing, exactly?"

The Sentinel cocked her head to the side, her lips spreading in a tight smile that showed no teeth. I recognized her then. It was Sandra, the Sentinel who'd come to my window the night I'd screamed in my sleep.

Lea glanced at us, eyes wide. "Okay. Weird," she murmured loud enough for only us to hear. She folded her arms and cocked her head. "It really stinks back here, okay?" she said in probably her snootiest voice ever. "So can we get this over with quickly?"

Caleb choked on his laugh.

Sandra's head turned toward him as she reached down, unhooking the Covenant dagger. Her fingers circled the hilt of the blade, her eyes still fastened on Caleb.

"Uh…" Caleb stepped back. His expression told me he wanted to laugh, but knew better. "No need to bring a dagger into this. We were just sneaking around."

"Yeah, we're happy half-bloods, totally daimon-free." Lea sent me a sly glance. "Well, two of us are."

"I'm going to seriously hurt you," I snapped, glaring in her direction.

Lea rolled her eyes and turned back to the Sentinel. "I have nothing to do—oh, my gods!"

"What?" I followed Lea's open-mouthed, horrified stare.

Sandra wasn't alone. Behind her stood three daimon pures, their ghoulish faces marked by dark veins and empty eye sockets.

I almost didn't believe what I was seeing. My brain tried to propel me into motion. The startled gasp we'd heard earlier and the Sentinel's strange behavior suddenly made sense. There were no visible marks on her, but I knew beyond a doubt she was a daimon—maybe even the daimon behind the attack on the young pure weeks ago. But how had she not been checked? The mystery of that would have to wait.

"Oh, man," I whispered.

"We so picked the wrong night to sneak around." Caleb's lanky body tensed and coiled.

One of the daimon pures stepped forward, not even bothering to use elemental magic to conceal itself. Which was strange to me, but then again, I wasn't a daimon expert. "Two half-bloods and…" He sniffed the air. "Something else. Oh, Sandra, excellent work."

Gods, were Seth's Apollyon cooties rubbing off on me? Now they could *smell* me?

"They talk?" Lea gasped, sounding as if the knowledge horrified her. She'd never seen a daimon, let alone talked to one.

"A lot," responded Caleb.

The daimon pure cocked his head to the side. "Should we kill them?"

Sandra, who was still staring at Caleb, raised her dagger. "I really don't care. I've waited long enough, so one of them is all mine."

His laugh sounded twisted. "You'd need more than just one if you bag a half, Sandra. They're nothing like pures, but the girl is… different."

"We've already killed the Guards at that bridge." The other daimon's gaze slithered over Lea and me, his mouth spreading in what appeared to be a smile. All I saw was jagged teeth. "You could've got some aether then. Kill the boy. We'll take these two with us."

My stomach turned over in revulsion. I pulled from deep inside of me, forcing the nearly overwhelming terror down. Fight daimons without titanium? Crazy and suicidal, but there still had to be Guards and Sentinels patrolling—*there had to be*. They'd hear us and they would come.

That is, if these four hadn't already killed them all. But I couldn't let myself believe that, because I knew Aiden and Seth were out there somewhere, and they wouldn't have gone down on a night like this—not a night when Caleb and I'd just wanted to grab some soda and watch movies with Olivia.

Lea bumped into me, her chest rising and falling quickly. "We are so screwed."

"Maybe." I dipped down and grabbed a lid off a garbage can. Straightening, I reached over and squeezed her arm. I heard her sharp intake of air, and then felt her body stiffen. I knew she was doing the same thing I did, calling on instinct and years of training. I let go of her arm.

Caleb shifted in front of me. "When there's an opening, make a run for it."

I didn't take my eyes off the daimons. "I'm not leaving you."

As those words left my mouth, the daimon pures flew at us.

CHAPTER 12

WHEN I SAY THEY FLEW, I WASN'T KIDDING.

I dipped down as the daimon swung at my head. I shot up under his arm, slamming my fist into his throat, hearing the sickening crunch as the cartilage gave way. He fell back from me, clutching his throat and wheezing.

"Dammit!" I heard Caleb yell, and then a body hit the ground. Panicked, I searched the alley and let out a sigh of relief when I saw Caleb standing over a daimon.

Lea spun on her heel, hitting the daimon in the chest. He staggered back, and she kicked him again. Hell, she was quick, sure-footed, and damn good. The daimon she fought didn't have a chance to recover from her blows. She *kept* landing them.

Flipping the trash can lid over, I watched the daimon with the crushed larynx climb to his feet. I whacked him over the head, and then inspected the nice dent his skull had left behind. Not too bad. I caught the one daimon who hadn't spoken upside the head. It was kind of like playing Whac-A-Mole.

Except the quiet one swung back, clamping down on my shoulder. He wretched me forward. Stumbling, I dropped the lid as I tried to yank myself free. The daimon latched onto my other arm and pulled harder, sending darts of pain through my shoulders. I dug my feet in, but I inched across the gravel.

Behind him, Lea sprinted forward and launched herself at the daimon. Wrapping her legs around his waist, she grabbed his head and twisted. Bones crunched and gave. The daimon released his hold and hit the ground, twitching in a messy heap.

"Damn, Buffy," I said, eyes wide. Part of me couldn't believe she'd intervened—and saved my life. "Thanks. I owe you."

Lea sent me a wild grin. "We need to make a run for it—"

A strong current of air hit her from behind, slamming her against the wall. She slid down, rolling onto her side and moaning.

"Lea!" I started toward her, but the daimon Sentinel cut me off. Breathing harshly, I skidded to a stop. Caleb was struggling with the daimon who had sent Lea flying, but the daimon half consumed my world. Fighting them—especially one trained as a Sentinel—was nothing like battling daimon pures.

And this daimon half knew it.

Smiling coldly, she stepped forward. "It's time to stop playing, little girl. You can't beat me."

Ice drenched my veins. Her hand struck out, catching me in the chest. I saw nothing but flashing white light when I hit the ground. Sharp gravel cut into my palms as I rocked onto my feet, lightheaded and stumbling.

Lea climbed to her feet and rushed the daimon half. I wanted to press stop and hit the rewind button. I couldn't move fast enough. I couldn't scream loud enough. And maybe, if I'd had a do-over, I could've stopped Lea. But everything was moving and changing with incredible speed.

Lea swung at the daimon half, her fist ramming the half's chin. It knocked the daimon half's head back, but that was about all. She slowly turned back to Lea, catching Lea's second throw. She twisted Lea's arm, and the sound of bones shattering overwhelmed the sound of the blood pounding in my temples. I shot forward, but I couldn't get to her.

Time… there wasn't enough time in the world.

Lea paled, but she didn't scream. Not a sound, and I knew she had to be in pain. She didn't even fall, didn't even flinch. Not even when the half daimon raised her arm, Covenant dagger in hand.

But Caleb was like lightning running past me, full of rage and purpose. He grabbed Lea by the waist, breaking the daimon's hold and tossing her out of the path of the dagger.

And the dagger found a new home.

A boy and a girl, one with a bright and short future…

"No!" The scream tore from my throat, from my soul.

The blade sank deep into Caleb's chest, all the way to the hilt. He stared down at his chest, staggering back. The front of his shirt looked like someone had thrown black paint on it, soaking it.

I wrapped my arms around his waist just as he started to fall. "Caleb! No. *No!* Caleb, look at me!"

He opened his mouth, but no words came out. His weight carried us both to the cold, dirty ground. Those bright blue eyes dulled, fixed on some unseen point.

"No," I whispered, brushing damp strands of hair off his forehead. "No no no. This isn't supposed to happen. We were just getting soda. That's all. *Please!* Caleb, wake up."

But he didn't wake up. Some part of my brain that was still functioning told me that people who died didn't wake up. They never woke up again. And that Caleb was dead. He was gone before he even hit the ground. Pain—so sharp and so real—cut through me, taking away a chunk of my soul.

The universe ceased to exist. There were no daimons, no Lea. There was just Caleb—*my* best friend, *my* partner in dysfunction, the only person who *got* me. My shaky fingers slipped over his boyishly shaped cheeks to his neck, to where his pulse no longer beat. A piece of my world ended just then, gone forever with Caleb. I pulled him into my lap, pressing my cheek against his. I thought that maybe, if I held him long enough and wished hard enough, all of this would be just another nightmare. That I'd wake up, safe in my bed, and Caleb would still be alive.

Hands delved deep into my hair, wrenching me backwards. I lost my grip on Caleb and fell onto my back. Stunned and vastly empty, I stared up at the daimon. She'd been a *half-blood*—once a Sentinel—sworn to kill daimons. Not their own kind.

She gripped my head, slamming it back against the concrete. I didn't even feel it. Dark rage filled me. It rushed through my system, so potent that I tumbled over the edge. She would die, and it would hurt.

Seizing the sides of her face, I shoved my thumbs into her eyes. She let go, shrieking and pulling at my hands. Someone was screaming and screaming… and I pushed harder. Tears and blood mingled, streaking down my face. I couldn't stop. All I could see was her shoving the blade into Caleb's chest.

Pain was everything. I had no idea if it was physical or mental. It swamped me in waves and waves of hurt. And then the daimon flew backward and someone dropped down beside me. Firm, strong hands caught my wrists in a gentle grasp and hauled me to my feet. I caught the familiar scent of sea and burning leaves.

"Alex, calm down. I've got you," Aiden said. "Calm down."

It was me who was screaming, and making a terrible sound that was so final, so shattering. And I couldn't stop. Aiden flipped me around, pressing me against the muck-covered wall. He whirled on his heel, slamming his blade deep into the chest of a daimon.

I slid down, turning to the side. The daimon half edged along the very same wall.

Blood ran in rivets down her face from her damaged eyes, but she could still *sense* me. Blue light erupted, briefly swallowing everything around me. The daimon half flew backwards, striking the ground beside Caleb. Screams filled the air—as did the smell of burning flesh.

Then arms were around me, lifting me to my feet. The moment his hands brushed mine, I knew it was Seth. He half-dragged, half-carried me out from the narrow alley behind the dining hall and into the darkness of the quad. I fought him the entire way, throwing punches and clawing. Sentinels and Guards rushed past us, but they were too late.

They were too late.

When Seth let go, I tried moving past him, but he grabbed my shoulders. "I can't leave Caleb like that! Let go!"

Seth shook his head, his amber eyes luminous in the darkness. "We're not going to leave him there, Alex. We wouldn't—"

I punched him in the stomach. He grunted, but did little else. "Then you get him! Get him out of there!"

"I can't—"

I hit him again. Seth'd had enough. He caught my wrists in one hand and held them between us. "No! You have to let me get him! You don't understand! Please—" My words broke off in a sob.

"Stop it, Alex. We will not leave Caleb's body behind the dining hall. You need to calm down. I need to make sure you're okay." When I didn't answer, he swore under his breath. I felt his fingers against the back of my head. They were quick and gentle. "Your head is bleeding."

I couldn't respond. Even though my eyes were open and Seth was in front of me, all I saw was the shock on Caleb's face. He hadn't seen it coming.

Neither had I.

"Alex?" Seth's arms eased around me.

The world started to unravel some more. "Seth?" I whispered. "Caleb is gone."

He murmured something as he brushed his fingers over my face, wiping away tears that continued to fall. I didn't speak again, not for some time.

†

Seth carted me off to the med center. The docs looked me over, determining that I only needed to be cleaned up and get some "much needed" rest. Someone washed the gore off my hands, and concerned looks were exchanged.

When they were done, I stayed where they'd left me. The white walls blurred. Seth returned just as I'd sat back down. I stared at him, feeling nothing inside me.

He came to my side, strands of hair hanging loose around his face. "Aiden and the rest have disposed of the daimons. There were only three of them, plus the half, right?" He paused, running a hand through his hair. "They managed to kill two of the bridge Guards, and they wounded another three Sentinels inside the Covenant. You're... lucky, Alex. So very lucky."

I stared down at my fingers. There was still blood under my fingernails. Was it mine, the daimon's, or Caleb's? Seth grabbed my hand, leading me out to the hallway.

He stopped briefly. "They have Caleb's… body. He's being taken care of."

I bit down on my lip until I tasted blood. I just wanted to sit down and be left alone.

Seth sighed, his grip on my hand tightening as we walked out of the med center. I didn't ask where we were going. I already knew, but Seth felt the need to make sure I understood.

"You're in a lot of trouble." He ushered me through the dark campus. It was near midnight, and Guards were everywhere. Some were patrolling, some huddled in groups. "Just to warn you, Marcus actually threw something. Lucian was woken up, and the gods know he didn't appreciate that. They're going to want to know why you were outside your dorm."

Numbness settled into my body. Perhaps that was why I wasn't worried about Marcus. I stumbled along behind Seth, stopping when he opened the Academy doors and the statue of the three furies came into view. Why hadn't they broken free? The Covenant had been breached again.

Catching what I was staring at, he squeezed my hand. "No pures were harmed, Alex. They… they don't care."

But Caleb had died.

Seth tugged me away from the statues. I was only barely aware of the crowd gathered at Marcus's door. The moment I stepped into the room, Marcus let loose. Lucian remained standing, which was new for him. Both of them yelled at me simultaneously, and then they took turns when the other appeared out of breath or out of words. What they said was pretty much the same old: I was irresponsible, reckless, and out of control. I didn't tune them out like I'd normally would. I soaked up everything they said, because what they said was true.

As I sat there staring up at my uncle and seeing real emotion in his face for the first time in a long time—albeit anger—I remembered another cryptic warning Grandma Piperi had left me.

You will kill the ones you love.

I should've stayed in my room like I was supposed to. There was a reason why a curfew had been imposed. The sanctuary of the Covenant had been violated once. I'd forgotten that, or I just hadn't thought about it, or cared.

I never stopped to think.

"I don't think any of this is helping." Seth stood behind me while I sat in the chair. "Can't you see she's upset? Maybe you should let her rest and ask questions tomorrow."

Lucian whirled around. "Of course none of this is helping! She could've been killed! We—*you*—could have lost the Apollyon. As the First, you should have been aware of what she was doing. She is your responsibility!"

I felt Seth stiffen behind me. "I understand that."

"And you?" Lucian snarled at me. "What were you thinking? You knew there had already been a daimon attack here. It was not safe for you or any student to be out there at night!"

There was nothing to say. Didn't they understand that? I'd been wrong, so very wrong, and there wasn't a damn thing I could do about it now. Closing my eyes, I looked away.

"Do not look away from me when I am speaking to you! You are just like your—"

"Enough!" Seth shot around the chair, nearly overturning it in the process. "Can't you see there's no point in talking to her right now? She needs some time to deal with the loss of her friend!"

Several Council Guards moved forward, ready to intervene. None of them looked like they wanted to. I'm sure they remembered what'd happened to the Guards in Lucian's house over the summer.

Lucian's nostrils flared with anger, but he backed down. A moment of clarity pushed through the grief. Why had Lucian backed down? Apollyon or not, Seth was just a half-blood and Lucian was the Minister. It was more than just strange, but before I could really catch hold of the realization, it slipped away as another thought pushed to the surface.

Seth remained where he was, between me and everyone else in the room. He was like a wall of fury, and no one dared to move a step closer.

It struck me then why everyone was afraid of there being two of us. Seth alone was a force to contend with. They were already fearful of him. Even Marcus seemed visibly affected, but Seth after I Awakened…?

"All right." Marcus cleared this throat. He strode forward, keeping a wary eye on Seth. "These questions can wait until a better time."

"Sounds like a plan to me," Seth replied casually enough, but he watched Marcus like a bird of prey.

Sidestepping Seth, Marcus stopped and crouched down in front of me. I stared at him. "Now do you understand that everything you do, every decision you make—even the slightest one—will have great consequences?"

I did, and I also understood he was talking about more than just Caleb, but also about Seth. However, Marcus had been wrong about one thing the last time he'd lectured me. My actions didn't just reflect upon Seth—they were a catalyst for how Seth would react.

CHAPTER 13

GRIEF WAS NOT SOMETHING THAT WENT AWAY WHEN I opened my eyes and found that the sun still rose in the morning. Nor did it pass when the sun started to decline and stars lined the sky.

I'd been mute and emotionless until I'd returned to my dorm and had seen the remnants of our movie party. Someone had gotten Olivia out of the room, but standing there, staring down at the Twizzler I'd thrown at Caleb's head hours before, I broke apart. All I remember was Seth picking me up and carrying me back to the bed.

Sometime in the afternoon, Seth left. Returning before dinner, he tried to coax me into eating. But I'd hit the dark abyss that followed such things. Maybe I'd never really dealt with Mom's death and the loss of Caleb had brought everything to the surface. I really didn't know, but when I thought about her, I thought about Caleb and our spirit boats.

All I did was sleep, and it was the deep sleep where the nightmares of reality finally couldn't reach me. During the random moments I was awake and fully aware of what was going on around me, I yearned for Caleb—and for my mom. I needed one of her hugs. I needed her to tell me everything was going to be okay, but that could never happen, and my heart couldn't bear the idea of mourning Caleb, too.

Seth stayed by my side, turning into this protectively fierce creature who wouldn't allow Marcus or any of the Guards into my room. He kept me in the loop, letting me know what was going on outside my room. Halfs were being searched again, but they believed Sandra was the culprit for the original attack. She'd been a Sentinel, so she'd been on and off the island so many times—enough times that they'd missed her when they'd searched the Sentinels and Guards. This whole time, their suspicion had been on one of the students, and it'd been a Sentinel.

He also tried telling me that what happened to Caleb wasn't my fault. When that didn't work, he went with the whole "Caleb wouldn't want this" tactic. Then he relied on the one thing that usually stirred me up—insults and witty banter. I think he told me I smelled by the third day.

Eventually Seth seemed at a loss for what to do. He stretched out, wrapped his arm around me, and waited. It took a while for me to realize the heartache I felt had transferred to him. Seth didn't know how to deal with it either, and at the beginning of the fourth day, it was like he, too, had lost his best friend. So we both lay there, silent and soul-sick.

Like two sides of the same coin.

Sometime during the middle of the night, Seth leaned over me. "I know you're not sleeping." A few seconds later, he brushed the limp strands of hair off my face. "Alex," he said softly. "They're having Caleb's funeral at noon tomorrow."

"Why… why aren't they doing it at dawn?" I asked hoarsely.

Seth shifted closer, his breath warm. "The Guards who were killed will be buried at dawn, but Caleb was only a half-blood student."

"Caleb… deserves a funeral at dawn—he deserves that tradition."

"I know. I know he does." Seth sighed deeply, sadly. "You have to get out of this bed, Alex. You have to go."

I steeled myself against the sharp pang, but it still cut through me. "No."

His head dropped to lie beside mine. "No? Alex, you can't be serious. You have to go."

"I just can't. I'm not going."

Seth continued to push the topic until frustration and anger took over. He jumped off the bed. I rolled onto my back and ran my hands over my face. My skin felt grubby.

Standing by the foot of the bed, Seth did the same thing with his hands. "Alex, I know this—all of this—is killing you, but you've got to do this. You owe this to Caleb. You owe it to yourself."

"You don't understand. I can't go."

"You're being ridiculous!" he shouted, not caring if he woke up everyone on my floor. "Do you know how much you'll regret this? Is that something else you want to eat away at you?"

There was a fine line between rage and sorrow, one that I tottered on. I tipped onto the side of rage this time. I pushed up, climbing to my knees. "I don't want to see them hoisting his body up in the air and burning it! His body—Caleb's body!" My voice cracked, along with my heart. "That's *Caleb* they'll burn!"

Just like that, the anger faded from Seth's face. He took a step forward. "Alex—"

"No!" I raised my arm, ignoring the way it shook. "You don't understand, Seth. He wasn't your friend! You barely knew him! And you know what? You want to know the most messed up thing about that? Caleb looked up to you. He *idolized* you, and did you even give him the time of the day? Sure, you spoke to him every once in a while, but you didn't know him! You didn't care to."

Seth rubbed his jaw. "I didn't know. If I thought—"

"You were too busy fooling around with the girls or being an arrogant jerk." After the words left my mouth, I immediately regretted them. I sat back down, heart racing painfully. "You can't do anything… about this."

"I'm trying to do something about this." Those eyes sparked to life, glowing amber. "I don't know what else to do! I've stayed with you—"

"I didn't ask you to stay with me!" I screamed so loud my throat hurt. I needed to calm down. Guards would rush this room if I kept it up. "Just leave. Please. Just leave me alone.

Seth stared at me for what seemed like an eternity and then he left, slamming the door shut behind him. I collapsed back on the bed, balling my hands over my eyes.

I shouldn't have said those things.

All this time I'd worried about having no control. Ironically, from day one I'd acted out-of-control. I didn't control my anger or my impulses to do whatever I wanted. How had I fooled myself this entire time? Having control meant acting in the right way, at least most of the time. But I'd acted wild—reckless. I'd let my heart decide when I'd questioned contacting the Covenant after Mom and I had left. There was no logic behind that. My heart had destroyed whatever friendship I'd had with Aiden. And my heart and my selfishness had led me to sneak around with Caleb. If we'd just stayed in my room—or if I hadn't moped around for a week—Caleb wouldn't have felt the need to cheer me up. We wouldn't have gone to get drinks.

He wouldn't have died.

I don't know how long I lay there tangled up in the blankets. My mind raced through my childhood with Caleb, the three long years without him, and every single moment I'd spent with him since I'd returned to the Covenant. Rolling over, I curled into myself. I missed him—missed Mom. Both of their deaths were linked to me, to decisions I'd made or hadn't made. Action. Inaction. Marcus's words came back to haunt me in those hours, over and over again. *Everything you do…*

On the fifth day, the day of Caleb's funeral, the sun rose early and it shone brighter than I remembered for a November morning. In less than four hours, Caleb's earthly remains would forever be lost. Five days since he'd died, one-hundred-and-twenty hours since the last time I'd touched him and heard him laugh, over seven thousand minutes of slowly adjusting to a world that didn't include him.

And only a few short hours since I realized I'd never had any control.

I sat up, threw the covers to the side and swung my legs off the bed. Standing made me woozy at first, but I went into the bathroom and stared at my reflection.

I looked terrible.

One of the daimons had left behind faint, purplish bruises along my jaw and cheekbone. My hair hung in thick, straggly clumps. Red tinged the rims of my eyes. Slowly, wearily, I peeled off the disgusting clothes and dropped them on the floor. In the shower, I leaned my forehead against the cool tile, letting my mind go blissfully blank.

Cold water bounced off my skin by the time I pulled myself from the shower and wrapped a large, white towel around me. It was when I mindlessly tugged a comb through the tangles in my hair that something occurred to me.

In the dim light, the scars covering my neck looked shiny and uneven. I always kept my hair down and wore long sleeve shirts to hide the red patches on my arms. Those scars had never seemed to heal like they should've. I did everything and anything to hide the scars. Scars left behind from my own reckless, thoughtless actions. So ugly—

Instructor Romvi's words came back to me. *You should be less worried about your vanity.*

The big-toothed comb slipped from my fingers. Hurrying from the bathroom, I went to the small kitchen area and straight to the wicker basket beside the microwave. I rummaged through napkins, clips, and other stuff I never used. Among them I found a pair of orange-handled scissors. Picking them up, I doubted they would cut through most things, but they'd do.

I went back to the bathroom and grabbed my hair, pulling it around my shoulder. My own wide, brown eyes stared back at me. The hair, wet and thick, hung past my chest. Without thinking twice, I positioned the scissors just above my bare shoulders.

A hand shot out, snatching the scissors from my grasp. So fast—so unexpected—I shrieked and jumped back. Seth stood there, dressed in all black. I clutched the front of my towel and stared.

"What are you doing?" Seth handled the scissors as if they were a snake about to sink its fangs deep into his skin.

"I… I'm vain."

"So you were going to cut your hair?" He sounded incredulous.

"Yeah, that was the plan."

He looked like he wanted to question that further, but he turned around and dropped the scissors on the dresser. "Get dressed. Now. You're going to Caleb's funeral."

My grip on the towel tightened. "I'm not going."

Ignoring me, Seth went into my bedroom. "I'm not arguing with you about this anymore. You're going to his funeral, even if I have to drag you there."

I didn't really believe that. So I was shocked when I tried to shut and lock the bathroom door, and Seth whipped around. He pried my hand off the door and yanked me out of the bathroom.

Exhaustion and hunger made me slow, and I had a death grip on my towel. Those were the reasons I ended up pinned to his chest, both of us on the floor in front of the bed. I could feel his heart hammering against my shoulder and his breath against my cheek.

Seth's hands were clamped on my arms, keeping me from delivering a nasty elbow to his face. "Why… why do you always act like this? Why? Why did you do this to yourself? All of this could've been avoided."

The sudden tightening in my throat warned that the yawning emptiness was still there, lingering. "I know. Please… please don't be angry with me."

"I'm not angry with you, Alex. Okay, maybe a little." He moved slightly, pressing his head against mine. Several moments passed before he spoke again. "How could you do this to yourself? You—*you* of all people should have known better."

I felt the tears start to well up again. "I'm sorry. We didn't—"

"You could have died out there, Alex—or worse." Seth let out a ragged breath, his fingers tightening around my upper arms. "Do you know what I thought when I felt your panic?"

"I'm sorry—"

"Sorry wouldn't have done a damn thing if I'd lost you, and for what?" He grasped the sides of my face, turning my head so I had no other choice but to face him. His eyes searched mine. "Why? Is it because of what happened with Aiden?"

"No." Tears rolled down my cheeks now. "I did it because I was being stupid. We just wanted to get some drinks. I didn't think anything would happen. If I could change it, I would. I would do anything."

"Alex." Seth closed his eyes.

"I mean it. I would do anything to change what happened! Caleb—he didn't deserve that. I did know better. If we'd stayed in my room, he would still be alive. I know that."

"Alex, please."

"I know I acted stupid." My voice cracked. "And if I could go back, I would. I'd switch places with him. I would—"

"Stop," he whispered, his thumbs wiping away my tears. "Please stop crying."

Everything inside me felt like it was tensing and twisting into one giant knot. "I'm so sorry. I want to take it all back. I want a do-over, because I can't do this again."

He made a strangled sound as he pulled me to his chest, holding me there until my heart stopped racing and the tears subsided. "You have to do this again and you don't get a do-over, Alex. None of us do. You can only move forward from here, and the first step is going to his funeral."

I drew in a deep breath. "I know."

Seth caught my chin with the tip of his finger, tipping it back. I think that's when he realized I wore nothing more than a towel. His eyes flicked down for a moment and then his entire body seemed to stiffen. It could have been all the extreme emotions rolling through both of us, or the connection we shared, but every inch of my body suddenly felt warm.

It was strange how the body could forget all these terrible things so quickly. Or maybe it was the soul that worked that way, seeking out warmth and touch, needing to prove that we were still in the world of living. I leaned in, resting my cheek against his shoulder. I closed my eyes.

"You're shaking," Seth murmured.

"I'm cold."

His hands slid over my shoulders. "You really need to put some clothes on. You shouldn't be dressed like that."

"You came in here. That's not my fault."

"Still. You need to put some clothes on."

I bit my lip and pulled back. Seth stared back at me, his eyes unnaturally bright. "Okay. But you're going to have to let go of me first."

His hands tensed on my back, and for a second… well, he looked like he wasn't going to let me go. I wasn't sure how I felt about that. Seth did let go, but he leaned in, resting his forehead against mine. "You do smell better now. I think we're making progress."

My lips twitched. "Thanks."

Some of the tension in his body seemed to seep out. "You ready?"

I breathed in deeply, and it felt like the first time in days. "Yes."

†

When I was little, my mother had once told me that only in death could a pure and a half be viewed as equals. Both would stand before the River Styx, waiting for their souls to be carried into the hereafter.

Everyone had already filed into the cemetery by the time Seth and I made it there. The pures stood up front, before the halfs, which made no sense to me. Caleb had been one of us, not them. So why should they stand closer to him? Aiden would say it was tradition.

It was still wrong.

I roamed the outer edge of the groups with Seth, dodging outright curious looks and even a few stares of condemnation. I tried to convince myself I wasn't looking for a certain, dark-haired pure as my gaze kept returning to the group at the front. Aiden was the last person I wanted to see.

Seth finally stopped, so I did, too. He hadn't spoken since we'd left my room, but he kept glancing at me. I think he worried I'd flip out again. Tucking my still-damp hair back, I looked up at him, chewing on my lip.

"You're going to thank me, aren't you?" Seth sounded amused.

"Well… I was. Not so sure about that now."

"Come on. I want to actually hear you say it. It'll probably be your first and last time."

I squinted against the sun's harsh glare. Far away, I could see the pyre, the body swathed in white linen. "Thank you for staying with me. And I'm sorry for being such a bitch toward you."

Seth unfolded his arms, nudging me with his elbow. "Did you just call yourself a—"

"Yes, I did, because I am one." I sighed loudly. "You didn't deserve it when I yelled at you… about Caleb."

He stepped closer as Lucian moved to stand before the pyre. As the Minister, he would give the parting speech, eternal life and all that. "I deserve a lot of things," Seth said.

"Not that." I tore my eyes from the scene before me. I focused on a nearby hyacinth bush. The single dense spike of flowers was a vibrant red, the blossoms shaped like little stars. They signaled grief and mourning, and they were everywhere in the cemetery, reminding all of us of the tragedy of Apollo's love for the beautiful Hyacinth. Back when the gods roamed the earth freely, people who ended up dying some tragic death became a flower if they were young and beautiful, male or female, and had earned a god's favor.

Twisted.

Seth shifted closer, his arm brushing mine. "You know, the connection between us didn't leave me with any other choice."

I rolled my eyes. "Well, thank you, anyway."

Lucian started in on the memorial speech, speaking about Caleb's spirit and strength. The ache in my chest grew and the sweetly scented air felt cool against my damp cheeks. When the pyre was lit, my insides twisted and I couldn't stop the shudder that kept running through my body. I turned halfway, pressing against the waiting warmth while the air filled with the sounds of crackling wood and quiet sobs.

I don't know what hurt more: the fact I'd never see him again or that I'd never hear his infectious laugh. Each realization sent a sharp pang through me.

It wasn't until the crowds began to disperse did I grasp the warmth I'd sought out actually belonged to a body—and that body belonged to Seth. Cheeks flushing, I stepped out of his embrace. I'd cried on him enough to last me a lifetime. "I need to…"

"I understand." Seth stepped back. "I'll wait for you outside."

Grateful that he got it without me actually having to say anything, I watched him head back to the cemetery gates. I wiped under my eyes again and turned around.

I froze.

Olivia stood in front of me, dressed in black slacks and a sweater. Her skin was shades lighter; her eyes, usually so warm and open, were now cold and angry. Tears ran down her face unchecked.

I stepped toward her, wanting to comfort her. "Olivia, I'm so—"

"Why didn't you do something?" Her voice broke. "You were his best friend. You could've done something!" She moved forward, her arm trembling as she pointed at me.

Luke reached out and wrapped an arm around her shoulders. "Don't. It's not Alex's—"

"You're the Apollyon!" Olivia cried out, her words ending in a broken sob. "Yes, I know! Caleb told me what you are, and I've seen you fight!" She turned to Luke, eyes pleading. "You've seen how fast she can move. Why didn't she do something?"

I knew—*I knew* there was nothing physically I could've done. I wasn't the Apollyon—not yet—but to hear her say that? Well, it was like hearing Marcus's voice in my head. *People expect more from you, because of what you will become.*

"I'm sorry, Olivia. I'm so—"

"Don't say you're sorry! That won't bring Caleb back!"

I flinched. "I know."

"Olivia, come on. Let's go back to your room." Luke sent me an apologetic look as he started inching her around.

Elena came forward, taking Olivia's hand. "It's okay. It's going to be okay."

Olivia slumped against Luke, her head falling to her chest. The full weight of her loss was visible for all of us to see.

Grief clawed its way through my chest. I turned away, feeling a rush of hot tears. Blindly, I stumbled away from them, roaming deeper into the memorial grounds. It wasn't until I bumped into someone did I look up, wiping under my eyes. "Oh, sorry—" I stopped, mid-apology.

It wasn't a person I'd run into, but a statue. A small laugh crawled out of my throat as I stared up at the striking, yet woeful face carved out of stone. The sculpture had been shaped so that he bent at the waist slightly, one hand reaching out toward something, palm open in a beckoning manner. My gaze drifted down to the base, where the name Thanatos had been scripted. Under his name was a symbol—a torch turned downward.

I'd seen it before… on Instructor's Romvi's arm.

CHAPTER 14

SIGHING IN FRUSTRATION, I SHOVED MY HANDS INTO the pockets of my hoodie and scanned the night sky. Stars broke up the darkness, some shining more brightly than the others. The last time I'd seen the dark sky had been more than a week ago. I'd been behind the dining hall, holding Caleb's cold body.

Caleb.

I squelched the rising tide of sorrow and regret before it consumed me again by focusing on something that had been nagging me since his funeral. Why in the world would Romvi have the symbol of the god of Peaceful Death tattooed on his arm? And wasn't he the same god that old book had claimed was responsible for killing Solaris and the First Apollyon? I wasn't sure it really mattered, but the image kept coming back to me.

"You okay?"

Every muscle in my body locked up. I reminded myself that it was only going to take eleven hours to get to the Catskills—eleven hours stuck in a car with the guy I loved, the guy I'd practically begged to love me in return. Maybe not in so many words, but that was how I felt. This was going to be easy. Yeah, really easy.

"Alex?"

I turned around. Aiden was tucking my suitcase into the back of the Hummer, watching me over his shoulder. My gaze skittered away, unable to really, really look at him. "Yeah, I was just thinking."

"Is this all your stuff?"

Nodding, I kicked the toe of my shoe along the asphalt. I needed to act normal or this was going to be the longest car ride of my life. "How… how is Deacon?"

A few seconds passed before he answered. "He's doing okay." He shut the rear door. "He wanted me to tell you that he's really sorry about… what happened."

I faced him, keeping my eyes trained on his shoulder—which was one really nice shoulder—when I spotted a silver chain around his neck. It disappeared under his sweater. Odd—Aiden never wore jewelry. "Tell him I said thanks."

Aiden nodded as he headed around to the side of the vehicle, but then he stopped so unexpectedly that I bounced off his back. He turned and caught my arm, setting me right. Our eyes met for a fraction of a second, and then he dropped my arm.

He stepped back. "I don't know what you were thinking." He broke off, glancing toward Leon, who waited under the awning of the Covenant.

"We just wanted to get some drinks from the cafeteria." I swallowed, but the lump in my throat didn't go away. "We were going to watch movies."

"Are we ready?" called Leon. "We should be leaving now if we want to reach the Catskills before noon."

"Yeah." Aiden turned away, but then faced me again. "Alex?"

Slowly, I lifted my eyes to his. That turned out to be a mistake of epic proportions. A different kind of hurting opened up in my chest.

His gaze drifted across my face. "I'm… so, so sorry about Caleb. I know how much he meant to you."

I couldn't look away, couldn't say a word.

He glanced over his shoulder and when he turned back to me, his eyes shone bright silver in the dim light. "Don't… don't ever do anything like that again. Please. Promise me."

I wanted to ask why he'd care if I threw myself in front of a daimon, but those words didn't come out. Something else did. "I promise."

Aiden watched me a moment longer, and then broke away. After that, we climbed into the Hummer. I took a seat in the back while Aiden slid into the one in front of me. Leon drove and the other Guard took the seat next to me.

Leaning my head back against the seat, I closed my eyes and wondered how I'd ended up in the car while Seth got the private jet with Lucian, Marcus, and the Council members. They'd flown out this morning. Half-bloods—even Sentinels—usually didn't get seats on the planes, but an exception had been made for Seth.

Car rides typically turned me into a bratty five-year-old, especially astronomically long ones, but I was too tired to really think about it. With all the sleeping I'd been doing, I probably should've been wide awake for days, but I drifted off quickly.

I woke up about two hours in when we stopped to get gas in Middle-Of-Nowhere, Virginia. Leon and the Guard went into the shack of a gas station, and I climbed out to stretch my legs. It was so dark out here, surrounded by woods and farms. The only sounds were the cows lowing in the distance. I strolled around the rear of the Hummer and found Aiden leaning against the bumper. He looked up when I stopped beside him. His eyes were nearly the same color as the moonlight.

"If you want to get something to eat, Leon or the Guard will get it for you." Aiden rolled a bottle of water between his hands.

"I'm not hungry." I moved past him, keeping my back to him.

"We don't want to stop unless we have to."

"I'm fine." I hopped up on the curb and proceeded to place one foot in front of another.

Mid-step, I glanced over at the convenience store—if you'd consider that place a convenience store. It looked like an old pizza shop and the blinking red sign out front read "OPE." Leon stood at the counter. "So… has Marcus confirmed that the Sentinel was responsible for the first attack?"

"There's no way to really confirm that, Alex. We believe so. Another round of searches is being conducted—" He paused when I stiffened, "—to make sure she was the one."

I reached the end of the curb. "I guess now I understand why the searches were so important. They missed her and… look what happened.

The Guards at the bridge, they probably didn't expect anything when she showed up."

"No. And the daimons are obviously getting smarter. She was on and off the campus a lot, making her a prime candidate. And her tags weren't visible."

I bent over backward, sprung off my hands, and landed perfectly on the narrow curb. I could have been a gymnast in a different life. Turning to face him, I found Aiden staring at me.

He glanced away as a strange, almost sad look crept across his face. Pushing off the bumper of the car, he shoved his hands into the pockets of his jeans. "You and Seth seem to be getting along a lot better."

I frowned at the change in subject. "Yeah, I guess so."

Aiden stopped in front of me. "That's a vast improvement from wanting to stab him in the eye."

Even though I stood on the curb, Aiden was still taller than me. I tipped my head back, meeting his pale gaze. "Why do you even care?"

His brows rose slightly. "It's just a statement, Alex. Has nothing to do with me caring or not."

I felt my cheeks burn as I nodded stiffly. "Yeah, I think I grasped the whole caring and not caring topic." I hopped off the curb and inched around the gas pumps.

Aiden followed behind me. "I saw you two at the funeral. He was there for you. I think that's good. Not just for you, but for him. I think you're the only person Seth cares about besides himself."

I stopped, wanting to laugh, but I felt… embarrassed. Like I'd been caught doing something wrong, but I hadn't. Confused by what Aiden was getting at, I started walking again. "Seth cares about himself. That's about it."

"No." Aiden followed my movements, meeting up with me at the edge of the pumps. "He rarely left your side. Seth wouldn't allow anyone—not even me—near you."

I whipped around, surprised. "You stopped by to see me?"

Aiden nodded. "Several times, actually, but Seth was determined that you needed time to come to grips with everything. That doesn't sound like someone who cares only about himself."

"Why would you come see me?" I stepped toward him, hope and excitement building inside me. "You told me you didn't care about me."

He fell back a step, clenching his jaw. "I never said I didn't care about you, Alex. I said I couldn't love you."

I flinched, cursing myself for the stupid window of hope I'd allowed to open. Smiling tightly, I headed back to the Hummer and slammed the door shut behind me. Unfortunately, Aiden followed me.

He got in the seat in front of me and turned around. "I'm not trying to fight with you, Alex."

My temper and hurt feelings took over. "Then maybe you should try not talking to me. Especially when you sound like you're trying to pawn me off on another guy."

Aiden's eyes snapped alive, flaring in the darkness. "I'm not trying to pawn you off on someone. You were never mine to do so."

I leaned forward, my fingers digging into my thighs as I spoke in a whisper thick with pain. "I was never yours? You should've thought about that before you stripped me naked in your room!"

He sucked in air sharply, then his eyes shuttered to a dull gray. "It was a temporary loss of sanity."

"Oh." I gave a harsh laugh. "Did your temporary loss of sanity last several months? Did it make you say all those things to me at the zoo? Did it—"

"What do you want me to say, Alex? That I'm sorry… for leading you on?" He paused, visibly trying to rein in his anger and frustration. "I am. Okay? I'm sorry."

"I didn't want you to say that," I whispered, stomach tumbling over.

Aiden closed his eyes and shook his head. "Look, you don't need this right now. Not after everything with Caleb and with us going to the Council. So, just stop."

"But—"

"I'm not going to do this with you, Alex. Not now. Not ever."

Before I could respond, Leon and the Guard returned, putting an end to this. I flung myself against the seat and glared at the back of Aiden's head. I knew he could feel me staring holes into him, because he sat stiffly with his eyes forced front.

Eventually I got bored with that and climbed over the back of my seat to dig out my music player. I tried going back to sleep, but my mind was too busy thinking about Caleb, the argument with Aiden, and whether or not Seth was as self-centered as I'd always thought he was.

†

After nine more hours of hell, we turned onto a winding road lined with towering pines and spruce trees so thick it reminded me of a Christmas tree farm. We were deep in the Catskills—no man's land. About a mile in, a nondescript fence poked out, surrounding what I assumed was the perimeter of the New York Covenant.

I snorted. "Nice security."

Aiden turned halfway around. "You haven't seen anything yet."

I ignored him and leaned forward, seeing nothing more than a wire fence and trees. Maybe it was one of those fences that electrocuted people, because I'd really expected more than this.

Then I saw the Guards standing in front of the pitiful-looking fence, armed with what looked like semiautomatic weapons. My eyes widened as they leveled the guns at our vehicle. Leon slowed down as the four Guards approached us cautiously.

"Alex, take your hair down," Aiden said quietly.

I didn't understand why, but the seriousness in his tone told me not to fool around. I unraveled the messy bun, letting it fall around my face. Leon rolled down all the windows, and at once, the Guards peered inside the vehicle, searching each of us… for *visible* tags.

I shrank back, but met the dark-skinned Guard's intense gaze as he looked me over once, then twice. The tags felt like they were burning under the mass of heavy hair. I wasn't sure what they would've done if they'd seen the scars. Shoot me?

Not quickly enough, they gestured at the one Guard who remained back. The tall gate shuddered and creaked opened. I let out the breath I hadn't realized I'd been holding. "Am I supposed to keep my hair down the entire time I'm here?"

Aiden glanced back at me, his lips forming a hard, tight line. "No. But I'd rather you not provoke a trigger-happy Guard."

I could understand that, I guessed.

We rolled through the gate and went another half a mile down the road before the trees started thinning out. I leaned on the back of Aiden's seat as the New York Covenant finally came into view.

Well, the twenty-plus-foot wall made out of white marble came into view.

After passing another set of gun-toting Guards, we finally entered the grounds. It didn't look much different than our Carolina branch. There were statues of gods everywhere, except where ours stood among the sand, theirs rose up from the greenest grass I'd ever seen.

The first building I got to see was a mansion—the kind I didn't expect to see in the middle of the Catskills. I'd once heard the Rockefellers had a house around these parts, but nothing compared to this monstrous thing. I counted six stories, several all-glass rooms, and possibly a ballroom with a skylight dome by the time the car stopped in front of the sandstone manor. I started to follow them, but Aiden stopped me.

"Alex, hold on a second."

My fingers froze on the handle. "What?"

Aiden had turned around completely and those eyes… gods, those eyes always drew me in, always filled me with such warmth that I could almost taste his lips on mine. Too bad his words kind of ruined the moment.

"Don't do anything here to draw unwanted attention."

My fingers tightened on the door handle. "I don't plan on it."

"I'm being serious, Alex." His eyes bored into mine. "No one here will be as forgiving as your uncle or stepfather. I can imagine that they won't go easy on you when you have your session. Some of the Council… well, they're not fans of yours."

An ache throbbed in my chest in response to his clipped, professional tone. I had no idea where the tender Aiden had gone, the one who'd sworn to always be there for me, the one who'd gently brought me back from the brink when I'd freaked out in training. Gods, there were so many more moments, but all of them were gone.

Aiden was gone. Like Caleb, but in a different way. I'd lost both of them. A lot of the anger leaked out of me then. I faced the window, sighing. "I didn't expect them to. I'll behave. You don't have to worry about me." I started to open the door again.

"Alex?"

Slowly, I turned to him. Aiden wasn't so guarded in that instant, and a deep, unsettling pain reflected in his gaze. There was more—almost like an uncertainty. But he pulled it together, like slipping on a well-worn mask of indifference, shuttering any and all emotions.

"Just be careful." His voice was strangely hollow.

I wanted to say something, anything, but a flurry of activity outside of the car made that impossible. Servants—droves of half-blood servants—descended on the Hummer, opening doors and retrieving luggage. My mouth dropped open as one, a fair-haired boy about my age, meekly opened my car door. A black circle with a slash through it had been tattooed onto his forehead. I glanced at Aiden and saw his gaze still fastened on me. He gave me a strained smile before climbing out. I couldn't help but wonder if the doubt I'd seen in his face had anything to do with me.

I was given a room on the fifth floor, one that connected to Marcus's room. Or at least, that was what the half-blood doorman inside the mansion said before stepping back into the shadows. I really had no clue, so I just followed the blond boy. I didn't see where Aiden and Leon were carted off to, but I bet they got rooms on the bottom floors—big, awesome rooms.

We crossed the grandiose lobby and entered a glass-enclosed breezeway. To our left was the entrance to what appeared to be the ballroom, but the twinkling lights didn't hold my attention. Right in the middle of the breezeway was the very same statue that stood in the Covenant lobby in North Carolina.

Furies.

Sucking in a sharp gasp, I hurried around the statues to catch up with the half servant. Their heavy presence remained after I left the breezeway, nagging at the back of my thoughts. We went up several flights of steps, and I couldn't deal with the silence any longer.

"So… um, how do you like it here?" I asked as we stepped into a narrow hallway adorned with oil paintings.

The boy kept his eyes fastened on the oriental carpet.

Okay… was there some sort of "no talking" rule? I glanced at the paintings, mentally listing the gods as we passed them: Zeus, Hera, Artemis, Hades, Apollo, Demeter, Thanatos, Ares—wait. Thanatos? I stopped to get a closer look at his painting.

He had wings and a sword. Thanatos looked like a pretty rocking angel, actually. But he shared the same woeful look the cemetery Thanatos had had on his face as he gazed upward. His left hand held a flaming torch turned downward. Why would Thanatos, who wasn't one of the major Olympian gods, have his picture here among them?

An opening door drew my attention from the painting. I glanced over my shoulder. The half servant held the door open, eyes downcast.

I pursed my lips, scanning the four dull-white walls within. A closet would have been too nice of a description for this… this thing considered a room. I walked in as the servant placed my luggage inside the door.

There was a bed—a twin size bed covered with an itchy-looking brown blanket and one flat pillow. A tiny bedside table offered a rusty lamp that'd seen better days. It took me two seconds to cross the room and peek inside the bathroom.

It was the size of a coffin.

My eyes fell over the scuffed-up tile, dirty mirror, and rust stains surrounding the drain in the shower stall. "You've got to be kidding me," I muttered.

"They expect you to sleep in this room—on that bed?"

Jumping at the unexpected sound of Seth's voice, my hip slammed into the washbasin. "Ouch!" I rubbed my hip as I turned around.

Seth stood at the foot of the bed, his ever-present smug expression tainted with disdain. It'd only been a day since I'd seen him, but strangely, it felt longer than that. His hair was down, curving around his chin. And he wore jeans and a plain black sweater—a rarity.

I was kind of glad to see him.

"Yeah, this room sucks." I left the bathroom.

Seth strolled to a door on the other side of the bed. He reached down, throwing the lock.

"I guess that's not the closet?"

"Nope, that's the door to Marcus's room."

He arched a brow. "They gave you a servant's room?"

"Nice." I looked around, discovering there wasn't even a closet in the room—or a dresser. I'd be living out of a suitcase for my whole stay. Yippee. "Why'd you lock it?"

Seth threw me a mischievous grin. "I can't have Marcus just walking in on us. What if I want to snuggle on these cold New York nights?"

My frown increased. "We don't snuggle."

He dropped his arm over my shoulder, and the scent of mint and something wild tickled my nose. "How about we cuddle?"

"We don't do that either."

"But you're my cuddle bunny. My little Apollyon cuddle—"

I punched him in the side.

Laughing, Seth steered me toward the door. "Come on, I want to show you something."

"What?"

He removed his arm and captured my hand. "The Council is starting their first session at one today. I think we should go watch it."

"That sounds boring." I let him drag me out of the room, though. It wasn't like I had anything else to do.

"We could always practice?" Seth pulled me into the stairwell, taking several steps at a time. "I'm feeling froggy—haven't thrown fireballs at anyone's head lately."

"That sounds more interesting than watching a bunch of pures postulate how great they and their laws are."

"Postulate?" Seth glanced over his shoulder, grinning. "I can't believe you used the word 'postulate.'"

"What?" I scowled. "It's a real word."

Seth raised a brow at me and then continued down the steps. In the stairwell we passed several servants in drab clothing. Each of them looked down. I watched them lift their heads once they'd passed us.

Seth tugged on my hand. "Come on. We're going to miss it."

Outside, the biting wind cut through my sweater and sent shivers through me. For once, I was grateful for Seth's hand. It felt incredibly warm in mine.

"Anyway, the Council session should be interesting. It's a hearing."

"I thought mine was the only hearing?"

"No." Seth led me around the west wing of the mansion. "There are several hearings. You are one of many."

I started to respond, but we stepped around back and my lips clamped shut. A labyrinth of waist-high marble walls separated us from the Greek style coliseum. Bright flowers, all in full bloom, sprung from the vines that covered them. Thick cords of a creeping plant climbed the statues and benches, covering everything in front of us in a mass of vibrant red and green. "Wow."

Seth chuckled. "If you stay on this pathway it leads straight to the Council."

I glanced down several of the walkways that branched off the main one. "Is it a real labyrinth?"

"Yes. But I haven't checked it out."

"Looks kind of fun, don't you think?" I looked up at him. "I've never been in a labyrinth before."

A real smile replaced the smug one. "Maybe if you're good—and I mean, really good—we can come play in the labyrinth."

I rolled my eyes. "Gee, really?"

He nodded. "You have to eat your dinner, too."

I didn't even bother responding to that. I got kind of lost in the scenery for a while. How in the world did the pures manage to keep these fragile flowers alive all year round? It had to be magic—old magic. The deeper we moved down the pathway, the thicker the vines grew and when we neared the end, Seth slowed.

"We have to sneak in," he said. "We aren't really supposed to be listening to the Councils."

"And if we get caught?"

"We won't."

Trusting Seth felt strange, mainly because I did… trust him. Not in the same way I would have placed my life in Aiden's hands, but almost there—almost.

Behind several thick columns made of stone, Themis, the Goddess of Divine Justice, stood at the entrance to the coliseum. She was quite formidable with that sword in one bronzed hand and balanced scales held high in the other, but her presence seemed kind of ironic to me—the pures knew nothing of balanced justice.

The building was something straight out of ancient Greece. Hidden as the New York Covenant was, they could get away with designs not normally found in neighborhoods boasting Wal-Marts and fast food joints. The closest thing we had was the amphitheater where the Carolina Covenant held sessions.

I followed Seth and we slipped through the side entrance used by the servants. Most of the halfs we passed cast their eyes to the ground as they carried goblets and plates of tiny appetizers. I had a hard time looking at them, harder than I'd realized I would. Back home, we rarely saw so many. They were kept separate from us, as if the Carolina Covenant didn't want us to see what the other side was truly like.

What did the servants think when they saw me—or any half who wasn't in servitude? Were they even capable of thinking? If I were one of them and I had some critical thinking skills left, I'd be outright hostile toward the "free" halfs.

The icky feeling in the pit of my stomach was hard to acknowledge, so I started jabbering as Seth led me past several small doors. "Stairs—more stairs? Would it kill them to put a damn elevator in one of the buildings?"

Seth started up them. "Maybe they think the gods would be unhappy with elevators."

"That's stupid." The long car ride had made my legs feel like jelly.

"We only have to go up eight flights. I promise."

"Eight?" I eyed two more servants heading down the stairs, hands empty. One was a middle-aged female in a plain gray dress. She wore thin-soled shoes and no socks. The skin around her ankles looked bruised and red, as if it had been rubbed raw. Cringing, I glanced at the male servant behind her.

A sudden cold shiver crawled over my skin.

The older male half had dark brown hair that curled around a strong chin and cheeks weathered by the sun. Fine lines jutted out from the corners of gentle brown eyes… that were looking straight at me.

His eyes weren't the glassed-over eyes of a servant. They were keen, intelligent—seeing. There was something familiar about him, something I should *know*.

CHAPTER 15

"COME ON," SETH URGED, TUGGING ON MY HAND. "We're going to miss it."

With surprising effort, I refocused on Seth's back and started up the stairs again. The line of Seth's shoulders seemed unnaturally tense. At the landing to the fourth floor, I spared a second to look over my shoulder.

The half-blood servant stood below, staring up at us. Our eyes met for a second, and the half stepped back, hands balling into fists. Then he spun around, disappearing down the stairwell.

"That was strange," I murmured.

"Huh?"

Hadn't he noticed how alert that servant had been? Seth stared at me like I'd just made out with a daimon. Guess not. "Nothing."

Seth inched open a door. "You ready?"

"I guess." I was still thinking about that servant.

"We have to keep back, but we should be able to see everything from here." He motioned me through.

I stepped onto what turned out to be a balcony overlooking the Council below. I started forward, but Seth pulled me back.

"No." His breath stirred the hair around my ear. "We have to stay back against the wall."

"Sorry." I wiggled free. "Can I sit?"

He smiled gamely. "Of course."

I slid down the wall and stretched out my aching legs. Seth did the same, managing to be as close as possible. I elbowed him, but he only grinned. "So what's the big deal?"

"Aren't you at all interested in the Council hearing?"

I faced the Council below, fiddling with the string on my hoodie. "Interested" wasn't the word that came to mind; "terrified" seemed more accurate. These pures could make or break a half-blood. Leaning forward, I scanned the crowds through the slats of the balcony railing.

A sea of red, blue, green, and white moved around the floor, taking seats with others who wore the same colored robes. I looked at the white robes and saw a coppery redhead moving with the grace of a ballerina through the throng of pures.

"Dawn Samos," I whispered. She made white sheets look good.

Seth leaned forward. "You know her?"

"Lea is her sister. Do you think she's come with Dawn?" I paused, remembering how Lea had fought beside me. "I… I'd like to talk to her."

"She didn't come, but she did stop by your room after… everything."

"She did?" Surprised, I watched the throng of pures. "That's surprising. Did… she look okay?"

"Her arm was broken and she was a little bruised up, but she'll be okay."

I nodded, watching Dawn sit down and smooth the robe out around her. She kept looking around—looking for someone. Before I could really study any more of the Council pures, I realized that non-Council members were also in attendance. Toward the back sat Marcus and a raven-haired beauty I'd only seen once.

"Laadan—the woman with Marcus is Laadan. She was the pure who pretty much came up with the deal to give me a chance to stay at the Covenant." I tucked my hair back. "I forgot she was here."

Seth nudged my leg with his. "I've heard of her. She doesn't seem too bad."

A familiar dark head slid into the seat beside Laadan. Aiden had changed into white slacks and a white buttoned-down shirt rolled up to the elbows, showing off his powerful forearms. The edges of his hair curled around the collar, giving him sort of an untamed look. I watched as he turned to Laadan and said something. She smiled and patted his arm while Marcus shook his head.

Something struck me. Marcus was dressed like he normally was—dark slacks, a suit jacket—looking more like a Wall Street stock trader than a demigod. Laadan wore a deep red dress made out of crushed velvet. I scanned the back crowd, noticing that some wore the colors that matched the robes. "Why is Aiden wearing white?"

"He's owed a Council seat."

I looked at Seth sharply. "What does that mean?"

Seth arched a brow. "Since his father's seat is still open and will remain so, he's owed a seat on the Council."

"So? He doesn't want that seat."

"That doesn't matter. Aiden still has to show his respect to the current Council members. That's why he's wearing all white. The other people dressed like that? They're either next in line or ones who will campaign for seats when others open up."

I turned back to Aiden. He'd leaned back, one arm thrown over the empty seat beside him. "He never told me that."

"Shouldn't you have known that?"

"I really don't pay attention in civics class."

Seth snickered. "He'll probably take his seat one day, when he settles down. All the pures do."

I wrapped my arms around my waist. "What do you mean by *settles down*?"

Seth's heavy stare settled on me. "I didn't mean anything."

But he did. His unspoken words hung between us. Most pures thought hunting and killing daimons were below their station, but the female pures found it dangerous and thrilling—sexy. My insides twisted into raw knots. The idea of him with someone else made me want to dropkick something—or someone.

A sudden silence descended on the crowd as the Ministers from all four Covenants entered. I recognized Lucian and Minister Nadia Callao, a tall female who I'd only seen a few times in Carolina. They took their seats together, as did the rest of the Ministers. One—a man with dark hair graying at the temples, a full face and piercing blue eyes—stepped to the center of the raised dais, his green robes heavily adorned with gold thread. A golden laurel wreath sat atop his head.

"Who is that?" I asked.

"Minister Gavril Telly. The house you're staying in is his. The woman in green is Diana Elders—the other Minister of New York—but Telly is the head of the Ministers. He's the one in charge."

Telly started the opening session with a prayer in ancient Greek. I had no clue what he was saying. The language was beautiful, almost musical, but went on for so long I leaned back and yawned.

Seth grinned. "Don't go falling asleep on me."

"No guarantees."

I didn't fall asleep though. Minister Telly eventually started to address the crowd in heavily accented English. I couldn't place where he was from, but his voice carried the same lilt Seth's did, just with a hell of a lot more authority.

"We have several urgent issues that must be addressed during this Council Session." Telly's voice rang through the building. "Most importantly, we are here today to discuss the… unsavory situation that has arisen over this past summer."

"They're going to talk about Kain, aren't they?" I perked up, eager to see how the pures would handle this.

Seth shrugged. "There are a lot of things they could talk about."

Telly paced the length of the dais, the long green robes trailing behind him. Raising one arm, he signaled to the section of the theater underneath us. I strained forward, but Seth got a handful of my sweater and held me still. Two Guards eventually came into view, escorting a woman dressed in nothing but a gray tunic that ended above the knees. She didn't even wear shoes. They brought her to stand below the center of the dais, and then forced her to her knees.

Apprehension blossomed in the pit of my stomach. The dark-skinned woman wasn't a daimon from what I could tell. She looked like a normal half-blood—perhaps a Guard or a Sentinel. Her legs were toned enough for someone who'd spent years training and fighting.

She lifted her head defiantly, and a hushed murmur carried through the crowd of pures.

"Kelia Lothos." Telly's upper lip curled. "You have been accused of breaking the Breed Order by having inappropriate contact with a pure-blood."

My eyes widened. Caleb had told me about her—and her pure-blood boyfriend, Hector. I twisted back to Seth. "Seriously? Their most pressing issue is a half having sex with a pure?"

Seth's amber gaze met mine. "So it seems."

Shaking my head in disbelief, I turned back to the drama unfolding on the floor below. "Damn Hematoi."

"How do you plead?" Telly demanded.

Kelia started to stand, but the Guards forced her to stay down. "Does it matter how I plead? You have already found me guilty."

"You have the right to tell your side." Minster Diana Elders rose, slowly approaching the center of the dais. An open kindness marked her expression, softening the set of her lips. "If you feel that you are not—"

"It is not her fault!" A voice cried out from deep within the audience as a pure in green robes came to his feet. His complexion was swarthy, much like Jackson's. "She has done nothing wrong. If anyone is to blame, then it is me."

"And so it begins," muttered Seth.

I ignored him, transfixed by this pure-blood coming to Kelia's defense. This was better than watching daytime soaps.

Telly drifted to the left of the dais. "Hector, no one here holds you at fault. Halfs can be just as beautiful as pures… and as manipulative as any daimon."

Hector—Kelia's pure-blood lover—pushed down the aisle. "Yes, she is beautiful, but manipulative? Never. I love her, Minister Telly. That is of no fault of hers."

Telly scoffed as he came to the edge of the dais. "A half-blood and a pure-blood cannot fall in love with each other. The idea is as absurd as it is disgusting. She has broken the law. Perhaps she should have thought of that before she acted as a common whore."

"Do not speak of her like that!" Hector's face flushed with anger.

"How dare *you* speak to *me* that way." Telly drew himself up. "Proceed carefully, or your next action might be mistaken for treason."

Kelia twisted around. Concern and fear filled her eyes—and so did love. My heart twisted for her—for them. "Hector, please don't. Just leave."

Hector's dark eyes fell on Kelia, mirroring the same emotions displayed across her face. "No. I can't let this happen. You've done no wrong. I should have never—"

"Hector, please leave," Kelia begged. "I don't want you to… see me like this. Please!"

"I'm not leaving," Hector said. "You're not guilty of anything!"

"I'm guilty of loving you!" She pulled her arms free of the Guards. They seemed too stunned by the explicit outpouring of emotion to do anything. "Don't do this! You promised me you wouldn't do this!"

Promised what? What Hector was doing was heroic, romantic, and swoon-worthy. How could she not want the man she loved to stand up against the entire Council for her?

Hector rushed down the main walkway, and the Guards finally snapped out of it. They positioned themselves between the half and pure.

Hector halted, his hands clenching at his sides. "Stand down."

"Are you going to allow this to continue, Minister?" asked Lucian, speaking for the first time since the session began.

Telly exhaled slowly. "Kelia Lothos, how do you plead?"

The crowd of pures watched, excited and horrified, eager to see how Kelia would respond. But it was Hector who did.

"She pleads not guilty."

An elderly female Minister stood. The red robes swallowed her frail body. She reminded me of the Crypt Keeper I'd faced when I was seven. "Enough. Sentence the half to servitude and remove this pure from the session!"

A clap of thunder *inside* the building sent me back from the railing into Seth. Above us, the air started to thicken and darken. As impossible as it seemed, dangerous-looking clouds began to form—and they were coming from Hector. He was using the element of earth, the electical power creating an indoor thunderstorm.

Hector met Telly's stunned gaze. "I will not allow you to take her."

Chaos broke loose on the floor below. Hector surged forward, and the cloud above us flashed with lightning, filling the air with an electrical charge. The ministers came to their feet, full of shock and anger.

"Please! We can discuss this civilly!" cried Diana. "Can we not—"

Another crash of thunder drowned out her words. I pressed my face into the gap beteen the slats for a better look at the what was happening below. Unsurprisingly, the Guards who'd held Kelia back didn't look willing to attack a pure. We were trained from birth to never do so, not even in extreme cases like these. They moved back warily as Hector grabbed hold of Kelia, pulling her to his chest.

"The half-blood is found guilty!" Telly shouted. "Seize the half and send her to the Masters! Remove the—"

Hector thrust Kelia behind him as the cloud cracked, shooting streaks of lightning throughout the room. Pures shot from the benches, pushing at each other as they hurried out of the way. Worried for Aiden, I searched him out in the madness. He stood in the center beside Laadan, his expression a steely mask.

"I will kill anyone who dares to take her." Hector's voice was low and steady.

"You would stand against your own kind—for a half-blood?" Telly's face was pale with anger.

Hector did not hesitate. "Yes. I would for the *woman* I love."

Telly backed off. "You have sealed your fate."

I didn't understand those words. Pures were *never* punished for messing around with halfs. About the only thing they were ever punished for was using compulsion or other elemental powers against other pures, but…

The cloud continued to darken, and Seth pulled on my arm, but I held onto the slats of the balcony railing.

"Guards!" Telly ordered, and Guards from every corner descended in a flurry of white. All of them were halfs, except one.

The pure-blood Guard had eyes the color of rich soil. He stared at Telly, his fingers wrapped around a Covenant dagger. The other Guards reached the two lovers, managing to break Kelia from Hector's hold. She screamed and fought them, breaking loose once to only be tackled to the floor.

Overhead, the cloud darkened even more. A bolt of lightning snapped from the cloud, striking the floor near Telly. "Take him down!" said Telly.

"No!" screamed Kelia. "Stop this, Hector! Please!"

The pure reached Hector before he could send another lightning bolt. A horrified scream rose in my throat, muffled by Seth's hand. The pure-blood Guard—the only one out of all them who could strike down another pure—shoved the titanium blade into Hector's back and twisted. A sucking sound shot through the building and the ominous cloud fizzled out.

Seth jerked me from the railing. "You can't scream, okay? I doubt they're going to be thrilled if they find us here. Promise me you won't scream." He eased off after I nodded. "We need to get out of here."

I barely heard Seth. Horror and anger slammed through my heart and my fingers dug into his arm. Kelia's screams filled the air until they were abruptly cut off. All of this was impossible, cruel, and horrifying.

Seth gave a weary sigh "I guess it's a good thing Aiden came to his senses."

Ice drenched my veins, stealing the very air from my lungs. I twisted around, facing him. "You knew this was going to happen. You brought me here on purpose!"

The tawny hue of his eyes glowed. "I didn't know it would go this far."

"I don't believe you." I pushed against his chest, feeling sick. "You knew what they were going to do!"

Seth looked away, the hollow of his cheeks flushed. "I only know what Aiden's future would've held if you two had continued with that insanity."

I pushed again, and this time, Seth let go.

I spent the rest of my first day in New York holed up in the dingy room. I didn't want to be here—or anywhere near here. Raw knots formed in my stomach, and I was furious with Seth.

But I was also furious with myself.

I plopped down on the edge of the hard mattress. *I only know what Aiden's future would've held if you two had continued with that insanity.*

As much as I hated to admit it, Seth had been right.

Aiden was the kind of man who would've done exactly what Hector had done. If Aiden had loved me and I'd ended up in Kelia's position, he would've fought an army of Guards and received a dagger in the back.

I lowered my head to my hands and drew in a strangled breath. My heart yearned for Aiden like he was the very air I needed to breathe, but at the same time I understood—really understood—that, even if Aiden had loved me in return, we could never be together.

What had he said to me that day in the gym? That if he loved me he'd take everything from me. What I'd seen proved that I'd also take everything from him—even his life.

A soft knock drew me out of my troubled thoughts. I crossed the two feet to the door and opened it.

Seth stood there, arms folded across his chest. "Alex—"

I shut the door and locked it. Seth may've been right, but I still didn't want to see him. If I had to deal with his gloating face, I'd really punch him. I sat back on the bed and scowled at the door.

A minute passed, and then the knob turned, first left then right. Squinting, I leaned forward. There was the unmistakable sound of the door unlocking.

"What the hell?" I sprang to my feet.

The door swung open. Seth stepped into the little room. "I fried your lock."

My mouth dropped open. "You arrogant son of—"

"Shush." He shut the door behind him and surveyed the room with another disgusted look. "I still can't believe they stuck you in this craphole. I'm going to have to talk to Lucian about this."

"Why would Lucian care?"

He strode past me and bent at the waist, pressing his open palm into the mattress. "Lucian cares more about you than you realize." He straightened and smiled. "You should come to my room. You'd like it."

I rolled my eyes. "Not going to happen."

Seth looked disappointed, and then his eyes fell on my skeevy bathroom. "I have a Jacuzzi tub in my bathroom."

"Seriously?"

"Yep."

The idea of a nice long bath teased me. I shook my head, dispelling the dream. "Seth, I really don't want to talk to you right now."

He dropped down on the bed and winced. "Well, we need to talk."

I tipped my head back, groaning. "Does what I want ever matter to you?"

"What you want always matters to me." His face was serious. "By the way, I liked the other jammies you wore that one night. The thermal and flannel shirt aren't very alluring, but those little shorts were nice."

My gaze narrowed on him. "It's freezing in this room and this," I marched over to the bed and tugged on the itchy blanket, "is not touching me. It probably has fleas." I turned back to him. "What do you want, Seth?"

He cast his eyes down. "I'm sorry you had to see that today."

That wasn't what I expected.

"But you needed to see it," he continued, his gaze flicking up, meeting mine. "I know you… love him. Don't deny it, Alex, I know you do. And I know that no matter what Aiden says to you, he still cares for you more than he should."

I opened my mouth to deny that, because Aiden had told me in many different ways that he didn't, but I stopped. Did it matter if Aiden really did care for me? I whirled around and sat beside Seth, staring at the frayed carpet.

"I think you know that, Alex," he said softly. "I've said it before. Eventually you two would've gotten caught. No one—not even me—would've been able to stop the Council. You know what Aiden would have done."

"I know." I rubbed my palm over my thigh. "He would have done exactly what Hector did. I just didn't think they'd do that to their own kind."

"This place is a different world. I've been here a couple of times. It's straight Old School. It doesn't take much to insult Minister Telly and he's no fan of half-bloods… even the Apollyon."

I lifted my head, looking at him. "What do you mean?"

Seth's lips thinned. "It's nothing that I've been told, it's just a feeling I get."

"Is he going to be the one questioning me during my testimony?"

"I don't know." Seth smiled then. "He's nothing to worry about."

I really didn't believe him, but I was too tired to poke further. "I hate this place."

He leaned over, brushing my hair back off my neck, exposing my scars. "You've only been here a day, Alex."

"I don't need more than a day to know." I turned my head, startled to find our faces mere inches apart. "Do… you like it here?"

Seth's eyelids lowered, fanning his cheeks with long lashes. "It's not the worst place." He was quiet for a few moments and then his eyes flicked to mine. "You really have realized that Aiden is sort of a lost cause, haven't you?"

I blinked tightly and turned away. I suddenly wanted to cry, because it was true. "I guess that fills you with some sick sense of satisfaction, doesn't it?"

"I'm not a terrible person, Alex."

His sharp tone brought me back to him. "I didn't say you were a terrible person."

Seth smiled tightly. "Then why would you think I'd like to see you hurt? And I know you're hurting."

Now I felt guilty. "Look, I'm sorry. I'm just out of it."

He relaxed. "That's the second time you've apologized to me. Wow."

"It'll be the last."

"Maybe." He scooted back, lying down on his side. He patted the tiny spot left. "This bed really sucks. You sure you don't want an upgrade?"

I sighed. "Seth, you can't stay here."

He shrugged. "I don't see why not."

"My uncle is right next door."

"So?" He patted the bed again. "He's not even in his room. He's downstairs with the rest of the pures. They're having their opening party fest."

"It doesn't matter." I climbed over his legs and sat beside him. "This bed sharing thing has to stop."

Seth looked up at me, his face the picture of innocence. "Why? It keeps the nightmares away, doesn't it?"

A retort died on my lips. Damn him.

"You haven't had one in a while. What did I tell you about needing—?"

"Oh, shut up."

Seth chuckled, and then told me about his first visit to the New York Covenant. I told him about some of the towns Mom and I had lived in. After a while, his eyes drifted shut and there were no more stories. I watched him for a few moments. What in the world was I supposed to do with him?

I eased down onto my side, careful not to wake him. I stared at the scruffy white wall for what seemed like hours. My mind wouldn't shut down, which was strange. Usually Seth's presence easily lured me into sleep.

Tonight was diffcrent. I missed Caleb, hated where I was, and wished more than anything that things could be different between Aiden and me. Tonight I felt more alone than I ever had before. Maybe everything seemed so much more real here, so much more cold and stark. Seeing Hector slaughtered had destroyed whatever little seed of hope I'd still carried deep inside me that there would be this wild, beautiful fairytale ending when it came to Aiden.

Beside me, Seth's breathing slowed into a deep, steady rhythm. I flipped onto my back and looked at him.

Seth was staring at me, definitely not asleep. He looked curious and even a bit confused. In this miniscule bed, lying on my back gave him little room. As it was, he already was using one arm as a pillow and his other was clamped to his side. I sucked in my lower lip and sat up. Reaching behind me I picked up the pillow and offered it to him. He took it, his eyes narrowing inquisitively. We stared at each other, and then Seth seemed to understand. I expected him to say something conceited or dirty.

But he said nothing. Quietly, he lifted up and slid the pillow under his head. Then he lay down on his back and stretched out his right arm. His chest rose sharply as he waited. I ran a hand over my face and squeezed my eyes shut. *What was I doing?*

I didn't really know. I was tired and I hated this place. The room was cold, the coarse blanket was left on the floor, I *wanted* Aiden… and I stopped making excuses. I lay down, resting my head on the crook between his shoulder and chest. My heart pounded strangely.

Seth remained still for a minute, maybe two. Then he moved his arm down, circling my waist, pulling me closer. My body fit against his, my hand resting on his chest. Under my palm, his heart hammered as wildly as mine.

CHAPTER 16

"ARE YOU FEELING UNWELL?"

"Huh?" I looked up from my untouched plate.

Marcus eyed me curiously. "You haven't eaten any of your breakfast."

I glanced over at Aiden. He also watched me. So did Seth. Laadan's eyes were on me, too, except she kind of had this nostalgic look about her, as if she really wasn't seeing me.

This breakfast was a whole lot of awkward.

My gaze settled back on Aiden and I couldn't stop the image of the pure-blood Guard stabbing Aiden in the back from flashing through my mind. I felt the blood slide out of my face.

Aiden put his glass of orange juice down. "Alex?"

"Yeah… I just didn't get much sleep last night." I could feel Seth's eyes boring through me. "It's just being in a new place and all."

"Is your room not to your liking?" asked Marcus.

"Have you seen my room?" I debated shoving forkfuls of egg in my mouth, but the way Aiden studied me over the rim of his glass, it didn't sound like a good idea. "If you can even consider that box a room."

Marcus sat back, crossing one leg over his knee. "I haven't seen your room, but I'm sure it's not that—"

"Marcus, what time are the sessions this morning?" asked Laadan.

Distracted, he glanced at his watch. "They should be starting shortly."

I sent Laadan a grateful smile, and she winked as she twirled her glass of champagne. Drinking champagne this early in the morning appeared sophisticated and cool to me, and so did the awesome green dress she wore. It was demure, with little cap sleeves.

The scratching of Seth's chair across the marble tile sounded harsh. "Alex, it's time for practice."

Aiden glanced over his shoulder at Seth. "She hasn't eaten anything."

"Then at least she'll eat her lunch," Seth replied.

Hardness crept across Aiden's face. "Or you could give her a few minutes to eat her breakfast before she starts practice."

"Hmm… I'm having this strange sense of déjà vu, except you were telling me to stay out of your training business, and I told you how weird—"

"That's funny." Aiden's full lips twisted into a smirk. "I'm having the same feeling, except I said you should—"

"Oh, for the love of baby daimons everywhere, I'm ready to start practice." I pushed up from the chair.

Aiden twisted around, his eyes narrowing into thin slits. I grabbed my glass of juice and took a healthy swallow while Laadan watched on with amused interest. "Happy?"

"Do they do this often?" she asked, taking a sip from her crystal flute.

Marcus cleared his throat. "Do you even have to ask?"

"What?" Seth scowled, turning his beauty even colder. "What do we—"

"Dean Andros, I've been looking for you. There are some things I'd like to talk with you—oh, is this the infamous Alexandria?"

I tensed, recognizing the voice. *Minister Telly.* I met Seth's stare for an instant, and then I forced my body to turn around. Seeing him after he'd ordered Hector's death caused my stomach to sour. I smiled—probably looked more like a grimace—but I tried.

Telly's gaze drifted over me in a wholly condemning matter. "So this is what all the fuss is about?"

That plucked the wrong nerve. "I guess so."

He smiled faintly. "Well, there has been a lot of uproar surrounding what you've accomplished. Many rumors have spread, claiming you have already killed daimons. I am curious if this is true. How many daimons have you killed?"

Vaguely, I sensed Seth moving around the table. Odd that I knew where he was in a room. "I've killed three."

"Oh." Telly's brows rose. "Impressive. And how many innocent people have you thrown into harm's way? Or gotten killed?"

Blood came rushing back to my face. Telly's smile spread, becoming genuine. He was getting off on seeing me squirm.

"Seth? Isn't it time for Alex's practice?" asked Aiden.

If Seth was humored by Aiden's sudden change, he didn't express it. "Why, yes. Excuse us, Minister Telly, but we must—"

I met Telly's icy stare. "One."

"One what, dear?"

Everyone behind me probably stopped breathing. "I've gotten one innocent person killed, and I don't know how many I've put in harm's way—maybe dozens."

Seth swore under his breath.

Telly's eyes flared wide for a second, filled with shock. "Is that so?"

Surprisingly, it was Marcus who came to my rescue. He slid in front of me, blocking the Minister's hostile glare. "Minister Telly, there were a few things I wished to discuss with you also. If it pleases you, would now be a good time?"

Without waiting for Telly's response, Seth grabbed hold of my arm and pulled me away from the table. He waited until we were a step away from the doors. "Gods, you just cannot keep your mouth shut."

"Whatever." I yanked my arm free and stepped outside. The thermal and sweats I wore were no protection against the biting wind.

Seth seemed unfazed by the chilly air. He held his hand up as we walked toward the labyrinth, a small ball of blue energy formed in his open palm. "He is *not* somcone you want as an enemy."

The little ball went up, then down, then up in his palm. My inner golden retriever couldn't look away. "I don't think he liked me to begin with."

"Still, you don't need to make it worse."

His tone pissed me off. "You know what, you need to stay out of my bedroom. You have your own."

He smiled. "I know I do. I see it quite often. I just prefer your bed. It smells better."

I made a face. "It smells better? What does your bed smell like? Regret and bad taste?"

Seth chuckled. "Wherever you sleep, it smells like you."

"Gods, that has to be the creepiest thing I've heard in a long time. And that is… that is saying something, Seth."

"You smell like roses and summer." He tossed the ball a little higher. "I like it."

I choked. "I smell like summer? For real? Summer?"

"Yeah, you know. Warm. You always smell warm."

Two pures passed us, glancing over their shoulders at Seth's little display of power. I started to smile at their shared looks of shock, but remembered I was supposed to be mad. "I don't care if you like the way I smell, you freak."

"It's not like Marcus is going to walk in." The ball grew bigger, swallowing his hand. "That's why I locked the door. He can't interrupt our cuddle-fest."

"That's not the point, and would you put that away!" I snapped.

Seth was quiet for a whole minute—a new record for him. "Don't worry; you'll be able to do this one day. And you'd miss me if I didn't want to cuddle."

"That's not true."

He cast me a sideways glance that said he remembered *me* cuddling up against him last night. I groaned, wanting to smack him with every fiber of my being. But he did put the ball of energy away as we cleared the labyrinth and the amphitheater came into view. A shudder ran through me that had nothing to do with the temperature. "Where are we going?"

"Not in there."

"Well, I figured that much." I followed him around the building, refusing to look at it. Just like the servants we passed on the way refused to look at us.

Behind the Council building I could finally see the actual Covenant. A wrought iron fence surrounded the campus grounds. While our school looked like something straight out of Greece on a good day, theirs looked like a medieval fortress with creepy turrets and towers that rose out of the fog. Behind the sprawling structure, I could see the tops of gray buildings I assumed were the dorms.

I noticed the designs in the fence as we neared it. "What's up with the torch thing?"

"Huh?"

"These downward torch things." I pointed one out on the fence, "They're everywhere here."

"Yeah, I've noticed that. They're a symbol of Thanatos."

"One of my Instructors at the Covenant has a tattoo of it on his arm."

His lips pursed. "Minister Telly has one on his arm, too."

"How in the world do you know that?" We cut across the frost-covered lawn to one of the covered walkways connecting smaller buildings to the main one. "Have you been sneaking into his room and cuddling with him, too?"

"Don't be jealous. You're my only cuddle bunny. But to answer your question, when I got here with Lucian, Telly was waving his arm around as he yelled at some servants. The sleeve of his robe slipped back and I saw the tattoo."

"I wonder if they belong to some secret society or something."

"A secret society of douchebags, maybe."

I snickered. "Sounds about right."

We passed two halfs walking to class and they came to an abrupt standstill. Eyes wide, they gawked at us. One boy elbowed the other. "That's him! And that has to be her—the other one."

The other boy's mouth dropped open. "Then it's true! There really are two Apollyons."

"By the gods," his companion ran a hand over his chest, "this is so cool."

Seth bowed at them. "Way cool."

Rolling my eyes, I pushed him to the side. The whole sensing Seth thing was getting annoying. "Where are we going?"

"Since it's freezing up here in the mornings, I figured we'd do our first session in a training room. Then move outside."

My shoulders slumped. "I have to practice with you all day?"

Seth spun around in front of me, the perpetual, cocksure grin on his face. "You have to spend *all* day with me. Every day. For as long as we are here."

I stared at him.

He clapped his hands together, letting out a rather high-pitched squeal before grabbing my hand. "Oh, we are going to have so much fun! Aren't we? Fun, Alex—we will have fun."

We weren't having fun.

I spun around, blocking first his kick then his jab. Sweat poured off me and my muscles ached from the never-ending onslaught that was Seth.

Then again, I preferred these morning sessions over the afternoon ones. Over the past three days, I'd come to dread the outside training sessions. The weather didn't warm up very much by then, and the frozen ground was unforgiving, even with the magically green grass springing up from it.

Seth tossed me a bottle of water. "Five minutes."

I retreated to the edge of the mats and took a long swallow. Seth, who never seemed thirsty, decided to entertain the ever-growing crowd of gawkers. In between class changes, half students had started gathering at the doors. Seth left them open since this kind of thing stroked his ego. All the halfs were pretty cool, though, and they didn't treat me like people did at my Covenant. Somehow—and I totally blame Seth—they'd found out I'd already made some kills, which upped my cool factor into uncharted territory. We had students and Instructors watching us try to tear each other's heads off.

This, in a way, was what we really wanted to do.

It seemed the only time we didn't fight was when we slept. There hadn't been another repeat of the night I'd used Seth as a pillow, and I think that ticked him off.

I strolled across the mats, catching that tail end of what Seth was saying to the pretty little half with eons of red hair and a chest that made me feel like I wore a training bra.

"Maybe after practice I'll show you my balls of—"

I chucked the water bottle at the back of Seth's head. He spun around and caught it before it connected. Gasping, the girl stepped back and stared at me. I had a feeling that if I were anyone else, she'd pull my hair out.

"Not nice." Seth threw the bottle to the floor.

"Five minutes are up." I bounced back a few steps, grinning.

Cross, a half-blood who'd become a regular at the door, elbowed his friend. "Hundred dollars they end up in a fight to the death by week's end."

"Who'd you think would win?" Will, another now familiar face, grinned.

"I'd put my bets on that one." Cross jerked his head at me.

I tossed my head back, smiling at Seth. "Me," I mouthed.

Seth looked bored.

Boobs stopped twirling her hair for five seconds. "Oh no, I'd say the First would come out on top."

My smile faded, and I decided to ignore them. I turned to Seth. "Ready, *sweetheart*?"

He moved to stand in front of me, his back to his—our—groupies. "I'm always ready for you, *cuddle bunny*."

My hand slipped past his block, slamming hard into his solar plexus. He staggered backward, grunting. "Moving a little slow there, Apollyon?"

Not to be outdone with the growing fan base by the door to witness, he tapped into the elements. *Jerk-face,* I thought. The first gust of wind missed me only by an inch, but the second was so far off that I stopped to laugh. The third punched me square in the chest. I hit the mats hard but rolled to my feet before he could pin me down. We went at it until we broke for lunch. Seth liked eating with the students. It provided more chances for his head to grow bigger.

Cross and Will invited us to a party they were throwing Saturday night. "It'd be awesome if you guys could come," said Cross. "The pures will be doing their own thing, so no one will be checking on us."

The pures had been doing their own thing every night. Even five floors up, I could hear their raucous laughter in the wee hours of the morning. Thinking about that soured my mood. I wondered if *he* was one of the pures partying it up.

Seth thought the party sounded like a great idea. So did Boobs. I wasn't so sure, because the secondhand hot flashes I'd caught from Seth had been bad enough from a distance. I really didn't want to experience them in the same room. At the end of our afternoon practice outdoors, Seth caught my hand before I could make off without him.

"What?" I desperately wanted a long, hot shower.

Uncaring of the cold mud covering every square inch of my clothes, he pulled me toward him. "You have to come to the party with me."

I arched a brow at him. "I didn't say I wasn't going."

"You didn't say you were, and you've been grumpy all afternoon."

"That's because I'm stuck with you, day and night."

"I don't believe that." Seth's gaze flicked up and behind me, and then he inched me closer. I braced myself by putting my hand on his shoulder, but he smiled down at me—a different kind of smile, one he usually reserved for girls like Boobs and Elena. Sudden wariness shifted through me, ratcheted up to the tenth degree when he reached out with his free hand and cupped my chin.

My pulse skyrocketed. "What are you—?"

Seth smoothed his thumb over my lower lip, sending a weird mix of shivers through me. His stare locked onto mine, and the yellow of his eyes flared. "You have mud on your lip."

"Oh." I wiped my hand over my mouth, twisting out of his embrace. "I have—"

Aiden stood under a statue of Apollo, appearing just as unmoving and fierce as the god. It took quite of a lot for me not to turn and sock Seth in the face.

"Hey there." Seth stepped around me. "Checking out our training sessions, are you? Don't fret; I've been taking really good care of her."

I decided right then and there: the first thing I was going to do once I Awakened was zap Seth.

"I'm sure you have." Aiden's voice was cold.

Seth moved past Aiden, clapping him on the shoulder as he did so. "How are the Council sessions going? Changing the world?"

Aiden's gaze settled on Seth's hand and then slowly lifted to his face. Whatever Seth saw in his eyes must've told him to remove his hand as quickly as possible. Chuckling as if it amused him, Seth glanced back at me. "See you later, cuddle bunny."

What came out of my mouth made Aiden's eyes widen, but only made Seth laugh harder as he strolled back toward the campus.

"Hey," I said, grateful that mud *did* cover half of my flaming face.

Aiden shoved his hands into his white trousers. "I can see training with him is going as expected."

"I hate him, really I do."

"'Hate' is such a strong word."

My chin jerked up. "You'd understand if you had to spend five seconds with him."

His gray eyes settled on my face, then my lips—lips that he'd seen Seth touch. "I guess so."

"So why are you here?" I sounded harsh, but I was bristling at the coldness in his eyes and still licking the emotional wounds Aiden had sliced open.

"I haven't seen you in a few days, so I was actually checking in on you."

I felt warm despite the brisk air and hated myself for it. "Why?"

He shrugged. "I'm not allowed to?"

Secretly, my heart was jumping around happily at the idea of Aiden searching me out. My brain, on the other hand, brutally ordered me to walk away. I stayed. "I guess so."

"Walk you back?"

"Is that okay—I mean, no one will care that a pure is walking with a half? I don't see many of them doing so here." I paused, frowning.

"Actually, I never see any pures talk to halfs here."

"Minister Telly is a bit archaic in the way the Council and the Covenant are run here. He wants things to be as if centuries of change has not occurred—a complete separation of breeds and races."

We started back toward the main house, together. "So that's why I haven't seen any mortals here."

Aiden nodded. "I think Minister Telly would go completely back to the old ways, to a time when our kind devoted every aspect of our lives to the gods. He doesn't even believe we should have any contact with mortals, not even through compulsion."

"Well, how does he expect to build up his half-blood army of daimon killers?" He gave me a straight look. It hit me. "He doesn't think there should be any half-bloods, does he?"

"He thinks that pures should be able to refrain from the carnal activities that lead to little half-bloods being made, and that we should be able to defend ourselves against the daimons."

I knocked back a mud-encased strand of hair. "Then what would you all do for servants? Actually take care of yourselves?"

He stared at the cloudy sky. "There are enough half-bloods in the world now to carry the pures through several generations. After that, I don't know what Telly would do."

"So he wants to see all half-bloods enslaved? Nice. I knew there was a reason why I thought he was a giant douchebag. My judgment wasn't as bad as I thought it was."

Aiden glanced down at me, a curious expression on his striking face. "Why would you think your judgment is off?"

I looked at him pointedly.

He pursed his lips and nodded stiffly. "Got it."

We continued on in silence for a few minutes. "So… how do you like it here?"

I wet my lips, thinking about Hector. "I miss… home."

Aiden continued to stare up at the overcast sky. "I miss it, too."

I drifted closer to him as we neared the Council building. I told myself that was normal. Aiden was my friend—only a friend. "This whole place makes me uncomfortable. I just wish I could get on with my hearing and be done with it. It's stupid that I have to be here all this time, when my hearing isn't even scheduled until the end of the session. Anyway, how have the hearings been?"

"Long. The Councils spend more of the time arguing than anything else."

That didn't surprise me. "Have they talked about halfs turning yet?"

His expression suddenly emptied. "That discussion provokes the most arguments, but anyway, what are you planning to do with your evening?"

"What am I planning to do?" I tipped my head back and sighed. "Shower."

Aiden laughed, sending a flurry of warm and fluttering feelings through my stomach. It'd felt like years since I'd heard him laugh. "You are such a mess right now."

I sighed pitifully. "I know. I think I have mud in my mouth."

"Well, I might have something that'll make you feel better." He reached into his pocket and pulled out a slender black tube about four inches long.

"What is that?"

Aiden smiled as he held it out from his body. "They've been working on new weapons since the discovery of halfs being turned. This is what they came up with."

"A black tube? Wow."

His smile turned into a grin. "Just watch." His fingers moved to the end of the tube, pressing down on a small button. Titanium blades shot out from each side. Aiden shook his wrist and the blade on the right side extended and curved in.

My eyes went wide. "Whoa. I like."

He laughed. "I know how much you like things that stab. Here." He handed me the blade. "But be careful. The ends are wicked sharp."

I took the weapon, holding it reverently. It was heavier than I expected, but still manageable. My fingers curved on the cool matter of the center. One end had been finished down to a sharp point, while the other reminded me of a sickle. Why had they shaped the blade this way?

Then I felt stupid for not realizing right off the bat. Cringing, I pointed to the sickle end. "This is for taking off heads, isn't it?"

"Yeah, we all can't harness akasha like Seth. And even he can't zap every daimon half. Using akasha soaks up energy, so he can only use it when he really needs to."

"Oh." I made a wide-sweeping motion, grinning in spite of the messy business it represented. "I wonder what it will be like after I Awaken. If he'll be able to use akasha easier."

"I don't know." Aiden eyed the blade warily. "Probably something you should ask Seth."

I remembered what Lucian had said about Seth pulling from me once I Awakened. "He's going to suck me dry, probably." The moment those words left my mouth I froze. Mom had said that. Was that what would happen?

Aiden noted my sudden stillness. "You okay?"

I blinked. "Yeah, I'm fine." I pressed the little button on the end of the metal tube. The sickle side straightened before both ends collapsed back into the tube. I handed it back to Aiden, forcing a casual smile. "Thanks for letting me see that."

"No problem." We walked a while in silence before he spoke again. "You sure you're all right?"

"Yep," I said, promising myself that Seth and I would have a conversation very soon.

Aiden stepped in front of me, opening the door to the main house. Inside, we stuck to the less-travelled areas as we made our way to the stairwell. We passed another one of those damn paintings with the torch, but this one had something written in ancient Greek.

"Hey, you read ancient Greek, right?"

Aiden halted in front of me and turned around. "Yes."

I pointed one dirty finger at the painting. "What does this say?"

He stepped closer. "It reads 'Order of Thanatos.'"

"I know that from somewhere." I crossed my arms. "What's up with all the Thanatos stuff here?"

He brushed messy waves off his forehead. "I really don't know what the fascination is, but the Order was a mystic group that existed centuries ago. It's in the Myths and Legends book I gave you."

"Well, that's currently being used as a doorstop in my dorm."

Aiden grinned at that, and I realized we hadn't argued or said anything mean to each other. This was progress. "The group died out centuries ago. I don't remember much about them, but they were pretty extreme about tradition and the old ways."

I thought about the tattoos Instructor Romvi and Telly shared. "What do you think it means if someone has a tattoo of Thanatos's symbol?"

"Nothing probably, since a lot of us have tattoos of various symbols."

"You don't." As soon as the words left my mouth, I regretted them.

His eyes turned from gray to silver in a heartbeat. I imagined he was remembering how I would know if he had a tattoo hidden somewhere.

"I'm sorry," I whispered.

"It's okay." Aiden stepped back, his eyes dropping to my lips again, then back up.

What passed between us in those tense moments could've caught the whole damn building on fire. A yearning—deep and powerful—sprung alive. My fingers dug into my own skin, but it did nothing to dampen the desire to be close to him, to be in his arms. I thought I saw the same look on his face.

I squeezed my eyes shut, letting the mad desire wreak havoc on my heart. Aiden was gone when I reopened them. Pressing my lips together, I headed up the stairwell used by the servants since I was sure Aiden had taken the main one, and being stuck with him in a stairwell… well, my overheated imagination supplied possible scenarios that would never happen. I rounded the fifth landing, almost plowing through a servant coming through the door to my floor.

"Sorry! I should have—"

The half-blood from the first day here—the servant with eyes that seemed so familiar, stared down at me, incredibly alert. A second passed before he jerked his chin down and hurried past me. I spun around, gripping the handrail. "Hey!"

He stopped.

I went down a step. "Do I know you from somewhere?"

No answer.

"I know you can talk—you especially." I inched down one more step. "You don't look like the rest." He whipped around so fast I leaned backward. His eyes searched my face, but he still didn't say anything. I took a deep breath. "Your eyes aren't glassed over like… like most of the servants here."

His head cocked to the side and he came up a step.

I held my hands up, my heart pounding. "I'm not going to say anything. I'm totally Team Half-Blood. Are there others like you, others that aren't all doped up?"

Probably not the best word choice, but he nodded.

I mulled that over, studying his features. He may've been handsome before the servant's life took a toll on him, but I kept going back to his eyes. They were such a warm brown. "Why won't you talk to me?" I made a face. "Why won't any of you talk to me?"

His hand clenched the rail, knuckles bleaching.

"Okay. Anyway." I swallowed nervously. Were the servants up here unstable? "You look familiar to me."

That seemed to be the wrong thing to say, because he backed off.

"Wait—just wait a second." Once again, he stopped and watched me, lips thinned into a tight line. "What's your name?"

The door opened and Marcus's voice rang out. "Alex, is that you in the stairwell?"

The servant's eyes narrowed then he disappeared down the stairs. Groaning in frustration, I pulled myself up the last couple of steps. "Yeah, it's me."

"Who are you talking to?"

I shook my head, sliding past him. "No one."

CHAPTER 17

RED MEAT AND POLITICS DIDN'T AGREE WITH ONE another.

"Marcus, things have changed, but in some aspect, things have not." Lucian twirled a glass of wine between his elegant fingers. "Minister Telly's stance on separation versus integration is gaining ground."

"Only because he believes that the gods are among us." Marcus leaned forward, voice low. "Telly's a fanatic—always has been."

Lucian sipped his wine. "I agree with you, but sadly, most do not."

"I'd like to believe that most see the error in his thinking." Laadan sat across from me, her hair pulled up into an elaborate twist. The silky, pale blue dress she wore was to die for. "We are on the brink of change. The Breed Order must also change."

I stabbed my steak, watching the juices run out of it. It sucked to sit here and be expected not to say anything. I could only imagine the words coming out of Seth's mouth if he were here, but he was MIA.

I kind of missed him.

A plate of tiramisu slid in front of me. Politics forgotten, I glanced at the gray-eyed pure sitting beside me. Whoever had designed the seating chart needed to be killed. "Thanks," I murmured.

Aiden nodded and went back to following the conversation. I dug my spoon in the bowl and tried not to read too much into his gesture.

"Nadia and I will do everything to ensure that the Breed Order is changed," said Lucian, "but I'm afraid there are many who plot against it, and will stop at nothing to see that things remain the same."

I choked on my dessert, and everyone stopped to look at me. "Sorry," I gasped, waving my hand in front of my face.

Lucian frowned. "Are you all right, dear?"

"You… you want to see the Breed Order changed?"

"Of course," he responded. "It is time that half-bloods have representation on the Council. Just a few short hours ago I was telling Seth that with you two, we are closer to that change than ever before. It will not be us, the pure-bloods, who bring up such wondrous things. It will be you and Seth."

My brows inched up my forehead.

Lucian patted my hand. "Pure-bloods like Telly believe that the gods would favor the road back to the old way."

I stared down at Lucian's pale hand, unable to let go of the innate suspicion I felt when it came to him. He patted my hand once more and smiled. "Dear, have you put any thought into what you will be wearing to the ball next week?"

"What?" I had no idea what he was talking about.

"The annual Fall Ball? You are invited, which is a great honor for you and Seth. You two will be the first half-bloods to be in attendance. You must find something decent to wear." He glanced across the table. "Laadan, would you help her?"

She nodded. "Of course."

Ball, what ball? I glanced around the table, bewildered. Aiden looked slightly amused at the idea of me attending their ball. I scowled.

"Then it is settled." Lucian turned back to Marcus, already forgetting about me. "Have you received any word from the Dean at South Dakota?"

Marcus shook his head. "It was a student who'd been turned—a half-blood. The pure wasn't killed."

How in the world did they just jump from politics, to a ball, and now to daimon attacks? And here I'd thought *I* had the attention span of an ant on Red Bull.

Aiden leaned forward. "So each Covenant has had an attack, but the Council believes that none of these events are related?"

I picked up my spoon, pretending not to listen.

Lucian reclined back in his chair, studying Aiden. "We are not so foolish to believe that the daimons do not have something up their sleeves, but what? They cannot truly believe they can take on the Covenants?"

Aiden's fingers tensed around the stem of his glass. "Haven't they already tried, Minister? The only things I've heard the Council discuss are what drinks will be served at the Ball, whether or not a new Covenant should be opened in the Midwest, and other insignificant items."

Lucian eyed him over the rim of his glass. "For someone who shows no interest in his Council seat, you are very opinionated about how the sessions are proceeding."

Two bright spots appeared on Aiden's cheeks. I felt the immediate urge to defend him. "He has a point, you know." Four sets of eyes turned on me. Crap. "Look at what happened at home. They got past our Guards and… and killed people. They are planning something—something big. Shouldn't the Council be concerned with that instead of a stupid dance?"

Marcus glared at me. "If you are finished with your dinner, you are excused."

I slammed my spoon down. "If you don't want my opinion then maybe you shouldn't talk about these things in front of me."

"Point taken." Marcus met my furious stare. "Good evening, Alexandria."

Embarrassed at being dismissed like that, I jerked to my feet. None of the pures seated in the elaborate dining hall looked up as I passed them, and neither did the servants removing trays and replenishing drinks. I scanned the hall, but the one servant I had an interest in finding wasn't bussing tables.

There wasn't anything for me to do besides go back to my room, and I'd rather shove my head in an oven then go back there. I roamed the halls aimlessly, as unnoticed as all half-bloods were in this magnificent hellhole.

I missed North Carolina even more—and Caleb. Gods, I wished I could hop online and chat with him like we'd planned. I blinked away the hot tears and stepped into a large, musty-smelling room—a library.

Strange that I would find myself in a library, since reading really wasn't my thing. A few lonely chairs sat beside the antique lamps, but they looked like they were covered with dust. I made my way through the stacks, trailing my fingers over the spines of books. Maybe I'd find one of those smutty historical romance novels—the kind Mom used to read.

Not likely.

Nothing in the room looked like it'd been in touched in years. I couldn't even begin to decipher most of the titles. But I continued on, anything to avoid the heartache that thoughts of Caleb always brought on. I tried pronouncing the titles, but gave up after five. Sighing, I tucked back my hair and crouched down.

"Unpronounceable. Unpronounceable. Unpronounceable." I tipped my head to the side. "Really unpronounceable. This one can't even be a real word. Oh, come—" My fingers stilled over a thick black book with gold lettering. I had no idea what the words were, but I recognized the symbol on the spine. "Downward torch…" I wiggled the book free.

A fine shiver coursed down my body. My head jerked up and I scanned the library. There was no mistaking the feeling of being watched.

"Alexandria, are you in here?"

I let go of the book and straightened. "Laadan?"

She appeared at the edge of the stacks. In the dim light and pale dress, she looked ethereal. A tentative smile pulled at her full lips. "I'm not interrupting anything, am I?"

"No. I was just looking for something to read, but everything is in ancient Greek."

Her gray eyes dropped to the books. "I don't know why Telly stocks the library with books most of us can't read."

I stepped closer, but kept a decent distance between us. "I thought all of you pures read the old language."

Laadan laughed softly. "All of us are taught it in school, but I promptly forgot it. Most of us can't."

Except Aiden, I thought. Thinking of him reminded me of the first time I'd seen Laadan, standing beside Leon and bargaining with Marcus to allow me to stay. "I never got a chance to thank you."

"For what?"

"You convinced Marcus to give me a chance. If you hadn't been there, I don't think he would've allowed me back into the Covenant." I bit my bottom lip and took another step toward the end of the stacks. "Why did you speak up for me? Did you know… what I was?"

She smoothed her hands down the front of her dress as she glanced toward the door. "Did I know you would become an Apollyon? No, but in a way, I did know you."

More than just a little curious, I walked out of the stacks.

"When I was your age, I attended the Covenant in North Carolina. Your mother and I were very close. To this day, I wish we hadn't grown apart, that I'd stayed in North Carolina. Maybe things would have turned out differently."

Surprise left me speechless. Laadan smiled again. At once, the nostalgic looks she'd get when she looked at me made sense.

She nodded. "You look so much like Rachelle did when she was your age. You're a bit wilder, but I think that's your father in you."

My chest tightened. "You—you knew my father?"

"Yes." She drifted closer, lowering her voice. "Much better choice and fit for Rachelle than Lucian, but your mother didn't really have a choice. A lot of people will tell you that she met your father after marrying Lucian, but that wasn't true. She knew your father first—she *loved* your father long before Lucian entered the picture."

"But… I don't understand. She married Lucian when she was young, and it was at least five years before I was born."

There was a far-off look in her eyes as she recalled a past I was not familiar with. "Then you can imagine the scandal when you were born, but don't let that tarnish what your parents had. Their love was the kind written about in those silly books your mom used to read. She and Alexander started off as just friends—the three of us actually—but over the years their friendship grew into something much deeper."

Hearing my father's name spoken felt strange and oddly wonderful—as if he was a real person who'd existed once upon a time.

"Rachelle tried to do the right thing. She stayed away from your father as long as she could after she married Lucian—marrying Lucian was what was expected from her. She was determined to follow the rules of our society, but love like theirs can't be denied for too long, no matter how wrong it is." She paused, eyes widening. "Alexandria, are you okay?"

"Yeah." I shook my head. "I'm sorry. It's just Mom never talked about him. Like ever. I had no idea it was this epic love affair."

She pressed her lips together and turned away. Walking off toward one of the lamps with green and gold stained glass, she shook her head. "I think it was too hard for your mother to talk about him after everything."

I followed her. "What was he like?"

"Alexander?" Laadan glanced over her shoulder with a sad smile. "A good man, loyal to a fault, very handsome, and Rachelle was his entire world." She turned around, folding slender arms across her waist. "You look so much like her, but you have his personality. When Marcus read off your files in his office that day, all I could think of was Alexander. He's incredibly strong-willed, a bit reckless, and wild."

The way she talked about Alexander, as if he were still here, made me wonder if she'd had feelings for him. "I wonder what he'd think of me." I laughed self-consciously. "That sounded so stupid."

"No, not at all. He'd be proud of you, Alexandria. I hope you know that."

"Well, I am an Apollyon."

She reached out, patting my arm. "Not because of what you'll become, but because of who you already are."

The sting of tears hit my eyes, which seemed so weak. I pulled away, fiddling with the chain on the lamp. "I don't know about that. I should've done something when Mom left the Covenant. And I really shouldn't have gone after her when she'd turned, or at least, when Caleb showed up, I should've gone back to the Covenant, but I didn't. I mean, what was I thinking?"

"You did what you believed was right." She drifted to my side, resting her hands on the old, scuffed-up table the lamp sat on. "Rachelle probably would've smacked you for doing something so incredibly dangerous, but you made sure she had peace."

"You think so?"

"Yes."

A little bit of weight lifted off my chest, but my breath still sawed in and out. "I've messed up, really bad, a lot of times." I squeezed the chain between my fingers. "I don't think he'd be so proud."

Laadan placed her hand over mine. "He would be proud. You followed your heart when it came to Rachelle, and yes, sometimes the decisions you've made have not been the right ones, but you know that. You've learned from them. And owning up to Telly about your role in what happened to your friend? That was brave and mature."

I looked up at her—a pure-blood. This all seemed strange to me. It took me a couple of minutes to make sense of my own mixed-up thoughts and emotions over what she'd told me of my mother and father. "How did she met him—my dad? There aren't many mortals around the Covenants. Did he work on Bald Head?"

Laadan's smile seemed off, nervous almost. She pushed away from the table, running her hands over her arms. "She met him in North Carolina."

There was more to it than that, which filled me with all the more curiosity. So Mom had loved a mortal for many moons. They weren't the first or last, I imagined. "What was he doing there? How did he die?"

A loud crash caused us both to jump. I whirled around, expecting to see a crap ton of books on the floor.

Laadan laughed nervously. "I forget that there are things here that move unseen."

I looked at her sharply. "What do you mean? Spirits?"

She blinked and laughed again. "Yes, spirits. I'm a bit superstitious. This library doesn't help, creepy as it is. I think one of the shelves collapsed in the stack." Laadan came to my side, scanning the rows quickly and I thought a bit anxiously. "It happens from time to time. Anyway, if you are anything like Rachelle, you love ice cream and pie."

I swung back to her. "Vanilla—"

"And pumpkin pie," she finished, smiling. "I know where we can score some. Interested?"

My mouth watered. "I'm always interested in anything food related."

"Good." She threaded her arm through mine. "Let's go gorge ourselves until we swear off food."

At the door, I shivered and looked over my shoulder. The feeling of eyes boring into my back was uncanny, but no one was there—no one that I could see.

†

My father would be proud of me, even after all the stupid things I'd done—and probably would still do? It seemed hard to believe, but Laadan had known him and she had no reason to lie to me.

"Alex, are you even paying attention to me?"

"Huh?" I blinked, glancing up from my rock. We were in a wooded area off of the labyrinth, a few hours into our afternoon practice. "Yeah, I heard you. Dodge. Run. Stuff."

Seth folded his arms.

"What?" I stood and brushed off my rear.

"I think you just fell asleep. That would hurt my feelings—if I had any."

"Sorry. You're kind of boring me."

"Well, okay then. Let's get to work." Seth held up his hand, like he was going to throw a baseball. A blue ball of flames formed in his open palm. He released the tiny ball, launching it straight at my head.

I ducked easily. "Boring."

Seth let go of another ball, but this time he sent it at my feet. I jumped onto the rock and yawned loudly. A devilish grin pulled at his lips as he slowly approached me. My foot caught him in the shoulder as soon as he came within reach. He retaliated by sending two balls of flames—one at my head and one at my legs. It took some fancy footwork to avoid them, but I did and I still managed to stay atop the rock.

I stuck my tongue out. "You can do better than that."

He threw up his hands and a gust of wind hit me square in the chest. There was nothing I could do to block something like that.

"Remember to tuck and roll," Seth called out, laughter in his voice.

If I hadn't been flying through the air, I would have flipped him off. However, I did remember to tuck and roll. I hit the cool patch of grass shoulders first. I didn't give my body a chance to recognize the impact. Rolling onto my feet, I suspected Seth would be making his move.

I was right.

A ball of fire grazed my head as I darted to the side. We went at this until he hit me with the element of air, knocked me down, and didn't let go. Pinned to the dirty ground, I glared up at him.

"Get up," he ordered, standing above me.

"I can't get up. And you know that."

Seth cocked his head to the side and sighed. "This is getting old, Alex. You excel at every aspect of fighting—not as good as me, but who am I kidding? No one is better than me."

I rolled my eyes. "You like to hear yourself talk, don't you?"

"Why, yes. Yes I do."

"That's why you don't have any friends."

"And the last time I checked, I'm *your* only friend."

My jaw clicked shut. Score one for Seth.

"But that's not the topic of discussion. We are discussing that fact that you cannot break through the air element, and it's the most common element pures and daimons can wield. That's a problem."

"Gee, you think so?"

He increased the pressure until it felt like someone was sitting on my chest. I squirmed, but that was about all. "What did I tell you about the elements, Alex?"

"Something about… magic being… all in the head," I gasped.

"No. The elements are very real—obviously. You have to force yourself through it, Alex. Push."

I still didn't get what he meant by *push*, but he kept telling me to do it every time this happened.

"If you can't push through it than you're going to be a daimon snack again, Alex. They're going to smell that aether in you and go crazy. You sure you want to be a Sentinel?"

Now he was just pissing me off. "Shut up, Seth."

He stepped over me, planting his legs on either side of my prone body. Crouching down, he brought his face close to mine. "Remember, you're not fast food to them; you're like the best steak this side of the continent."

"You say that… like it's a good thing."

Seth smiled like he knew some kind of private joke. "Concentrate. You need to concentrate on moving forward. Picture yourself sitting up, Alex."

I stared at him.

He sighed, rolling his eyes. "Close your eyes and picture yourself sitting up."

Cursing under my breath, I did as he asked. I closed my eyes and pictured myself sitting up. "Okay."

"Focus on that image. Hold it in your mind. Focus."

I did as he asked, but all I managed was to get one leg to bend. And that exhausted me. "This is ridiculous. A daimon would've already killed me by now."

"A daimon would've already bitten into your skin by now." His eyes fastened onto mine, refusing to let go. "But you know that, don't you?"

A ragged breath leaked from my tightly pressed lips. My skin practically burned at the reminder, and Seth knew it.

"How many times were you tagged, Alex?" Seth reached down and brushed the hair off my neck. "I can count at least three on this side of your neck."

"Stop," I hissed.

His fingers moved over the scars on the other side. "I see three more, Alex." Then his fingers dipped under the collar of my thermal, brushing over more scars. "How many here? Two or three… or even more than that? Want to add more? No? Then sit up."

I tried, because I badly wanted to knock him upside the head. Every muscle in my body tensed, but I still couldn't break through the hold. "Stop it now."

Frustration flared in his eyes. "How many are there on your arms?"

"Stop it!" Something shifted in me, a sense of deep awareness. Suddenly, everything around me seemed acute and vivid. The overcast sky was more muddled, the cawing of the crows sounded closer, and the golden hue of Seth's skin became a pearly luster.

"Then sit up! Break this hold, Alex!"

A couple of things happened next.

I felt the rage snap deep inside my core—a tightly coiled ball of energy unraveled. It was so strong, so vibrant, that I imagined it looked like the cord I'd seen wrap around Seth and me the first time we'd touched.

Seth leaned in, going for my arm this time. Too close, he was *way* too close. The coil raised, my heart stopped, and something—the rock I'd stood on—blew up.

The shattering boulder startled Seth enough that he let go of the crushing wind. Every muscle in my body had been straining to sit up. So when he let go, I flew up so fast I rammed right into him. The impact of my body knocked Seth flat on his back. His arms immediately swept around me.

I wasn't sure what that had to do with practice.

We remained that way for a second, both of us struggling to breathe. I couldn't process it or even begin to understand what had happened.

"Alex…?"

I pushed off his chest and stared down at him. The marks of the Apollyon shifted over his skin crazy fast. I'd never seen them move quite like that before. "Um…"

Seth's eyes were wild, practically glowing. "I didn't do that."

"Me, neither."

"Bull." His expression was full of amazement.

I swallowed. "Okay. Maybe I did."

"What did it feel like inside, when it happened?"

"I don't know, kind of like a coiling feeling in my stomach."

His lips parted, working slowly. "This can't be possible, but it is. You're Awakening already. I don't believe it, but it explains how you've been able to sense my emotions."

"What?" I started to sit up, but his hands dropped to my hips, holding me in place. "What do you mean I'm Awakening? Am I like ahead of schedule or something?"

Seth tried to laugh, but it came out more like a gasp. "No. I don't know. I mean, who knows? Right? The other two Apollyon were never around each other before Solaris Awakened. He only sensed Solaris *after* she Awakened. Maybe… maybe this is what happens. Has anything like this happened before?"

"Yeah, I blow up rocks in my spare time. Jeez. No." I started to move again. "Seth, you can let go."

He smiled the kind of smile that warmed his features. "I don't think I'm ready to. And get that freaked look off your face. This isn't a bad thing, Alex. No—nope, not at all. This is good. We can start working on your powers and…"

I tuned him out. The freaked-out look on my face had nothing to do with blowing up rocks. I had long come to terms with the fact that I'd be some weapon of mass destruction one day. The look came from the fact our bodies were touching in all the strategic places bodies liked to touch.

"Alex, are you listening to me?"

"Yes." I stared at the runes gliding down his neck. When they reached his pulse they throbbed. I shifted my weight. A raw ache hit me hard. I wanted to touch them—needed to touch them. Something, I was sure, would happen if I did.

"You are so not paying attention to me." Seth sighed. The movement brought us closer. "You know," Seth was saying, "this opens up so many possibilities. We—"

I reached out my right hand and touched the rune on his neck, where his pulse pounded, with just the tip of one finger. A burst of crackling blue light flared. The light split, one strain shooting through the tip of my fingers, the other pulsating over his neck. Pinpricks of pain burst across my hand, searing and intense.

Seth's back bowed as his fingers dug into me. Under my left hand, his chest rose and fell rapidly. His eyes snapped open, wide and unseeing. The glyphs on his face shifted shapes and changed color, becoming a shade of blue that mirrored the sky seconds before dusk.

The air popped and fizzed as the blue light spilled onto the ground, and out of that blue light, another shone much brighter, more intense.

An amber cord radiated from the glyph on his neck, quickly twining itself around my finger, twisting over my hand, up my wrist… trying to connect us once again.

CHAPTER 18

I JERKED MY HAND BACK AND IT FOLLOWED ME, AN amber line arching through the space between us. I needed to get up—get away, and put as much distance between us as possible, because this was weird as hell. "I—"

The amber cord vanished, as did the blue light. Seth fell back to the ground, letting out a ragged sigh.

"Seth? Are you okay?" I clutched my throbbing hand to my chest. Seth wasn't moving, wasn't talking. Fear blossomed in my chest. What if I'd killed Seth? I knew I'd said I wanted to kill him—I'd said it a lot—but I hadn't meant it. Not really. "Seth, please say something."

An eternity passed before his eyes opened. "That… felt wonderful."

A sudden wave of dizziness crashed over me and my stomach dropped.

Seth's head lolled to the side, his smile lazy and faint. "I'm pretty sure I could stop a truck with my hand right now."

"Okay…" I took a shallow breath. "That tells me nothing. And I really want to know what happened when I touched your marks—"

Seth twisted up, rolling me onto my back in one fluid motion. Hovering above me, he used one arm to support himself. Only our legs touched, but it still felt like… well, like every part of us was still touching. "Angel, that's like Apollyon foreplay right there."

"For real?"

"For real." He reached out and brushed a strand of hair off my cheek.

I swallowed. "I didn't know that. My bad, but that's kind of weird. Usually takes more with most guys." I had no idea why I just said that.

Seth's fingers trailed over my cheek, down to my chin. "Does it, Angel? Well, what does it take?"

This was probably a conversation not to have with Seth, especially when he was practically lying on top of me. "I think you of all people would know."

His hand slipped to my neck. "I have a secret to tell you. It's not Apollyon foreplay; I'm just messing with you. I have no clue what that was."

"Gods, I hate you." Flushed with embarrassment, I knocked his hand away.

Seth caught my hand and sat up, pulling me along with him. "How do you feel?"

"Fine. I'm just a little dizzy."

He nodded. "I'll tell you what, my skin still tingles. Man—that was one hell of a rush. I've never felt anything like it." He turned my hand over, palm up. "We should try it—*what the hell?*" His fingers slid over my palm as he studied it, then his eyes widened. "Oh. Wow."

"What?"

He held my hand up between us. "Look."

I squinted at my hand. "I don't see anything." Sighing, he flipped my hand over, and my jaw hit the ground. A faint blue line marked the center of my palm with a smaller line through it. It would've looked like a cross, except the horizontal line was slanted.

"Oh. My. Gods." I jerked my hand away, scrambling back. "I have a rune on my hand. It's an Apollyon rune, isn't it?"

Seth rested his hands on his knees. "I think so. I have one like that."

"But why is it still there? Why is it there at all?" I flipped my palm over several times, shook it, but the faint blue tattoo was still there. "You can see it, right? Like right now, you can see it?"

"Yes. It hasn't faded." Seth leaned forward, catching my hand. "Stop shaking it like it's a damn Etch-A-Sketch. That doesn't make them disappear."

I met his eyes with my own wide ones. "What makes them go away? Yours go away. They're not there all the time. I haven't Awakened, have I? Wait—what if I have? Need or want something, and I'll see if I want it, too. Go ahead. Try it."

His brows flew up. "Whoa. Alex, calm down. Take a deep breath. I mean it. Take a nice, long and deep breath."

I inhaled and let it out slowly. "That didn't help."

He looked like he wanted to laugh. "Alex, stop freaking out. You haven't Awakened. I would know, and while I do feel a somewhat different—"

"How do you feel different?"

"I feel… more charged, but you haven't Awakened."

I exhaled roughly. "Then what happened?"

Seth's face softened and all traces of smugness and coldness vanished, revealing a youthful, earnest quality I'd never seen before. "I think… it's just another product of the connection between us. Minutes before, you used the earth element—earth, Alex. That's one of the most powerful elements. And I don't know how you did that, but I think you were probably feeding off me. That makes sense."

"It does?"

He nodded. "I think so. I also think that's what happened when you touched me—by the way, why did you touch me?"

I glanced down at my mark, blushing. "I… don't know."

"You really don't know why?"

I scowled. "No."

"Whatever." Seth didn't sound like he believed me. "All right, this is nothing to freak out about, right?"

"Right."

"Nothing has changed, really, and everything is okay. You following me? Everything is okay. We're in this together."

In that instant, he reminded me of Aiden—when I'd found out about being an Apollyon and Aiden had coached me through it. I climbed to my feet. My legs felt like rubber. "Are we done with practice?"

He stayed on his knees, lifting his head. "Yes."

I nodded and turned away, but Seth called out to me. "Alex, I don't think we should tell anyone about this, all right?"

"Okay." I could agree with that. I started back to the main house, mind reeling. I looked down at my hand. I had a mark of the Apollyon already.

One that didn't seem to fade.

During dinner, I excused myself after the first course. They did the four-course meal thing and I usually stuck around for dessert, but tonight was different. My mind was on my tingling palm.

Aiden eyed me curiously, but didn't remark on my lack of appetite. However, I felt Seth stand and follow me out of the dining hall.

"Are you feeling okay?" asked Seth.

My gaze flicked up to his eyes. They looked abnormally bright tonight, like two mini suns burning. "Yeah, I'm just not hungry."

He gave me a knowing look as he reached down and picked up my right hand. He turned it over. "It's still there."

I nodded. "I tried to wash it off earlier."

Seth gave a startled laugh. "Oh, Alex, you can't wash it off."

My cheeks flushed. "Yeah, I know that now."

He ran his thumb over the rune's straight line, eliciting a sharp gasp from me. I felt the butterfly touch all the way to the small bones in my fingers. I yanked my hand free and backed up.

His eyes narrowed on me. "What did you feel?"

I curled my hand, covering the rune. "It just felt weird."

Seth reached for my hand again, but I dodged him. He shot me an annoyed look. "What are you planning to do now?"

I debated on telling him it was none of his business. "I'm feeling a little keyed up. I think I'm going to work it off or something."

He smiled. "Want me to go with you?"

"No." I shook my head. "I need some time alone."

Surprisingly, Seth dropped it and went back into the dining hall. I rushed upstairs and grabbed my hoodie, then took off for the training arena.

It didn't take much for me to get worked up, swinging and kicking a dummy. Seth didn't prefer to work with them. He was into the whole contact thing.

Go figure.

I don't know how much time had passed as I beat the crap out of the dummy, but when I stopped, I was panting and covered in sweat. I rested my hands on my knees. The dummy swayed in front of me. Fighting had done nothing to get rid of the overall frustration of… *everything.*

I straightened and turned over my right hand.

The blue rune was faint but there. I stalked over to where I'd dropped my hoodie and pulled it on.

A fine shiver crept over me. Turning around, I scanned the empty training room. It was the same feeling I'd gotten the night I'd left Marcus's office. Like a warning, telling me I wasn't alone. I wasn't going to ignore it.

The overhead lights flickered once and then went out, plunging the room into darkness. I wished I had super-vision or something, because I couldn't see crap. Not even where the door was, and I really wanted to get out of this room. All my senses were screaming at me to go. Something was wrong, something wasn't—

Air stirred behind me, lifting the damp hair at the base of my neck, caressing the skin with a lover's touch. I whipped around, striking out into nothing but air.

My breath came out harsh, my voice pitched high. "Who's there?"

Nothing… and then I heard, *"Alexandria, listen to me."*

The words—oh, gods, the words smoothed over my skin like the richest silk. My arms fell to my sides as my eyes drifted shut. A small part of my brain that was still working recognized the compulsion, but that thought flickered out.

I felt the air stir again. A hand slipped around the nape of my neck, a soft voice whispered in my ear. My thoughts flashed in and out until they were devoid of any meaning. Then they were filled with instructions the conscious part of me couldn't recognize, but I would follow nonetheless.

"Okay," I heard myself say in this dreamlike voice.

Vaguely, I was aware of the air stilling around me and the lights coming back on. I floated out of the training room. Outside, in the near frigid temperatures, maybe I'd just float right up into the night sky.

I think I'd like that.

I found myself standing at the mouth of the dark labyrinth. I was supposed to be here. My body knew that. I bent down slowly and untied my shoelaces. My fingers slipped over the knots a few times, but I finally got them and my socks off. I placed them side-by-side on the frozen ground. I pulled off my sweatshirt and folded it neatly. I placed that atop my shoes.

Then I entered the labyrinth, smiling as the cool air washed over my bare arms, still slick with sweat. I roamed aimlessly, having no clear purpose other than to keep walking until I was too tired to walk. That was what I was supposed to do—place one foot in front of the other.

It started snowing.

Beautiful, large flakes fell from the sky, landing on my arms. Each piece felt like it belonged there—like I belonged here. The grass crunched under my toes as I continued further into the maze. Snow encased my hair, sticking to my cold skin. My breath puffed out in pockets of steam, eventually slowing.

Hours must have passed, because each step became more difficult than the one before. I stumbled, hitting the hard ground on my knees and the palms of my hand. My skin looked strange beside the snow-covered ground. Blue? Not entirely blue, but like the veins under my skin were leaking, tinting my flesh with a faint violet hue.

It was so pretty.

I pushed to my feet and swayed off balance. I was tired, but I could make it a little further. I kept walking. Well, tripping really. I couldn't feel my toes, and my skin felt pleasantly numb. Stumbling again, this time into an ice-cold statue, I slid down the marble, feeling the rougher edges pull at my skin. It should have hurt, but as I sat there, I realized I didn't feel anything.

Somehow, I was on my back, staring up at the winged statue. He looked down upon me, arm outstretched, palm open. I willed my arm to move but it wouldn't lift. My gaze drifted beyond the statue as I drew in a shallow breath that didn't seem to fill my lungs. The sky was dotted with small flakes that eventually made their way down to me. My lids grew too heavy to stay open, and it was only seconds before the snow caked my lashes. I thought I heard a desolate cry in a beautiful language, but then there was nothing.

CHAPTER 19

"WHAT WAS SHE DOING OUT THERE?"

"I don't know. I find it hard to believe she somehow mistook it for summer! Why hasn't she woken up yet?"

The voices sounded familiar to me. My right palm burned. Everything burned actually—really freaking burned.

Someone moved something warm and heavy over me. It made my skin scream.

"She'll be fine," a woman said. "She just needs rest."

"Needs rest?" That sounded like Seth, but he didn't sound right to me. His musical voice was pitched wrong. "She *was blue* when Leon brought her in."

Leon brought me in? From where? Why had I been blue? Blue didn't sound good.

"The girl is lucky. A few more minutes and she would have lost a finger or four, but she is fine," the woman said again, irritation lacing her words. "There is nothing more to be done."

Wait? What the hell? Lose fingers?

I heard a door shut, and then the bed dipped beside me. Someone brushed my hair back off my face. Seth. I tried to open my eyes, but they felt annoyingly heavy.

"Where did she say she was going when she left dinner?"

My heart sped up, recognizing Aiden's voice. Why couldn't I open my eyes? And why was I so damn tired?

"She said she was going to practice," answered Seth.

“And you let her go by herself?” That was my uncle speaking. Only he could sound so coldly displeased and yet cultured.

“I’m not her babysitter,” snapped Seth. “She didn’t want me to go with her.”

“Alex shouldn’t be roaming around here alone.” Aiden’s anger filled his voice. “Dammit, she knows better than this.”

Seth snorted.

“Even though Alex is prone to idiotic behavior, I seriously doubt she’s responsible for this one,” said Aiden.

Gee, thanks, I thought sleepily. I kind of wished they’d all shut up so I could go back to sleep. My skin didn’t burn when I slept.

“She wouldn’t go skipping through a maze dressed like it’s summer and almost die from hypothermia,” Aiden continued. “Someone did this to her.”

“You’re suggesting a compulsion?” Seth’s voice lowered. “You know pures are forbidden from using compulsions on halfs who aren’t indentured. Would one dare?”

“What do you think?” asked Aiden.

“I think I’m going to kill someone,” Seth replied casually.

Marcus sighed. “I’ll speak with Minister Telly first thing in the morning. He assured me there would be no trouble here.”

They continued on for a few moments, their voices drifting further away as I fell back into the blissful oblivion where my skin felt normal. I awoke a little while later, shivering uncontrollably. The room was quiet and dark when I opened my eyes.

I wanted to get up and grab a thermal, but my muscles didn’t want to cooperate. Whimpering, I fell back to the hard mattress and willed a nice heavy blanket to appear out of the thin air. Too bad I didn’t have any powers like that.

Suddenly, the bed shifted and a dark shadow leaned over me. If it weren’t for the bright yellow eyes, I would’ve screamed. “How are you feeling?”

“I’m c-cold,” I gasped out.

“They brought in extra blankets. You’re still cold?”

"Uh-huh." My teeth chattered. I heard Seth sigh, and then I felt his hands sliding underneath me, rolling me onto my side. "W-what are you doing?"

"Getting you warm, since we already have every blanket known to mankind on this craptastic bed." He pulled me back against his chest and wrapped his arms around me. "Wow, you are cold. Like a little popsicle."

I squeezed my eyes shut. "I wasn't s-suggesting this."

He rested his chin against the top of my head. "Do you have any better suggestions?"

"Yeah, g-go get more blankets?"

"That wouldn't be nearly as fun as this."

I didn't respond to that, because truthfully, Seth was really hot. Hot in a totally platonic, body-warming way. Then his leg slipped in between mine and my eyes snapped open. "S-Seth!"

"Just making sure you are warming up. Is it working?" Seth shifted his arms under the blanket, one hand finding the curve of my hip.

I bit down on my lip. Yes, I was warming up.

"Alex?"

"Yeah?" I wiggled uncomfortably and stopped when Seth's hand tightened on my hip.

"What were you doing in the maze tonight with half your clothes off?"

"What?" I squeaked.

"You… don't remember?" Seth slipped his hand under the hem of my shirt. "Your stomach is ice cold."

And his hand was really warm. I told myself that was the reason why I didn't break his arm. "N-no, I don't k-know what you're talking about."

"Okay. Do you remember talking to me after dinner?"

What a stupid question. "Yes."

"Did you go to the training rooms?"

"Yeah."

"What happened after that, Alex?"

"I worked with the dummy for a little while and then…" I frowned. Then what? I remembered walking over the corner and putting on my hoodie. "The lights went out."

"In the training room?"

I nodded, still concentrating. My memories floated just out of reach, like a word lost on the tip of my tongue. "I don't know."

Seth stiffened. "You don't remember anything else?"

There was a huge blank spot where nothing existed. I rolled onto my back, only making out his eyes in the darkness. "Can you fill me in on what happened?"

"I was kind of hoping you'd be able to do that, Alex. We don't know what happened. Leon found your shoes and sweater at the beginning of the labyrinth. Obviously, that concerned him greatly. He found you in there, half-frozen."

"What? I didn't do that." I reached down and placed a hand on his creeping one. It was moving a little too far north. "Well, I don't remember doing that, and that sounds really stupid."

Seth's fingers curled beneath my ribs. "Do you remember talking to any pures?"

"No. I don't remember anything after the lights going out." I paused, feeling slightly nauseous as I picked up on Seth's suspicions. "Do… do you think a pure used compulsion on me?"

He didn't answer immediately. "Yes."

"But that doesn't make any sense. Why would a pure compel me to walk the maze? Of all the things they could compel me to do and they…" I closed my mouth. I had no idea what the pure had compelled me to do. Walking through the maze could have been just one part of it. Anything could've happened. I had no idea and that made me sick. Compulsion was a violation, pure and simple. It stripped a person's free will, and their ability to say no.

It was straight out mind-rape.

But why couldn't I remember what'd happened? I'd only been compelled once, and that had been when Aiden made me sleep the night they'd found me in the warehouse. I remembered everything about that.

"Alex?" Seth moved his hand out from underneath the blankets and cupped my face. My stomach kind of missed his hand. "Are you remembering something?"

"Do you think I was compelled to forget the compulsion? Is that even possible?"

"It is possible. A compulsion is limitless."

I swallowed. "I had clothes on, right? Just my shoes and sweater were missing?"

"Yes," His voice sounded strained. "I think it's best that you don't go anywhere without someone being with you, Alex. I know you hate that idea—"

"They sent me out to freeze to death," I said, stunned by the realization. "I would've died if Leon hadn't found me."

"Like I said, I think it's best that you don't go anywhere without someone with you."

I wanted to punch someone. I also wanted to cry. I didn't like this helpless feeling, this not knowing. I drew in a breath and let it out slowly. "I want to know who did this."

"We'll find out. Trust me on that. But you need to get some rest now."

Sleep didn't seem like an option, but Seth rolled onto his back, bringing me along for the ride. I was too caught up in my own thoughts to protest his possessiveness. My head rested against his chest as I stared into the darkness.

Quiet as he was, I knew Seth didn't sleep that night either.

A few hours into light practice a day later, Council Guards arrived and stated that Minister Telly wanted to see me. Clearly only my presence had been requested, but Seth refused to leave my side.

The Council session had paused for lunch, and we were led to an elaborate office inside the Council building. I'd never seen so many gold-plated things in my life. What was left of my family was present: Marcus and Lucian. They were seated on luxurious leather chairs. I decided to stand, which meant Seth stood directly behind me.

Telly gazed out a circular window, a glass of dark wine in his hand. He turned around, his pale gaze flickering past me, narrowing on Seth. "Miss Andros, I apologize for interrupting your training, but I wanted to express my sincere relief to see that you were not permanently injured due to such a misfortunate event."

He didn't sound sincere. "Someone used a compulsion on me," I said. "I wouldn't consider that a *misfortunate event*."

"I would have to agree," Lucian said. "My stepdaughter is not given to flights of fancy."

Telly pushed away from the window, his eyes settling on my stepfather. "I would hope not, but I can assure you there is no one here who would be so audacious to use a compulsion against a guest of mine."

"Then what are you suggesting, Minister?" asked Marcus. Today he was dressed in a navy blue suit. I'd kill to see the man in jeans.

"I am as curious as you to find out how Miss Andros ended up in that predicament," Telly said. "I have my best Guards investigating the matter. Perhaps they will discover what truly happened."

"You say it like I'm somehow responsible for what happened," I said, which earned me a bland look from Telly.

"I know we are rather lax around here in regards to drinking." Telly took a leisurely sip of his wine. "Did you have anything to drink with your dinner?"

My mouth dropped open. "I wasn't drunk!"

"Alexandria," Marcus's head snapped in my direction. Turning back to the Minister, he smiled politely. "I can attest that Alexandria didn't drink at dinner."

"Hmm? What about afterwards?" asked Telly.

"I spoke with her afterwards and she went straight to the training arena." Seth's annoyance with the whole thing radiated from him.

Telly's brows rose. "You'd cover for her, would you not? Since she is yours and your fates are so intricately tied together?"

"I'm not—"

"Are you calling me a liar?" Seth cut me off, his annoyance flipping right into fury.

Lucian stood, smoothing his robes. "Minister Telly, I trust you are taking this event seriously. If not, I cannot agree to keeping Alexandria here."

"She must give her statement at Council."

"She also must be kept safe and that is the priority," replied Lucian. "Not her statement."

Telly took another drink, his pale gaze falling back to Seth and me. "Of course I take her safety very seriously. After all, she is such a rarity, and we would not want anything to happen to the Council's precious Apollyon."

†

"*The Council's precious Apollyon,*" I spat, swinging out harder than I probably should. They hadn't been Seth's words, but he was the only target I had. He barely dodged me. "This 'precious Apollyon' is going to shove her foot so far up his—"

Seth caught my fist. "Alex, if you don't take it down a notch we're going to stop. I don't know why I agreed to spar with you when you're in this kind of mood."

Stepping back, I wiped my forearm across my forehead. "I loathe the way he speaks, the way he looks at us like he wished he could zap us into oblivion."

"And you shouldn't be practicing this hard," Seth continued as if he hadn't heard me. "You were an ice cube not too long ago. You need to take it easy."

"Stop babying me. I feel great." That wasn't a lie, even though the chilly air whipping through the clearing made me feel a little icky.

Seth sighed. He was getting really good at the sighing thing. This one said *I don't know what to do you with sometimes.*

"And he hates half-bloods. Did you know that?" I continued, lashing out with a fierce back kick. Seth deflected that. "Aiden told me so. Did you also know that he'd like to see all half-bloods enslaved? Even Lucian thinks he'd like to see things go back to the old way. Jerk-off, stupid mother—"

Seth caught my shoulders, giving me a little shake. "Okay. I get it. You hate Telly. Guess what, everyone does, but he controls the entire Council, Alex."

I was breathing heavily, sucking in cold air. "I know that!"

He smiled. "With him controlling the Council, nothing will change. The Breed Order will remain the same. If anything, the lives of half-bloods will get worse."

"Oh, well, that makes me feel so much better. Thanks."

"But—but listen to me, Alex." A look of eagerness crept over his face. "When you Awaken, we can change the Council. We have supporters, Alex. People who would surprise you." He brushed a strand of hair off my check.

I swatted his hand away. "Don't touch me. I don't need any more never-fading-magical-runes to appear."

Seth dropped his hands, grinning. "Still hasn't faded?"

I shoved my hand in his face. "Still there?"

"Yep."

"You don't have to sound so happy about it." I dipped around him, stopping. We had company.

Cross, Will, and Boobs stood at the edge of the field. Will held a small cooler in his hand. "We thought you guys could use some drinks since you missed the party."

Seth fell into an easy banter with them while I fiddled with the string on my pants. "Drinks" consisted of cheap wine coolers that Caleb would've laughed at, but I was so thirsty I wasn't complaining. Once Seth shut up long enough to allow someone else to talk, Will began drilling me about the daimon battles I'd taken part in. Cross watched on with this sort of hero-worship look on his face, which was so different from the ones sent my way in North Carolina. None of them here knew the whole story surrounding my rise to fame—or the crash and burn I'd taken on my way down. I wanted to keep it that way. I relaxed on the rock eventually, sipping my drink while I answered their questions.

“So how many times were you tagged?” asked Cross, two wine coolers in hand.

Will turned to his friend slowly. “Dude, that’s not a question you ask someone. You fail.”

I froze. Unintentionally, I had exposed my neck by flipping my hair back. Flushing, I tipped my head so my hair fell forward in a heavy curtain. Seth, who’d been in a deep conversation with Boobs—probably about himself—pulled his head out of gods know where, and twisted around to us.

Cross grimaced. “I’m sorry. I didn’t mean to… offend you. It’s just that I think it’s awesome that you fought daimons and survived. Not that you were tagged, of course. That’s not awesome. That’s pretty messed up.”

Will rolled his eyes, groaning. “Just shut up, Cross.”

“No. It’s okay.” I cleared my throat, deciding if I didn’t make a big deal about it then none of them would. “I don’t know how many times. A couple, I guess.”

Cross looked relieved, but then Seth stood, and Cross shifted further back. I watched him stride between us and stop, blocking both Cross and Will as he faced me. I had no idea what he was doing, but what came out of his mouth wasn’t even on the possibility list.

“Dance with me.”

I stared up at him. “What?”

Seth bowed gracefully, extending one arm to me. “Dance with me, *please*?”

“Why do you want to dance in the middle of a field, Seth?”

“Why not?” He wiggled his fingers. “Dance with me, *pretty please.*”

“With sugar on top,” Will added, chuckling.

Seth’s grin grew to epic proportions. “Dance with me, Alexandria.”

Over his shoulder, I spotted Boobs eyeing the whole thing with a pouty, displeased look. I don’t know if that made me take Seth’s hand or the fact he was embarrassing the hell out of me. Seth yanked me to my feet, keeping my one arm outstretched while placing my other around his back.

Then he started waltzing around the field—with no music.

It was so ridiculous that I had laugh. We rounded a boulder, tripping over the uneven ground. Seth knew how to dance—really dance—like the kind people did in ballrooms. With one arm, he spun me out from him.

I giggled. "Did you pick this up from watching *Dancing with the Stars*?"

"You mock me." Seth spun me so my back was against his chest. "You wound my sensibilities when I'm trying to help you."

"Help me with what?"

Seth twirled me around. "You need to know how to dance without a pole if you're going to the ball."

I smacked him on the chest. "I don't dance like a stripper and I'm not going to that stupid ball."

He didn't respond. Grinning, he slipped his hand up my back and dipped me over his arm. I laughed and let my head fall back. I could see Boobs on her rock. Very slowly, when she was sure she had Seth's attention in that nanosecond he had me bent backward, she licked her lips.

Seth dropped me.

Much later, after the sun had fallen and we were covered in mud, Seth and I slipped past the dining hall. Trying not to bring attention to ourselves, we moved as quietly as possible.

I rubbed my aching rear and caught Seth watching me. "Your fault," I whispered.

"You're never going to let me forget that, are you?"

"You dropped me on my butt."

He tipped his head back, laughing softly. "I blame the wine coolers."

"I blame Boobs."

Grinning madly, Seth grabbed my hand and hurried me down the hall. We passed several quiet rooms, and then we heard Marcus, loud and clear. "I have no idea if Lucian is planning anything!"

We stopped and looked at each other.

"Are you not close with him?" I heard Telly ask.

"Lucian keeps a lot secret, just like every one of you does," Marcus responded angrily.

Seth pulled me under the stoop beside the room Marcus and Telly occupied, pressing me against the wall. He didn't have to get *that* close. "Come on, Seth. Back—"

"Shh." He tipped his head toward mine, strands of his hair swept against my cheeks. "This feels naughty."

I shot him a dirty look.

"I know he's up to something!" said Telly. "He thinks he can control him, but he is foolish for believing so."

Seth straightened an inch, a slight frown pulling at his lips.

"Even Lucian is not that foolish," Marcus responded.

Telly made a disgusted sound. "It is my job as a Minister to protect them—my duty! If you know something—"

"I know nothing of the sort!" Marcus slapped something down. "You are being paranoid, Minister."

"You call it being paranoid, and I call it planning for the future. There are certain precautions we could take—just in case. Ways to ensure that they are never threatened."

I wondered what they were talking about. Seth also had a puzzled look on his face, which almost made me giggle. Maybe the wine coolers were still in my system. He must've felt the laugh bubbling up in me, because he looked down at me and smiled.

"What are you suggesting, Minister?"

"There are ways of eliminating the threat—ways in which no one is harmed. Some of the Council members agree that it may be best to do so."

When Marcus spoke next, his words were cold and flat. "Has the Council already acted on this?"

Telly scoffed. "What are you insinuating, Marcus?"

There was a stretch of silence. "And how would you eliminate the threat, pray tell?"

The tension that followed Marcus's question was so thick I could feel it. "We already have one here," replied Telly. "Why not keep them both here?"

There was a stretch of silence. "That is out of the question. I am sorry, but I cannot agree to that."

"Perhaps you just some need time and motivation. You want that Council seat very badly. I could make it happen."

Seth dropped his head, his breath warm against my neck. I tried to move back, but there wasn't anywhere to go. "Do you know what they're talking about?" he whispered.

For a second I had to think about what he was asking. I felt kind of out of it. "No clue."

"I do not believe my mind will change," Marcus finally responded. "It is late, Minister. And this conversation is over."

Seth's lips brushed against my neck, right under my ear. I jerked from the unexpected touch, and then socked him in the stomach. He chuckled softly.

Telly laughed mirthlessly. "My offer stands until the end of sessions."

"Good evening, Minister Telly."

We ducked into the adjoining room, shutting the door just in time. Telly exited seconds later, followed by Marcus. Seth and I stared at each other. There was something in his eyes, mischief definitely, but something else. He prowled toward me, grinning.

I put my hand up, flattening it against his chest. My pulse sped up. "Playtime is over, Seth."

He placed his hand over mine. "Sounds like a bit of bribery going on."

"That doesn't surprise me." I gave the room a brief glance. We were in another sitting room. How many of these things were there? "I'm a little surprised over how much Marcus dislikes Telly."

Shrugging, Seth went to the door and peered out. "All clear." He paused, grinning over his shoulder. "Unless you want to stay here a little while. That couch looks comfy."

I shoved past him. "Can't you think of anything else?"

He followed me out. "No. Not really."

"Wow. You're so multi-dimensional, Seth."

Chuckling, he sidled up to my side and dropped his arm over my shoulders. "And you're such a killjoy."

CHAPTER 20

OVER THE NEXT COUPLE OF DAYS, SETH CONSUMED most of my time. I saw very little of Aiden and Marcus. Once, when Seth wasn't attached to my hip, I hung out with Laadan while she got a mani and pedi for the ball. I opted out of the indulgence.

People touching my feet creeped me out.

Seth and I had snuck into one of the training classrooms between practices and sparred with some of the halfs the other day. I think we caused more mayhem than anything else, but I'd enjoyed fighting people other than Seth. Goofing off eased some of the pent-up frustration of being in this place, and the growing unease that occupied each day closer to my Council session.

But time with Seth hadn't been all fun and games. We'd spent most of our training sessions working on avoiding the use of elements in battle. Throwing balls of flame around really wasn't an indoor sport, so we were forced outside.

We also argued. A lot.

He got pissy because he claimed I'd been watching Aiden when he'd shown up one day during our practice and worked out alongside us. Seth also claimed that I'd drooled on myself.

Not true.

Flushing with embarrassment and anger, I'd stormed off and left him standing in the middle of the field we'd practiced in. A short hour later, Seth reappeared with hamburgers and fries—my favorite—and I kind of forgave him. He'd had hamburgers; what else could I have done?

I still had no recollection of how I'd ended up in the maze. Not knowing what'd happened—or why a pure would do that—nagged at me. So did the conversation we'd overheard between Marcus and Lucian. I couldn't shake the feeling that those two events were connected.

But that could just be my paranoia.

Today's practice had been cut short as Seth had something important to discuss with Lucian. When I'd asked what it was, he'd told me not to worry my pretty little butt over it and to go hang out with Laadan.

I hate boys.

And I couldn't find Laadan anywhere.

Even though it irked me that no one wanted me to roam around alone, I didn't want to end up a pure's compulsion toy again. Thinking about that filled me with enough anger I could have put my fist through the wall. After checking out a million sitting rooms, I gave up on my search for Laadan. Another long and boring evening staring at the white walls in my room awaited me.

With barely restrained aggravation, I turned the corner and froze.

Up ahead, a female servant trembled on her knees. She'd dropped a stack of dishes on the carpet. The man towering over her wore the unmistakable—and terrifying—garb of a Master. I'd only seen one once before, and that had been when Mom had brought me before the Council when I was seven.

I'd never forget the blood red tunic or how they shaved their heads and *all* facial hair.

The Master kicked one of the empty plates, shattering it. "You careless, stupid half-blood. Is carrying plates too complicated for you?"

She cowered, lowering her head and clasping her knees. She didn't speak, but I could hear her soft cries.

"Get up." Disgust dripped from the Master's voice. The girl didn't move quickly enough for his liking. He reached down and grabbed a handful of her tangled hair, yanking her to her feet. Her gasp of surprise and pain brought forth a cruel laugh from the Master and something far worse. He lifted his free hand to hit her.

I didn't even think.

Rage propelled me into action. I struck out, catching the Master's fist before it landed a blow. The Master whirled around. Lack of eyebrows gave his startled expression an almost comical aspect. He recovered quickly and tried to pull his hand free.

I held on. "Didn't your mother ever teach you not to hit a lady?"

Anger and contempt filled his eyes, sharpening them. "You dare to touch me and interfere in a situation that does not concern you? Do you have a desire for the elixir, half-blood?"

I smiled, tightening my grip until I felt the bones in his hand rub together. His lips thinned in pain, filling me with sick satisfaction. "Oh, I'm not just a half-blood."

"I know what you are." He wrenched his hand free, lips curling with disgust. "You think that will save you? If anything, that ensures that one day you will be under the Masters' control… or worse."

His words should've scared me, but they just pissed me off. "Go screw yourself, you eyebrowless freak."

The Master laughed as he twisted back to the silent girl, but then he swung around so fast I hadn't a chance to raise my hands in defense. The fist intended for the servant ended up smashing right into my jaw.

Fierce pain exploded along my face as I stumbled back into the wall. My eyes immediately filled with tears; the throbbing sent darts of dizziness through me. I held my jaw, almost certain he had broken it. And then Seth was standing in front of me, a towering inferno of fury. I don't even know where he'd come from or how he'd gotten there so quickly.

"That will be the last thing you ever do," Seth snarled. He threw back his hand. Not to hit to the pure, but to *kill* the pure.

Many times in practice I had seen akasha start to build in his hand, but always as just a small ball of energy. When he'd taken down Kain, Aiden had blocked most of it, but now it was all that I could see. The blue energy shot from somewhere under the sleeve of his shirt, filling his hand, crackling and snapping blue fire.

Pain forgotten, I pushed off the wall and grabbed Seth's other arm. "No! No!"

"Get back, Alex, now."

I got in front of him, blocking the Master. The mark of the Apollyon stood out in contrast against his pale face. "You can't do this, Seth! You need to calm down."

"Do it," urged the Master. "Seal your fate, Apollyon. As your bitch's fate has been sealed."

Seth's eyes glowed, his lips pulled back in a snarl. Akasha spread, spitting flames.

"Ignore him," I balled my hands in the front of his shirt. "Please! You can't do this!" This wasn't working. He wasn't listening to me. His arm went back, readying to release the most powerful element known to man. I twisted around. "Get out of here! Now!"

The servant took off, but the Master stayed, daring Seth with his smile as if he had no sense of self-preservation. Then it struck me—he wanted Seth to do this, knowing that for a half to kill a pure in any situation meant death.

Possibly even for the Apollyon.

I turned back to Seth, hands trembling. I pressed against his chest as if I could somehow burrow my way into him and make him understand that the penalty for hitting me wasn't capital punishment. I could taste the fear in the back of my throat; panic overshadowed the physical pain

Seth shuddered and then his arms swept around me. I almost cried out in relief. The Master's cruel laugh echoed around us, seeming to hang in the air long after he left the hallway.

He stared down at me, still furious. "I want to kill him."

"I know," I whispered, blinking back tears.

"No, you don't. I still do."

"But you can't. It was my fault. He was about to hit a servant and I stopped him. He—"

"Your fault?" he said, eyes widening with disbelief now. He reached out and caught my chin, turning my head to the side. "No. This wasn't your fault."

I swallowed, closing my eyes. Crisis adverted… for now. "Is it going to bruise?"

"Most definitely."

"I think… I'm going to be in trouble." I stepped back, staring at the floor. This Seth—this hard and lethal Seth—was frightening. "You're going to be in trouble, too."

"Yes." Seth sounded as if he didn't give a crap about that.

I touched the left side of my face and winced. "Oh, crap."

Seth pulled my hand away from my face. "I think if we make it to dinner without anyone saying anything, then we're in the clear."

"You think so?"

Seth smiled, but everything about him still seemed on the verge of destroying something. "Yes."

We didn't make it until dinner.

About twenty minutes later, Marcus and crew stormed the sitting room Seth and I were kind of hiding in. Aiden was with them, his eyes immediately finding me. His gaze glided over my face, stopping on what I knew was a nasty-looking bruise. He came to a complete stop and inhaled sharply. Potent anger rolled off him in waves, nearly as overwhelming as what was still radiating from the one next to me.

"What were you thinking, Alexandria?" demanded Marcus.

I pulled my eyes from Aiden's, but didn't look at Marcus. I watched Seth instead. His face was still a picture of hard lines and chilling beauty. "I know I shouldn't have stopped the Master, but he was going to beat a girl for dropping plates. I had to do—"

The door swung open, revealing Minister Telly and a slew of Council Guards. I stiffened, but Seth stood. "What is this?" he demanded, hands balling into fists.

"What is this?" Minister Telly repeated, striding across the room, tall and graceful, his green robes flowing. He stopped before Marcus and Lucian. "What is it that I hear about Alexandria attacking a Master this afternoon?"

"Attacked?" I sputtered. "I didn't attack anyone. I stopped—"

"She did interfere with a Master, but she did not attack the man," Marcus cut in, sending me a dangerous look. "However, he did strike Alexandria."

Telly spared me a brief glance. "Half-bloods know to not interfere with a Master and their treatment of servants. To do so is a breach of the Breed Order!"

My mouth dropped open. Had I expected to be in trouble? Yes. But not to be accused of breaking the Order.

"Are you serious?" Seth stepped forward, eyes narrowing into thin slits.

"Get your Apollyon under control this instant, Lucian," Telly spat, "or my Guards will."

Lucian swung toward Seth, but I knew there was nothing that he could say or do. I grabbed Seth's arm and tugged hard. "Sit," I whispered.

He glanced over his shoulder at me, brows raised. "I'd rather stand."

Gods, he so wasn't helping matters. Not like it would stop him, but I held onto his arm.

"Minister Telly, I understand that Alexandria should not have interfered, but accusing her of breaking the law?" Marcus shook his head. "I think that's a bit extreme."

"That half-blood is extreme," Telly responded. "Neither of you have any control over her. She's threatening Masters now? What will she do as an Apollyon? Massacre them in their sleep?"

I laughed. Everyone looked at me. "I'm sorry, but this is ridiculous. All I did was stop him from hitting a girl. That's it! I didn't hit him, but he did hit me." I pointed at my jaw. "And I wouldn't massacre people in their sleep."

Telly turned, facing me fully. "You, little girl, have shown no regard for the law or for rules from the moment you could breathe. Oh yes, I've seen your files."

Had everyone seen my files? Gah. I felt exposed.

"You are uncontrollable and a constant problem for the Council," Telly continued, turning back to Lucian. "She belongs here, where the Council can control her, since neither of you have been able to ingrain a sense of respect in the girl."

Fear stopped me dead in my tracks. "What?"

"That will not happen," Seth said so low that I wasn't sure anyone else heard him. But then everyone in the room froze.

"Are you threatening me, Apollyon? Threatening the Council?" Telly demanded. I'd swear he sounded happy about this, but that would be crazy, because Seth would kill him.

Seth would wipe the ground with Telly's face.

I tore my gaze from the Head Minister and saw the marks of the Apollyon swirling across Seth's face. And then I realized Aiden had moved, standing on the other side of me. I thanked the gods that everyone was focused on Seth, fearing he was about to lose it. The look on Aiden's face said he was about to rip through everyone in this room.

My heart sank as I looked between the two guys. This wasn't going to end well at all. I stood, my knees shaking. "I'm sorry."

"Don't apologize. You did nothing wrong," Seth hissed.

"But I did. I shouldn't have interfered." I met Telly's eyes and swallowed my pride at the same time. "I forgot… I forgot my place."

Seth whirled on me so quickly I thought he might actually zap *me*. I met his furious stare, willing him to just sit down and shut up.

"Minister, as you can see, Alexandria sees her error." Lucian moved in front of Seth, his hands clasped together. "She is strong-willed, stubborn even, but she broke no law today. As you know, if she had attacked the Master, I doubt he'd be well enough to spread such atrocious exaggerations."

"She thinks without acting sometimes," Marcus joined in. "She is reckless, but she never has ill intentions. As for controlling her, I can promise you that she won't even speak out of turn for her stay here."

I opened my mouth, but shut it.

Telly drew another breath before turning to Lucian. "This kind of behavior she has repeatedly displayed is concerning not only to me, but the Council. But that is something you are already aware of, Lucian." He paused, scanning the room. His gaze, full of condemnation, fell on me. "I will not forget this." With that, he turned and stalked from the room. The Guards followed him, stiff and silent.

I collapsed on the couch, exhausted. I'd barely escaped the noose with that one. I felt Seth sit back down, but I didn't look at him.

"Alexandria, what have I told you time and time again?" asked Marcus.

"Enough," Lucian said. "It is in the past now. It is done."

"It just happened," Marcus retorted, "and this one here threatened the Master with akasha, for crying out loud! He is lucky that the Master didn't report him."

"What did you expect?" Lucian countered wearily. "He will defend what is his."

I sent my stepfather a death glare. "I am not *his*. Would you please stop referring to me as a possession instead of a person?"

Lucian smiled. "Either way, Seth cannot be blamed for defending her. Or would you rather he'd allowed the Master to continue to beat Alexandria?"

"That is preposterous, Lucian!" Marcus's hands balled into fists.

They went back and forth for a little while. Eventually my head ached as badly as my jaw did. On the positive side, Seth began to relax and no longer looked like he wanted to wipe out an entire village of pures. Once I'd gathered I wasn't in *that* much trouble, I slipped out the double doors and breathed in the brisk air.

I didn't roam off too far, staying just around the corner from the sitting room. I kept thinking about what the Master had said. My fate had already been sealed? Had the Master known something or had he just been taunting Seth?

"Alex?"

I turned to the sound of Aiden's voice. His eyes were a flinty silver. "Hey," I murmured. "I know I messed up again and—"

"I'm not here to yell at you, Alex. I just wanted to make sure you are okay."

"Oh. Sorry. I'm just used to everyone yelling at me."

He tipped his head to the side, eyes a dark gray. "I understand why you did what you did. Honestly, I wouldn't have expected you to do anything differently."

"Really?" I looked around skeptically. "Are you on drugs?"

Aiden smiled, but then his eyes flickered to my jaw. The smile faded. "Does it hurt?"

"No," I lied.

He looked like he knew better. Before I knew what he was doing, he reached out and brushed his fingers around the edge of the bruise. "It's swelling. Have you put ice on it?"

I had actually, but I'd grown bored holding the ice bag Seth had rifled together. Staring at Aiden now, though? I completely forgot what he'd just asked me. His fingers were still against my cheek and that was the only thing in this world that mattered.

"You still show so much strength." A small smile appeared on his lips. Then he dropped his hand, the heady connection brief. "No other half-blood would have done what you did."

"I don't know why you keep saying that." I leaned against the smooth wall as if it could somehow ground me back into reality.

"It's the truth, Alex. And I'm not even talking about what you did for the half-blood. It's what you just did in there. I know damn well what it took for you to apologize and say what you did. That took strength."

"It wasn't strength. I was scared out of my mind, actually. Maybe a little irrational, you know?"

Aiden glanced away, toward the labyrinth. From here, all I could see were the tips of the vine-covered statues. "I was wrong."

My breath caught in my throat. "Wrong about what?"

He turned back to me, eyes silvery. "About a lot of things, but I always thought your irrational nature was a flaw. It's not. It's what makes you so strong."

I stared at him, my heart doing all kinds of crazy things in my chest. "Thank… you."

"Don't thank—"

"I know." I smiled even though it made my jaw hurt. "Don't thank you for that, but I did."

Aiden nodded. "I better get back in there. Don't wander off too far, okay?"

I nodded and watched him turn around. He got to the French doors and stopped. Turning around, the expression on his face was unreadable, but his words were precise.

"Part of me wishes Seth had killed that Master for touching you."

†

Dinner was served early on the night of the ball and the mad bustle of servants drove me up to my room. My nerves were stretched tight from my impending Court session, my run-in with a Master's fist, Seth's psycho akasha killing power, and Aiden's parting words.

Part of me wishes Seth had killed that Master for touching you.

Two days later and I still couldn't forget what he'd said.

That had been a serious statement, but what could it mean? Did it matter? No, I told myself. Even if Aiden loved me as much as I loved cake, it didn't matter. There was no future there, only death and despair.

A soft knock on the door pulled me out of my thoughts. Since Seth never knocked, I knew it couldn't be him. I scooted off the bed and went to the door.

Laadan stood in the hallway, dressed in a beautiful deep green dress that clung to her hips before billowing out around her in soft, wispy material. Her hair was done up in an intricate twist, adorned by several fresh rose blossoms.

I glanced down at my sweats and shirt. Gods, I never felt more boring and ugly in my entire life. And here I thought Lea was the only one who could evoke such feelings.

Laadan smiled faintly. "If you're not busy, which I can tell you're not, I want to show you something."

I glanced back at my bed and shrugged. It wasn't like I had anything to do. We passed several servants on the way to her room on the floor above, and Laadan smiled at each of them graciously.

Once inside her room, she circled one arm around my shoulders and steered me to an overstuffed chair by her closet. I sat down and pulled my legs up to my chest. "You… wanted to show me your closet door?"

Laadan's laugh was throaty and infectious. I found myself smiling at her. "You're so much like your mother." She shook her head as she leaned against the doors. "The things you say—it's like hearing Rachelle speak."

My smile faded a bit and I wrapped my arms around my knees. "My mom never said half of the stupid stuff that comes out of my mouth."

"You'd be surprised." She paused as a soulful look crept across her features. "Do you know what your mother loved most about the Council sessions?"

"No."

Laadan spun around and threw open her closet doors. She stepped back and spread her arms in a sweeping gesture. "All the dancing and beautiful dresses."

Curious, I leaned forward to get a look inside the closet and nearly fell out of the chair. "Wow. That's a lot of clothes."

She gave a saucy grin over her shoulder. "A girl can never have too many clothes. Come on. Take a look."

I pulled myself from the chair. The gowns caught my eye. Like being under a compulsion that'd turned me into a girlie girl in under two seconds flat, I stepped forward and ran a hand over the soft material.

"You like them?" She tugged on a deep purple dress in crushed velvet.

My fingers lingered on a red silk dress. I couldn't see the cut of it, but the color was divine. "These are the kinds of dresses you'd give up your firstborn child for."

She laughed, dropping the purple dress and gently unhooking the red one. She held it up between us. "Why are you so dead set against going to the ball?"

I shrugged, eyeing the sleeveless dress. It had scalloped edging around the bodice, a high waist, and a skirt cut to cling to the legs. "I don't even know why I'd be invited since halfs aren't."

"But you are different." She hung the dress on the closet door and smoothed out the silk. "Being an Apollyon sets you apart from the rest of your kind, Alex. Once you Awaken, I've been told that both you and Seth will even be able to attend Council sessions."

I hadn't known that, but I seriously doubted at eighteen I needed to be in that kind of position of power. Maturity didn't happen overnight. My eyes and mind were fastened on *that* dress. "There's not going to be anyone there I know. And no offense, but my idea of fun isn't spending a night with a bunch of pures."

"None taken." Laadan pulled out the skirt. The hue of the red caught the light, casting a faint glimmer over the dress. "Seth will be there. So will Aiden."

I looked at her sharply. "Why would I care if Aiden will be there? He's a pure. Where else would he be tonight?"

Laadan smiled faintly. "Would you like to try it on?"

"No thank you."

"Humor me, why don't you? Your mom wore a dress like this once, and I only have a little while before I'm due downstairs."

The yearning to try the dress on was a physical ache, but I shook my head. Laadan persisted until I found myself standing in front of a full-length mirror with the red silk dress on. She stood behind me, hands on my shoulders. "You look beautiful."

The dress was stunning. It was made to fit me—or at least altered to do so. The silk hugged from my chest to my hips before gliding out around my thighs. I twisted to the side, grinning. The back looked just as good as the front. Red was definitely my color. For a moment, I let myself drift into a dream where Aiden actually saw me in something this elegant and sexy.

And what if Seth saw me in this? Even my dirtiest imagination couldn't capture his response accurately.

"I should probably take this off before I ruin it."

Laadan pulled me away from the mirror and sat me down in front of a small table full of makeup and other suspicious-looking things. I started to stand, but she planted her hands on my shoulders again. "Alex, there is no reason for you to stay in your room tonight while everyone else is enjoying the ball. So be still and let me do something with this hair of yours."

"I don't want to go." I twisted around so I faced her.

She turned me back around and picked up a brush. "Why? Is it because you have your session tomorrow? Wouldn't that be even more of a reason to relax and enjoy tonight?"

I frowned and tried to ignore the soothing way the brush moved through the tangles in my hair. "It's not because of the session tomorrow. I just… don't want to go."

Ignoring me, she picked up a curling iron and started twisting long sections of hair around the barrel. I gave in to the primping pretty quickly, still having no real intention of going to the ball. It was nice to have someone make me pretty, even if all the hard work would be wasted on my pillow. Chattering on about my mother, she moved on to the makeup and when she was done, I barely recognized the smoky-eyed girl staring back at me.

Laadan had outdone herself.

She'd piled the curls atop of my head, but pulled several thick strands down to cover my neck and tease the bodice of the dress. The curls seemed strategically placed, as they hid the scars.

"What do you think?" she asked, a powder brush in her hand.

I had no idea what to say. The blush accented my cheekbones, making them appear higher than normal. She'd covered the bruise on my jaw without coating my face with makeup. The mascara and artfully applied shadow turned my eyes into the warmest chocolate instead of the dirt color they usually favored. Red stain plumped my lips in a way that begged to be kissed.

"Wow. My nose looks small."

Laadan laughed, setting the brush down. "Wait. The only thing you are missing is…" Drifting off to a dresser and opening a large velvet box, she rooted around for a few moments and pulled out a silver chain with black stones surrounding a ruby.

The necklace probably was worth more than my life, but she dropped it around my neck and clasped it. "There! Now you'll be the belle of the ball."

I stared at myself, wanting a picture of this moment. I don't think I'd ever look so… unlike me again. If Caleb could've seen this, I think he might've complimented me.

Laadan glanced at a clock gilded in gold. "And we're finished just in time. The ball has only just begun, and you will make a fashionably late entrance."

My gaze drifted down the mirror. "I can't go."

"You're being silly. You're going to look more beautiful than any pure-blood in that room, Alex. You'll belong."

I stood, shaking my head. "You don't understand, Laadan. I do appreciate all of this and it was fun, but I… I can't go."

She frowned. "Perhaps I don't understand. Would you explain it to me?"

Slowly, I turned back to the mirror. The girl staring back at me looked beautiful if no one looked *too* hard or *too* close. If anyone did, the picture of perfection would start to fall apart. There wasn't a pretty dress in Laadan's closet that could fix that.

"Alex?"

"Look at me," I said quietly." You don't see… them? I can't go down there and have everyone stare at me."

Laadan's concerned face appeared above my head in the mirror. "Honey, everyone will be staring at you because you look beautiful."

"Everyone will be staring at my scars."

She blinked and took a step back. "No. They're not even—"

"I know they will be." I turned around, fingering the delicate chain around my neck. "Because it's what I notice first on someone. And look at my arms, they're pretty gross."

And they were. The skin had never quite returned to the original skin tone. They'd paled, like all daimon tags did, but the tiny teeth marks left behind were uneven and red, lining my forearms, starting right above my wrist and ending along the tender skin of the inside of my elbow. The skin was just as uneven and patchy as my neck, but at least the scars on my throat had faded into a shiny color a shade or two lighter than my normal complexion. The bit of cleavage the dress showed off took away from those scars, but my arms totally made up for it.

Laadan suddenly smiled, which I found really inappropriate considering she should be commiserating about how much of a freak I looked. She moved to her closet and pulled a large box off the top shelf. Taking it to her bed, her smile grew wider. "I have the perfect thing."

Doubtful, but I followed her to the bed.

She flipped up the lid and pulled out two elbow-length gloves in black silk. "Problem solved."

I took the gloves gingerly. "I'm going to look like Rogue from *X-Men*."

Her nose wrinkled. "Who? It doesn't matter. Try them on. The gloves will work now. If it were the summer, it would be a tad bit questionable."

I slid one on and it did cover the scars quite nicely, but gloves? For real? Who wore them but old grannies? "I don't know about this."

Laadan sighed, shaking her head. "This is a formal ball, Alex. Have you been to one before?"

"Um, no."

"Trust me when I say that you will not be the only girl wearing gloves. Now, come on. We don't have much more time to stand up here and feel sorry for ourselves. You look beautiful, Alex. More so than even your mother ever did."

I wiggled my fingers in the silk gloves, feeling excitement bubble for the first time. Half-bloods didn't go to grand balls, and they didn't have pure fairy godmothers, either. So I'd never really expected to attend anything like this, especially not in this killer dress.

But here I was.

A slow smile crept over my face. "Laadan?"

"Yes?" She stopped at the door.

"Thank you."

Her hand flew to her heart. "Honey, you don't have to thank me. I'm just glad I could do this for you."

"You had this planned ever since Lucian mentioned something at breakfast, didn't you? That's why this dress fits so well."

Laadan gave a sly smile. "Well, I always thought red would be your best color."

The ball was in full swing by the time Laadan and I made it downstairs. The soft hum of an orchestra filled the corridors as we moved closer to the ballroom. A display of dazzling candles lit the way.

My excitement quickly turned into nerves. I've never worn anything like this before and attending something like this just went against everything a half-blood knew. Also, orchestra music just wasn't my thing.

Would I be expected to waltz? The last time—and only time—had been with Seth and he'd dropped me. I couldn't hit the ground in this kind of dress—that would be a sacrilege. And who would even dance with me? Was I going to be hugging the wall all night?

That's when I started sweating.

Laadan grasped my hand with hers and led me forward. "You've fought daimons and the idea of a ball scares you?"

"Yes," I whispered.

She laughed, the sound reminding me of wind chimes. "You're going to do beautifully. Just remember that you belong among them. More so than any of them can even realize."

I looked at her warily. "You really do love some half-bloods, don't you?"

Her cheeks flushed a fierce red. "I… I just believe that all of us are equal and should be treated that way."

I doubted that was the main reason, but I didn't push it. She pulled me out of the soft shadows of the hallway, past the frozen furies, and right into the ballroom. I think I may've had a minor heart attack standing there, taking it all in.

The room was massive, the walls entirely made of glass. Crystal vases full of roses sat in every corner and on every table, and flower-covered vines hung from sparkling chandeliers in a dazzling display of light and darkness and streamed across the ceiling. At the far end of the room, a small orchestra sat—mortal musicians. Mortals were easy for both pures and halfs to pick out. It was more than just the physical attributes that set them apart. Their movements were jerky and slow, while the pures glided gracefully around them. Compared to the pures, their expressions were bland. They were probably under compulsion to play here and not acknowledge anything weird.

Pures could get a little freaky after a few drinks.

Behind the orchestra, Thanatos rose above the mortals to loom over them like some kind of angel of death. His wingspan had to be at least eight feet and the ever-present sad expression had been carved into the marble. Someone had laid a wreath of roses on the god's head.

Nice touch.

Two servants appeared in front of us. One held a tray of champagne flutes and the other carried a platter of finger sandwiches and what smelled like raw fish. I had a sudden mad desire for tater tots.

Laadan graciously accepted two glasses of champagne and handed me one. She caught my hand before I could down the glass. "Careful," she warned softly. "This isn't like mortal champagne. It's much stronger."

I stared down at the bubbling liquid. "How much stronger?"

She tipped her head to a table where a pure girl laughed hysterically while her companions looked on in annoyance. She had a glass of champagne in her hand. "That's probably her second. You sip this champagne."

"Advice taken."

Lucian drifted out of the throng of pures and grasped my free hand. His eyes drifted over me in a mixture of shock and appraisal. "Laadan, you have outdone yourself. She looks just like Rachelle did when she attended this very ball."

It was official. I felt creeped out on a whole new level.

"And you can't even see her scars," Lucian continued. There was a weird sheen to his eyes, and I wondered if he was drunk. "Utterly amazing job, Laadan."

Straining back, I tried to maintain a polite smile. "Uh… thanks."

Laadan looked as put off as I felt. Smoothly, she engaged Lucian's interest. I scanned the room for friendly faces as my fingers clutched the fragile stem of the glass.

Everyone—all the pures—looked magnificent in their finery. Most of the females wore the kind of risqué dresses I'd love to, showing off expanses of perfectly smooth skin and long, graceful necks.

I didn't belong here. No matter what Laadan said, I didn't belong here.

Taking a deep breath, my gaze skittered over the crowd. Out of them, I recognized Minister Diana Elders. She wore a white diaphanous gown that reminded me of something a goddess would wear. Beside her, my uncle looked extremely interested in whatever she was saying. In awe, I watched as he actually smiled and when they turned toward us, those emerald eyes shone like jewels.

That is, until he saw me.

Marcus stepped back, blinking. Shock splashed across his face. He reacted like he'd seen a ghost. Recovering slowly, he and Minister Elders approached us. He nodded at Lucian and Laadan. "Alexandria, you decided to join us after all."

Uncomfortable, I nodded and *sipped* my champagne.

Diana smiled warmly enough, but she looked nervous when she addressed me. "Miss Andros, it is a pleasure to meet you."

"Same here," I murmured dumbly. I was never good at exchanging pleasantries, but the good thing was that the pures surrounding me gravitated toward each other and I was able to drift off to the side. I continued searching the crowd… well, for Aiden if I was being honest with myself. I knew he wouldn't speak to me, but I wanted him… to see me. Lame, yes, but I wanted that.

Go figure it was Seth I saw first.

Or he saw me first. I'm not sure. Either way, I was surprised to find both Aiden and Seth standing with another pure-blood male I didn't recognize. Several pretty pures had crowded them, possibly fascinated by the fact that an Apollyon half-blood was in the mix—or they'd just been drawn to the general hotness of the group.

Dawn Samos was one of those pretty pures. Her dress was a white sheath that ended above her knees. She stood the closest to Aiden, her slender tan arm brushing his as she spoke. I hadn't seen her since the first day of sessions and I'd forgotten about her, but there she was.

Seth stood facing Aiden and the entrance. He wore a tux like the rest of the pures, except he'd managed to find an all-white one and still look good in it. A grin pulled at my lips.

Like Seth needed any extra help sticking out.

His gaze moved around the edge of the ballroom and landed on me. The expression on his face was almost comical. His brows inched up his forehead, eyes widened with surprise. Apparently, I looked like a doofus most of the time. Me being in a dress must be a sight to behold. A smug quirk to his lips was quick to replace the startled expression. He nodded at me approvingly.

I tipped my glass at Seth.

He must've said something, because Aiden's muscles stiffened under his black tux. Then slowly, almost reluctantly, Aiden looked over his shoulder. The moment our eyes met, I felt like Cinderella.

Aiden's lips parted as his gaze drifted over me in a way that made the glass tremble between my fingers. When his eyes made their slow journey back to mine, all the air fled my lungs. The silver burned so fiercely, so hot, that a warm blush swept over my skin. My hand fell to the side, the barely touched glass of champagne forgotten as it hung from my fingertips.

Aiden turned around fully, his chest rising and falling sharply. He didn't smile. He seemed only capable of staring. Just like me, because he looked truly magnificent in the sharp cut of the black tux, the wild waves of hair tumbling over his forehead, and those soft lips still parted in surprise, eyes still full of hunger.

As if in a daze, Aiden crossed the ballroom floor, his piercing eyes fastened on me. I knew I looked good, but not *that* good. Not so good that everyone else seemed to fade and disappear to Aiden. I thought of what he'd said outside the sitting room, how he'd been wrong about a lot of things.

I think I knew one of those things he'd been wrong about.

So caught up in Aiden, I hadn't realized Seth had moved, but I felt him before he placed his hand on me, his fingers curving over my bare shoulder. Anger flashed over Aiden's face. He stalled, silver eyes dropping to my shoulder. I could almost feel it in the air—the primal jealousy, his raw urge to physically remove Seth's hand.

Seth leaned close, his warm breath stirring the hair at the nape of my neck. "People are starting to stare."

Were they? I couldn't say I really cared, which was wrong, but Aiden was staring at me—staring at me with so much passion, so much want—it was the only thing I could think about.

And then Aiden pulled it together. Halting mid-step, he clamped his jaw shut. Those eyes were still like quicksilver, smoldering in the soft light. His gaze drifted over me once more. Shivering under its intensity, I imagined that he was filing the image of me away.

Seth's hand slid down my arm, fingers tightening around mine. "You know he's not for you."

"I know," I whispered. And I did know that, and maybe that was why I felt so hollow inside.

Aiden turned away then, smiling at something Dawn said. But it was a fake smile. I knew Aiden's smiles. After all, I lived for them.

"Do you want to dance?" Seth suggested.

Coming to the ball had been a bad idea. The emptiness I felt spread, leaving a gaping hole. I didn't belong here, but Aiden did. Aiden belonged here with pures like Dawn. Not with me, not a half-blood.

I tore my gaze from Aiden and looked up at Seth. "I don't want to dance."

Seth's amber gaze drifted over me. "Do you want to stay here?"

"I don't know."

He smiled and leaned forward. When he spoke, his lips brushed my ear. "We don't belong here, Alex. Not with them."

I wanted to ask exactly where it was we belonged, but I knew what Seth's answer would be. He'd say that *we* belonged *together*. Not in the way I wanted to belong to Aiden, but in a different way. A way I hadn't figured out yet.

"Let's go," he coaxed softly.

I could stay here and continue pretending that I belonged, or I could leave with Seth. And then what? My fingers trembled as I set the glass down on the nearest table. I let Seth lead me away from the ball. A sudden heaviness settled over me. I felt like I'd made some sort of irrevocable choice.

And maybe I had.

CHAPTER 21

"LET'S DO SOMETHING STUPID."

I turned to Seth, oddly nervous. "You want to do something stupid right now?"

"Can you think of a better time to do something stupid?"

I considered that. He kind of had a good point. "Okay. I'm down with stupid."

"Good." He started off, pulling me through the labyrinth. We rounded the Council chambers and headed into the campus. Seth cut toward the dark and silent building I'd spent the majority of my waking time in.

"You want to train?"

He shook his head, jaw clenched. "No. I don't want to train."

Seth picked up his pace. I had no idea what he was up to, but I'd learned a while ago to just go with it. The door to the arena was unlocked. A wide grin broke out across his face when he spotted the double doors inside the dark corridor.

"You want to go swimming?" I asked.

"Sure."

"It's like forty degrees outside."

Seth pushed open the door. The smell of chlorine was everywhere. "So? It's not forty degrees in here, is it? More like sixty."

I pulled away from him and stepped to the edge of the pool. Glancing over my shoulder, I saw Seth kick off his shoes. He caught my eye and winked.

"You're ridiculous," I said, fighting a grin.

"So are you." He slipped off the dress jacket, dropping it on the cement. "We are a lot alike, Alex."

I started to deny it, but I stopped and actually thought about it instead of dismissing it. There *was* something about Seth that called to my wilder and yes, stupider side. We were both reckless, a little wild, and aggressive, and neither of us knew when to ever be quiet. I guess there were two types of people in the world, those who sat around a fire, staring into the flames, and those who started the fire.

Seth and I started the fire, and then we danced around it.

"Was it so obvious back there?" I asked quietly.

Seth had been yanking his white shirt out of his pants, but he stopped and looked up. He appeared to be choosing his words. "I don't know what goes on in your head, Alex. I can't read your thoughts. I just picked up on your emotions."

"Good to know."

"I second that." He started unbuttoning his shirt. "Anyway, I don't even need to be able to sense your emotions to know. I don't think you want to know what it looked like."

"No. I do." I shifted my weight to my other foot. These heels were killing me.

Shaking his head, Seth sighed. "You were staring at him like an ugly chick stares at the last cute guy at the bar when they make the last call."

I choked on my laugh. "Oh. Wow. Thanks."

He raised his hands in a helpless gesture, which looked so strange for him. "I told you."

"Yeah." I pushed strands of hair off my neck. "So I looked like an idiot to everyone?"

"No, everyone saw a beautiful half-blood. That's all anyone saw." Seth glanced away, a wry smile on his face. "Can I tell you something?"

I turned back to the pool. "Sure."

"I prefer you without gloves." His breath stirred the tendrils of hair against my neck. I had no idea how he moved so quietly.

"Oh." I said, watching Seth as he moved to my side. Quietly, he peeled off one glove, and then the other, tossing them both away from the water. His fingers slid around the scars before he dropped my arm, stepping back. My tags never seemed to bother him. I looked at him through my lashes. "Better?"

"Much."

I glanced down at the beautiful gown. Laadan would be so upset if I ruined her dress. I turned slightly, catching my reflection in the windows of the pool room. It didn't look like me. I looked like a doll, a carbon copy of my mom. So much so that even Lucian had looked at me in a way that made me puke a little in my mouth. Had that been what Laadan wanted? To fashion me like her long-lost friend?

"Can you get silk wet?" I asked.

Seth made a funny noise behind me. "I'd say probably not."

"That's a shame." I kicked off my shoes. My toes immediately sighed and thanked me.

"You really are going—"

I dove in. The water wasn't as heated as I'd thought and was a shock to my system, but after a few seconds I grew used to it. Staying underwater, I swam to the opposite side of the pool.

The water immediately killed all of Laadan's hard work. Twisting around, I found Seth at the pool's edge. Amusement and satisfaction played out across on his face, which made him look sort of normal.

"So childish, Alex. You've ruined her dress."

The vibrant red silk floated around me as I treaded water. "I know. Bad me."

"Very bad." He sounded more appreciative than chastising.

Grinning, I sank underwater again and closed my eyes. Under the water, it was a quiet, blissful world. I didn't have to think, or worry… or love.

I inched my way back up and caught Seth shrugging off his shirt. I saw maybe a second of his bare upper body before I hastily ducked underwater. It wasn't bad—all golden skin and hard muscles.

Seeing his chest wasn't a big deal, for crying out loud.

On the nights Seth stayed with me, he did so fully clothed—thank the gods—but it was just weird. Seth was weird—*I was weird*—and

I couldn't stay underwater all night. Using my legs, I pushed off the bottom of the pool.

Seth had moved to the center of the room. His head was tipped back, arms stretched high in the air as he stood on the tips of his toes, completely at ease. "Stop staring."

I floated forward. "I'm not staring."

He chuckled. "How's the water?"

"Nice."

His arms dropped to his sides. "Do you remember the last thing I told you in training?"

I pushed through the water, coming to where he stood. "You tell me a lot of stuff in training. Honestly, I don't pay attention."

He snorted. "You do wonders for my self-esteem."

Rolling my eyes, I pushed off the cement wall and floated on my back. The dress streamed out around me as water glided over my skin. "I feel like a mermaid."

Seth ignored that. "Tomorrow, when they ask you about what happened in Gatlinburg, only answer their questions."

I sighed. "I know. What do you guys think I'm going to say? That I love daimons?"

"Just don't elaborate on anything. Answer yes or no, and that is it."

"I'm not stupid, Seth."

Seth arched a brow. "I didn't say you were. I just know you tend… to talk a lot."

"Oh. Like you're one—"

Seth dove in, sending a wave of water crashing over me, and I lost my balance. I sank under, only to find him swimming toward me. Recognizing the wild grin plastered across his face, I pushed back, but he caught the edge of my dress. I smacked his hand away and resurfaced. He came up a few feet away, shaking his head, sending beads of water flying.

I splashed him. "You talk more than I do."

He floated over to the side and swung one arm over the edge. Squinting through water and hair, he made a face at me. "You look like a drowned monkey."

"What? I do not." I ran a hand over my hair, then under my eyes. Come to think of it, I probably had brutal raccoon eyes right now. "Wait. Do I?"

Seth nodded. "Honestly, you look like a mess. This was a bad idea. What was I thinking?"

"Shut up. You don't look so hot yourself."

That wasn't entirely true. Seth looked rather… nice soaked. The whole shirtless thing probably helped. A little bit. Not much. For some bizarre reason, I thought about the day the rune had appeared.

His lips curved into a mad sort of grin as he placed his hand over the water. "Watch this."

I tried keeping the edges of my dress from floating all the way up. "Watch what?"

The water under his hand spun, much like water going down a drain. Then it shot straight up in the air, reaching for the ceiling. The cone of water twisted in midair, arced, and then came down.

I couldn't move back quickly enough.

Water funneled around me, pulsating and drowning out everything. Then it froze. I couldn't see beyond the wall of still water. I tilted my head back and smiled. Being stuck in a Seth-made typhoon was strange, but also cool. Tentatively, I reached out and poked a finger through it. Wrong move. It all came crashing down.

The weight of the water pushed me under, and when I came back up, an all-out water war ensued. We both were acting like two bored kids who'd snuck away from their parents, but this was *fun*. It didn't matter I was sorely outmatched in the water arena and Seth seemed intent on drowning me.

I wasn't thinking about Aiden, or the Council, or *anything*.

Laughing and swallowing way too much water, I backed off while Seth pushed clumps of blond hair out of his eyes. "You're such a girl, Seth. Do we need to take a grooming break?"

"You need to give up." He reared back, sending his arm crashing against the surface of the water. "You can't beat me. Ever. At anything. Give it up."

I swam back, slipped under and resurfaced quickly. "I don't give up, Seth."

He inched closer. "Well, we all have to learn how to someday. Besides me. I'm secure in my awesomeness."

"More like you're secure in your douchiness."

"You are such a goner." He shot across the water, and I dropped underneath. I aimed for his legs, thinking that if I could take them out, I could take him out.

But it didn't quite go as planned.

I got one arm around a leg and tugged. Seth retaliated by reaching down and tugging me back up to the surface. The moment my head broke through the water, I struggled and cursed. Unsurprisingly, a long, wet gown really hindered the use of one's legs.

"That's cheating, Alex." Seth planted both hands above my hips. "You know what happens to cheaters."

I tried prying his fingers from my waist. "Don't you dare!"

He lifted me until over half of my body was out of the water. I stared down at his face. His smile went up a notch as I dangled above him. "Cold up there, huh?"

Yeah, it kind of was. "Stupid down there, huh?"

Seth's brows flew up. "For one in such a precarious position, you sure don't know how to talk yourself out of it."

"That's because it's hard to reason with idiots." I gave him a cheeky grin. "Why bother?"

"Oh? Is that how it is? Well, my little Apollyon-in-training, have a nice flight."

"Seth! I swear I will—"

Using the air element, he launched me out of the water, cutting off my words. I went up… and up another couple of feet, and back down in a mess of arms and red silk several feet away. Water went up my nose as I sank to the bottom of the pool.

Breaking the surface, I immediately started yelling things only Seth could truly appreciate. A lot of four letter words that rhymed with other four letter words. This resulted in me flying back through the air again and again.

"Okay. Okay," I gasped, hanging above him. "You're awesome."

"And?"

"And… you're not a douche… all the time—Wait!" I stalled as my knees came out of the water. "You're just a *great* person."

Seth frowned. "That doesn't sound very sincere."

My hands slipped off his. "Okay. You're the best Apollyon there is."

He tipped his head to the side and arched a brow. "I'm the only Apollyon there is right now."

I grinned. "You're still the best."

He sighed, but he lowered me back down. "Now you really do look like a drowned monkey."

"Thanks." I started for the shallow end of the pool, but Seth pushed through the water like a damn fish. He circled one arm around my waist and flipped me back around.

"Where do you think you're going?"

I went to push against his chest, but remembered there was literally nothing between my hands and his skin. I opted for his shoulders, which turned out to be rather pointless. "Don't throw me again."

"I'm not going to throw you."

I considered that for a moment. "Then I win the water war?"

"No."

"Damn. Well, I guess you have to be better than me at something. Congratulations."

"I'm always better than you. I'm—"

"Egotistical?" I supplied helpfully. "Narcissistic?"

He pressed forward, and I backed up, trying to keep as much space between us as possible. Not that it did any good in water. My legs floated everywhere I didn't want them to—like closer to him. "I have some words for you, too. How about stubborn? Impudent?" he countered, slowly pushing on until my back hit the rough edge of the pool.

"Was 'impudent' your word choice of the day?"

He put his finger on my lips. "Well, yes it is. I could even use it in a sentence if you like."

"That won't be necessary."

He removed his finger and planted his hands on either side of me, effectively caging me in. I looked up and our eyes locked. An immediate level of awareness passed between us. It was powerful, almost like the charge that'd shot through us when I'd touched his rune.

Something I never planned on doing again.

The atmosphere was no longer playful or light, and as the silence grew, so did the nervousness in the pit of my stomach. Seth had *that* look on his face—all intent and purpose-driven, and it was directed at me. He liked to flirt, liked to the push the line between us, but this—this was different. I felt *it* inside me, waking up and stirring.

Suddenly I thought of the heaviness I'd felt leaving the ball. "I think… we should head back now. I'm cold and it's getting late."

Seth smiled. "No."

"No?"

"I'm not done being stupid yet." He leaned in. Strands of his wet hair brushed my forehead. "Actually, there's a lot of stupid left in me."

At once, I placed my hands against his chest to stop him. His skin felt incredibly warm for being above the water. I opened my mouth to respond, but found myself at a loss. A strange edginess swamped me. Somehow, he managed to get closer and I… I didn't push him away or move my hands. Seth seemed to read something in that, because his hands slipped away from the edge and fell to my waist.

"You know what?" His breath was warm against my cheek. "There are a lot of stupid things to do, but I really want to do the stupidest thing possible."

"What's that?"

"I want to kiss you."

My stomach hollowed. "That is crazy. I'm not Elena… or any other number of girls."

"I know. Maybe that's why I want to."

I turned my head in the other direction. Or at least I thought I did. That was what I planned, but for some reason my head went the direction I didn't want it to—toward him and his warm breath. "You don't want to kiss me."

"But I do." His lips brushed against my cheek, sending shivers that had nothing to do with the cold air over me.

My hands slipped from his chest and I gripped the edge of the pool. "No, you don't."

Seth chuckled against my cheek. He slipped his fingers up my spine, curving his hand around the nape of my neck. "Are you arguing with me over what I want?"

"You're arguing with me."

"You're ridiculous." I felt him smile as his lips brushed over the line of my jaw, over the bruise. "It's such an annoying quality, yet strangely endearing."

My heart was beating way too fast. "Well… you're annoying, too."

He laughed again and pulled me against his chest. My fingers lost their tenuous grip on reality, falling into the water. "Why are we still talking?"

I rested my cheek against his shoulder and closed my eyes. "This is your one chance to talk without me telling you to shut up, because we aren't doing... anything else."

"Do you know how amusing I find you?" He shifted, pressing my back into the pool edge. His hand left my waist, smoothed down over my hip and thigh. Jerking back, I grabbed for his hand. Too late, he hooked my leg around his.

"What are… you doing?" I hated how breathless my voice sounded, confused by the need burning through me.

"Do you know why I think you're so amusing?" He slid the hand over my thigh.

"Why?"

"Because I know how badly you want me to kiss you." Seth cupped my chin, tipping my head back with his other hand.

"That's not true."

"You lie. Why? I have no idea." He pressed his lips against my cheek, then against my throat, my shoulder. The hand on my leg slipped between my thighs. My blood pounded, sending my heart into a frenzy. "I can feel what you're feeling. And I know you want me to kiss you."

I grasped his arms "It's not…"

"Not what?" He lifted his head, brushing his nose against mine.

"I…"

"Just let me kiss you."

Gods, I needed him to kiss me. I needed him to keep doing what he was doing with his hands. But was any of this was about the heart… or even the body? Or was it just what existed in both of us? The connection, the bond—whatever it was—controlling what we wanted. It sang between us, tightening until it was all that existed. But what I felt with Aiden wasn't a product of a connection, and it didn't fade away because he didn't return my feelings. I didn't even question what it was, but this? I had to question everything.

I opened my eyes. "Is this real?"

"Very real." He leaned back and brushed strands of wet hair off my face.

I did want to kiss him and I also wanted to wrap myself around him. The ache his hands created was almost too hard to deny, but as I stared at him and saw the runes slipping down his neck, slowly reaching toward where my hands rested against his skin, I had no idea if I could trust what I wanted. There was something between us that neither of us fully understood. We didn't know what the connection actually controlled, what it could make us want.

His breath danced over my cheek, then my lips. "Angel, just let me kiss you."

With Aiden, with what I felt for him, there was nothing external—or internal—pulling me toward him except what I *felt* for him. It didn't matter that it was forbidden or that he didn't want me.

Seth dropped his hands suddenly. I hit the edge, wincing as the cement scraped my skin. The mark of the Apollyon shifted over his chest, swirling and moving. "You're thinking about Aiden."

I bit my lip. "Not in the way you think I am."

He ran both his hands over his head. Then he pushed forward, suddenly right in my face. "You know, I don't know which is worse. That I was stupid enough to want to kiss you, or the fact that you're still hung up on someone who doesn't even want you."

I blinked. "Wow. That's a little harsh."

"It's the truth, Alex. Even if he did profess his undying love for you, you can't have him."

I whirled around and hauled myself out of the pool. Standing above him, water ran off the ruined dress. "Just because I can't be with him doesn't change the way I feel."

In an instant, he was out of the water. "If you have this epic love for Aiden, why did you want to kiss me as badly as you did?"

I flushed hot with fury, the kind that only came from Seth making a point I couldn't argue. "I didn't kiss you, Seth! That should answer your question right there!"

"You wanted to. Trust me, I know you did." He smiled that smug smile. "You really wanted to."

"I don't know what I want!" I yelled, my hands balling into fists at my sides. "How do you know, Seth? How do you know it's not the damn connection between us instead of something real?"

The anger faded from Seth's eyes, replaced by surprise. "You think it's just the connection? Do you really think that's all I feel for you?"

I laughed harshly. "You say it yourself all the time! Anytime you do something nice for me, you say it's the connection forcing you to do so."

"Did you ever consider that I was joking?"

"No! Why would I? You said the connection would grow stronger between us," I said. "That's why you want to kiss me! It's not real."

"I know why I want to kiss you, Alex, and is has nothing to do with either of us being Apollyons. And apparently it has nothing to do with your common sense, either."

I narrowed my eyes. "Oh, shut up. I'm done talking—"

"I know exactly why." Seth stalked forward, backing me up until I hit the cement wall behind me and he stood inches away. "I can't believe I'd even have to spell it out for you."

Shivering in the cool, damp air, I flattened my hands against the wall. "You don't have to."

"You're the most frustrating person I know."

I rolled my eyes. "And that makes you want to kiss me? You're twisted."

His eyes burned like liquid gold. “Do you feel the connection between us right now?”

I frowned, searching for the telltale signs the connection was doing its thing. I didn’t feel that swamping heat or edginess, so I was going to go with no. “Not really, but I don’t know what it feels—”

Seth grasped the sides of my face and brought my mouth to his. I froze, shocked that he’d actually kiss me after all of that, but he was. Soft, tentative, questioning kisses, as if he was doing this for the very first time, and I *so* knew that wasn’t the case.

I knew I should stop him, because allowing him to kiss me totally defeated the point of the argument we’d just had, but I found myself closing my eyes instead. His mouth was so warm and sweet, dizzying actually. Then it deepened, stealing my breath and sending my heart racing.

Kissing wasn’t a big deal, so this kiss shouldn’t be any different. But by the gods, I’d never been kissed like this before.

I looped my arms around his neck, tangling my fingers in his hair, and then I was kissing him back. Kissing him with the same wild abandonment he’d dived into, and gods, I liked kissing Seth.

He was really good at it.

Seth nipped at my lower lip as he pulled back just enough that I could breathe. “You can’t tell me you didn’t like that.” He pressed his lips to mine again, soaking up my response. “And don’t you dare tell me you didn’t kiss me.”

I let my hands slid down to his chest. I knew, if I opened my eyes, I’d see the marks. “I… don’t know what that was.”

He chuckled and brushed his lips across mine. “You have a choice, Alex.”

I opened my eyes then. The marks stretching across his face were faint, but I still had the insane desire to run my fingers along them. It took everything in me not to. I met his eyes. “What choice?”

His hands dropped to my shoulders, then made their way to my waist. They fisted the soaked material, holding me still. “You can choose to continue wasting away for something you can never have.”

I swallowed. “Or?”

He smiled. "You can choose not to."

"Seth, I—"

"Look, I know you aren't over him," he said *him* like it was some kind of venereal disease, "but I do know you like me. I'm not suggesting anything. Not asking for stupid little labels or promises. No expectations."

I took a shallow breath. "What are you suggesting?"

"You choose to see what happens." Seth let go of my dress and stepped back, running his hands through his wet hair. "Between us—you choose us."

Choose us? I shivered and wrapped my arms around me. Choose between what? Aiden was completely off limits, and Seth and I—even though we were stuck with one another—couldn't go a day without wanting to knock each other's heads off. This didn't seem like a great choice.

Seth smiled faintly. "Think about it, at least." He turned around and went back to where he'd left his clothes.

I sagged against the wall and sighed. Seth had done some pretty nice things for me. He'd stayed with me after Caleb's death, defended me against the Master. But then there was Aiden and all that I felt for him, and the way he'd looked at me tonight.

But choosing Aiden meant choosing nothing.

Choosing Seth meant submitting to a whacked-out fate.

Or did it?

My gaze fell to my hand. The rune on my palm shone an iridescent blue, as if it were pleased by Seth's suggestions. And his suggestion didn't sound so bad. No labels. No expectations. No feelings. And that was good, because my heart… my heart was somewhere else. Soon, I'd be heading home to North Carolina, where there would be no Caleb, no halfs who really wanted to be around me, and no more Aiden.

But there would be Seth.

I pushed off the wall. Seth had his back to me, head bent in concentration. *What was I doing?* I stopped a few feet behind him, my heart jumping in my throat. "Seth?"

He turned sideways, fingers finishing the last of the buttons. "Alex?"

"I… I choose you—or whatever it is that you're saying." I flushed. Gods, I sounded stupid. "I mean, I choose the whole seeing what—"

Seth's mouth cut my words off. His arms swept around me, dropping something warm and dry over my shoulders. I realized it was his suit jacket, but then I was thinking about how warm *he* felt. Before I knew it, I was gripping his shirt, arching against him, soaking up his warmth.

Then I felt it waking up like some kind of slumbering giant, sending sparks of electricity over my skin. My palm itched—burned, really. I gasped against his lips. The kiss wasn't enough. I slid my hands under his shirt, over the hard expanse of his stomach.

He jerked back, breathing heavy. A fleeting, satisfied look shot across his face—gone so quickly I couldn't be sure what I'd seen. Then he smiled, and I knew I couldn't have seen that calculated edge to his stare. The transformation that occurred was nothing short of amazing. "You're not sleeping in that bed—in that terrible little room—tonight."

CHAPTER 22

I DID SLEEP IN MY BED, IN THAT TERRIBLE ROOM.

And I did so alone.

It'd taken every ounce of my self-control to convince Seth that sharing the same bed wasn't a good idea, which was difficult, mainly because my body had thought it was an awesome idea. Surprisingly, my brain had won that battle.

I didn't know why I'd kissed Seth—once, then twice. Hell, I didn't even know why I agreed to *seeing what happens*. The smart thing would've been to punch Seth and make a run for it.

But I never did the smart thing.

"That *was* a beautiful dress." Laadan wore a slight, curious frown. "I guess there are several ways to ruin silk, and I suppose a midnight swim would be one of the more daring ways to do so."

Cringing and flushing, I ran my hands down the only pair of dress pants I owned. They were made of some thin, black material and they swallowed my feet, which sucked. Even after I'd destroyed Laadan's dress, she'd let me borrow some sexy black pumps that made me feel tall and clever.

"I'm really sorry about the dress." I glanced back at the double doors adorned with a golden eagle. "I have some money saved up. I can pay for it."

"No. Don't worry about it." She patted my shoulder. "Although I am curious to what actually provoked you to leave the ball so quickly, and then go swimming. You left with your Seth. I'm assuming you went swimming with him?"

My cheeks flamed at the mention of Seth. If *my* Seth had been here to catch that, I'd never hear the end of it, but he wasn't allowed in the Council building. "He's not *my* Seth."

Marcus and Lucian rounded the corner before Laadan could do more than give me a knowing smile. Oddly, I felt grateful to see them.

Lucian floated up to me, clasping my cold hand in his. Or maybe his hand was so warm that mine felt chilled to the bone? "Dear, you look so nervous. There is nothing to be worried about. The Council will ask you a few questions, and that is all."

I met Marcus's stare over Lucian's shoulder. He looked like there was something to be worried about. Sliding my hand free, I resisted the urge to wipe it across my pants. "I'm not nervous."

Lucian patted my shoulder as he slid around me. "I must go in and take my seat. It's about to begin."

It being the whole reason I'd come up here. Watching the Council Guards hold the doors for Lucian, I decided I *wasn't* nervous. I just wanted to get this over and done with.

Marcus's lips were drawn tight when I faced him. Passing a meaningful look at Laadan, he waited until she nodded and followed Lucian into the Council before he spoke. "Alexandria, I expect you to be on your best behavior in there. Do not allow yourself to get drawn into any arguments. Only answer their questions—nothing more. Do you understand?"

My eyes narrowed as I crossed my arms. "What do you all expect me to do? Go buck wild and start cussing people?"

"Anything is possible, really. You're known for your temper, Alex. Some probably expect you to lose your cool," said a deep, familiar voice from behind me.

Every cell of my skin recognized and still responded to that voice. It didn't matter than I'd chosen Seth last night. Wasn't that what I'd done? My brain screamed at my body to not turn around, but it didn't listen.

Aiden looked every inch a pure-blood. One lock of his otherwise tamed, dark hair kept falling forward, brushing against thick, sooty lashes. Dressed in that white, mafia-style getup, he appeared even more untouchable to me.

Marcus cleared his throat, and I realized I was staring.

Blushing fire-engine red, I turned to Marcus. "I know. Just answer their questions, blah, blah. I got it."

Marcus glared at me. "I hope so."

I didn't know how else to prove to them that I wasn't going to jump out of my chair and body-slam someone.

Marcus checked his watch. "We must head in. Alexandria, the Guards will call you when the Council is ready."

"I won't go in with you all?" I asked.

He shook his head and disappeared into the Council, which left Aiden and me alone with the silent Guards. Ignoring him was out of the question. "So… how have you been?"

Aiden stared somewhere over my head. "Good. You?"

"Good."

He nodded and then glanced at the doors.

The awkwardness of all of this pained me. "You can go in. You don't have to wait out here."

His gaze fell on me finally. "I do have to go in."

I nodded, biting the inside of my cheek. "I know."

Aiden started toward the door, but then stilled. Seconds went by before he pivoted back to me. "Alex, you can do this. I know you can."

Our eyes locked, and I sucked in air. Speechless, I stood there as his gaze left mine and roamed over my face. I couldn't remember if I'd put on any makeup today. Maybe some lip gloss? My hair was under control so it fell around my cheeks and covered my neck perfectly. I touched my lips, happy to find they felt glossy.

His eyes zeroed in on my movements before he broke away, running a hand over his head. He let out a ragged sound and when he spoke; his voice was so low that I barely heard him. "I think… I'll remember how you looked last night for the rest of my life. Gods, you were so beautiful."

I may have stroked out.

The next thing I knew he'd disappeared beyond the heavy Council doors. He left me spinning in confusion. Hot then cold, kind and then standoffish. I didn't get it. Why tell me that… and then walk away? Like the day he'd said he wished Seth had killed the Master for hitting me. Why admit any of that?

Leaning against the wall, I let out a long, tired sigh. Now wasn't the time to obsess over Aiden's manic mood swings. I needed to focus on—

The door to my left opened, revealing a Council Guard. "Miss Andros, your presence has been requested."

Well, that came sooner than I'd expected. I pushed off the wall and followed the Guard into the Council. It looked different from what I remembered. Granted, the only time I had seen it was from the top balcony, hidden from the pures below. Titanium trim graced the curved benches that filled the ground floor of the coliseum. The symbols etched into the tiles were artfully done—nothing like the chicken scratches in the pathways back home. Things had to be bigger, better here.

Those in attendance swiveled around in their seats as I made my way down the center aisle. Openly curious stares met mine. Others were not so curious—more like downright hostile and suspicious.

Steeling myself, I focused on the raised dais ahead instead of the violent roiling in my stomach. The Ministers sat like gods about to rain down some great and terrible divine justice. They watched my progress, picking apart everything about me before I'd even reached them. Only one didn't seem bothered by me. Reclining in one of the smaller thrones, dressed in lavish white robes, Lucian stared at Telly. Or perhaps he was staring at Telly's throne, imagining himself in the seat that offered the closest thing our world had to absolute power.

An open chair faced the audience in front of the Eight, directly between two thrones occupied by Head Minister Telly and Diana Elders. I stared at the seat, unsure if I was supposed to wait until I was given the okay to sit or make myself at home.

I sat.

A hush of disapproval swept through the crowd of pures. Apparently, that'd been the wrong action. This was starting out great. Lifting my eyes, I glanced at the balcony and caught a shadow flickering back from the railing.

Seth.

I felt Telly rise behind me, but I didn't dare look. Somehow I knew that would also give rise to another murmur of censure. Casually, I rested my hands on the arms of the chair and stared out at the crowd in front of me. I searched out Aiden immediately. He was leaning forward in his seat, eyes fastened on the Ministers behind me.

"Alexandria Andros." Head Minister Telly drifted around my chair. He stopped beside me, tipping his head to the side. With an elegant wave toward the audience, he smiled broadly, making him look like a demented cherub past its prime. "We must ask that you swear an oath to the Council and to the gods that you will answer each question today with the utmost honesty. Do you understand?"

I nodded, eyeing the Head Minister. Was it just me, or did the gray clinging to the hair around his temples appear to be spreading?

"Breaking this oath would be an act of treason not just against the Council, but also the gods. Doing so would result in your removal from the Covenant. This is also understood, I assume?"

"Yes."

"Then do you, Alexandria Andros, swear to disclose all information regarding the events that took place in Gatlinburg?"

I met Telly's pale eyes. "Yes."

His smile turned brittle as he held my gaze. "Good. How have you found your accommodations here, Alexandria? Have they been to your liking?" Telly tsked softly. "Look only at me, Alexandria."

The arms of the chair groaned as my fingers dug into the wood. "Everything has been *lovely*."

One dark brow arched as he glided to the other side of my chair. "That pleases me to hear. Alexandria, why did your mother leave the Covenant three years ago?"

I blinked tightly. "What does that have to do with what happened in Gatlinburg?"

"You have been asked a question—no, do not look out to the audience. Why did your mother leave the Covenant three years ago?"

"I… I don't know why." I kept my eyes on Telly this time. "She never told me."

Telly glanced at the audience while he rubbed his thumb and index finger together. "You do not know?"

"No." I heard myself say, staring at his hand.

"That is not true, Alexandria. You know why your mother left the Covenant."

Jerking my eyes away from his hand, I shook my head. "My mother never told me why. All I know is what other people have said."

"What were those reasons?"

Where was he going with this? I followed his slow, purposeful movements. He was circling me. "She left because the oracle told her I would become the next Apollyon."

"Why would that make her leave?"

I couldn't help it. My gaze moved to the balcony, to where I knew Seth watched.

"Alexandria, do not look away!" he snapped.

Now I understood why Marcus had looked so worried. My entire body thrummed with the desire to plant my foot into Telly's gut. I glared at him. "She wanted to protect me."

A different Minister spoke next. The older pure woman's voice rubbed like sandpaper over my skin. "From whom would she have wanted to protect you?"

Was I supposed to continue looking at Telly or the Minister? "I don't know. Maybe she was worried about the gods getting upset over there being two of us."

"That would be a concern," she responded. "There should not be two of you in the same generation."

"What other reasons would there be?" asked Telly.

Words tumbled out of my mouth. Not good or smart ones. "Maybe she was afraid of what the Council would do."

Telly stiffened. "That is absurd, Alexandria."

"It's what she said."

"Really?" His brows rose. "I thought she never told you why she pulled you from the Covenant?"

Dammit. I could imagine the look on Aiden's and Marcus's faces. "She never told me why before she was... before she changed."

"But she told you after she chose to become a daimon?" asked a male Minister.

"My mother didn't choose to become a daimon!" I gripped the arms of the chair again, drawing in several deep breaths. "She was forced to become one. And yes, she told me that I wouldn't have lived if I'd stayed at the Covenant."

"What else did she tell you about why she left?" asked Telly.

"That was it."

"Why did you never report her during the three years you were missing?"

"She was my mom. I was afraid she would be punished."

"Rightfully so," said the elder Minister. "What she did was unforgiveable. From the moment she was told of your true nature, it was her duty to tell the Council."

"That is true, Minister Mola." Telly paused, placing a hand on the back of my chair. "How is that you did not know your mother had turned?"

Air couldn't fill my lungs quick enough. "I found her and I thought she was dead. I killed the daimon that… was hurting her."

"Then what happened?" Telly asked so softly I felt sure no one else could hear him.

My throat burned. "There was another daimon, and I… I ran."

"You ran?" repeated Telly, loud enough for the entire Council to hear.

"I thought she was dead." I swallowed, my gaze falling to the floor. "I was trying to get back to the Covenant."

"So it took the perceived death of your mother for you to remember your duty to the Covenant?" Telly didn't wait for me to answer, which was a good thing. I had no answer for that. "You were found in Atlanta? With four daimons, is that not correct?"

What did any of this have to do with what'd happened in Gatlinburg? "They were following me. It wasn't like I was hanging out with them."

"Your tone is one of disrespect," snapped the elder Minister. "It would do you well to remember your position, *half-blood*."

I bit down on my lip until I tasted blood.

Telly drifted to the right of me. "Where you aware of your mother's whereabouts after you returned to the Covenant, Alexandria?"

A fine trickle of sweat traced down my spine. "No."

"But you left the Covenant in August to find her, did you not? After she took part in the Lake Lure massacre? And you did find her?" Telly's full lips twisted cruelly.

Telly had tripped me up *again*. I closed my eyes and inhaled. "I didn't know *where* she was. I didn't even know she was alive until Lucian told me."

"Ah, yes." He glanced behind me at Lucian. "What did you do once you found out she was alive?"

Punched and kissed a pure-blood, but I doubted he wanted to know that. Actually, he'd love to know that; he'd use it to send me to the Masters within the hour. "Nothing."

Telly clucked his tongue. "But—"

Anger pulsed through me, pounding in my temples. "What do these questions have to do with what my mother told me the daimons were planning? They want to overtake the Council. Turn halfs and send them back to the Covenants to kill. Isn't that more important?"

Surprisingly, Telly handled my temporary loss of sanity well. "It has everything to do with it, Alexandria. What provoked you to leave the Covenant in search for your mother?"

The need to lie was almost too great. "When I realized she'd killed at Lake Lure, I left. I figured she'd find me and she did. I felt like… she was my responsibility, my problem."

"Interesting." Telly roamed to the edge of the dais. Looking out over the audience he spoke louder. "Is it true you did not fight Rachelle when you saw her in Bald Head?"

I glared at the back of Telly's head. "Yes."

He cocked his head to the side. "Why?"

"I froze. She was my *mother*."

"Half-bloods see through the elemental magic. We cannot. How could you see past the monster she'd become?" He pivoted around, smiling at me. "This is what we do not understand, Alexandria. You left Florida, claiming that you believed she was dead. You came back to the Covenant, and your mother followed you, leaving behind a trail of slaughtered pure-bloods and Guards."

"What? There was only the attack at Lake Lure. She didn't—"

"You've been sadly misled." His smile grew wider, truer. "She was responsible for over twenty attacks across the southeastern coast. We were able to track her progress right to the doorsteps of the North Carolina Covenant. She sent a daimon half-blood back to the Covenant. Was that to draw you out?"

Twenty attacks? No one had told me that. Not Aiden, Marcus, nor even Seth. They had to have known. Why wouldn't they've told me that?

"Alexandria?"

I lifted my eyes. "Yes… I guess she wanted to draw me out."

"It worked. You left the day after Kain Poros had returned and murdered several pure-bloods." Telly strode across the dais. "Tell me Alexandria, a half-blood named Caleb Nicolo was also with you in Gatlinburg?"

My chest clenched. "Yes."

Telly nodded. "Did he try to stop you in Bald Head?"

"Yes."

"Is this the same half-blood who died a few weeks ago?" asked a female Minister. "In a daimon attack while he was with this one?"

"I believe so," Telly answered.

"How convenient," the Minister murmured, but it sounded like he had screamed those words. "While you were in Gatlinburg with Rachelle, what did she tell you the daimons planned to do?"

Somewhat sick to my stomach, I told the Council what Mom had planned. Remembering my instructions, I didn't tell them it was actually Eric who elaborated on the whole thing. Nothing crossed Telly's face as he watched me. Honestly, I don't even think he cared about what I was saying.

"They plan to attack the Council and bring us down?" The old Minister snorted. "This is ridiculous. All of this."

Telly chuckled then. "It is to think that a bunch of addicts could form a cohesive plan."

"Addicts? Yes, they're addicted to aether, but they are the most dangerous kind of addict," said Minister Diana Elders, speaking for the first time. "We cannot dismiss what they are capable of. Knowing they can turn half-bloods changes things. And obviously the gods are questioning our ability to rein the daimons back in."

This started a battle of wills for the next several minutes. A few Ministers didn't like the idea of ignoring the daimons' plans, while the others simply didn't take the threat seriously. Suggestions were thrown around, like increasing the number of Sentinels and sending them out to target large infestations of daimons, but the majority of Ministers didn't see any reason to do so. The talks kept coming back to *me*.

My stomach filled with dread as understanding dawned. Telly and much of the Council outright dismissed the daimons' plans. Suddenly I knew what my mother had told me was not the whole reason why I'd been ordered to attend this session. Marcus had been *sadly misled*. Or maybe he'd known all along. Distracted by the other Ministers, I was able to look out over the crowd without Telly bitching me out.

Aiden whispered to Marcus, his hands tight and white-knuckled on the back of the bench in front of him. I looked up at the balcony. I could only imagine what Seth thought of all of this.

Telly finally returned his attention to me. "Rachelle planned on turning you into a daimon?"

I wanted to say *no shit,* but I decided against it. "Yes."

Telly turned his hawkish nose into the air. "Why?"

I rubbed my hand over my forehead. "She wanted me to become the Apollyon as a daimon. She thought she'd be able to control me then."

"So she wanted to use you?" asked Telly. "To do what?"

"She wanted to make sure I didn't come after her, I guess."

"What would you do for her?"

I met Telly's stare. Somehow, I think he already knew this part. "She wanted me to take out the other Apollyon… and she wanted me to help the daimons with their plans."

"Oh yes, their plans to take out the Council and enslave the pure-bloods?" Telly shook his head, smiling. "How many times were you tagged, Alexandria?"

My entire body tensed. "I don't know. A lot."

He appeared to consider this. "Enough to be turned, you think?"

Nightmares of those hours locked away with Daniel and Eric haunted me still. I remember that last tag—the one I'd felt sure would finally darken my soul, shatter it into nothing. One more tag and I would've crossed over to the dark side. A fine sheen of cold sweat broke out across my forehead.

"Alexandria?"

I blinked, bringing his face back into focus. "Almost enough."

"Did you try to stop them? Trained or not, you had already killed two daimons by then."

Disbelief coated the back of my throat.

"Tagging is very painful," Telly continued, stopping beside me for what felt like the hundredth time. His face seemed fuller when he stood close. "How could you allow that to happen repeatedly? It seems that a half-blood would do everything and anything to prevent from being tagged."

"I couldn't fight them."

His dark brows rose in incredulity. "You couldn't or wouldn't?"

I closed my eyes, struggling with patience. "I promised her I wouldn't if she didn't kill Caleb. I had no other choice."

"There are always choices, Alexandria." He paused, disgust curling his lip as he stared down at me. "To allow something so revolting seems suspicious. Perhaps you wanted to be turned."

"Head Minister," Lucian spoke up then. "I understand that some of these questions are necessary, but Alexandria did not submit to those atrocities willingly. To even suggest something like that seems unnatural and cruel."

"Is that so?" Telly sneered at me.

"Wait a second," I said, his words finally sinking in. "Are you suggesting that I wanted to be turned into something that evil? That I asked for it?"

Telly raised his hands haughtily. "How do you think we'd interpret it?"

I looked at the audience then, briefly catching a pained look on Marcus's face. "Do you know that sounds like a rapist's motto? She wore a short skirt, therefore she *wanted* it?"

Several gasps could be heard from the audience. It seemed the word "rapist" was unseemly. The smug look slowly slipped from Telly's face. "Alexandria, you are out of line."

My brain clicked off at that point. What Daniel had said to me before he'd tagged me filled my mind. It was like Telly thought the same thing. That I *wanted* to be tagged, that I enjoyed it. I stood. "You're telling me I'm out of line?"

"No one gave you leave." Telly drew himself up to his full height.

"Oh, I'm not leaving." All eyes were on me. I reached down and pulled my sweater up and over my head. There was a moment when no one seemed to breathe. I met the open mouthed stares; I'd think I didn't have a camisole on underneath the sweater by the looks on their faces.

"What in the world are you doing, Alexandria?" demanded Lucian.

Ignoring him, I stepped away from the chair and held my arms out in front of me. "Does this look like something I wanted to go along with? That I asked for this?"

Against their will, dozens and dozens of eyes fastened on my arms. Most gasped and shuddered, looking away quickly. Others didn't. As if they couldn't tear their eyes from the patchy red skin and its unnatural shine. My gaze flitted across the floor as Telly looked like he was having a heart attack beside me. I saw the proud tilt to Laadan's chin. A few rows in front of her I saw Dawn's horrified gaze. Further back, behind the Council members, Marcus paled. It kind of hit me that he'd never seen my scars, only caught glimpses of the ones on my neck. I don't think he'd known how bad they were. I felt a hot flush crawl up my neck, but the stunned look of pride on Aiden's face gave me the confidence to face the Ministers.

I wondered what Seth's expression looked like. He was probably smiling. He loved it when I was irrational, and this was *really* irrational.

Twisting around, I showed them my arms. "They look like they hurt, don't they? They did. It's the worst kind of pain you can imagine."

"Alexandria, sit down. We get your point." Telly reached for me, but I stepped aside.

A Guard moved in, picking up my sweater. He held it, his eyes nervously bouncing between Telly and me.

I glanced at the other Guards, hoping they weren't planning on body slamming me to the ground. All but one were half-bloods and none of them seemed willing to stop me. Tipping my head at the Ministers, I tried to keep the smile off my face. "So do you really think I went along with my mother? That I wanted this?"

Diana paled and looked away, shaking her head sadly. The remaining Ministers reacted much like the audience had. Either way, I'm pretty sure I'd gotten my point across.

A furious shade of red covered Telly's cheeks. "Are you done, Alexandria?"

I met his scowl with my own. Leisurely, I went back to my chair and sat down. "I guess so."

Telly ripped the sweater out of the Guard's hand. I could tell he wanted to throw it at me, but with amazing self-control, he handed it over. I didn't put it back on. "Now where were we?"

"We were at the point where you were accusing me of wanting to become a daimon."

Several Ministers inhaled sharply. Telly looked seconds away from exploding. Leaning down so that our faces were inches apart, he spoke low and quick. "You are an unnatural thing, do you understand me? A harbinger of death to our kind and to our gods. The both of you."

I shrunk back, wide-eyed. "Harbinger of death" sounded extreme and crazy.

"Head Minister," called Lucian. "We could not hear your question. Would you care to speak again?"

Telly straightened. "I asked her if there was anything more she would like to add."

My jaw hit the floor.

He smiled evenly. "There are areas besides the event in Gatlinburg that concern me greatly, Alexandria. Your behavior before you left the Covenant and the fighting you have taken part in upon your return have served you a great disadvantage, I'm afraid. And how is it that the night the Covenant was breached in North Carolina, you were outside your dorm after the curfew implemented for half-bloods?"

I so knew where this was going, so I cut to the chase. "I didn't let the daimons in, if that is what you're suggesting."

Telly's smile turned sour. "So it appears. Then there is your behavior since you arrived here. You accused a pure-blood of using a compulsion against you, did you not?"

"She did what?" screeched the old female Minister. "To accuse a pure-blood of such an act is shocking. Was there any proof, Minister Telly?"

"My Guards could not find anything to support the claim." Telly paused dramatically. "And then you attacked a Master who was disciplining a servant."

Several Ministers lost it then. Telly preened as they demanded to know exactly what occurred. I pictured rushing across the dais and kicking Telly in the groin over and over again.

When it calmed down a bit, Telly addressed the Council. His voice rang loud through the coliseum. "I fear that we have a greater concern than daimons pulling together and attacking us in droves. What you see sitting before us may look like an ordinary half-blood, but we all know that is not the case. In a matter of a few months, she will become the second Apollyon. If she is even half as uncontrollable as she is now, what do you think will occur when she Awakens?"

My heart stuttered, missing a beat.

"As the Head Minister, it pains me deeply to suggest this, but I fear we have no other choice. We must protect the future of our true Masters. I petition that we remove Alexandria Andros from the Covenant and place her under the supervision of the Masters."

I jerked forward blindly. I couldn't even move as the rush of fear coated my mouth and churned my stomach into raw knots. This was what Telly wanted—the whole reason for me being here. It had nothing to do with what the daimons planned.

From above, I felt a tempest building. It drifted over my skin, raising the tiny hairs on my body. Seth was a storm about to explode.

"Minister Telly, my *stepdaughter* has committed no crime that warrants servitude," Lucian objected. "She has to be found guilty before you can expel her from the Covenant and place her into servitude."

"As the Head Minister—"

"You have a lot of power as the Head Minister. You can expel her from the Covenant, but you cannot sentence her to servitude without due cause or by vote of the Council," Lucian said. "Those are the rules."

I looked up, my eyes meeting Aiden's. This was one of those rare moments in my life that I knew *exactly* what Aiden was thinking.

I twisted around in the chair. Telly glared at Lucian, but I saw that Lucian was right. Telly could expel me, but he couldn't send me into servitude on a whim. He would need the Council to do so, and I had a feeling if the Council agreed it would be the last thing they ever did.

"Then I call for a vote." Telly's voice was like ice.

I calculated the distance from where I sat and the door to my right. My muscles tensed as I let go of the chair and twisted sideways. My sweater fell from my lap. I didn't want to hurt the half-blood Guards, but I was going to get past them.

Then what?

Run like hell.

"How do you vote?" asked Telly.

The first "yes" sent a shiver through me; the second caused the air to ripple with electricity. The audience shifted as the third "yes" skyrocketed the tension. I wanted to look at Aiden one last time, but I couldn't take my eyes off the door. It would be my only chance.

Three of the Ministers said "no," and Telly stalked toward the end of the dais. The next said "yes," and my stomach dropped. I wanted to cry out, but fear clamped my throat shut. Facing down daimons was one thing, but a lifetime of servitude was my worst fear.

"Head Minister Elders, you are the last vote." I could hear the smile in Telly's voice.

Silence filled the room, holding the pures transfixed and stretching my nerves into taut lines. *This was it... This was it...* I closed my eyes, drawing in a deep breath.

"She has proven to be… a problem," Diana said, her voice as clear as Telly's. "There are many areas which concern me greatly, but I have to vote 'no.' She has to break the Breed Order to be placed in servitude, and she has not, Minister Telly. Everything that has been provided has been circumstantial."

Sagging against the chair, the air expelled from my lungs. Violent energy pulled back, slithering from my skin as it made its way back to its host.

Telly didn't take that well, but there was nothing he could do. He returned to my side, glaring. I wanted nothing more than to karate chop him in the neck.

"Then Miss Andros, you shall continue as you are, for now." Telly smiled tightly. "One more mistake, Alexandria, one more time and that will be it. You will be placed into servitude."

CHAPTER 23

AFTER COUNCIL, MARCUS ESCORTED ME TO MY ROOM with explicit instructions. "Do not leave this room unless someone is with you."

Had he seen this room? Spending the rest of however long it took for Seth to show up or Laadan to take pity on me felt like punishment. I hadn't done anything wrong. It wasn't my fault Telly was a lunatic, hell-bent on sending me into servitude.

But I spent the rest of the day and the better part of the evening in my room, picturing the look on Telly's face after I Awakened and lit him up with enough Apollyon juice to obliterate him into nothing. And all those pures who'd looked at my scars with such disgust? I'd give them something to freak out about. Okay. Maybe I was overreacting a tad bit. But Telly's antagonistic attitude chafed at me. I needed to get out, needed to do something.

What I really needed was to hit something.

Just when I was about to go crazy, there was a soft knock on my door. Rushing toward it, I threw it open. Laadan stood in the doorway, two crystal glasses in her hands. Her cheeks were flushed, eyes bright.

Please be here to let me out of this room.

Her eyes weren't really focused on me as she smiled. "I figured you could stretch your legs." She stepped back. "Coming?"

Thank you, gods. I followed her graceful form down the hall and the steps. Downstairs, the pures were in full celebratory mode. From the sounds coming out of the ballroom and reception hall, they sounded trashed already. No one would be paying attention to me. They were too busy partying it up. Their blasé attitude toward everything was infuriating and frustrating.

"I thought you could use the company," she said slowly, speaking for the first time since she'd appeared outside my door.

We stopped outside the crowded reception hall. Laadan stood beneath a painting of the Goddess Hera. The resemblance between the two was striking. She offered me a glass of the luminous red liquid. "Here, you deserve this after the day you had."

The glass felt warm in my hand. "What is it?"

She smiled as her gaze drifted away. "It's something special for a special girl. You'll love it."

"Are you buzzing?" I giggled.

Laadan sighed dreamily. "It's a beautiful night, Alex. How is your drink?"

I lifted the glass and took a cautious sniff. It smelled magnificent—like wild orchids, and a hint of honey and sesame. Looking up, I saw Laadan float into the entrance of the reception hall. I trailed behind her, my gaze gliding across the crowd as I brought the glass to my lips. I saw Marcus and Diana standing super close. Once again, the smile on Marcus's face confused me. He never smiled like that, especially not when I was around.

Giggles erupted across the room, drawing my attention. Young pure girls surrounded a good-looking male, clamoring over each other to be the closest to him. Several Guards stood behind the happy little group, looking equally bored and aloof. Among them stood the pure-blood Guard whom Telly had called on during the first session. I shuddered, holding the glass tighter. Then my eyes flitted further into the hall and settled on Aiden.

Dawn stood by his side, looking stunningly beautiful and staring at him with large eyes the color of amethyst. Seeing them together didn't bring the warm and fuzzies. He'd never showed her an ounce of interest outside of being friendly, but she was the kind of girl Aiden would be allowed to date—should date.

Maybe he'd marry her one day—or another pure like Dawn. He'd settle down and commit. *Stop*, I ordered myself. That didn't matter—not even if he had a dozen pure-blooded babies. I'd accepted I couldn't be with him. Besides, I'd kind of chosen Seth. But hurt climbed deep inside my chest, taking root around my heart. I deserved a swift kick in the butt for standing here, staring at him like some kind of obsessive stalker chick.

"Your drink, dear, are you not going to try it?"

"Oh." I glanced down. It still felt wonderfully warm in my hand. The drink burned my lips and the tip of my tongue, but went down surprisingly smooth. It actually tasted minty—a warm wintergreen. "It tastes…"

Laadan was gone.

Surprised by her vanishing act, I looked around the hall, finding Aiden instead of Laadan. He'd moved, standing at the end of the hall now. Minus Dawn, he spoke to another pure, but he appeared focused on me.

His disapproval stretched beyond where he stood and slammed into me. Was it because I was outside my room? If so, that irked me. What also irked me was the fluttering in my chest.

Aiden broke away from the pure, stepping forward and looking very, very angry. My heart leapt in my chest. He was coming to me—not Dawn, not some other pure, but *me*. The fluttering in my chest increased.

Any attention was good attention.

Suddenly, I hated that idea. Hated the fact I would be *satisfied* with that. I tipped the glass back and took a long swallow. It was either that or throw myself on the floor, sobbing and flailing.

I took another sip, expecting the burning this time. It did taste good, really good. I looked up again and found that a tall, blond pure partially blocked Aiden, but his furious gaze still found me. I quirked a brow at him and brought the glass to my lips again, taking another draft.

Aiden cut around the pure and made a beeline straight for me.

Out of nowhere, and I mean freaking nowhere, Seth appeared and whipped the drink out of my hand, splashing red drops all over my sweater.

"Jeez!" I ran my hand over my mouth. "Was that necessary?"

Seth brought the glass to his face and sniffed it. Swearing under his breath, he shoved it at Aiden. "Who gave you this?" Seth demanded.

"Why do you care? It's just a drink."

"Alex, who gave you this drink?" Aiden's quiet voice left no room for me to push his buttons.

"Laadan gave it to me. What's the big deal?"

Seth's mouth dropped open, but Aiden's reaction was far stronger. "Shit. Unbelievable."

"What?" I looked between the two. "What's going on?"

"Freaking pures," Seth spat. "I can only begin to imagine what they hoped to achieve with this."

The glass looked like it would shatter in Aiden's hand. Fury radiated off him in waves and his eyes burned, but he wouldn't look at me now. Not at all. "Dammit. Was this your first glass?"

"Yes." I stepped forward. "Aiden, what's going on?"

Seth exhaled harshly. "Half a glass is more than enough."

"There is no way Laadan would have given her this." Aiden scowled. "She knows what this drink will do."

"Laadan did give it to me. I wouldn't lie about that. Tell me what the hell is going on."

Seth ran a hand over his head. "I think I'm going to hit someone."

I shot a look at Seth. He wouldn't look at me either. Was there something wrong with my face? I put my hand to my cheeks and the only thing I noticed was my skin felt warm.

"I can't leave now." Aiden spoke in crisp, short words. "Telly and the other Ministers want us here. She can't be left alone, Seth."

Seth nodded. "I'll keep an eye on her."

Aiden barked a short laugh. "Yeah, I don't think so."

"Then what do you suggest we do?" Seth demanded. "Let her roam free?"

My temper snapped. I reached out and grabbed Aiden's arm—a bad thing to do to a pure in public, but they were acting like I wasn't even standing here. "What is going on?"

Aiden whirled around and grasped my hand, pulling me between the two of them. "There is no way Laadan would have given you this drink freely. Did she seem strange to you? Acting different in any way?"

"Yes," I whispered. "She seemed buzzed."

His eyes snapped fire. "She was compelled to give you this drink."

"No way, that's impossible. It's completely illegal to compel another pure. You have to—"

"Someone set you up, Alex, and they wanted to badly enough to break the rules themselves. All pures know what that drink is just by looking at it. You were given Aphrodesian Brew, Alex."

"Brew? Oh. *Oh*. Oh, my gods." I felt cold and hot all at once. I'd just drunk the equivalent of an Olympian roofie. Disbelief set in. "You have to be wrong. A pure wouldn't compel another pure and Laadan would never give me something like that. I don't care what you say."

"Alex," Aiden said gently. "There are pures who know you're close with Laadan."

"Aiden, we need to get her out of here. Soon," Seth interjected.

I glanced at him. "I feel fine. I must not have had enough."

Seth laughed dryly. "Yeah."

Aiden let go of my hand, staring at Seth. "I don't like you—let alone trust you."

A muscle feathered along Seth's jaw. "You don't have any other options at this point. I won't let anything happen to her, Aiden. And I wouldn't… take advantage of her."

I shot Seth a dirty look. "No one is taking advantage of me unless I want to be taken advantage of."

Whoa, that didn't come out right.

"Out of the question," Aiden said in a low, dangerous way.

"Guess what? I don't like you, either. But you don't have any other choice. Either you risk this or you trust me enough to know that I'll keep an eye on her." Seth paused, his gaze meeting Aiden's. "I have just as much invested as you."

I scratched my leg. "Invested in what?"

They ignored me.

Aiden sort of growled. "If anything—anything happens to her—"

"I know," replied Seth. "You'll kill me."

"I'll do worse," Aiden growled. "Don't take her to her room. We don't need Marcus knowing about this. Take her to… your room. As soon as I can, I will come." He turned to me and forced a smile. I hated that kind of smile. "Everything is going to be okay. Just please, please listen to Seth, and whatever you do, don't leave his room."

I stared at Aiden. "Wait. I want—"

Aiden had already turned and disappeared into the crowd. Then Seth took hold of my hand, leading me from the hall. I really didn't know what to expect. I'd heard rumors at the Covenant about the Brew, knew that Lea had supposedly had some, but I'd never seen anyone under its influence.

Seth didn't say anything as we navigated the hallways and headed upstairs. Several flights of stairs later, I still felt okay. "I really feel fine. Nothing is wrong with me. I'm sure I can go to my room. I won't leave."

Seth pulled me down the hallway.

"Look, why won't you talk to me? Especially after last night—"

He shot me a dangerous look over his shoulder. "This right now has nothing to do with last night."

I glared back at him even though I thought his hand felt incredibly smooth around mine. "Are you mad at me?"

"Alex, I'm not mad at you. But I am pissed right now. It's best I just don't speak. I might end up burning down this building." Letting go of my hand then, he pushed open the door to his room and motioned me forward. "In."

I shot him a haughty look. Really, they were making this into a bigger deal than— "What the hell?"

Seth kicked the door shut behind him. "What?"

"How come you get this awesome room?" I turned around, amazed by the cathedral ceilings, plush carpets, and a big screen television that took up half the wall. And the bed—it was the size of a boat. My current predicament was temporarily forgotten. "I've been sleeping in a closet. This isn't fair."

He dropped his key on a dresser. "I'm the Apollyon."

"So? I am, too, and I got a matchbox for a room. A coffin would've been bigger."

"You're not an Apollyon yet."

That was the extent of our conversation for several minutes. I watched him prowl around the room, and then over to the window. There he stayed.

"What're you doing?"

Seth leaned against the windowsill, attention fastened on whatever he saw outside. Several strands of hair had slipped from the tie and obscured most of his expression. "Help yourself to whatever you want in the room. Watch some TV or go to sleep."

My temper stretched and snapped. "You're an ass."

He didn't respond.

I shifted uncomfortably, wishing I'd thrown on a shirt under the hoodie. The room felt steamy, nearly unbearable. I went to the bed to sit down, but stopped. A strange sensation crawled up my spine. It felt different—incredible. Like an incredible rush of—of happiness. Yes. Like waves of sunshine and all things good.

Everything suddenly seemed okay—great even.

Seth turned from the window, his eyes narrowing on me. "Alex?"

I twisted around slowly. The room seemed lighter, soft, beautiful. Everything seemed beautiful. I think I may have sighed.

"Oh, gods," Seth groaned. "It's starting."

"What's starting?" I barely recognized my own voice.

Seth looked at me pointedly. I thought he looked funny, so I laughed, and it was like a switch being thrown. I wanted to run and dance, and sing—and I couldn't sing, but I wanted to—and I wanted to… do stuff.

His slouch vanished and his expression took on a hard edge. "Go sit down, Alex."

I tipped my head back. Well, it kind of fell back, and I liked the weight of my hair falling into empty space, just hanging there. It felt good on my neck.

"Seriously, go sit down."

"Why?" I lifted my head, swaying a little. My skin tingled, like, all over—tingled like electric shocks—like when Aiden used to touch me or when I'd kissed Seth last night. I'd liked that, too, but I'd liked Aiden's kisses better. Seth's touch evoked something different. Gods, my brain wouldn't shut up. It just kept going and going.

He pushed away from the window. "You look ridiculous, Alex."

I stopped moving, having no clue exactly when I'd started swaying back and forth. "Yooooou look mooooore ridiculous," I sang. "You're brooding. Brooding doesn't fit you."

He rubbed his chin as his gaze followed me with the intensity of a hawk stalking its prey. "This is going to be a long night."

"Maybe." I inched closer to him, because I wanted to be closer to something, someone. "Hey. You smiled."

He dropped his hand. "Don't."

I giggled. "Don't what?"

"Don't come any closer, Alex."

"You had no problem being close to me last night. Why, are you scared of me?"

"I'm not."

"Then why can't I?"

Amusement flickered across his face for a second before vanishing. "Alex, you need to go lie down."

I spun around, suddenly overcome by the urge to dance. When we'd waltzed in the field—that'd been fun. I wanted to do it again, and I wanted Seth to join me. Dancing alone was kind of lame.

"Alex—"

"Okay. I'm sitting down." Then I darted for him. I must've taken him off guard, because he didn't move, and come on, Seth could've moved out of the way if he'd wanted to.

But he didn't.

I wrapped my arms around his waist like an octopus, and I didn't want to dance anymore. "This feels good," I murmured, rubbing my cheek against the front of his shirt.

Seth didn't react at first, and I *knew* he thought it felt good, too. Then he grabbed my arms and untangled them from his waist. "Alex, please go sit down."

"I don't want to." I tried to reach for his neck, but he stepped back. I frowned. "Why do you keep moving away from me? Are you scared of me now?"

"Yes. Right now, I am."

I threw my head back, laughing. "The big bad Apollyon is afraid of me? I'm hot. Can't you open up a window?"

Seth spun around and went to the window. "Why did I suggest this?"

"Because yooooou like me," I sang, turning and turning until I felt dizzy. "You really, really like me. Gods, I need to drink this stuff more often. I feel awesome."

Groaning, he looked for the window lock. "You won't later."

"Huh? You drank it before? You have! You dirty, dirty Apollyon." I threw myself on the bed. It was *so* comfortable. "I love your bed." I rolled onto my stomach, smiling. "I love it so much I'd marry it if I could."

Seth laughed out loud. "You'd marry my bed?"

"Mmm." I flopped onto my back. There was a painted mural on Seth's ceiling. Angels and other winged creatures painted in pretty pastels. "I would if I could marry, but we can't marry. Not even inanimate objects. Kind of takes the fun out of falling in love."

"Does it?" murmured Seth.

I pushed off the bed, unable to sit still. Seth was still at the window, but he'd forgotten about the lock. "Haven't you ever been in love, Seth?"

He blinked slowly. "I don't think so. Does loving yourself count?"

I laughed. "No. It doesn't. But good try. Seth?"

"Yes?"

"It's hot in here."

Shaking his head, he turned back to the window. "Yeah, let me find the damn lock on this thing and I'll fix that for you."

It was too hot. Just too hot in here, and I couldn't stand the itchy material against my skin anymore. Seth was taking too long. I tugged the hoodie over my head and dropped it on the floor. I immediately felt a thousand times better.

Seth stiffened and let out a strangled sound. "Please tell me you did not take off your clothes."

I giggled. "No."

He ran his hands over his head. More silky strands sifted through his fingers. "I'm going to regret this. I'm so going to regret this."

"I'm not naked, you idiot." I tugged my hair off my neck and started twisting it. "And you've been trying to see me naked since I met you."

"That may be the case, but not like this."

"Naked is naked," I reasoned.

Slowly, Seth turned around and froze. His chest rose and fell unsteadily. "Oh, for the love of the gods, Alex, where is your shirt?"

I didn't understand why he was making a big deal about this. I had a bra on. It wasn't like… the thought evaporated. "I'm so hot. Just give me a shirt. Your shirt would work."

"Yes… you're hot. I can tell." His voice sounded thick and edgy.

I laughed and let go of my hair, but I was still hot… and out of control. The last time I'd felt this way, I'd kissed Aiden. That is, after I'd punched him in the face. I stopped moving, not liking the nervous fluttering in my stomach. I looked down, expecting to see my skin move. I poked my tummy once, but it felt like I'd jabbed my finger into the skin a thousand times. My heart skipped a beat.

"What are you doing?" Seth asked.

"I don't know. My stomach feels all light."

"It's the drink. You'll feel better if you just sit down. I'll get you a shirt. Just hold on a sec."

I looked up then. Seth had moved to the dresser, rummaging through the drawers. His back was to me—a vulnerable position—and he seemed to be concentrating awful hard on finding a shirt.

A new, although somewhat old, idea consumed me. I don't think I'd ever moved so quietly in my life. I was ninja stealth. Seth didn't realize until it was too late. He shot up and whipped around, eyes wide.

"Alex, just let me get you a shirt. Stay put." He moved to the left.

I followed him, shadowing his movements much like I did in training. Giving up on the shirt, he darted away from the dresser—away from me. But I was quicker. Once again, I had my arms around him. Then an even better idea took over.

"Kiss me?" I asked.

CHAPTER 24

SETH TIPPED HIS HEAD BACK, SIGHING LOUDLY. "ALEX, you don't want this. It's the drink."

"That's not true. Nothing's wrong with me. Don't you want to kiss me?"

"It's not about what *I* want." He clasped my arms. "I'm not doing this when you're like this."

"I'm not drunk," I said indignantly.

"You were just dancing like some wood nymph five minutes ago. You took off your shirt and now you're latched onto me like a little monkey. So don't tell me you're in complete control of yourself."

Damn. When he said it like that, I had to stop and think about what I was doing. Thinking lasted all of five seconds, maybe six. Thinking was overrated. "You want to kiss me and you liked kissing me last night."

Seth made a low sound in his throat as he grabbed my shoulders, giving me a little shake. "Do you know why you feel this way right now? It has nothing to do with me or you," he said roughly. "Someone wanted to ruin you, Alex. They wanted to get you on your back with some pure so you'd be removed from the Covenant and placed into servitude. Don't you get it? This—*this* is not you."

"No. This is me, really me. Or the connection thingy, but who cares? I want you to kiss me again. I like you, Seth. I really don't know why. You're arrogant and rude, but I like you. Don't you like me?"

"Alex." He said my name as if he was in some sort of exquisite pain. "I'm trying to be a good guy right now, and you're not helping."

"I don't want you to be a good guy."

He choked on his laugh. "You are making this really hard."

I pressed against him. "You're making this harder."

His hands slid down my arms again, sending shivers over me. Could it be possible to be so hot and so cold all at once? "Alex."

"Seth."

"There are a lot of things I want to do to you right now, but it wouldn't be right."

I tipped my head back and looked him in the eye. Faint marks of the Apollyon started to creep across his face. "Don't you want to kiss me?" I reached up, running my fingers over his parted lips. "I know you do. I can tell."

Seth's grip tightened and his eyes fell shut. I slipped a hand under the hem of his shirt. He inhaled and tried to step back, but I followed him… a bit too closely. My leg got snared with his. For someone normally so graceful, he wasn't right then. He went down, half on his side and half on his back.

And I, well, I was right where I wanted to be. Giggling, I pressed my mouth to his neck. "Yay me," I murmured against his skin.

Seth jerked his head back, but his hands dropped to my hips, fingers digging through the denim. "Alex! Get off—"

I lowered my mouth to his. Seth pushed at me, but I had a really good hold on him and he didn't push too hard. And then he stopped pushing me and was pulling me closer—so close that I melted into nothing. Restraint and good intentions vanished when my lips brushed over his. This kiss wasn't soft or filled with tentative exploration. Seth's hands got tangled in my hair, and for a while, I got lost in that kiss, lost in all the insane sensations. Then his hands were on my shoulders, my back, and then the clasp of my bra. Seth's lips never left mine once, not even when he rolled me onto my back.

Things kind of got beautifully out of control at that point. His shirt came off. My jeans ended up clear across the room. My fingers found the button on his jeans and so on. Crazy as it sounded, Seth held back when I tugged him closer, lifted off me when I tried to wrap myself around him. And even though my body burned for more—demanded it, really—a small nagging voice picked up in the back of my mind, asking questions I didn't want to answer. Pointing out that this *wasn't* real. Or was it? I didn't know anymore. I knew I should care, but I didn't. Everything became about feeling.

Seth's lips moved across my skin. His hands cupped my cheek before drifting down. My own hands followed his lead, mimicking everything he did until the tips of my fingers no longer felt tingly, but numb instead.

Seth pulled away again, his breathing heavy and ragged as his fingers traced the curve of my neck. "I shouldn't do this. Not when you're like this, but I can't help myself. What does that say about me?"

His words confused my already jumbled thought process, but then he kissed me again. This was the powerful, deep kind—the kind I'd had little experience in handling. Only once had I been kissed like this.

Aiden.

Oh, *my* Aiden. My heart, the very air I breathed equaled Aiden. But his name disappeared in the mad rush of Seth's touch. I shifted restlessly, needing to be closer, and I thought I'd moved at first, but I hadn't moved at all. I tried to again, but my body wouldn't respond.

"We should stop here, Angel," Seth whispered against my lips, even as he slid a hand under my hip, lifting me, bringing me closer.

Closer. Hadn't that been what I wanted all long? Didn't I still want that? I just couldn't get closer. My hands slipped off his back and then my arms fell limply to my sides.

Seth lifted his head and two bright, nearly iridescent eyes filled my vision. They were hazy, clouded with passion. I think he frowned, but then his face blurred in and out.

"Alex? What…? Oh, hell."

Concern replaced lust, passion—whatever he'd felt. He sat back, pants sliding low on his hips as he pulled me into his lap. "Alex, are you in there?" He brushed the hair off my face.

"I'm… so tired. Sorry…"

He smiled, but it rang false. "I know. It's okay."

I shivered, unable to wrap my arms around myself. Where had all that heat gone?

Seth got his other arm around me and stood, cradling me like he'd had a lot of experience carrying girls. Judging by his recent actions, I think he did. He placed me on the bed and hovered over me. "You still there?"

I blinked slowly, his face going in and out. "I'm… sleepy."

"Okay." Seth leaned in and brushed his lips over my forehead. I squeezed my eyes shut, stomach twisting when he disappeared.

A few seconds later, he returned to my side and helped me get into a shirt that fell to my knees. Things were kind of hazy after that. Numbness settled so deep in my bones, I started to believe that my limbs weren't connected anymore. Unable to move, unable to say more than a few words at a time, I lay there and tried to figure out what was going on with my body.

Lust and all those other warm, wonderful feelings had vanished. So had the numbness, and in their place was a godsawful feeling in the pit of my stomach. I squeezed my eyes shut again and tried to breathe through the sharp rise of nausea. It didn't help. A twisting and churning motion swept through me. Oh, gods, this wasn't going to be good. I was going to puke. I could feel—taste it—and I couldn't move. A soft whimper escaped my lips.

The bed dipped beside me and a warm hand brushed across my cheek. "You hanging in there?"

"Sick," I gasped out.

Seth scooped me up in one swipe and carried me to the bathroom. The part of my brain that still functioned on normal Alex level noted that his bathroom was bigger than my entire room, and much nicer. So not fair. But then I stopped thinking altogether. The moment he held me over the toilet, I started heaving. Once I started, I couldn't stop.

I really don't know how long I remained latched there or how in the world Seth stomached all of it, holding me up and keeping my hair out the way. Only when my sides ached and my eyes leaked did the painful heaving subside.

"Better?" Seth smoothed the damp strands off my forehead.

"I want to die," I moaned pitifully. "I think I'm… dying."

"No, you're not." Seth shook his head. "Water will help. Just hold on to—" He tried to keep me upright, but I slipped to the floor. "Or just lie down. That works, too."

I pressed my forehead against the cool tile. It helped with the hot feeling, but my head throbbed something fierce. Moaning, I wrapped my arms around my waist and curled into a ball.

Seth cursed under his breath. I felt him stand and go back into the bedroom. I hoped he left me there. I never wanted to move ever again. I could rot there, as long as the pounding went away and the room stopped spinning.

But he returned a few seconds later and forced me to sit up. He barely got one bottle of water in me. I struggled, slapping his hands away a dozen times. Seth was halfway through forcing a second bottle when someone knocked at the door. We heard it swing open.

Seth swore again, put the bottle of water down, and eased me back to the floor. Ah, the cool floor was my friend—*friend?* I missed Caleb. I missed him so terribly.

"Where is she? Seth?" Aiden's firm voice called from the bedroom.

"Dammit," Seth muttered, standing. "She's fine," he called out. "Just needs a few more minutes to hang on to the floor."

I wanted to hit him.

Seth left the bathroom then, and the silence from the other room stretched out long, becoming ripe with tension. My mind provided the images of what the room must've looked like to Aiden. And shirtless, pants-unbuttoned Seth. Surely—*surely* Seth would've taken five seconds to button them?

I heard Seth sigh. "Look, I know all this looks really bad. It's not what you think."

"This isn't what it looks like?" Aiden growled, and I'd never heard his voice sound that way before, so hard and flat but with an edge that trembled with the promise of violence. "Really? Because I think *this* belongs to Alex."

I cringed, wishing I could sink through the floor and disappear. A mass of confusion and unease formed in my delicate stomach. Then Aiden stood in the doorway to the bathroom, and I knew I must've looked a mess. Damp hair clung to my skin; the room smelled of sickness, and I was dressed in Seth's shirt and little else.

"Aiden," I said weakly. "It's not—"

"Seth, I trusted you." Aiden's voice was filled with cold steel.

"Look, I know. This wasn't—"

The sound of a fist connecting with flesh came from the next room. A body slammed into something—a dresser? Something heavy crashed to the floor, shattering. The really sweet TV came to mind. Curses exploded from each of them.

I pushed myself off the bathroom floor, standing on wobbly legs. The white walls and gilded mirror spun in wild circles for a moment. Pushing through the dizziness, I staggered out of the bathroom and into the middle of a major throwdown between a highly trained Sentinel and the Apollyon.

"Guys, come on… you both are being so stupid." I swayed to the left. Cold sweat clung to my forehead.

They either didn't hear me or didn't care. Aiden, who looked surprisingly unscathed, backed Seth across the room. He lunged at Seth, knocking him to the floor. They rolled, each of them exchanging and receiving blows.

"Aiden! Stop it!" I lurched forward, swearing as my stomach rolled violently. "Seth—don't choke him!"

Seth had gained the upper hand, rolling Aiden onto his back. He reared back, throwing one arm in the air. Blue light shimmered around his fist. *Akasha.* I panicked—which maybe wasn't the greatest thing to do considering my reflexes and even basic walking skills were subpar at the moment. I stumbled to them, intending on pulling Seth off Aiden, and then I planned to knock the crap out of both of them.

I wrapped my arms around Seth's waist the same moment Aiden slammed his fist into Seth's stomach. When Seth fell backwards, so did I. My shoulder smacked off the edge of the bed first and then Seth's weight crashed onto me. I hit the floor for the second time that night.

Aiden popped to his feet and grabbed Seth, tossing him to the side. I turned over and there was my bra—lying right there, laughing at me. I closed my eyes, utterly mortified.

"What the hell?" another voice rang out. A clear, distinct voice I knew belonged only to Leon. "Have you all lost your godsforsaken minds?"

Seth rolled to his knees, wiping his hand over his bloodied lip. "Oh, we're just wrestling."

Aiden shot him a dark look as he dropped down. "Alex, are you okay?" He slid his hands under my arms and helped me to sit up. "Say something."

I peered through the mess of hair covering my face. "I'm… great."

Aiden brushed the hair off my face. "I'm sorry. I should have never—"

"Aiden, I know you're pissed—"

"Pissed? You took advantage of her, Seth." Aiden rose to his feet. "You son of a—"

"Stop it!" Leon ordered. "You two are going to bring every Guard in this building to this room. Seth, get out of here now."

"This is *my* room," Seth protested, climbing to his feet. "And if this dickhead would give me five—"

Aiden growled low in his throat. "I'm going to kill you."

"Oh, that's *it*." Seth whirled around, eyes flaring. "Let me see you try."

I staggered to my feet and reached for Aiden. The room swayed off kilter, but I ignored it.

"Don't. Please. This isn't Seth's… whoa." The wall spun suddenly.

"Alex?" Aiden said, but he sounded so far away, which was weird, since he was right beside me. I reached for him, but then I think I keeled over.

When I woke up, I felt like hell and I hadn't even opened my eyes yet. A drummer lived inside my head and my mouth was a desert. I groaned and tried to roll over, but I couldn't move. Something stopped me. Slowly, I pried my eyes open and looked down.

A heavily muscled arm lay across my waist—not my arm.

Well, this was odd.

I tilted my head to the side, blinked once, and then twice. It couldn't be him… Waves of dark hair fell over his forehead and along his cheek. It was Aiden's flawless face inches from mine, but a younger version of him. At rest, he looked vulnerable, peaceful. My fingers itched to trace the smooth line of his jaw, to touch his parted lips and see if he was real. It had to be a dream, something my heart had produced, because he couldn't be here.

"Stop staring at me." Aiden's voice was gruff with sleep.

I jerked back an inch. Okay, maybe not a dream. "I'm not."

He pried one gray eye open. "Yes, you are."

Accepting that this was reality, I glanced around. We were still in Seth's room. "Where's Seth?"

"I don't know. He left a couple of hours ago." Aiden seemed to realize then that his arm was around me. Looking confused, he pulled back and sat up. "I sat down for a little while. I must've fallen asleep. How are you feeling?"

Everything seemed hazy at first. Then, slowly, the memories clicked into place: Laadan giving me the super sex cocktail drink, Aiden ordering me off with Seth, and then… everything with Seth.

"Oh. My. Gods," I moaned. "I want to die. Like right now."

Aiden hovered beside me. "Alex, it's okay."

I covered my face with my hands. When I spoke, my voice was muffled. "No, it's not. I'm going to kill someone."

"I think you're going to have to get in line for that."

"Have you found Laadan?" I asked. "Is she okay?"

"Yes, I found her in her room just before I… I checked on you. She's fine, but she doesn't remember a thing. It's just like the night Leon found you in the maze. To compel someone that strongly and to make them forget is a hell of a compulsion. And to use it against another pure is unheard of."

I mumbled incoherently against my hands. Delayed as it was, it struck me then that Aiden had spent the night with me—in a bed. And I'd been passed out for it. Gods, that royally sucked, but it didn't suck as badly as it would have if someone found out about it. "Why did you stay here? What if someone—"

"Only Seth and Leon know what happened. And Laadan. No one else knows we're here." He pulled my hands away. "I wasn't leaving you alone. The drug was still in your system and I wasn't taking a risk on something else happening to you. You were sick again in the middle of the night. You don't remember that?"

"No," I whispered, trying to ignore the warmth his protective words brought. "I don't remember that."

"Probably a good thing, it was pretty rough."

"Great," I muttered.

A brief smile appeared. "You were… talking a lot, too."

"This just keeps getting better. What did I say?"

"You told me you wanted to marry Seth's bed, and then you told me you'd marry me if I asked. After that, you started to—"

"Enough," I groaned, wanting to crawl under the blankets.

Aiden laughed. "It was actually kind of cute."

More embarrassed than I'd ever been, I had a hard time looking at Aiden. His face didn't show any signs that he'd duked it out with Seth. Maybe I'd imagined it. "Did you and Seth… fight?"

One eyebrow arched. "Yeah, we did."

"Oh, gods, Aiden, it wasn't Seth's fault."

"I'm sorry," he said. "I'm sorry that you had to go through any of this. You have nothing to be ashamed of. You did nothing wrong, but he did."

"Don't apologize. Please. None of this is your fault." I drew in a deep breath. "It wasn't Seth's, either. Aiden, he tried. Really, he did, but I just…" I couldn't believe I was going to say any of this. "I just kept pushing him. I couldn't stop, but I knew what I was doing. I just couldn't stop myself."

"That doesn't matter, Alex. Seth should've shown restraint. He knew you were vulnerable, that it didn't matter *who* you were with." He paused, drawing in a deep breath. "Alex, look at me."

I lifted my head slowly. I expected there to be some sort of judgment or disappointment in his gray gaze, but all I saw was infinite understanding, which made the ball of conflicting emotions feel that much worse. His eyes shut briefly. When they reopened, they burned an unnatural shade of silver. "Did he… did you two…?"

"No. We… didn't do that. He stopped." I figured it was best to leave out the exact reason why he'd stopped.

We fell into silence for a little while. My mind worked through the events of last night, the implications of them. Someone had wanted me to screw up in a bad way. And to go to that kind of extreme—even the idea sickened me. What if Aiden and Seth hadn't seen me?

"You really think someone was waiting for me?" I swallowed down the taste of bile, shuddering. "Waiting to catch me with a pure?"

Aiden looked me straight on. "Yes."

It was hard to wrap my head around that kind of tactic. I shuddered again. Aiden reached down and tucked the blanket around me, but then I jerked up, ruining his hard work.

"Are you feeling sick again?" He moved as if he would carry me off the bed.

I wasn't sure. The walls did feel like they were closing in around me, but it wasn't the effects of the brew. "I could've lost everything."

Aiden didn't respond, because really, what could he say?

My mind raced. There were so many things I could do with the power I would have. I'd learned one thing at the Council—I needed to be able to do something to change the lives of my kind. Seth had been right; we could do something about that as long as I made it to eighteen without being forced into servitude. If I were put on the elixir—which was what someone had intended last night by hoping to catch me with a pure—I might never Awaken. I'd lose such a huge opportunity—more than any half had ever had.

And someone had tried to take that from me at least three times in the last couple of weeks: the compulsion, the Council session, and now this? Telly had warned me if I messed up one more time, I'd be kept in New York.

Sleeping with a pure, willingly or not, would have classified as messing up.

"Alex, are you okay?"

My gaze dropped to his. I don't know what I saw in his eyes. I couldn't read them anymore. "Do you think Telly did this?"

Aiden blinked. "Minister Telly? I don't know, Alex. He's a lot of things, but to do this? And why?"

"He doesn't like me."

"Not liking you is one thing, but to destroy you? It has to be more than dislike, Alex. There has to be a reason."

Aiden had a point. "Then I need to find out why."

"We will find out why."

I nodded. "Right now, I just… I just want to leave here. I want to go home."

He leaned forward and placed his hand over mine, easing my fingers off the blanket I'd been gripping. "There's a late afternoon session, and we'll leave immediately afterward."

Surprisingly, I didn't feel very relieved by that. The plus side in all of this was I now knew not to take drinks from… it hit me then. I laughed.

Aiden's eyebrows furrowed with concern. "Alex?"

I shook my head. "I'm fine. It's just that damn oracle was right again. She warned me, did you know? She told me not to accept gifts from those who meant me harm." I laughed again. "Of course, she failed to mention that it would be a secondhand gift from someone who didn't mean me harm. Gods, if that woman were still alive, I'd hit her. Seriously."

His lips stretched into a lopsided grin and his hand tightened over mine. An old and familiar ache sprung alive at the sight of his smile, forcing me to look away. I swallowed, wanting nothing more than to climb into his arms. "Do you know where Seth is?"

"No. He left when he realized I wasn't leaving. He's around here somewhere."

I ran a hand over my face. I was surprised and kind of stung that he'd actually left me with Aiden, but I was happy that he had. Because that gave me time with Aiden—time in bed with Aiden. Which didn't make any sense. "I need to find him."

Aiden's hand left mine. "You shouldn't be worried about him right now. And I don't want you running around looking for him. It's not safe here."

"I know it's not, but I have to see him. You don't understand. Things—"

"Things are what, Alex?"

I turned toward him. He was frowning, eyes a deep and dark gray. "I don't know. Things are different with him." That was all I could say.

Aiden stared at me a moment, then straightened. "Are you two… seeing each other?"

My cheeks turned several shades of red.

His eyes turned silver in a nanosecond. "I thought you were against this whole *fate* thing."

"I am! But… I don't know. Things have just changed and… he's been there for me," I finished lamely.

A muscle started ticking along his jaw. "And I haven't been. So you decided to be with Seth?"

I gaped at him, but then my temper shot to the surface. "No, you haven't been. But that's not why I'm with Seth."

"Really?" He pushed off the bed. Standing, he ran his hand through his hair. "I find that hard to believe since you told me a few days ago you hated him."

I flushed, partly because he was right and that pissed me off. "Why do you even care, Aiden? You can't—*and* don't—want me. And you even said you thought Seth cared about me. Or is this one of those lame lines like 'I don't want you but I don't want you with anyone else?' Because that's so not cool."

He dropped his hand. "That is not what this is about, Alex. I just don't want to see you getting wrapped up in something… so serious for the wrong reasons."

My gaze flicked up, meeting his. His eyes burned so brightly, taking up his whole face. "You've told me we can't be together and—and I know. I know we can't, but—"

Aiden bent quickly, leaning down so our faces were only inches from one another. "But that doesn't mean you should settle for Seth, Alex."

I crushed the blanket in my hands. "I'm not settling for Seth!"

He quirked an eyebrow and held my glare with his own.

Then it hit me and my heart sped up. "This isn't even about Seth. This is about you! You don't want to see me with him or anyone else! Because you still care about me!"

Aiden jerked back, shaking his head. "Of course I care for you."

I drew in a deep breath, trying to quell my racing heart. "Tell me… tell me that you feel the same way I do about you, because if you do…" I couldn't bring myself to actually say it. If he told me that he felt the same way—that he loved me—then to hell with everything else. To hell with it all, because I would not—could not walk away from that. No matter how wrong it was, how I'd resolved to let him go, and no matter how dangerous it would be for the both of us. I simply couldn't.

Aiden inhaled sharply. "I won't."

"Or you can't?"

He shook his head again, eyes flickering shut. A quick grimace pulled at his lips, and then he looked me dead on. "I don't."

I exhaled harshly, suddenly wanting to curl up in a ball and cry. But I didn't. I'd brought this on myself. "Okay."

"Alex, I want—"

"No. I don't want to hear anything else." I pushed off the bed. "What I have with Seth is none of your—" A rush of dizziness made me stumble. I bent, grabbing the edge of the bed for support.

"Alex?" Aiden moved around the bed, reaching for me.

"Don't!" I threw up my hand. "Don't pretend you care. That takes douche-baggery to a whole new level."

Aiden stopped, opening and closing his hands. "Good point."

The room righted itself and it felt safe to move again. Ignoring Aiden and the need to wail like a baby, I started the mortifying search for my clothes. I gathered up my jeans and hoodie, tucking them under my arm. One very important, very embarrassing item hadn't been located. I scanned the floors rather desperately.

"I think this belongs to you."

Cursing under my breath, I turned around. Aiden dangled something black, small and flimsy from his fingertips.

Color burst across my face. I snatched it out of his hand. "Thanks."
Aiden didn't smile. "It's my pleasure."

CHAPTER 25

I WENT THROUGH MY MORNING ROUTINE SLOWLY, still feeling a bit whacked. Part of me wanted to dive under the covers, another part wanted to strangle Aiden, and I still needed to find Seth.

I also needed to deal with the fact that someone seriously didn't want me to turn eighteen. I pushed down the ball of conflicting emotions to dwell on some other day—which I felt sure would be a day very soon—and opened the door. Aiden stood there, waiting. He was there because I obviously couldn't be allowed to be anywhere by myself, but I still wanted to punch him in the face.

Our walk downstairs was awkward.

A few Guards who had been present during the Council session nodded respectfully as I passed them. That was an improvement from being ignored. Aiden left me when I stopped at the linen-covered tables. I guess he figured I was safe within eyesight.

I stared at the plate of fresh croissants and bagels, swallowing thickly. I didn't think I could ever eat again. I grabbed a bottle of water and shuffled to where Aiden sat beside Marcus. Marcus didn't look up from his newspaper when I dropped into the seat beside him.

I could feel Aiden's eyes on me and I wanted to bang my head on the table. Instead of doing that, I twisted around and stared across the cafeteria. I pretended to be engrossed in the wall until I noticed the two servants standing by it.

It was *him*—the clear-eyed one I'd seen the first day here and tried to talk to in the stairwell. He leaned toward the other half-blood, a boy.

I couldn't help but wonder how the pures—the Masters—couldn't see how alert this Brown Eyes was.

Brown Eyes must have sensed me watching, because he turned and looked me straight in the eye. Not quite a hostile look, maybe a little curious. He quickly turned back to the other servant. I don't know why I watched them for so long. It may've been how tense their conversation seemed. Half-blood servants rarely argued, even among themselves. They were usually too medicated to even hold a decent conversation, but these two were different.

"Where were you last night, Alexandria? This morning, you were not in your bed."

Marcus's question jerked me around. I said the one thing that I knew Marcus wouldn't question and was sort of true. "I was with Seth. We were talking and I fell asleep."

"Really?" He nodded at the double doors leading to the patio. Seth stood there, his back to us. "So are you the one who gave him that black eye?"

"Uh…" I was already standing. "I'll see you guys in a little bit."

Marcus made a noise that sounded a lot like a chuckle and went back to his paper. I found it disturbing that he'd find the idea of domestic violence so humorous.

Taking a deep breath, I cut between the empty tables and followed Seth outside, not daring a look back to see Aiden's expression. Seth didn't turn around, but I knew he felt me. His shoulders tensed as he leaned against the one of thick marble columns.

I shivered in the chilly air, wondering why I hadn't brought a jacket. I stopped next to him and stared across the grounds. The top of the mammoth wall surrounding the place peeked over the tree line. I hoped he'd say something first, but the minutes passed and Seth remained silent. He wasn't going to make any of this easy.

"Hey," I said, immediately feeling stupid.

"Hey."

I rolled my eyes and stepped in front of him. Seth stared down at me coolly. Up close, the purple and blue ring around his left eye looked brutal. "Does that hurt?"

"Don't you think that's a stupid question?"

"Do you want another black eye?" I snapped.

He arched an eyebrow. "I think I prefer the drunken version of you. She's much nicer."

I stepped back. "You know what? Forget it."

Seth reached out and caught my arm. "What do you want to talk about? How disgusted you are with me?"

"No," I stared at him in surprise. "That's not what I was going to say at all."

Some of the coolness slipped from his expression, but he still regarded me warily. "Then why did you want to talk to me?"

"I want to talk about… last night." I felt my cheeks burn. "It wasn't your fault."

His brows flew up. "Not my fault?"

"No." I glanced over his shoulder, spotting the pure-blood Council Guard who had taken out Hector. He stood by the glass door leading out to the patio, trying to appear as if he wasn't watching us. "Can we go somewhere private?"

Seth looked over his shoulder. "Let's go."

We ended up a few rows into the labyrinth. Being in here left a bad taste in my mouth, but there was really no other place that was private. Seth leaned against the stone wall and folded his arms. "So talk."

I swallowed uncomfortably. This would be so awkward. "I wanted to apologize for… well, for everything that happened last night."

"You're apologizing to me?" He sounded stunned.

Shifting to my other foot, I nodded. "I know you tried to get me to sit down and not do what I was doing. You tried to—"

"I didn't *try* hard enough, Alex." He pushed off the wall. "Aiden's right—gods, I can't even believe I'm saying that, but he is. I knew you weren't yourself. So I should've stopped it."

My gaze followed him. He plucked a rose off a bush next to an armless gray statue of a woman in an ill-fitted toga. "You did stop, Seth."

He shot me a bland look over his shoulder. "You and I both know why I stopped. It wasn't out of chivalry."

I didn't believe that—not entirely. "Seth, you aren't the bad guy in this. You were sort of drugged, too—through our connection. And you took care of me afterward."

He shrugged. "What else was I supposed to do?"

"You held my hair while I puked. You didn't need to do that. You could have left me in the bathroom. That's pretty hardcore."

"It was also gross. Just so you know." Seth turned around, not looking at me, but at the rose in his palm.

Irritation surged to the surface. "Why are you acting like this? I'm trying to tell you that you weren't at fault for last night, and you're being a jerk!"

Blue fire sprung from his hand, folding over the rose. It smoked a wispy blue before disappearing into nothing.

I dragged my eyes from his hand and struggled for patience. Was every conversation today going to end in argument?

His eyes flicked up, meeting mine finally. "It appears you were well taken care of after I left. Were you thrilled that Aiden stayed with you? I'm sure you were."

I felt stung and confused by Seth. "I don't want to argue with you."

The blue flames licked at the rose between his fingers much slower this time. Plumes of blue smoke puffed into the air. "Then you should probably stop talking to me."

I stepped back, chafing my arms. "Why are you being so pisstastic with me?"

Seth blinked and the blue fire evaporated, leaving the rose whole. "I don't believe pisstastic is a real word, Alex."

Hiding underneath the covers for the rest of the day started to look even better. "All right, well, this was fun. I'll see you around."

Seth moved then. He reached out and caught my arm again, the rose dangling from his other hand. "I'm sorry."

I gawked at him. Seth never apologized. Ever.

The impossible happened. The mask he wore slipped off his face. Suddenly, he looked very young and unsure. "I felt you this morning. You were embarrassed and upset, and then so angry. I'm sorry for putting you through that. I should have… restrained myself."

It took me a few moments to realize what Seth referenced. "That had nothing to do with you, Seth."

"Why are you trying to make me feel better?"

"Seth, I'm embarrassed. I danced around your room and molested you. So yeah, I'm a bit embarrassed about that. But the other things you picked up on? That was because of Aiden."

"Isn't it always about Aiden?" He dropped my arm and turned away. "Did he finally profess his undying love for you?"

I laughed brokenly. "Not quite."

Seth glanced over his shoulder. "My eye socket has a hard time believing that."

"He stayed with me because he fell asleep."

His head dropped, and I wondered what he was doing. "And you believe that?"

I blinked back sudden tears. I would've risked everything this morning if Aiden had said he loved me, but he hadn't. "Does it matter?"

He turned around, studying me like he was trying to figure something out. "Does it?"

A breeze rolled through, rattling the leaves and kicking my hair into my face. I pushed the hair away, but it blew right back. "Seth, you asked me to make a choice the night before. And I did."

Seth glanced down at the rose before peering up through thick lashes. "And that choice still matters today?"

That was a good question. How could it, when an hour ago I would've given up everything for Aiden if he'd told me just once that he loved me. But he hadn't. I looked away, once again wondering what exactly was I doing. Was this fair to Seth? Because Aiden had been right, I was kind of settling for him. But Seth hadn't said he had any hardcore feelings for me. He hadn't even asked me to be his girlfriend. What he *had* suggested was for us to see what happens—no labels and no expectations. And if I was honest with myself, I did care for Seth. A lot.

I bit my lip. "I chose you. Does that still matter to you?"

He laughed suddenly and then fell silent. I could see him trying to pull the shutters back up, but failing. I'd never seen him so vulnerable. Trying to give him space, I moved back to the wall and watched him.

"Yes, it does matter to me."

Something fluttered in my chest faintly. "Okay, so… um, where does that leave us?"

Silently, he handed me the rose. A small jolt ran over my fingertips. The stem felt warm to the touch and a faint trace of blue still clung to the blossom, turning the dewy petals violet. Without warning, he lifted me onto the wall. He placed his hands on either side of my legs. "Alex."

I looked around, dangling my legs. "Seth?"

"Well, all of this is weird."

"Yeah, especially right now."

"It's about to get weirder. Be prepared."

"Great." I twirled the rose around with one hand and tapped my thigh with the other. "I can't wait."

Seth smiled. "I can tell you're freaked out."

My eyes narrowed. "You're doing it now? Reading me, aren't you? How in the world do you do that?"

I was surprised when he answered the question. "I just open up my mind to you, tune into the connection. It's like a two-way radio signal. Your feelings come through in waves, sometimes loudly. Other times, it's just a twinge at the edge of my mind. You probably could pick up on them now, if you tried."

"Is it always going to be like this? When I Awaken, will I constantly be feeling you and vice versa?"

"You could shield your feelings."

I popped forward. "How do I do that?"

Seth laughed softly. "I could teach you, work it into your training if you want."

"Can we start now?"

A slow smile appeared as he dipped his head. "That's not what I want to do right now."

Parts of my body tingled—some parts more than others. "Seth…"

Seth kissed me. It wasn't like the heady and deep kisses from the night before. His lips were sweet, soft. His hand caressed my cheek before sliding around the nape of my neck and delving into my hair. I let my eyes drift shut, soaking up the dizzying warmth of his lips. For the briefest moment, I didn't think about *anything*. And that's what I liked most about Seth's kisses. I didn't think or want anymore. In Seth's arms, with his lips trailing kisses over mine, his presence overshadowed the hurt, eased it.

The tingling in my body suddenly grew stronger, like little sparks dancing over my skin. My palm itched, burned. I gasped as his mouth dropped to my throat, where my pulse had gone from pleasant to throbbing.

Seth pressed his lips there, inhaled deeply and pulled back, fingers trailing over my flushed cheeks. "Interesting."

"Yeah… that was different," I said breathlessly.

He chuckled. "Not the kiss. Don't get me wrong, that was interesting too, but look."

"Huh?" I followed his gaze and squeaked. The rose in my hand was on fire again. Blue flames licked over the stem, curling around the fragile petals, smoldering into thin wisps of azure. The rose shuddered once and then collapsed into itself, leaving a fine blue dust covering my hands.

"Akasha," Seth explained quietly.

"Okay." I let out a breath, relaxing for the first time in days—weeks even. "Okay. I don't know what that really means, but okay."

He hopped up on the wall beside me. We sat there for a little while, legs swinging above the ground. "What do you want to do? We have a couple of hours before you leave."

"You're not leaving after the session?"

"Nope. Lucian wants to leave in the morning, so I'm stuck here another night."

Dammit. Another eleven-hour car ride with Aiden.

Seth nudged my shoulder. "What?"

"I was kind of hoping you could convince Lucian to let me fly back with you."

He looked surprised. "You hate flying. It scares you to death, you little wimp. But you can't stay here another night. You have to leave tonight with Aiden."

"And with Leon."

"Yeah," he sighed, kicking his legs off the wall. "Want to go swimming?"

I laughed. "No."

"Damn. I was hoping you'd fall for that one again."

I stared at the moss-covered walkway, knocking my heels off the wall. "Seth?"

"Yep."

"Who do you think was responsible for slipping me that drink?"

His expression hardened. "I don't think it was the Council's decision."

"Then who could it be if it wasn't the Council?"

"I didn't say it wasn't one or more of them, but I know it wasn't something approved by the Council. Lucian would never allow something like that to happen."

I snorted. "You give Lucian way too much credit."

"Don't get me wrong, he's still a pompous ass." Seth flashed a grin. "But he wouldn't allow something like that to happen to you. I'm sure it could be a Council member, but they don't have the official backing of the Council."

"Sorry. I don't trust Lucian."

Seth twisted around. "You need to start trusting him. He wants to make sure you Awaken, Alex. There isn't a damn thing he's going to do to jeopardize that."

"And that is another thing I don't trust. Why does Lucian want two Apollyons, when every other pure is scared to death of that idea?"

"Because Lucian wants to see change—and we are the vessel for that change. You want to change this society, make it better? Lucian wants that, too."

"Since when did Lucian become such a half-blood lover?"

"You don't know your stepfather, Alex. You never really tried."

I shook my head. "Sorry. You didn't spend fourteen years with him. Lucian is cold, conniving, and has never been a fan of halfs. You're not going to get me to believe otherwise."

Seth sighed. "I'd put my bets on Telly, but that seems too obvious and he's too old school. But it's one or more of them."

I wrapped my arms around me, shuddering when I thought about what could've happened. "They didn't have to do something so vile."

He reached over and pulled me down so my head rested in his lap. It felt weird at first, but after a few seconds, I rolled onto my back and stared up at the gray clouds. "We'll figure it out once we get out of this damn place. Lucian is already—"

"You told Lucian?"

"He needed to know." He brushed a strand of hair off my forehead. "Needless to say, he was pissed."

I groaned and placed my hands over my eyes. "Did he throw something dainty? He usually throws something small and expensive."

Seth laughed. "Yes, he did actually. I believe it was a Fabergé egg."

"Oh. Sweet."

He picked up my pinky and peeked down at me. "What are you hiding from?"

I considered that. "I don't know. Everything?"

"Sounds like a plan."

I lowered my hands to my stomach, but Seth still held onto my pinky. "Childish, huh?"

He wrapped his hands around mine. "It's all right. You can hide for a little while longer, but then you've got to face… everything."

"I know."

He grinned down at me. "But for right now, just relax."

Once we got back to North Carolina, there would be classes, and Olivia now hated me, and we still needed to find out who'd set me up last night, and… crap, Instructor Romvi. I cringed. "Can we stay… here for a little while?"

"Sure." He bent down, pressing his lips against my forehead. "If that's what you want."

It really didn't matter what I wanted, but I closed my eyes and smiled anyway.

The sun had set by the time the servants lugged my bag downstairs. Seth and I waited in the glass breezeway outside the ballroom. I tried to not stare at the furies, but my eyes kept going back to them.

"Do you think I'll get to see Laadan before we leave?" I asked.

Seth leaned against the wall opposite from me. "I'd think so."

I slid down the glass and crossed my legs. "I just want to see her before I leave. I hope she doesn't feel..." I stopped, glancing around me before I continued, "guilty or anything."

"Understandable." He shot an irritated look back toward the ballroom. "How long is this crap going to take?"

"Who knows?" I muttered. Telly had all the pures gathered, doing some kind of stupid closing ceremony. I stretched out my legs and eyed Seth. He had changed into his Sentinel uniform, blades and all. Squinting, I noticed the new blade attached to his thigh. "Can I see that one?"

"Hmm?" He glanced down and unhooked the blade. "This one?"

I wiggled my fingers. "Let me see it."

He walked it across and handed it to me. "Be careful with it, both edges are deadly sharp when released."

"Yeah, I know. Aiden showed me one earlier." I pushed to my feet, imagining chopping a daimon half's head off with it. "You know, using this thing is going to be really messy."

Seth made a grab for the weapon, but I stepped back. He gave me a droll look. "Haven't used it yet, but I'm sure it's not going to be pretty."

I whipped the sickle blade through the air again, and then remembered what I'd realized when Aiden had showed me the blade. I peered up at Seth. "What about after I Awaken? You'll just have unlimited zapping powers, right?"

"I don't know." He watched the blade with wary eyes. "I imagine it will be different. Could even be different now. Remember, we don't know all the fine details."

I looked at Seth, but he still fixated on the blade. "What happens to me when you pull from my energy?"

Seth's eyes snapped to my face. "I don't know."

My fingers tightened around the blade. "I'm not sure I believe you."

His eyes bored into mine. "I've never lied to you before."

I swallowed hard. Seth had a point, but if he did know that something bad would happen, would he actually tell me?

Leon strolled into the foyer, coming to a complete stop when he saw me holding the blade. "For the love of the gods, who gave that to you?"

I pointed the sharp edge. "Seth."

Seth arched a brow at me. "Wow. Thanks."

"Please give it back to him before you do damage." Leon frowned as I twirled the blade. "You're going to cut off your hand or arm. The sickle blade is by far the sharpest."

Rolling my eyes, I stopped twirling it. But I kept it. I liked it. "Are they almost done in there? Because I'm getting really—"

A siren blasted off in the distance, starting as a low pitch and building into a never-ending loop of eardrum-breaking noise. I jumped a good five inches off the floor. The three of us looked at one another and seemed to share the same mind for a moment. Even though I'd never had the misfortune of hearing a Covenant siren, I knew they meant only one thing: security breach.

Usually a very big and very bad security breach.

CHAPTER 26

I TURNED TO THE GLASS WALL FACING THE YARD.

Behind me, several Guards burst into the hall, and beyond them excited voices came from the adjoining ballroom. Guards rushed past us, one of them yelling, "Secure the gates! Lock down the school!"

Then the sirens ceased their blaring, and a cold shiver ran down my arms. "False alarm?"

"Not sure." Seth whipped the blade out of my hand. "But I'll be taking this back now. Thank you."

I barely paid him any attention. The light from the scattered lamp-posts outside began to dim and flicker. I glanced back, finding Leon with a sickle blade in one hand and a dagger in the other.

"Everyone calm down!" A Guard yelled over the panicked voices. "The siren has ended! Everything is fine. Everyone just needs to calm down and stay in the hall."

Marcus and Aiden brushed aside curious and frightened pures as they entered the room. My overactive imagination said that Aiden's eyes searched the crowd until he found me and that there was a flicker of relief on his face.

Aiden crossed the room, dagger in hand. He must've changed into gear before the closing ceremonies. He stopped beside Leon. "What's going on?"

"I don't know." Leon shook his head. "But I got a bad feeling about this."

I turned back to the glass, squinting. Further off, near the tree line, it looked like something moved—several things, actually. Guards and Sentinels, I thought.

Marcus joined our little group. "Telly is keeping all the pures in the ballroom as a precaution." He paused, glancing down at me with a little frown as if he'd forgotten about me.

"Hello." I wiggled my *weaponless* fingers.

Marcus frowned. "Alex, you're coming with me."

I scowled. "I'm not hiding in a room with a bunch of freaked-out pures."

Aiden turned to me, eyes thundercloud gray. "Don't be ridiculous."

I glared right back at him. "Can I be irrational instead?"

Aiden looked like he wanted to shake me… or worse.

"Alex, do not argue with us," Marcus snapped. "You are going in that room."

My temper snapped. "I can fight if one of you would give me one of those neat blades."

Seth grabbed my arm. "All right, little Apollyon—who is not completely trained and is on the verge of becoming annoying—go with your uncle."

Pulling my arm free, I whirled on Seth. "I can—"

The lights outside shuddered off, casting the grounds in utter darkness. Temporarily forgotten, I turned back to the glass. Squinting to see through the reflection of the lighted interior, I saw the shadows of the Guards forming a line. But something looked off about the formation. It moved forward instead of away from the house.

"Uh, guys…" I started to back up.

Leon stepped forward. "Miss Andros, get into that room. Now."

Someone grabbed my arm, pulling me backward. I glanced up, expecting Seth but finding Aiden. His eyes were trained on the glass wall. "Alex, for once in your life—"

A loud crack drew our attention back to the glass. My mouth dropped open. Glass splintered and fissured under the impact of a body.

I flinched back. "Holy crap!"

The glass exploded, shooting large shards through the air as several bodies thudded onto the marble floor. The color of their uniforms made them unmistakable, although blood stained their white shirts and pants. The Council Guards hadn't even *drawn* their weapons. All of their throats had been ripped open, revealing pink and jelly-like tissue. Some still twitched before their eyes glossed over.

Aiden pushed me toward Marcus. "Go!"

With a tight grip on my arm, Marcus rushed across the room as Sentinels entered, drawing weapons—*weapons*? I broke free and went in the opposite direction.

"Alexandria! No!" shouted Marcus.

"Give me a second!" I skidded over to one of the bodies, trying not to look too closely at it. Wincing, I unhooked a sickle and a dagger. There was no way I was going to be weaponless in a daimon siege.

A shrill, heart-stopping cry broke through all the commotion, drowning out everything else. Shivers of dread dug deep into my muscles as the soulless howls hit an intense pitch. I wrapped my hands around the blades and jerked up. Shadows descended, like a wave of death moving incredibly fast.

Daimons—buttloads of daimons.

The sight of so many pale faces—black veins throbbing under papery-thin skin and empty holes where eyes should have been—freaked the holy hell out of me. My nightmares had come alive in vivid, startling detail. There were at least a dozen of them, screeching with mouths full of razor-like teeth. But scattered among them were faces that looked no different.

Daimon halfs.

The Sentinels—Aiden and Seth included—rushed them, disappearing into the mob. Blades clattered and fell to the floor, screams and shouts mingled with the ripping and tearing of clothing and flesh.

"Alexandria!" Marcus shouted. "Let go of me! I have to get her!"

I spun around. A Council Guard pulled Marcus toward the reception hall—toward the stronghold. Another Guard appeared, helping remove Marcus to safety. Taking off after them, I reached them just as they pushed Marcus into the hall and slammed the titanium-lined door shut.

Marcus beat on the door, his words muffled by the thick metal separating us.

"This door does not open again." The Guard looked me straight in the eye. He was the pure—the Guard who'd carried out Telly's orders.

"Thanks," I said through clenched teeth. Then, taking a deep breath, I turned around and faced hell.

It was a bloody mess, literally. In that instant I knew that all the smaller scale attacks on the Covenants over the last couple of months had been practice runs. They'd been testing how to infiltrate the Covenant, gearing up for a grand-scale attack on the Council. Mom had warned me, and I'd warned the pures—but they'd dismissed it.

Idiots.

I caught sight of Seth as he engaged a half-blood daimon. He slammed the half in the chest with a booted foot, knocking it to the ground. In a stunning display of brutality and grace, he whipped the sickle blade through the air.

Then there were Aiden and Leon, their backs against one another as four pure daimons circled them. They looked screwed.

Fighting was in my blood, not running. This was where I was supposed to be and this definitely wasn't my first time at the rodeo. I bolted across the room, dodging bodies of the good, the bad, and the downright ugly. The ones closing in on Leon and Aiden didn't even see me coming. I shoved the dagger deep into the back of the daimon closest to Aiden.

Leon knocked aside one of the daimons, going blow-to-blow with it. Aiden went after the other two, trying to keep them both focused on him. "Alex, behind you!"

I whirled around, gripping the dagger in my right hand. A female daimon dove at me, but I ducked out of her grasp. Swinging around, I caught her in the chest with my sneaker just as Seth had done. She went down on one knee, and I lurched forward, jabbing the blade into her stomach. Looking through the poof of blue dust, I grinned at Aiden. "That's two."

"Five for me," he grunted, sinking his dagger into the throat of his daimon.

I flipped the dagger. "Well, la-dee—"

Hands grabbed my shoulders, throwing me backward. I hit the mess of glass and blood, skidding a few feet on my back and losing my grip on the dagger. Stunned, I stared up into the face of a daimon half.

"Alex!" yelled Aiden, sounding truly panicked.

It leaned over me and sniffed. "Apollyon…"

I could easily remember what'd happened when I'd tried to fight the last half-blood daimon. It hadn't gone well. Pushing those memories down, I scrambled across the floor. Glass dug into my palms, mixing my blood with the blood of the fallen. My hand brushed against something wet and soft. A thousand gruesome images flashed through my mind of what I'd possibly backed into.

The daimon half—a trained female Sentinel—opened her mouth and howled. She jumped in the air, swinging a Covenant dagger right at my head. There was a popping noise and then she was a ball of flames crashing down on me. I rolled out of the way as she hit the floor, screaming and thrashing.

I jerked toward Aiden. He nodded at me, then lowered his hand and swung at another daimon. Glancing back at the daimon on the floor, I winced. She slowly climbed to her feet, a charred, stinky mess of skin and cloth.

"Good gods," I muttered, wanting to yak. "Don't even touch me."

She opened her mouth, and then her head went in one direction and her body in the other. Leon stood behind her, sickle in hand. "Miss Andros," he said politely. "I do believe you were supposed to go to safety?"

"Yeah, that was the plan." I looked around the room. There were a lot of bodies on the floor—some of the halfs who'd been turned, while others were of our kind. Seth had two daimons cornered, fighting rather gleefully. I grinned, even though it was sort of twisted.

Aiden followed my gaze. "Leon, that one there counts half for me. So that's six and a half." Then he pivoted around, heading toward another daimon who had a Guard pinned on the floor.

Leon shrugged. "That's okay. I have ten, loser."

A howling sound spun me around. Two daimon halfs charged, going right for Leon. It was as if I wasn't even standing there. "It's about to be twelve," Leon said casually.

"Eleven." I switched the sickle blade to my right hand.

Leon glanced down at me. "Do try not to get yourself killed."

With that, we met them halfway. The male, finally noticing me, made a grab for my arm, but I feinted to the right. He was much bigger than me, maybe the size of Aiden, and I knew I couldn't let this one get me on the ground. I got a good kick in, but he barely moved.

Not good.

I blocked his punch, but it still knocked me back a few steps. I kept my balance, whipping the blade through the air. He dipped quickly, retaliating with a vicious swing aimed to take me down. I felt the wind of the blade whizzing past my head. I jumped to the side, but the daimon half moved so damn fast. His fist came around, slamming into my stomach. I staggered back, gasping for air.

The daimon half laughed. "Ready to die?"

"Not really." I straightened. "The pale and addicted look isn't a good one. You look a little strung out. Need some aether?"

He tilted his head to the side and smiled. "I'm going to rip you apart, you stupid—"

Dipping down, I swept his legs out from underneath him. He went down—leaving only an instant to attack. Jumping up, I brought the sickle blade down on his throat. It met no resistance.

Wide-eyed, I lifted the blade. "Damn, that *is* sharp." I turned around, about to point that out to Leon when the daimon pure was suddenly right in my face.

It licked its lips. "Apollyon…"

"Oh, come on, can you all really smell it?" I flipped the sickle over and shoved it into his stomach.

"You smell like warmth and summer." Seth appeared at my side. "I told you, you smelled good."

"Well, you smell like… like…"

Seth waited, brows raised.

My eyes widened. Over his shoulder, I saw at least five more daimon pures coming down the hallway. "Daimons."

"I smell like a daimon?" He looked let down.

"No, you idiot, there're more daimons coming."

Seth glanced over his shoulder. "Oh. Well, damn. They must've broken through the entrances."

"That's not good."

Another cracking sound shattered through the hall, different from the breaking glass. It reminded me of an artist chipping away at marble. Seth and I turned at the same time, but I don't know who noticed it first. Both of us took a step back.

A network of fractures split the white marble encasing the furies. Chunks of stone broke off, dropping to the floor. Pink, luminous flesh appeared through the larger gaps in the marble. A fine current of electricity shot through my body.

"Oh, my gods," I whispered.

Seth's arm shot out, slamming his dagger into the chest of a daimon pure without even taking his eyes off the crumbling statues. "Indeed."

A soft, tinkling laugh overcame the sounds of battle, halting everyone and everything in the hall. Transfixed, I watched the rest of the marble slip away like a snake shedding its skin. And there they were, the three of them hovering above the makeshift battlefield. And oh, my gods, they were savagely beautiful.

The gods had unleashed the furies.

Their diaphanous white gowns stood in sharp contrast to the surrounding blood and gore. Pale, blonde, and perfect, the three cast their all-white eyes toward the carnage before them. They moved through the still air on pale, transparent wings, delicate-looking and soundless. The furies were lesser goddesses, but their presence took over the hall.

I'd never seen a god before, let alone three of them, but they appeared the way I'd imagined them: compelling, and beautiful. Frightening. I even took a step toward them, barely realizing that Seth had done so, too. Neither of us could help it. They were gods—freaking gods appearing before us. None of the other halfs or pures moved, seeming too stunned to do much of anything.

Around the room, the daimons backed off from their opponents, all their attention fixed on the furies as they sniffed the air. Some started to whine, others growled. It was the aether flowing through the gods, I realized. If Seth and I were steak, then the furies had to be the most succulent cuts of filet mignon.

One of the daimons, a half-blood, let out a low howl and charged forward.

The furie in the middle lowered to the floor, sinking her bare feet into blood and glass. Thick blonde curls floated around her head as her noiseless wings fluttered around her. A pearly glow radiated from her skin as she tipped her head to the side and smiled. The daimon lunged at her, but she simply raised one hand and froze it mid-attack.

Her smile was innocent, child-like, and yet held a barbed edge to it that was cruel. She reached back with her other arm and slammed her hand clean through the daimon's chest. She shot straight up in the air, bringing the frantic daimon with her. Floating above us, she ripped the daimon in two.

I gasped. "Holy…"

"Shit," Seth finished.

In an instant the furies shifted, shedding their beautiful bodies. Their skin and wings turned gray and milky, their hair darkening and thinning into stringy black ropes that snapped at the air around them. Snakes, not ropes, I realized. Their hair was *freaking snakes!*

The middle one screamed, bringing several pures to their knees. I backed up, knocking into Seth. He wrapped an arm around my waist, hauling me against him. One of the furies swooped, snatching up a daimon and launching it through the air. Another arced down, grabbed a Sentinel with her clawed feet, and sliced him apart as he screamed. The third landed near a crop of daimons, one strand of her snake hair zipping out and right through the eye of a Guard as she eviscerated a daimon pure.

It didn't matter who stood in their paths—the furies were destroying everyone.

I caught sight of Leon ducking under a gray wing and pulling Aiden out of reach of one of the furies. An expression of awe and horror marked

Aiden's features as he swung a blade into a nearby daimon that wasn't even paying attention to him.

A furie swept the ceiling, her all-white eyes glowing much like Seth's did when he was pissed. A second later, the furie swung toward us, shrieking shrilly. It stared straight at us, arms extended and claws sharpened into fine points.

Seth grabbed my free hand. "Come on!"

I let him pull me back. "But what about Aiden and Leon?"

"They don't have a furie gunning for their asses. Now, come on!"

We rushed toward the reception hall. The Guards still held their ground at the doors, protecting the pures. Looking back, my heart dropped; the furie was coming after us.

"Seth!"

"I know, Alex, I—" Seth stopped as we rounded the corner.

I slapped into his back. Peering over his shoulder, horror twisted my insides. The hall was choked with daimons. Half-blood servants littered the floor, necks broken or ripped open. As medicated as they were, they'd been utterly defenseless against the daimons. Guards struggled with the flood, trying to hold them back.

The furie screamed, dipping down. Seth spun around, knocking me to the floor and throwing his body over mine. By the grace of gods, I didn't accidentally stab him with the sickle. My heart thundered and fear stuck to my skin as the furie's wings stirred the air around us. Seth tensed as the furie swooped again, but sensing a god chock full of aether in their presence, the daimons swarmed the furie.

Jumping to his feet, Seth pulled me up and we started back down the hall. We rushed past rooms full of carnage and disaster. In the midst of the chaos, I saw Brown Eyes fighting back daimons along with the younger half he'd spoken with in the dining room this morning. He moved as gracefully as any Sentinel, taking down a daimon with a titanium candelabrum.

Seth and I reached the ballroom just as a sudden burst of panicked and terrified screams whirled the Guards around. As they yanked the door open a stampede of pure-bloods trampled the Guards, pushing and clawing to get away. Then the herd of frightened pures descended on us, tearing my hand from Seth's. The wave of red and white robes slammed into me from all sides. Trying to stay upright, I screamed, "Seth!"

Bodies rocked into me from every direction, and I was knocked to the floor by one of the Ministers. Sharp pain exploded in my head. I tried getting up, but the hysterical crowd kept pushing me down. Dropping the blade, I curled into a ball and protected my head. Feet were everywhere, stamping down on me, kicking into me. This was how I was going to die—not in battle, not from the plot of some Council member hell-bent on destroying me, but trampled to death by a bunch of pure-bloods. *Of all the ways to die.*

I was so going to haunt every last one of them.

My side throbbed, and I was pretty sure I had a broken rib. In the mad rush, daimons were running and killing right beside the pures, and I had no idea where those damn furies were. I squeezed my eyes shut, whimpering as each sandal-covered foot dug into me. Seconds after I didn't think I could take anymore, the crowd thinned enough for me to lower my hands and grab the blade.

Shaken and bruised, I climbed to my feet. Pures cluttered the hall, smelling of smoke, sweat, and fear. I didn't see Seth anywhere. Stumbling toward the ballroom, I went against the tide of pures. Marcus had been in that room, along with Laadan and Lucian.

Inside the once-grand ballroom, I staggered through the destruction, scanning the bodies littering the floor. Marcus and I didn't get along for longer than five seconds, but he was the only person left in this world who shared the same blood as me. I didn't want to see his body among the ones on the floor. I didn't know what I'd do. I just didn't.

Several side doors of the reception hall had been busted in, and some daimons stalked the remaining pures like prey. I watched one pounce on a pure—a coppery-headed one, super tan and beautiful.

Dawn Samos.

It sank its teeth into her arm. Screaming, she tried to wretch her arm away, but the daimon had her in a death grip. She was lucky, though. He could've gone for her throat. A small voice in the back of my head whispered, *let her go; she likes Aiden.*

But that was all kinds of wrong—super messed-up.

Pulling on my remaining strength, I ignored the aches and rushed toward them. The only easy daimon to kill was a daimon tagging some hapless fool. Didn't I know? My eyes met Dawn's amethyst ones as I plunged the sharp edge of the blade into the daimon's back. He exploded into blue dust all over her pretty white robes.

Dawn scuttled back, face sharp with pain and terror. Dismissing her, I faced the carnage. The daimons, both half and pure, were giving in to all the aether, feeding on the fallen. I started toward them, but a raw shriek stopped my heart.

I turned around.

The three furies hovered in front of the door, their snake hair nipping at the space around them. An unfortunate Guard stood between me and the furies, but not for long. The ugliest of them, her gown stained with blood, snapped his neck with a twist of her wrist.

Rage and fear swept through me, dulling the ache deep in my bones. Coiling, responsive power expanded in my stomach and spread through my limbs. A jolt of energy shot through my palm, lighting my hand on fire. It traveled up my arm, and then it twisted down to my core where it licked at a muscle never used. Maybe it was akasha, maybe it was something far stranger—far deadlier—because everything shone like a tawny jewel, as if someone had dipped a paintbrush in amber and spread it over the room.

Stepping forward, my fingers spasmed over the center of the sickle blade. One of the furies laughed. The other two tittered and brushed past the really ugly one. Behind me, I could hear the Guards fighting the daimons, but I focused on the furies.

The two glanced at one another and licked their lips. One of them spoke, "Pretty little Apollyon, siphoning off the First, are you? Or is he throwing his power to you? He better be careful doing that."

"It won't be enough," the other said. "You can't kill us."

"I can try." I clenched the blade.

The furie laughed. "Try and die."

Then they flew toward me. I wheeled around and raced toward the wall. Launching myself up, I kicked off the wall and flipped over the two furies, bringing the blade down in a wide, arcing sweep.

I landed in a crouch behind them, arms widespread. The two furies staggered backward, their bodies falling forward without their heads. Blue fire shot from their necks, swamping and consuming their bodies.

The ugly furie cackled, and I whirled around, facing her. She drifted several feet off the floor, her hair wriggling. "You didn't kill my sisters, but Thanatos will not be pleased upon their return."

"Sorry to hear that."

She smiled, slipping back into the form that was so beautiful it almost hurt to look at her. "You're a threat, and we must deal with the threat. It's nothing personal."

"I didn't threaten anyone. I'm not the problem."

"Not yet, but you will. We know what you will do." She reached for the blade, striking unbelievably fast.

I lashed out, kicking her arm back. "What will I do?"

"Why fight me? You kill me and I will come back." She jumped out fast, catching the front of my shirt. I narrowly escaped her claws. "That is what we do. We will keep coming back, hunting you till the threat is eradicated."

"Great. You're like herpes. The gift that just keeps on giving."

She blinked. "What?"

I spun into a scissor kick, ignoring the sharp spike of pain as her claws caught my arm and pulled me forward. Using the momentum, I crashed into her. The furie was under me for a second, snarling as I gained the upper hand. I shoved my knee into her, delighting in the flicker of surprise.

She stared up at me, a picture of beauty and innocence. "What a path, what a path the Powers have chosen. You will be their tool. That is why you're a threat."

I stilled. "The oracle said that—"

The furie shifted again, her hair snapping at me. Coming up, I lopped the sickle across her neck and rolled off. Seconds later she went up in blue flames, but her laugh still lingered. For a moment I lay on my back, staring up at the ceiling. Did taking down each furie count triple? Surely they were enough that I blown Aiden and Leon out of the water.

Rolling to my feet, I ran the sleeve of my sweater over my cheek. I turned around, seeing so many blue piles of dust and dead halfs that had been turned. Only one Guard remained in the reception hall—the pure-blooded one. Of all the people to survive, it had to be him. I should feel terrible about that thought, but I didn't.

Sighing, I slowly approached the Council Guard. He had a fresh bruise blooming across his jaw, but was otherwise unscathed. "That was insane."

He flipped the dagger in his hand and turned toward the two remaining pures. Dawn huddled behind a statue of Themis, her arm cradled to her chest. Blood dripped onto her white robes. A male pure several decades older than her had his arm around her, whispering something to her. The chick looked freaked out. I couldn't blame her. She'd been *this* close to meeting her end.

I wiped my hand under my nose, not surprised to see my blood smeared across my skin.

"Is she okay?" the Guard asked.

The male lifted his head. A deep, angry-looking tag bled from where his shoulder and neck met. "Yeah, I think so. We need to get her checked out." He looked at me. "You were amazing. I've never seen anything like that."

"I was, wasn't I?" I murmured, wanting to feel great about winning the fight, but the furie's words left a jolting echo in my mind. She had given me an additional part of the puzzle, finishing what the oracle had said. But it still made little sense. Who were "the Powers" and how would I become a tool?

The pure had turned back to Dawn. "It's over," he soothed her, "all over now."

It was, but I was still unwilling to put the sickle down—just in case. I kept having visions of horror movie monsters jumping out at me. I moved to the broken doors and peered out. Nothing moved, which I believed to be a good sign. But when would the furies be back? Five seconds from now? A day, a week, or a month?

"Alexandria."

I wheeled around. "What?"

The Guard pressed his lips into a smile. "You did do really well. I saw you. You may be the first person in history to face down a furie and live. And you took out three of them? That… that was amazing."

Reluctant warmth cascaded through me. That meant something coming from a pure-blood Council Guard, even if he'd been ordered to kill Hector. A smile spread across my face. "Thanks."

He put his hand on my shoulder and squeezed. "I'm really sorry for this."

My smile started to fade. "For what?"

"The furies were right. There can't be two of you. You are a risk."

A shiver of warning went up my spine. I stepped back, but the Guard's grip tightened on my shoulder, holding me in place. I looked up with wide eyes and met his. Only one word came out. "Please."

There wasn't an ounce of regret or doubt in the Guard's eyes. "We must protect the future of our race."

Then he swung his blade at my chest.

CHAPTER 27

HE'S GOING TO KILL ME.

The words flashed through my mind, and I reacted out of instinct. In the back of my mind, I recognized the act of shoving the sickle into his chest was far different than shoving one into a daimon's or even a furie's. The blade felt heavier in my hand, the sucking noise the skin made when pierced by the sharpest metal seemed louder.

And the thing that was the most different? Pure-blood Guards didn't collapse into themselves and fade to nothing but a fine shimmer of blue dust. The Guard kept standing, a horrified look on his face. I think he'd actually believed he could outmaneuver me, that there wasn't a blade stuck deep into his chest.

I screamed, yanking the sharp end of the sickle out. Then he fell. First to his knees, then face first onto the marble floor. I lifted my head, the bloodied sickle clenched in my shaking hand. I didn't even know the Guard's name… and I'd killed him.

The male pure must have risen to his feet at some point. He stared back at me, equally horrified. He opened his mouth, but nothing came out.

"I had to do it," I pleaded. "He was going to kill me. I had to do it."

Dawn whimpered from behind the figure of Themis. The statue had been damaged during the battle. The scales had tipped—no longer equal.

So many rules governed the half-bloods. I really couldn't keep them all straight. But there were two I always remembered: never get involved with a pure-blood, and never kill a pure-blood. Self-defense didn't matter. A pure's life was and always would be valued higher than mine. Being an Apollyon didn't make me above that law. Breaking one rule had seemed bad enough, but both of them?

Well, I was so screwed.

Footsteps thundered into the reception hall, the only sound that seemed greater than the pounding of my heart. Innately, I recognized the two. How had they known where I was? Of course, Seth would know—always know—where I was.

Aiden was the first through the door. Both he and Seth halted a few feet away. I could only imagine what they saw—piles and piles of blue dust, the bodies, the broken doors, and two pures cowering under the statue.

Then they saw me, standing with a bloodied sickle in-hand and a dead Council Guard lying at my feet.

"Alex, are you okay?" Aiden crossed the room. "Alex?"

He stepped around the fallen Guard and stood in front of me. A bruise shadowed under his right eye, and a scratch slashed across his left cheek. His shirt was torn, but the blade hooked to his pants didn't have blood on it.

"Alex, what happened?" He sounded desperate as his eyes searched mine.

I blinked, but I kept seeing the look on the Guard's face.

Seth surveyed the mess with a cold, almost feral look to him. "Alex. Tell us what happened."

It all came out in a nervous rush. "I was fighting the furies and he told me I did a good job, Aiden. Then he apologized. I had to do it. He said there couldn't be two of us and that he had to protect his race. He was going to kill me. I—I had to do it. I don't even know his name and I killed him."

Pain and panic flared in Aiden's eyes, and then they took on a hard, steely edge. Resolve burned from them while a red-hot fury built behind him. Seth dipped down and rolled the Guard over.

"Okay." Aiden reached out to pry my fingers from the dagger. "Let me have the blade, Alex."

"No." I shook my head. "It has my prints on it. It's *mine*."

"You have to let me have it, Alex."

I shook my head, holding the sickle tighter. "I had to do it."

Aiden gently pried the blade loose. "I know, Alex. I know." He glanced over his shoulder before turning back to me. "Do not speak a word of this to anyone. Do you understand?"

"But—"

"Alex." His voice rose sharply. "Do not speak about this to anyone. *Ever.* Do you understand me?"

"Yes." My breath was coming out in sharp, little gasps.

He spun toward Seth. "Get her out of here. Take Lucian's jet to North Carolina. Use compulsion if you have to to get them to leave without him; I don't care. If anyone stops you or asks why you're leaving now, tell them the daimons had plans to take the second Apollyon. That the risk was too great for her to remain here."

Seth nodded, his eyes glowing. "What about them?"

Aiden glanced back at the pures. "I'll deal with them." His voice was low. "What happened in here will never leave this room. You can trust that."

"Are you sure?" Seth frowned. "If you change your mind, it's all over for Alex. We could just take care—"

"We will *not* kill them," Aiden hissed. "I know what I'm doing!"

Seth's eyes widened. "You're insane—as insane as Alex. If anyone finds out what you're about to do, you're—"

"I know. Go—go now. Before anyone else comes. I'll take care of this."

Would Aiden use compulsion on another pure? That alone was another forbidden act, another rule to be broken. How else would he get them to keep this secret? Especially Dawn? She was a Council member, obligated to report what'd really happened.

Aiden would compel the pures. Everything else would fall into place. The halfs who'd been turned had all used daggers. People would find the Guard and believe a daimon half had ended his life.

But if anyone ever found out the truth, Aiden would be deemed a traitor.

He would be killed for it.

I shot forward. "No. You can't do this. I won't allow it. You won't die—"

Aiden spun around and grasped my shoulders. "I will do this and you will allow this. Please, for once, don't fight with me. Just do as I say." His eyes met mine and when he spoke again, he did so barely above a whisper. "Please."

I closed my eyes against the sudden rush of tears. "Don't do this."

"I have to. I told you before I'd never let anything happen to you. I meant it." Aiden turned toward Seth. "Leave now."

Seth took my hand in a firm grip. There was so much I wanted to say to Aiden, but there wasn't time, not with Seth dragging me past the bodies and the shell-shocked pures. I did get one last glance, though.

Aiden was already setting his plan into motion. He crouched in front of Dawn, speaking low and quick—the same way he'd spoken to me that night in the warehouse.

A compulsion—he was really using a compulsion on another pure.

Seth pulled my hand. "We have to hurry."

The two of us raced through the hallways, avoiding the more heavily populated areas. We passed rooms where soft cries filled the space between our footfalls, corridors where bodies of half-bloods covered the floor. As Seth swiped a set of keys from a dead Guard, I looked into a dark chamber. Half-blood servants littered the floor, all of them dead or dying, and no one seemed to even care. No one tended to them. There were only moans and pleas for mercy. Pleas for help—help that would never come. I started toward them.

"We don't have time. I'm sorry, Angel. We just don't have time. We have to go." Seth wrenched me away from the room.

Numb—I was numb inside. So numb that I really didn't feel the bruises the hits had left behind, the ache that each step jarred out of me. Finding a Hummer wasn't hard, but ignoring the sounds of fighting all around us was difficult. Instinct demanded that I throw myself back into the fray, but I doubted Seth would appreciate that.

I scanned the dark grounds, relieved to see that Guards still held a line around the school. The daimons hadn't broken through. At least the students were safe.

But what about the servants?

On the way to the airport, Seth carried out Aiden's plan. After several unsuccessful tries, he was able to reach Marcus. I stared out the window, still numb with shock.

Seth said exactly what Aiden had instructed, telling Marcus that the daimons had tried to take me. "—and get her out of here in Lucian's plane tonight."

It sounded as though Marcus agreed with the idea of getting me out of New York. "Lucian is among the survivors. I'll pass on the information."

Some of the tension in my body eased off knowing that Lucian and Marcus were alive, but there were still many more whose fates were unknown at this point. There'd been so many bodies, so many daimons. What about Laadan?

Seth and I didn't talk until we'd boarded Lucian's jet. I took a seat beside a window while Seth *encouraged* the pilot and the servants to take off without Lucian.

I rested my head against the cool pane, squeezing my eyes shut. My stomach felt hollow. At some point after the plane took off, I stopped thinking. I just sat there, existing in a world where I might not even have a future. So many things could go wrong at this point. What if the compulsion failed to work? If so, Guards would be waiting for us the moment the plane landed. And even if Aiden was successful, compulsions weren't guaranteed to be permanent. They could wear off after time.

Then what? Both Aiden and I would lose everything.

Seth dropped into the seat beside me. I lifted my head and glanced at him. He held two glasses in his hands, filled with something that looked a lot like liquor. "What is it?"

"It's not the brew." His joke fell flat, but I smiled weakly and took it. "It's just scotch. It should help."

I downed the glass and handed it back. "Thank you."

"You really stopped the furies?"

Nodding, I handed the glass back to him. "Cut their heads off. They said they'd be back, though."

"Only a god can truly kill another god." He paused. "Or a god killer, but if you cut off their heads I can imagine that would put them out of commission for a while."

"Seth, they said… they said I was the threat." I bit my lip, shuddering. "Oh, gods, I killed a pure."

"Shh. Don't ever say that again. You know how much Aiden is risking. Don't let it all go to waste." Seth leaned over, draping his arm around my shoulders. After a few seconds, he spoke. "He really… isn't like the other pures, Alex."

"I know," I whispered. Aiden wasn't like anyone I knew, and there was no way I could accept that his actions tonight were a sense of duty on steroids.

But there was nothing I could do about that right now.

I looked out the tiny window, out into the dark night. Below, diamond-shaped lights grew smaller and smaller, becoming insignificant and vanishing as we moved into ominous clouds. I drew in a deep breath, but it got stuck in my throat. I'd killed a pure-blood and the man I loved was down there, covering it up, risking everything for me.

What had I done?

Thinking back on those seconds when I'd seen the pure raise the dagger, I knew there'd been time to avoid the deadly plunge of the blade. I was fast. I could've moved out of the way. I could've run. I hadn't needed to *kill* him.

Seth's arm around my shoulder's tightened as if he could read my mind. "You were defending yourself, Alex."

"Was I?"

"Yes. They declared war on us. You had no other choice."

"There are always choices." I pulled my gaze from the window and looked at Seth. *There are always choices.* I just had this terrible habit of making the wrong ones and now I had to deal with it. So did Aiden. So did Seth.

Seth reached out slowly, as if he was afraid to startle me. His caught my chin with the tips of his fingers. He didn't say anything. Not that he needed to—the connection between us was there, sparking alive.

I *needed* it right now—*needed* Seth.

Closing my eyes, I let him guide my head to his shoulder. And after I could take the first deep breath of air without choking on it—after I'd made my choice—I finally let the connection in completely. Seth's presence—*his warmth* surrounded me. Waves of comfort washed over me, easing the knots in my stomach. Not filling in all the cracks, not replacing ones that lingered back in the Catskills, but filling enough that I felt a little better, a little saner.

Keep reading for a sneak peek of:

Deity

The Third Covenant Novel by

Jennifer L. Armentrout

CHAPTER 1

RED SILK CLUNG TO MY HIPS, TWISTING INTO A TIGHT bodice that accentuated my curves. My hair was down, silky around my shoulders like the petals of an exotic flower. The lights in the ballroom caught each ripple in the fabric so that with every step, I looked like I was blooming from fire.

He stopped, lips parting as if the mere sight of me had rendered him incapable of doing anything else. A warm blush stole over my skin. This wouldn't end well—not when we were surrounded by people and he was looking at me like that, but I couldn't make myself leave. I belonged here, with him. That had been the right choice.

The choice I… hadn't made.

Dancers slowed around me, their faces hidden behind dazzling bejeweled masks. The haunting melody the orchestra played slipped under my skin and sunk into my bones as the dancers parted.

Nothing separated us.

I tried to breathe, but he had stolen not just my heart, but the very air I needed.

He stood there, dressed in a black tux cut to fit the hard lines of his body. A lopsided smile, full of mischief and playfulness, curved his lips as he bowed at the waist, extending his arm toward me.

My legs felt weak as I took the first step. The twinkling lights from above lit the way to him, but I would've found him in the dark if necessary. The beat of his heart sounded just like mine.

His smile spread.

That was all the reinforcement I needed. I took off toward him, the dress streaming behind me in a river of crimson silk. He straightened, catching me by the waist as I looped my arms around his neck. I burrowed my face against his chest, soaking in the scent of ocean and burning leaves

Everyone was watching, but it didn't matter. We were in our own world, where only what we wanted—what we'd desired for so long—mattered.

He chuckled deeply as he spun me around. My feet didn't even touch the ballroom floor. "So reckless," he murmured.

I smiled in response, knowing he secretly loved that part of me.

Placing me on my feet, he clasped my hand and placed the other on the small of my back. When he spoke again, his voice was a low, sultry whisper. "You look so beautiful, Alex."

My heart swelled. "I love you, Aiden."

He kissed the top of my head, and then we spun in dizzying circles. Couples slowly joined us, and I caught glimpses of wide smiles and strange eyes behind the masks—eyes completely white, no irises. Unease spread. Those eyes… I knew what they meant. We drifted toward a corner, where I heard soft cries coming from the darkness.

I looked over his shoulder, peering into the shadowy corners of the ballroom. "Aiden…?"

"Shh." His hand slipping up my spine and cupped the nape of my neck. "Do you love me?"

Our eyes met and held. "Yes. Yes. I love you more than anything."

Aiden's smile faded. "Do you love me more than him?"

I stilled in his suddenly lax embrace. "More than who?"

"Him," Aiden repeated. "Do you love me more than him?"

My gaze fell past him again, to the darkness. A man had his back to us. He was pressed against a woman, his lips on her throat.

"Do you love me more than him?"

"Who?" I tried to press closer, but he held me back. Uncertainty blossomed in my belly when I saw the disappointment in his silvery eyes. "Aiden, what's wrong?"

"You don't love me." He dropped his hands, stepping back. "Not when you're with him, when you chose him."

The man twisted at the waist, facing us. Seth smiled, his gaze offering a world of dark promises. Promises that I'd agreed to, that I'd chosen.

"You don't love me," Aiden said again, fading into the shadows. "You can't. You never could."

I reached for him. "But—"

It was too late. The dancers converged, and I was lost in a sea of dresses and whispered words. I pushed at them, but I couldn't break through, couldn't find Aiden or Seth. Someone pushed me and I fell to my knees, the red silk ripping. I cried out for Aiden and then Seth, but neither heeded my pleas. I was lost, staring up at faces hidden behind masks, staring at strange eyes. I knew those eyes.

They were the eyes of the gods.

I jerked straight up in bed, a fine sheen of sweat covering my body as my heart continued to try to come out of my chest. Several moments passed before my eyes adjusted to the darkness and I recognized the bare walls of my dorm room.

"What the hell?" I ran the back of my hand over my damp and warm forehead. I squeezed my watery eyes shut.

"Hmm?" murmured a half-awake Seth.

I sneezed in response, once, and then twice.

"That's hot." He blindly reached for the box of tissues. "I can't believe you're still sick. Here."

Sighing, I took the box of tissues from him and cradled them to my chest as I pulled a few free. "It's your fault—achoo! It was your stupid idea to go swimming in—achoo!—forty-degree weather, jerk-face."

"I'm not sick."

I wiped my nose, waiting a few more seconds to make sure I was done sneezing my brains out, and then dropped the box on the floor. Colds sucked daimon butt. In my seventeen years of life, I'd never gotten a cold until now. I hadn't even known I could get one. "Aren't you just so damn special?"

"You know it," was his muffled response.

Twisting at the waist, I glared at the back of Seth's head. He almost looked normal with his face planted into a pillow—my pillow. Not like someone who'd become a God Killer in less than four months. To our world, Seth was sort of like any mythical creature: beautiful, and could be downright deadly. "I had a weird dream."

Seth rolled onto his side. "Come on. Go back to sleep."

Since we'd returned from the Catskills a week ago, he'd been up my butt like never before. It wasn't like I didn't understand why, with the whole furie business and me killing a pure. He was probably never going to let me out of his sight again. "You really need to start sleeping in your own bed."

He turned his head slightly. A sleepy smile spread across his face. "I prefer your bed."

"I prefer that we actually celebrate Christmas around here, and then I'd get some Christmas presents and get to sing Christmas songs, but I don't get what I want."

Seth tugged me down, his arm a heavy weight that pinned me on my back. "Alex, I always get what I want."

A fine shiver coursed over my skin. "Seth?"

"Yeah?"

"You were in my dream."

One amber-colored eye opened. "Please tell me we were naked."

I rolled my eyes. "You're such a perv."

He sighed mournfully as he wiggled closer. "I'll take that as a no."

"You'd be correct." Unable to fall back to sleep, I started chewing on my lip. So many worries surfaced at once, it made my brain spin. "Seth?"

"Mmm?"

I watched him snuggle further down into the pillow before I continued. There was something charming about Seth when he was like this, a vulnerability and boyishness missing when he was fully awake. "What happened when I was fighting the furies?"

His eyes opened into thin slits. This was a question I'd asked several times since we returned to North Carolina. The kind of strength and power I'd displayed as I faced the gods was something only Seth, as a full-blown Apollyon, could've accomplished.

As an un-Awakened half-blood? Yeah, not so much.

Seth's mouth tightened. "Go back to sleep, Alex."

Seth refused to answer. Again. Anger and frustration rushed to the surface. I flung his arm off me. "What aren't you telling me?"

"You're being paranoid." His arm landed on my stomach again.

I tried wiggling out of his grasp, but his grip tightened. Grinding my teeth, I rolled onto my side and settled next to him. "I'm not being paranoid, you asshat. Something happened. I've told you that. Everything… everything looked amber. Like the color of your eyes."

He blew out a long breath. "I've heard that people in high stress situations have increased strength and senses."

"That wasn't it."

"And that people can hallucinate while under pressure."

I swung my arm back, narrowly missing his head. "I didn't hallucinate."

"I don't know what to tell you." Seth lifted his arm and rolled onto his back. "Anyway, are you going to go back to class in the morning?"

Instantly, a new worry surfaced. Classes meant facing everyone—Olivia—without my best friend. Pressure built in my chest. I squeezed my eyes shut, but Caleb's pale face appeared, eyes wide and unseeing, a Covenant dagger shoved deep in his chest. It seemed I could only remember what he'd really looked like in my dreams.

Seth sat up, and without even looking, I could feel his eyes boring holes in my back. "Alex…?"

I hated our super-special bond—absolutely loathed that whatever I was feeling fed into him. There was no such thing as privacy anymore. I sighed. "I'm fine."

He didn't respond.

"Yeah, I'm going to class in the morning. Marcus will have a fit when he gets back and realizes I haven't been to class." I flopped onto my back. "Seth?"

He inclined his heard toward me. Shadows cloaked his features, but his eyes cut through the darkness. "Yeah?"

"When do you think they're coming back?" By they I meant Marcus and Lucian… and Aiden. My breath caught. It happened whenever I thought about Aiden, and what he'd done for me—what he'd risked.

Easing down on his side, Seth reached across me and grabbed my right hand. His fingers threaded through mine, palm to palm. My skin tingled in response. The mark of the Apollyon—the one that shouldn't be on my hand—warmed. I stared at our joined hands, not at all surprised when I saw the faint lines—also the marks of the Apollyon—making their way up Seth's arm. I turned my head, watching as the marks spread across Seth's face. His eyes seemed to brighten. They'd been doing that a lot more lately, both the runes and his eyes.

"Lucian said they'd be back soon, possibly later today." Very slowly, he moved the pad of his thumb down the line of the rune. My toes curled as my free hand dug into the blankets. Seth smiled. "No one's mentioned the pure-blood Guard. And Dawn Samos has already returned. It appears Aiden's compulsion worked."

I wanted to pull my hand free. It was hard to concentrate when Seth messed with the rune on my palm. Of course, he knew that. And being the tool that he was, he liked it.

"No one knows what really happened." His thumb now traced the horizontal line. "And it'll remain that way."

My eyes drifted shut. The truth of how the pure-blood Guard died would have to remain a secret, or both Aiden and I would be in deep trouble. Not only had we almost hooked up over the summer—and then I had to go and tell him that I loved him, which was totally forbidden—I'd killed a pure-blood out of self-defense. And Aiden had used compulsion on two pures to cover it up. Killing a pure meant death for a half-blood, no matter the situation, and a pure was forbidden to use compulsion on another pure. If any of it came out, we'd both be totally screwed.

"You think so?" I whispered.

"Yes." Seth's breath was warm against my temple. "Go to sleep, Alex."

Letting the soothing sensation of his thumb against the rune lull me away, I drifted back to sleep, momentarily forgetting all the mistakes and decisions I'd made in the past seven months. My last conscious thought was of my biggest mistake—not the boy beside me, but the one I could never have.

Angelina's Secret

As a child, Angelina spent years in counseling learning that Josie, her imaginary friend, wasn't real, but it turns out her childhood friend wasn't imaginary after all.

Lisa Rogers

978-0-9831572-8-1

BETRAYED

A GUARDIAN LEGACY BOOK

Being one of
the Nephilim
isn't as easy
as it sounds.

June 2012

EDNAH WALTERS

January 2013

Having poison running through your veins and a kiss that kills really puts a dent in high school.

Kelly Hashway

Touch of Death

ACKNOWLEDGEMENTS

Acknowledgments are so tricky. I always feel like I'm forgetting someone terribly important. So I'll start with the business side of things. Huge thanks to Kate Kaynak and the team at Spencer Hill Press—Rich, Kendra, Marie, Osman, Carol, and Rebecca. Without you guys, *The Covenant Series* wouldn't even exist. Or if it did, it would be pretty bad without your editing, marketing expertise and general awesomeness.

Much thanks to my family and husband for your continuing patience and support when I ignore you while writing. Love you guys. Thank you to my agent Kevan Lyon, for rocking it out.

To my friends: Lesa Rodrigues, Julie Fedderson, Dawn Ransom, Cindy Thomas, Carissa Thomas, and everyone else, you know who you are, thank you for always being there for me when I need a break away from people that aren't real or when I need to brainstorm.

Speaking of brainstorming—I don't know what I would do without Lesa, Julie, Carissa or Cindy. You guys rock my socks. You are the awesome sauce with an extra helping of sauce.

Julie—you are still my rockstar.

A huge, GIGANTIC thanks to all the book bloggers out there, spreading their love of reading and their passion for it along with discovering new authors. You guys do this for free, in your spare time and are my go-to peeps. Without you guys, honestly, *The Covenant Series* wouldn't be half of whatever success it may be. You all don't nearly get the thanks you guys so very much deserve.

Photo by Ken Cappelli

Jennifer L. Armentrout lives in West Virginia. All the rumors you've heard about her state aren't true. Well, mostly. When she's not hard at work writing, she spends her time reading, working out, watching zombie movies, and pretending to write. She shares her home with her husband, his K-9 partner named Diesel, and her hyper Jack Russell Loki. Her dreams of becoming an author started in algebra class, where she spent her time writing short stories... therefore explaining her dismal grades in math. Jennifer writes Adult and Young Adult Urban Fantasy and Romance.

Come find out more at: **www.jenniferarmentrout.com**